PERSEUS RIFT
An Expansion Novel
Book two

By
Jack Edward

Other Jack Edward Novels

~ ~ ~

The Expansion Series
Book One Perseus Transit

Expansion Universe Novels
The Rangers

PERSEUS RIFT

The Expansion Book 2

By Jack Edward

First Edition
Copyright © 2017 John B Dorman
Cover art by iStock
Cover design by Jack Edward

ISBN-13: 978-0-9964092-1-6
ISBN-10: 0-9964092-1-1

Library of Congress Control Number 2015908975

Edward, Jack
Perseus Rift/ Jack Edward
        p.   cm.
ISBN 978-0-9964092-1-6 (pbk. v. 2)
1.Perseus Transit
2.Perseus Rift
I. Title.

P.O.D. Printed in the U.S.A.

"Appear weak when you are strong, and strong when you are weak."
    — *Sun Tzu, The Art of War*

DEDICATIONS

To all the warriors who bear the scars of defending our
way of life, you are never alone.

Thank you to my amazing family who have given me
the courage to explore.

CONTENTS

FCS Nyx Command Crew

Coline Amélie Lune, Rear Admiral Fleet Senior Officer out system, Flag Officer Nyx

Adam Stuart, Fleet Captain Fleet Special Commando Operations, Captain of Nyx

Samantha Leeane, Commander Fleet Intel, Executive Officer and Chief of Administration Nyx

Dr. Brynn Driscoll, Colonel, Marine Medical Officer, Chief Medical Officer Nyx

Helen Elizabeth Dower PhD, Commander Fleet Special Engineer System Officer, Chief Engineer Nyx

Asteria Hypnea, Commander Fleet CyberOps, Chief of Tactical Nyx

Callis Kane, Major Marine Flight Systems Officer, Chief Pilot Nyx

Michael (Mickey) Delaney, Major Marine Special Commando, Chief of Operations Nyx

Natalia Volkov Delaney, Lieutenant Commander Fleet Special Weapons, Chief of Combat Systems Nyx

Simay Demir Binici, Lieutenant Fleet Intelligence, Chief of Navigation, Senior ships Lieutenant Nyx

Jacob Lavagnino, Lieutenant Fleet Engineering, Assistant Chief Engineer Nyx

Harold "Hammer" Petrokov, Master Chief Warrant Officer Marines, Chief of Gunnery Nyx

Xander Beaumont, Chief Warrant Officer Fleet Combat Intelligence Analyst, Tactical Bridge Officer Nyx

Josephine (Joe) Santiago, Chief Warrant Officer Fleet Communications, Master Communications Technician Nyx

Shia O'Connell, Master Chief Petty Officer Fleet Military Police, Senior Ship Security Specialist Nyx

FCS Nyx
Cadets and Midshipmen

Katherine Carroll, Marine Cadet, Fifth year Fortress Hills Marine Academy Hades.

Jennifer Ashford Worley, Fleet Midshipmen, Fifth year Bastion Fleet Naval Academy Acheron

Olaf Gustafson, Fleet Midshipmen, Fifth year Bastion Fleet Naval Academy, Acheron

Aaron Bailey, Fleet Midshipmen, Fifth year Bastion Fleet Naval Academy Acheron.

Jorge Perez, Fleet Midshipmen, Fifth year Bastion Fleet Naval Academy.

William David Scott, Fleet Midshipmen, Fifth year Officer Training Corps, Derwin Advanced Ed Institution.

Sitting fifteen thousand light years from Earth outward along the Orion-Cygnus arm of the Milky Way lays the region of space where the Perseus Arm crosses known as the Perseus Transit. The Perseus Transit marks the absolute limit of human expansion in the galaxy along the Orion-Cygnus. The Federated Colonies, a democratic government consisting of three planetary systems, that lies just inside that limit. For decades the Federated Colony has guarded that frontier and no one has ever traveled beyond. Rough and difficult to manage the furthest out system of Elysium sits barely two lightyears away from the stellar crossroad. The vanguard of human expansion.

The region between the Orion-Cygnus and the Perseus arms of the Milky Way have become to be known as the Perseus Rift. Some one hundred plus lightyears wide the vast emptiness holds no resources. It's size creates difficult economic as well as physical barriers to human expansion.

The Perseus Transit is a bridge between the two arms. The only way for economical human expansion to occur away from its singular galactic arm…

CHAPTER I
Homecoming

Marine Cadet Carroll looked out the viewport at the ship outside. It was stunning! She couldn't believe she had been selected when they told her what ship she was assigned. Her head was still spinning. Outside was the most advanced ship ever built by the Fleet.

As she looked at it she saw a long oval cylinder flattened on the top and bottom extending out to a flat shovel nose. The heavily armored bridge hung just under the nose. On each side it had large thick braces that looked like grasshopper legs and attached to the legs were four massive graviton engines spaced off center two on each side. She had the four molybdenum rods of the Dower drive jutting from large metal shields on her shoulders. You could see a fifth short rod just above the bridge on the nose of the ship. The two aft rods extended out from under the first pair of engines and sparkled in Tartarus's light.

The ships name was lit up in massive white letters on the hull just behind the bridge and in front of the engine brace. *Nyx*, the goddess of night. She had looked it up as soon as she found out the name. It seemed fitting that the goddess of night watches over them in the deep darkness of space, she thought.

She looked down at her pressure suit uniform to make sure it was spotless for her report time. She wore the light blue bottoms and dark blue top of Marine dress. Her right arm was marine crimson and her right forearm bore the single gold three-inch dot of her cadet rank. She was incredibly nervous and couldn't even eat breakfast this morning.

"Hey it's a Marine!" she heard off to her left. Turning she saw four Naval Midshipmen approaching from the inner station. Their pressure suits were the standard fleet black bottoms and their upper bodies were the purple with white piping of Midshipmen. They carried the nova and anchor Midshipmen rank on their right forearms. They came up to her and looked at the viewport.

"Is that the *Nyx*?" one of them asked looking at it in shock.

"Yea they say it has the fastest CoNeE drives in the Fleet, if you can call those things CoNeE drives." another said.

A fifth Midshipmen came up behind them and walked up to her, "Hello Cadet, I'm William. Are you assigned to the *Nyx*?" he said to her.

"Why would they assign a Marine Cadet to a starship? Only Midshipmen do initial cruises." one of them said with a grimace.

"Actually that's not true Jennifer; there is just very few Cadets and typically none on smaller ships. They usually don't mix with the Midshipmen." William said.

"Yea well, stop mixing then…" she said as she walked toward the boarding tube.

The five of them walked up and scanned their orders at the console. They walked up the tube without even noticing the Staff Sergeant sentry that was watching them carefully.

Katherine picked up her Marine gray duffel and walked over to the console. She scanned her orders and read the assignment. To her horror she was assigned to the Midshipmen quarters and her senior officer was a Naval Lieutenant.

She sighed heavily and turned to see the Marine Staff Sergeant silently watching her without moving or turning his head. His level two pressure suit was commando green and fitted perfectly. As she approached he went rigid in the position of attention.

She paused a brief second and looked at him, "Good morning Staff Sergeant." she said nodding.

"Morning Ma'am, welcome aboard the *Nyx*." he greeted her officially as she passed.

She smiled slightly. She loved being a Marine, loved Marines, and would never be anything but a Marine. She walked up the tube and caught up with the Midshipmen at the entry to the main hanger and cargo hold.

Yawning out in front of them was a massive deck easily fifty meters by twenty meters. Above them it rose five decks tall surrounded by catwalks and crane rails. There were three combat shuttles stacked on the port wall and one on the deck. Crew were hurrying about moving cargo and maintenance equipment around everywhere. It looked like chaos.

She turned and looked at the starboard wall and took a sharp breath. There were four Marine Corp. Phoenix Multi-role fighters hanging above her. She had dreamed of flying one since she could walk. She stood staring up at them imagining what it might be like to sit in one.

"They are beautiful aren't they?" someone said from behind her.

"Oh yes, very much so." she said as she looked to see who had spoken. Her eyes stopped on a tall muscular Marine Major who was looking up at the ships. She jumped to attention and saluted.

"Sir!" she said suddenly intimidated.

He looked at and smiled, "At ease Cadet?"

"Carroll, Sir." she said.

"Welcome Cadet Carroll. You seem interested in the fighters; do you want to be a pilot?" he asked.

"It has crossed my mind sir." she replied hastily.

He smiled. "Well hopefully you'll do a rotation in my department and we'll see if you got the chops." he said as a beautiful Warrant Officer walked up in the orange of Signal Corps.

Katherine realized he was wearing the sky blue of

Aviation Corp and her eyes went wide. He must be the chief of flight!

"See you around Cadet Carroll." he said as he walked off with the Signal Warrant Officer.

Even the Midshipmen were speechless for a minute.

"Oye Middies, get clear of the deck. Got a flight coming in." an old deck chief hollered at them. They grabbed their bags and hurried off toward the lift tubes at the front of the hanger.

Helen Elizabeth Dower
Family Quarters Three Eighty-Four
Federated Colonial Station Dianaides, Hades System
173.0188 FCUDT 13:10:40

Commander Helen Dower leaned back in the comfortable sofa and put her head on Xander's shoulder. She had brought him home to meet her parents after the long and dangerous mission on the experimental ship *Hypnos*. Xander had reluctantly agreed to come because he knew she needed to come to terms with a few things. He loved her greatly.

Helen had not yet emotionally recovered from the loss of her right leg from the knee down and her right hand from the forearm down. She had been attempting to reach the lower decks when the ship was attacked and was nearly fatally injured. Due to a set of extremely unusual circumstances her injuries could not be healed in the usual manner. She had ended up with highly advanced cybernetic prosthetics.

If that was the only thing it would have been easily overcome. It turns out Helen had been responsible for solving one of the most difficult engineering problems in the history of the Colonies. She had unknowingly created the framework for Lorentzian traversable wormholes. Unfortunately, nobody told her until she stood face to face with the semi working prototype technology in deep space.

Helen was extremely resilient and had overcome the shock and disappointment eventually. It had taken its toll though and this trip had obviously renewed her. Helen's mother Alexandra had taken to Xander immediately and spent hours telling him stories about her childhood.

Her father had been so happy to see her mostly in one piece he had cried. He had been shocked when she told him she met Grace O'Malley and what Grace said about knowing him. The relief and pride he had as he told her about his past exploits with Commander Stuart was palpable.

Then they spent several more hours examining Helen's new cybernetics. Her father had several suggestions that Helen was excited to try out concerning the cybernetics. He had been incredibly jealous she could literally feel electromagnetic waves and measure spectrums like he could smell or taste. He even jokingly threatened to cut off his hand to get a new one. The ease with which her father had accepted her modifications had gone a long way in her acceptance of the new limbs.

Eventually they had come to the end of their visit. Helen was disappointed they had to leave so soon but she also was looking forward to getting back to the ship. Her parents had completely understood because they too had felt it in their years aboard. They had hugged and her father made Xander swear to watch out for her. Her mother cried a little and made her promise to write even though she knew she couldn't.

Helen and Xander now sat at the civilian departure lounge of Salmaneus waiting on their flight. Across from them three Marine's in medium armor stood watch as their ever present guardians.

"I like your parents." Xander said to her.

"Well that's good, they really liked you." she replied with a smile. "Have you decided if you want to share my quarters aboard?" she asked a little hopeful.

He seemed to be in thought for a bit and smiled at her,

"Well if you're serious, of course I will. You get way nicer quarters and better fabricators!" he said teasing her.

"Well as long as you're using me for the fabricator and not anything else…" she smirked.

Xander laughed putting his arm around her. "Are you excited to get back?"

"Yes, they were almost ready to install the Higgs components when we left so it should be pretty nearly finished. Plus, that ultra-dense carbon shielding should be installed as well and the reactors can come on line. I am pretty excited!" she said happily. "Those reactors from the Ottomans are really powerful but they didn't shield them nearly enough. They must have a pretty high fatality rate."

"Simay said their medical technology was pretty far behind ours," Xander said sadly, "They couldn't cure the radiation poisoning."

"That's horrible!" Helen said imagining the worst.

Xander nodded. They sat silently for several minutes and watched the other passengers arrive around them. People would periodically look at them and smile. The Fleet had a good reputation here especially after defending the system in the recent action.

Part of their last mission had included finding out the Ottoman Empire had instigated a conflict by invading Hades. Some twenty thousand people had lost their lives in that attack. They were still rebuilding several portions of the system. That was one reason they were at Salmaneus in the inner system instead of the more common Tantalus in the outer system. Tantalus had been nearly completely destroyed by the attackers.

"What do you think about our new mission?" she asked quietly.

"Sounds like a repeat of the last, only this time we have bigger guns," he said smiling.

"I'm going to miss *Hypnos*." she said sadly. "I spent a lot of time putting her back together."

"Yea, I know what you mean. I hope it isn't too rigid."

He was referring to military protocol. Their last mission was covert so there was very little military discipline. This time there were going to be nearly three hundred fleet crewmen aboard.

"Have to be a little bit I would assume, there's a lot of crew." she said thinking about it.

The station AI came on and announced the boarding of their flight. Helen stood and smiled at Xander. "Come on let's find our cabin for the next couple of weeks. Just think this will soon be a trip that will take an hour." she smiled.

"Yep, thanks to your huge sexy brain!" He teased her as they walked up the boarding tube behind one of their guardians. She jumped out of his reach as he grabbed for her and hurried ahead of him towards the room with the Marine following after her.

A few moments later he saw the Marine at a door up ahead. As he approached the Marine nodded, "The Commander is inside Chief. If you need anything just call, I will be on first watch."

"Thank you Sergeant Adams." Xander activated the hatch and walked in just as she unsealed her suit and dropped it. She smiled over her shoulder at him as he walked up to her.

Admiral Terzi
Imperial Ottoman Ship Phalanx, Flag Bridge
Barbary Anchorage, Deep Space Sector Four
189.0188 UDT 16:11:51

Admiral Terzi stood on the bridge of his Ship of the Line. He watched the precise maneuvers of his fleet as they moved into position. Breathing a mental sigh he tried to relax. After six months of travel they had arrived at this waypoint. He still had another six months to go but felt as if a weight had been lifted when he arrived here to find the diversion force already waiting.

He looked at the reports in front of him about the battle

at Hades. Several things bothered him but the loss of the *Caster* had burned the worst. He had to admit the bold courage it must have taken for that cruiser captain to fly into their shields was incredible. He would love to fight them. A battle of true warriors.

At least they saved him the need to shoot the *Caster's* captain. Behind him an officer walked in and waited. He turned and looked at him.

"Sir, we have contained the situation at Port Royal. The Brigantine *Revenge* was sighted being towed out system shortly before our arrival. The ship that towed them was the one identified by the Empire as a class one capture." he reported.

"Do we know where they were headed?" the Admiral asked.

"We are unable to determine their course. The nature of the drive they use is unpredictable." he answered. "However a spy has reported sighting the ship on the Briton frontier. Apparently it was instrumental in preventing the war from starting as we had planned. Our spy is unsure of its origin but the ship displayed registry from Clare." he said.

"Clare… How long to get ships to Clare?" he asked.

"Sir, Clare is currently ninety-seven light years away. It is one hundred seventeen days' travel sir."

He looked at the display in front of him. Clare was fairly well fortified and patrolled by several Barque sized vessels. "It is unlikely that the ship came from this system, it is populated by pirates and thieves." he said to himself. He turned to the officer, "Dispatch two divisions. Two Frigates, six Barques, and twelve Brigantines immediately." he ordered.

The man nodded, "Yes sir. Right away."

"Inform them to capture the ship or find any information concerning it. Contain the system for the Empire, it will be an excellent anchorage and provide a flanking point." he said disgusted.

He walked over to the view port and stared out.

Displayed in the window was the magnificent pink, blue, and white pastels of the Perseus Transit spread like a broad scarf across the black of space. He imagined it as a massive brush stroke from the hand of God. It seemed close enough to touch but he knew it was one hundred light years away. It had been a long flight across the Perseus Rift.

Sitting on the other side was the home of the nonbelievers. They would be purged and converted. His mission was ordained by the Emperor.

Floating in front of his Flagship was his massive fleet. Nearly fifty divisions of warships were anchored here. He had some five hundred ships at his command and soon they would be put to use.

"I am but a messenger, I shall deliver the word of God from the tip of my sword."

Admiral Terzi sat down and leaned back in his chair grinning in anticipation.

Senior Master Chief Shia O'Connell
City Center Park
Planet Erebus, Jonestown
175.188 FCUDT 10:48:22

Shia stood on the edge of the large green park and held her face to the sun. This was the first time she ever visited Erebus and she immediately decided she liked it. It was early summer here and the temperature was quite pleasant. People were scattered across the green expanse enjoying the day. A few children ran by yelling and laughing obviously playing some sort of game.

On the far edge of the park stood the impressive historic building that housed the judicial arm of the Federated Colonies. Its large white open colonnade glowed in the dazzling sun. She thought it strange that she had worked for the Judiciary and never actually been here before. She shook off the memory and began casually walking toward the shimmering colonnade.

She relaxed a little as she breathed the smell of the sweet grass in the park. She stepped onto the path that wound into the courtyard of the Judiciary and walked toward the main entrance.

The memories of her time as a Ranger ebbed and flowed as she made her way around the building. She had decided to come here purely on the spur of the moment. She hadn't actually meant to visit the Chief Justice but she had received an invitation only an hour after her shuttle landed. It was not surprising he kept tabs on her, he was the leader of the Rangers.

The cool air of the main atrium flowed across her face as she entered. Off to the side a peacekeeper manned the entry desk and he smiled as she approached.

"Hello I have an appointment." she said to him.

"Greetings Ranger O'Connell, you are expected. Take the lift to level six and someone will meet you who can escort you to the Chief." he said politely.

Shia raised her eyebrow at him, "I'm not a Ranger... well sort of I suppose."

He nodded and indicated the console, "My data says you're still active. You can speak to someone in administration if there is some kind of error." he said smiling.

She just frowned and turned towards the lifts, "Thank you." she said as she walked away.

The lift doors quietly opened and she stepped out into a large open space. The floors were covered in rich honey colored wood surrounded by three walls of windows. Several sofas and chairs were placed in sitting areas and a large iron wood desk sat off to the left. Sitting behind the desk with his boots up on it sat the Chief Justice of the Federated Colonies.

Shia walked over to the desk and paused in front of it. "Chief Justice Jeffery Dumont, why am I registered as an active Ranger?" she demanded.

He looked up at her and grinned, "What's that? Did Shia O'Connell just ask to be an active Ranger?"

She frowned at him, "No, I said why am I already active..."

"Don't know what you're talking about. But if you're active you can't talk to me like that." he said.

She huffed at him, "You activated me in the system... what are you after?"

He tilted his head to the side and looked at her, "I didn't and don't." he said evasively.

"Seriously Dumont it's been ten years and in two minutes I already want to shoot you."

He stood and stepped around the desk to look at her. "I'm not the reason you ran away. I didn't ask you to come to Erebus, you did that on your own." he said smiling. "It's really good to see you by the way. Lost track of you about the time that Ottoman craziness went up in Hades."

She looked at him carefully. His brown hair was now nearly all white and his square face had more age to it than she remembered. His bright blue eyes were exactly the same though. She sighed and stepped over to him embracing in a hug. "You smell the same..." she chuckled.

He pushed her to arm's length and smiled, "It sure is good to hear you laugh again. Come on let's have a drink! You have some storytelling to do to catch me up."

An hour later Shia sat quietly admiring the wonderful view out the windows. "I've actually missed you. Strange." she said still staring outside.

Dumont nodded, "I've missed you too, and that's why I keep track of you."

Shia looked back at him with a smirk.

"Yes I put you back on the roster, many years ago in fact. Just in case." he said. "Eventually I want you to be a training officer, but for now... I think you can learn from ol' Adam Stuart."

"Oh please." Shia snorted. "Just come clean Dumont."

He looked at her seriously for a moment. "Ok, you win. I didn't lie; you've been on the books for years. But, if you hadn't come to see me I would have come to see you before you ran off on this crusade with the Fleet. There's something coming, I know you know that."

Shia squinted at him suspiciously.

"Don't look at me like that; I get the same briefs as the President. Congress is in massive denial and running scared. The Fleet is cleaning its underwear after seeing the data you brought back and I have suffered so many budget cutbacks I have half the number of Rangers I actually need," he shook his head and stared at his whiskey. "You're going on a special mission and I want a presence out there. Just by coincidence I have two Rangers who happen to be Senior Fleet personnel... My two best Rangers by the way."

"Stars Dumont, I don't even know what our mission is." she said sarcastically.

"Well I do, I was in the planning session. It's important Shia. You'll understand eventually. I have to plan the long game. Stars know you and I may be here for another hundred years."

Shia suddenly felt a chill run through her, that deep hidden fear crept up in her mind at his comment. She put her hands in her lap to keep Dumont from seeing them shaking. "That's not funny." she whispered.

"No it's not, but it's the truth and you need to accept it," he said softly. "You can't run forever."

"We're done." she said lurching to her feet. "Keep me on the roster, I don't care. See you again in another ten years." she said trying to hold her fear and anxiety in check. She fled out the door slamming it.

Katherine hurried across the cargo deck toward the forward lift tubes behind the other Midshipmen. They stopped and waited for the lift that would take them to the crew deck.

The other Midshipmen didn't notice her or they acted like they didn't notice her. She watched as a shuttle eased across the shimmering fields that kept the atmosphere in. It glided forward and settled into the magclamp ringing out with a metallic clang. The deck crew scrambled around the ship attaching power cables and fueling tubes.

Katherine turned just in time to see the Midshipmen named Jennifer waving evilly goodbye as the lift doors closed. "Dammit!" she said to herself.

"Well lass, if you're just going to stand there give me a hand for a second." said an old grisly Warrant Officer standing next to her.

She jumped at his voice, "Oh, yes Sir..." she said quickly dropping her bag.

"Just hit that green button and slide this monstrosity back a bit." he pointed to the handle of a lifter.

She carefully did as he said and slid back the device.

"Ah, right there. Perfect. Thank you Lass." he said moving a crate into the free space.

"What is this?" Katherine said examining the device she had just moved.

"Well that is a top secret fancy piece of weaponry. It's called a graser." He motioned her over and pointed to a tiny silver reactor. "It uses Dower physics here to create a coherent beam of gravitons. It pushes them out through these pointed shafts and smashes the bad guys. I'm told it's like getting hit by a meteor moving at half-light speed..."

Katherine's eyes went wide. "I've never heard of something like this, it really uses Higgs reactors?" she asked, in almost disbelief.

"Aye, built by one of our own," he said smiling, "Now off with you, your lift is here." He nodded at the entryway.

Katherine turned to see the lift arrive and she hurried to step inside. The Warrant nodded his goodbye as the door snapped shut. There was a chief petty officer looking at his tablet idly. Katherine stared at the console trying to figure out which deck she wanted.

"There's only thirteen to choose from…" the chief said.

"Sorry, I am looking for the crew deck…" she said without looking up from the console.

"That would be twelve or thirteen, top floors." he said chuckling. "Don't worry you'll figure it out in a few days, if not, ask a chief."

She tapped the button and looked at him, "Thank you Chief."

He nodded as the door opened and he left the lift. Several more people got on and they chatted among themselves. She suddenly remembered her duffel was not in her arms. She rode the lift up and back down to the hangar bay and as the door opened the same Warrant was standing there holding her duffel.

"You might need this." he said smiling.

She felt her face burn as she carefully took it from him. "Thank you Sir." she said embarrassed.

He smiled at her, "I was new once too, don't sweat it Marine."

She suddenly realized he was also a Marine and felt her heart sink in terror. She was not making a good impression.

A few minutes later the doors opened on level thirteen and she stepped out into a very busy passageway. Crew came and went from all over the deck. Several were carrying duffels; others were moving about helping people settle in. She could smell the crew dining hall down the passage and her stomach rumbled loudly as she realized her last meal was many hours ago.

She looked at the confusing numbers on the wall, zero zero thirty seven. It was a listing of section and compartment numbers. Her quarters were in section eight compartment twelve room four. She turned left and headed forward from the lifts looking for section eight. She bumped into people and was nearly knocked to the ground as she made her way down the narrow passages.

The passageways were designed in military fashion. Basically thin metal between bulkheads with no outer walls. Katherine was awed at the sight and found it a bit frightening to think about why everything was exposed. The conduits, ductwork, and computer channels were all exposed to the passage so it was easier to perform repairs when everything was already uncovered. This was a ship of war and damage was expected and anticipated.

After several minutes she found the hatch and with a sigh she heaved it open and stepped inside. The room was six by ten meters and had five double berths spaced every meter along the center. The head and foot of the berths were bracketed by two-meter-tall personal lockers. The dull grey metal walls were covered in large cloth squares to dampen the sound. She walked across the soft cushioned plastic floor and looked for an open berth.

The other Midshipmen had claimed all the bottom berths.

"Snooze you lose…" One of the Midshipmen said to her as she looked for a berth. They laughed as they put away their gear.

Trying to ignore them Katherine walked to the locker of the first upper berth. She placed her hand on the reader and it popped open and her name appeared on the bright green digital display on the front of the locker door.

As she opened the door several cleaning buckets and two mops clattered out around her. The Midshipmen burst out in laughter.

"You owe me five credits; I told you she would pick the

first row!" one of them said.

She tossed her duffel in and shut the door red faced. She climbed up to her berth and lay down staring at the ceiling. Things never change she thought sadly.

"Stop worrying Simay, you'll be fine." Doctor Brynn Driscoll said smiling at her. "In a previous life you did many things more difficult."

Simay looked at Brynn sitting at her personal console. She knew she was referring to her past as an Ottoman Imperial ship Executive Officer. That seemed like such a long time ago even though it was only last year that she defected. She was a completely different person now thanks mainly to Brynn's compassion. If the crew of *Hypnos* hadn't saved her from the atrocious torture she was subjected to by her depraved Captain she would have died. As it is she cannot even comprehend who she was before that episode.

"You know I am not that person any longer." Simay said shaking her head.

Brynn reached out and took Simay in her arms. "That person is within you regardless. Part of who you are, was her. The Simay I love will succeed as you always do." Brynn said looking into Simay's face.

Simay frowned, "Why did Captain Stuart choose me though? Why do I have to be responsible for the Midshipmen? I can barely function as an officer all by myself..."

Brynn took a deep breath, "You will teach them to integrate into the ship just as you yourself still need to do. Do it together, be what they need, and trust the Captain."

Simay relaxed in defeat. "Of course I will do my best.

I'm just scared."

Brynn held Simay at arm's length, "I know you're scared, that's why I know you'll do a fine job. You care about this." She smiled at Simay as she leaned down and kissed her. A few seconds later she stepped back and handed Simay her coffee.

"Now I need to get to work and let you form a plan. We have almost finished installing the new nanite systems." Brynn said excited as she slipped past Simay. "See you later Lieutenant."

"See you at dinner Colonel..." Simay answered.

Brynn left Simay alone in their quarters. Simay sat down in their small sitting area and leaned back. Taking a deep breath, she tried to calm herself down. She wanted to be a part of this crew so badly she was upsetting herself needlessly.

After being saved by Captain Stuart, Simay had become intensely loyal to the core crew of this ship. The terms of her being allowed to stay here had included her confinement to the ship during its time in Federated Space as well as multiple exams by psychological operations staff. She had passed her exams with ease and endured the months aboard the ship. It was far easier enduring it with Brynn, of course.

The ship alerted her of a neurocom message and she accepted it. Neurocom was still somewhat new to her. The Ottoman Empire was far behind in similar technologies. She had received her neuro implant onboard the *Hypnos* shortly after arriving.

"Lieutenant Binici, the Midshipmen have arrived and are boarding. I thought you may like to know." the Staff Sergeant on duty had sent to her. Simay recognized his name, James Colfax. She had met him during her daily physical fitness training a month back. He has become one of her semi regular workout partners since then.

"Thank you Staff Sergeant Colfax. I owe you one." she sent in reply.

She activated the com system and called Commander

Samantha Leeane. The call was answered quickly.

"Simay good morning, what can I do for you?" Samantha asked.

"XO, the Midshipmen have arrived. I will be performing their initial brief as we have planned." Simay said.

Sam smiled, "Excellent, I will see you at the morning briefing then." she said smiling.

"Yes Ma'am." Simay said disappointed. She had been hoping to be released for this mornings' brief so she could focus on the junior crew. She signed off and quickly finished her coffee.

She exited the quarters and headed down the passage to the stairwells. As she passed the medical bays she saw Brynn inside through the observation windows. She was with her staff of four doctors and fourteen medics installing the new components of several advanced medical devices. Simay thought of how Brynn had been extremely excited when she had secured them for the bay. The medical on special warfare ships were class one treatment centers. They need to be the most comprehensive centers in all Federated Space because they often work alone for extended periods. Simay expected massive upgrades when they returned sometime next year.

She smiled to herself as she entered the stairwell and headed up to the crew deck.

The crew deck was a riot of activity as she entered. It had been a den of chaos since last week when the majority of the crew began to arrive. There were supervisors and new crew hurrying back and forth trying to get everything settled for departure in the next few days.

She casually walked over to the dining hall and headed over for the drink fabricator. She was a few minutes early and decided to pick up another cup of coffee. The room was busy with crew eating breakfast and having excited conversations. She walked along the wall of the large room. It could feed a hundred at a time in three scheduled shifts.

There was a similar dining room forward for the officers but only sat thirty. She liked to stop in here because it gave her the feeling of being closer to the crew.

"Good morning Lieutenant." Chief Petty Officer Shia O'Connell smiled as she passed with her security team in tow.

"Morning Chief!" Simay answered. Shia was a member of the original crew and had a fantastic sense of humor. She is an ex-Ranger law officer from Hades system. A notorious and rough place that has a reputation for organized crime, Shia says it is like stories of a place called the Wild West. Considering that it lies in the galactic west of Federated territory that seems appropriate, even if Simay didn't know what it meant.

She watched them head for the food line as Shia easily laughed with them. She headed for the door and turned to the forward sections. In her months of time aboard ship she had gotten to know her way around quite well. In a matter of minutes, she stood in front of section eight compartment twelve room four or forward eight twelve four as it would have been said by the crew

She stood there taking breaths and listening to the ship. The Midshipmen were quartered right at the beginning of Officers quarters in the forward sections of the crew deck. The enlisted crew called it 'Officer Country' and avoided it scrupulously. Several Ensigns and Junior Lieutenants walked by and smiled as they saw Simay standing at the door.

"I always knew the Senior Lieutenant did that!" an Ensign said smiling as he passed.

Simay smiled at him and with a breath opened the door and stepped inside.

"Hello Sam, how are you this morning?" Helen asked as she walked into the room.

"It's another busy day Helen…" Sam said smiling.

Helen walked over and took her usual seat near the head of the table. As a full commander she was now fourth in line of command. Her head spun when she thought about it. She had been only an Ensign three months ago!

Sam shook her head at Helen, "I remember the first briefing you came to with me…"

"Oh stars! Please don't remind me. I was so scared of you…" Helen said putting her head down.

Sam put her hand on Helen' arm, "Don't worry you will always be that Sparks to me little lady."

Sparks was Helen's nickname given from the magnificent display of a wormhole materializing in a Higgs field. Her discovery that allowed the ship she was in to travel so far so fast.

The ships pilot Callis Kane, strolled in behind Josephine Santiago, the chief of communications.

"Awe my three favorite ladies all in one room!" Callis exclaimed.

"Callis! Joe! I heard you arrived this morning. How was your trip home?" Helen asked.

"Oh it was ok…" Joe said sarcastically as she put her hand out for Helen and Sam to see. She had on a beautiful sparkling green ring.

"Oh my! Is that what I think it is?" Sam asked smiling at Callis.

"My Mothers engagement ring, yes." he said smiling.

"Oh Josephine! Congratulations." Helen said jumping up to hug her. "We must celebrate tonight with some Red!"

Helen said.

"Did someone just say the words celebrate and Red…
because I am in!" Major Michael Delaney said walking in
with his wife Lieutenant Commander Natalia Delaney.
Master Chief Warrant Officer Gunny Petrokov followed
behind smiling.

"Callis you young pup what have you done now!"
Gunny called out loudly.

They all congratulated the couple and Natalia approved
of the beautiful ring.

Shia walked in and laughed at the group, "I was going to
spill your secret you know…" she said to Joe. Shia, Joe, and
Callis were good friends and Joe had called Shia as soon as
they arrived on the ship.

At one minute to nine hundred Simay ran in looking
flushed followed by Commander Asteria Hypnea the chief
of Tactical and the only cybernetic life form known in
existence. They found their seats and activated their tablets.
Simay was trying to not breathe too hard as she settled.

The Admiral's tone sounded announcing Admiral
Coline Amélie Lune's arrival. The *Nyx* was built without an
Artificial Intelligence due to certain vulnerabilities exposed
by Arthur the AI on *Hypnos*. As a result, many older
traditions have returned including tones announcing the
Admiral or the Captain.

Admiral Lune swiftly crossed to her seat at the head of
the table followed by Captain Adam Stuart the ships
commander. The rather odd scenario that placed an
Admiral onboard without giving her command was a result
of certain political pressures. She was assigned to be the
Fleet admiral for a Fleet of one.

Regardless of political reasons she was widely accepted
by the command crew and had spent some time on the
Hypnos with them. They valued her leadership and guidance
as much as they did the Captain Stuart's.

She looked at them and smiled, "Good morning, I hope
everybody is as excited as I am about the upcoming

departure," she said happily, "I will save my comments till the end today." She sipped her coffee, "Except for telling Helen and Simay thank you for the excellent new coffee addition." She set her coffee down and nodded to each of them.

Helen had been slowly adding food from Simay's cultural home in the Ottoman Empire and had recently added a blend of coffee named Arabic. Rather dark, heavy, and earthy it was quickly well received.

Captain Stuart looked at Sam, "Go ahead XO."

Sam nodded and displayed her file on the holo screen in the middle of the table. "As you can see the remainder of the crew will be aboard today. Arrivals are mostly gun crews, operations, and some stragglers here and there. We expect to be at projected strength by this afternoon. There are two main briefings scheduled in the cargo bay please ensure you get all your staff to one of them so everybody knows what we're doing. We will begin full operations this afternoon and begin flight simulations tomorrow. Administratively there is no issues at present other than the typical pay, and orders difficulties." she finished her quick brief.

Helen put her data up and looked at the Admiral, "Engineering is on schedule for completion as planned. There will be a few outstanding issues but they can be completed enroute to the engine test site. We have the full systems test scheduled for today and will have everything online for the first shift this afternoon. Pending the outcome of the test, engineering is ready to depart." Helen said happily.

Asteria's data appeared without her appearing to move, "Ma'am, tactical is fully staffed and settled. We are continuing to review available data and create simulations based on analysis. As of yet we do not have any scenario that we can say is likely after the failure of the Ottoman's last attempted maneuver."

She was referring to the attempt to bring Briton and the

Federated Colony into protracted conflict by framing Briton in an attack of the Hades system. It was the exposure of the misdirection that *Hypnos* had successfully brought to light. Asteria looked at them and nodded.

Callis nodded to the group, "Flight is building a training program and standard flight deck crew for the shuttles and fighters. I am working in conjunction with Commander Hypnea on the future deployment of the fighters in tactical situations." he said smiling. Everyone knew he was itching to get out in one of their new fighters.

Michael Delaney put up his data, "Ma'am, Operations is working out our mission protocols and will have that data out this afternoon. We have the rotation schedules and operational tempo worked. The timeframe is set for a forty-day flight under graviton engine and then Dower engine testing for an unspecified time frame. We will then proceed on to Clare for first stop. Just like last time…" he said grinning.

"Let's hope not… Gunny wouldn't like that." Shia said. The *Hypnos* had performed a similar flight and been attacked by the Ottoman Empire last time. Gunny had been pinned under a wayward missile when the gunnery deck took damage.

Michael smiled at Shia then looked at the Admiral, "My other job as Senior Marine is beginning. The Marine Commando platoon has arrived and is trashing their squad room right now. They approve of the ship and cannot wait to get going. Marine Lieutenant Sheffield is the platoon leader and so far seems to run a tight unit."

Natalia smiled at the previous comment, "Speaking of Gunny, all the hard lines have been checked and verified by the combat systems team. We are still receiving a couple today but should be at personnel capacity soon. I will have a much more comprehensive assessment when we complete the systems test today with engineering."

Simay looked at the group. "Navigation is complete with personnel. We have been working closely with Tactical and Operations in laying out our actual and simulated courses. The Midshipmen have arrived this morning and will be reporting to their first rotations this afternoon. We have five naval Midshipmen and one Marine Cadet down in forward eight twelve four. Please inform me if you have any issues and I will see to it." She looked at Shia who was sitting next to her.

Shia smiled, "Security is getting along well and I have a pretty cohesive team. We had a couple of minor issues with tempers flaring last night but so far things seem to be quite good. There was one report of minor theft and we are investigating. We will begin training with the Marine commando platoon tomorrow morning."

The Admiral smiled, "Thank you, everyone for doing such fantastic jobs. I have only a few comments…"

The quiet compartment in front of Cadet Carroll seemed more like the library back at Fortress Hills Marine Academy than the operations center for the ship. As she looked around trying to figure out who to ask where she was supposed to go she spotted a tall muscular Officer with Marine rank. She stepped a meter farther in the room and cleared her throat. The tall Marine Major noticed her and smiled.

"Sir, Cadet Carroll reporting as ordered." she said.

"Howdy Cadet Carroll, you're right on time. Please step into my office so we can talk." He headed for a hatch on the port side of the room. He stepped behind a desk littered with data chips and various types of tablets, he motioned her inside to a seat.

As she sat down he closed the hatch and sat behind his desk. "So welcome to the *Nyx*. I'm Major Michael Delaney the senior Marine Commando on the ship. And you are Cadet Katherine Carroll fifth year Cadet of Fortress Hills Marine Academy." He looked up from her file on his tablet. "How are you settling in?"

She shifted a bit uncomfortably in her seat, "Fine Sir, no issues."

He chuckled, "Well it seems that sometime during your training and psyche evaluations someone thought you would be a good Commando Officer and you were assigned to us. It is important for you to understand how unlikely it is that you ended up here. This ship has a full platoon of enlisted and seven officers who are fully Commando certified. That represents a full one fourth of all commandos in the fleet. This ship is beyond special. Only a handful of Marines are selected for Commando and never right out of the academy." he stared at her intently.

"You are officially here to prequalify for Commando Officers training. I assume that because you are here on this extremely special ship that you are equally special. When the crew sees a Cadet on this ship they will assume you are beyond qualified. That is because the Officers on this ship are all extraordinary." he picked up another tablet.

Katherine's heart was slamming in her chest. It was true that she had performed well in the academy but she was certainly not at the top of the class. Quite the opposite. She had suffered terribly through most of her training. She never quite fit in and was constantly harassed by the training officers. Despite being in a class of thirty Cadets she was extremely isolated and the treatment by the cadre only made it worse. The knowledge that she was expected to meet the standards of legendary Marine commanders like Captain Stuart and Major Delaney was almost suffocating.

"It will be my recommendation that either allows or denies this training for you. You will rotate through sections and absorb everything you can. These will not be jobs Marines typically do, I am absolutely certain you can shoot, direct fire teams, board ships, and fight in any combat situation from zero-G to close quarters. You will therefore begin in Tactical with Commander Hypnea, then move on to Engineering, Administrative, Combat systems, Signal, Navigation, and finally Operations here with me." He sent her a data file.

"That file is your rotation schedule; you will file reports regularly on your progress. Along with your rotations you will perform physical training with the Marine Officers every night at twenty-one hundred, this is in addition to your morning routine with Lieutenant Binici. You have thirty days to qualify with every sidearm and crew served Marine weapon on board, you have sixty days to qualify on all ships weapon systems on the Gunnery deck. You will qualify on main missiles and grazers during your combat systems rotation." He handed her a training data chip and smiled.

"This is all the systems onboard. You will report to the Marine deck right after this and receive your standard ships issue. Class three standard ship armor is to be worn every day, class two for external operations and every fifth day of the week. You will receive class one commando armor and the training to use it immediately. As far as I am concerned you are a fully qualified Commando Officer until you prove you are not." He stood up and looked at her. "When operating with the Marines you will report to Lieutenant Sheffield and act as his XO."

She stood up quickly.

"This will be the most difficult thing you have ever done but even if you fail you will be more highly trained than any other Marine Officer in your class," he reached out and shook her hand. "Dismissed."

She went ridged at attention and exited his office. She walked numbly across the compartment and out the main hatch. In a state of shock, she could barely see straight.

Dear stars she thought, she would never be able to do this! All those weapon qualifications and armor training and physical training… and work in Tactical! What have I done…? Why did I ever think I could be a Commando? I think I'm going to be sick!

"Cadet, are you ok?" a Petty Officer asked her.

She realized she was standing in the passage staring at the floor. "I'm fine, sorry, lost in thought," she said hurriedly, "Could you tell me where the Marine section is…?"

He looked at her funny, "I never thought I would hear a Marine ask that. It's aft deck three in the 'hell hole'." he said as he stepped around her and headed away.

She sighed and headed for the lift on wooden legs. "Hell hole" she thought?

She was the only person to exit on deck three and it was deserted, quiet, and hot. The deck vibrated in a strange rhythm as she headed further down and the air seemed odd and bitter. She swore it was darker here as well but it couldn't be, could it?

As she approached the main brace that denoted the aft of the ship she saw a massive hatch that was sealed. Scrawled across the hatch in red paint was the words 'Vampyre Platoon' and below that in a different handwriting 'Welcome to the hell hold'. Hold she thought not hole... She reached out to open the hatch and it swung in before she could reach it. She jumped back in shock.

"Sorry Ma'am, didn't mean to startle you." a corporal said as he stepped out, just off to my shift." He held the hatch open and motioned her inside.

She nodded to him and stepped in.

"Officer on deck!" a Marine said as she cleared the hatch. She looked up in surprise to see four Marines jump to attention. She looked behind her confused for a second before she realized they were referring to her.

"Um as you were..." she said a bit unsure.

They relaxed and a Master Sergeant stepped up to her. "Howdy Ma'am, welcome to the Vampyre hold," he said easily, "What can we do for you Ma'am?"

"I need to find the armory and receive my ships issue." She said uncertain.

"Ah, no problem, follow me Ma'am, I will set you up." He nodded and led her down a few passageways to a large hatch that seemed to already be scratched and dented in several places. Across the door a big green sign stated 'Safety First'. The Master Sergeant opened the hatch and walked in. The room was filled with gear on shelves, and workbenches were scattered with boxes and helmets.

"Ma'am, have you ever been issued skin before?" he asked looking at her critically.

"Skin? Not that I am aware of." she said unaware of what he was asking.

He smiled, "Jimmy! Get our sister here a full set of... size fives." he called out.

There was some commotion behind some crates in the back and she heard a reply. Several minutes later a short stocky man peered out and looked at them.

"Size five should work Master Sergeant." he said and carried several boxes out placing them on the desk.

"Ma'am, I'm Master Sergeant Franklin Goody senior enlisted Commando of this platoon. That is Lance Corporal Jimson or Jimmy." he said smiling.

"Nice to meet you Master Sergeant, I'm Ships Marine Cadet Katherine Carroll." she said.

"You mean Cadet Commando, right… You're about to receive gear that is earned not given." he said smiling at her.

His words were a warning but they were delivered as an encouragement. She nodded, "Yes, Cadet Commando Carroll."

"Don't forget it, be proud," he said, "How much time do you have?"

"I need to report to Tactical in an hour thirty." she said.

He nodded, "No problem, now if you would drop your dress uniform and hop into the scanner. You can have your new commando pressure suit and level three armor before you go. I will have your level two's delivered to your quarters and you need to go through level one training before we will let you take those babies. Send me your schedule and I will get you trained as soon as possible." he said as he walked over to the desk and began sorting her new gear.

Katherine nodded and walked over to the old scratched and dented scanner. She activated her suit and it peeled away. Completely nude she climbed into the scanner and it activated in a bright blue glow. A few minutes later it turned off as it finished its cycle. She climbed out and walked over to the Master Sergeant. In training the military eliminates embarrassment over nudity and it is not a problem for any member of the military to be naked in front of others.

Master Sergeant Goody handed her a pressure suit, she stepped into it and activated the controls. It sealed up around her and she looked down. Her suit was the same as the Master Sergeants, black bottoms and dark green top with silver piping. Her forearm had the silver dot of cadet and above it the crossed arrows over nova of commando branch. As she stared at the insignia she reached out and touched it, she couldn't stop herself as she smiled.

Master Sergeant Goody grinned at her. "You should see your face Ma'am, there is no doubt you're in the right place."

She stepped over to the counter and looked at the level three accessories for her suit. Slim thigh plates, shoulder and arm plates and a chest harness that held her sidearm and extra ammunition.

"All the things a commando needs," Sergeant Goody said smiling, "They are bioneural so all you do is place them. They seal and connect to your interface." He held her shoulder plate to her left arm and it melted into her suit. She could immediately feel the connection.

Grinning she attached the remaining parts and looked at the sidearm on the counter. "I haven't qualified yet." she said to the Master Sergeant.

He looked at her amused. "You're a commando now Ma'am, you never go unarmed regardless of qualification. I am pretty sure you got to this point in time with the knowledge of how not to shoot the crew."

She nodded and picked up the pistol. Flipping the docking lever, she cocked the pistol receiver and performed a safety check then snapped it shut toggled the safety and registered her bio sign to the weapon. The Sergeant smiled as she slid it into her chest harness.

"Textbook Ma'am. Good job," he said, "Let me show you around the hold. I assume you will be spending a lot of time down here."

"Thank you Corporal Jimson." she said as she followed Goody out the hatch.

"Aye Ma'am, let me know if you need anything." he replied.

"So Miss Carroll you just saw the quartermaster, also in this passageway is the training room, weapons range, and classroom." he said pointing to the various hatches.

She could see three Marines in massive armor going through drills in the training room. The suits were huge black metal exoskeletons. They looked massive and powerful.

Master Sergeant Goody pointed to the Marines. "Have you seen level one armor up close before?" he asked.

"No, only in the hall of armor at Fortress Hills. They wouldn't let us get close." she said frowning.

He laughed, "That old thing, its generation two. These are cutting edge generation five suits. They come standard with rail gun mounts, micro drone net, and anti-personnel sensors. Fully integrated into our neural implants. The suit reacts faster than the mind can process so they come with inhibitors. Without training you could literally tear your own body apart." he said pointing out the parts.

She looked back at him in fear.

"Don't fret Ma'am, I'll train you up fine." he reassured her.

Reluctantly she followed him out into the main room. "So over there are quarters and next to it our own mess. Guess the Fleet is afraid of us when we eat..." he chuckled, "There we have the ready room for gear and briefing. Last but not least the platoon leader's office and quarters." he said walking over to the door. "Sir, Cadet Carroll is here." he said leaning into the office.

A tall thin Lieutenant stepped out and offered his hand. "Lieutenant Sheffield platoon commander of the Vampyres." he smiled.

"Commando Cadet Carroll," she said shaking his hand, "Pleasure to meet you Sir."

"Ah call me Sheffield or LT; commandos are pretty informal," he said, "I see Goody has shown you around and gotten you into the proper uniform."

"Yes he is being very helpful." she said.

He nodded his approval, "Well you're one of us now so you're welcome here anytime. If you have any issues, please feel free to come see me. I can't imagine being a Cadet on this ship with our mission, I was on a very uneventful mission in Hades on my cruise... Your first is not only on a special mission but as a commando surrounded by commandos..." he shook his head slowly.

CHAPTER 2
Tactical Trouble

Cadet Katherine Carroll
Deck Seven, Tactical
Light Destroyer Nyx, Dry Dock
Asphodel Fields, Tartarus System
191.0188 FCUDT 12:27:30

An hour later Katherine hurried down the passageway in her beautiful new level three commando armor in route to the Tactical compartment on level seven. Master Sergeant Goody had taught her how to correctly attach her armor and thrown in a few secrets to help her out in daily use. She had taken to quite enjoy his easy manner and sarcastic sense of humor.

She stepped into the proper compartment a few minutes early and saw an amazing holo of the Orion arm. She literally was standing in space surrounded by the beautiful stars and nebulas. She nearly collapsed from vertigo as the scene turned and zoomed into the forward frontier of the Colonies.

"Careful Cadet Commando Carroll... it takes a bit to get used to the simulated expanse." a woman's voice said to her from nearby.

She looked around to identify the source and a figure seemed to appear several meters away. She walked over and looked at Katherine. Katherine was shocked and speechless at the sight of the 'woman'.

A six-foot-tall well-proportioned figure in all black, level two plate armor with a pink glow emanating from underneath stood there. She had extremely human looking features but definitely was not human. Katherine had tried to imagine what a cybernetic lifeform would look like when she found out about Asteria Hypnea, but this was beyond her wildest imaginings.

33

Asteria Hypnea was the offspring of the artificial intelligence named Arthur who was destroyed in a conflict aboard the *Hypnos*. In a final act before his destruction he created her from an amalgam designed to fit in a miniaturized computer core. That core resided in a cybernetic frame and for all practical purposes was the frame. She is so complicated that the government decided to create a new lifeform designation for her. Katherine tried to remember the details but was promptly standing before the beautiful machine.

"Katherine Carroll reporting for duty Ma'am." she said officially.

Asteria laughed lightly, a surprisingly human sound. "Relax Cadet Carroll, I propose to work you hard enough that formality is needless," she smiled at her, "Follow me, I will familiarize you with your first several days of work."

Commander Samantha Leeane
Deck Six, First Officers Quarters
Light Destroyer Nyx, Dry Dock
Asphodel Fields, Tartarus System
191.0188 FCUDT 12:30:02

Sam closed her eyes and she was walking barefoot through the green grass raising her face into the suns warm rays. She could hear her daughter Eva laughing as she ran past chasing the family dog. Then she heard Eva call out to her father. Sam opened her eyes and looked across the grass field.

Eva had just met her father for the first time twelve days ago and taken right to him. Sam was still shocked to hear Eva call out to her "Daddy".

Edward Charles Windsor ran up swooping Eva into his arms smiling happily. Eva laughed and giggled in his arms. He carried her back over and Eva held out her arms to Sam. She took Eva into her arms and held her tightly.

"Hey silly girl why are you chasing that dog…?" Sam

asked her.

"We're playing mommy!" Eva cried as Sam tickled her. She carried Eva back to the blanket where they were having a picnic lunch in the wonderful afternoon sun. As she set Eva down she took off running again.

"Don't go far little girl!" Sam called after her.

Edward sat down on the blanket and picked up his drink. "Thank you for this." he said to Sam.

She sat down and looked at him, "I should have done it long ago. I'm sorry," she put her hand on his arm, "Now that you're here though you must know she won't let you leave."

He smiled as Eva ran by. "Yes, I don't think I can. I have requested to remain the attaché; I don't think they actually want me back." he smiled.

They were both covert agents for the government. Different governments… Sam had been assigned to spy on him in the closing years of the war with Briton and had eventually fallen in love. She terminated her assignment when he revealed to her he knew she was a spy and asked her to marry him. She had run away only to find out she was pregnant with Eva.

Ten years later Edward had been following leads on the Ottoman Empire when he encountered the crew of the *Hypnos* on Clew Bay Station. He had seen Sam get kidnapped and had followed to try to find her. He eventually happened to run into her on the streets of a pirate base named Libertatia and she was badly injured. Deciding that turning himself in was the only way to help Sam he risked prison as a covert British spy and carried her to her ship.

Sam had eventually told him about Eva and she brought him home to meet her as soon as she had leave.

It turned out to be a great thing. Sam could feel her old feelings for Edward resurfacing and Eva just loved him. She tried not to think about having to leave in a few days.

"Will you be able to spend time with her?" Sam asked.

Edward looked at her. "I will spend as much as you will allow me." he said immediately.

"You are listed as her father; you have all the legal rights in Tartarus as such. Trusting you was never a problem Edward. I simply ask you don't take her from Tartarus without me." she said seriously.

He cocked his head, "You mean I could have her live with me on Acheron? You wouldn't object to that?" he said hesitantly.

"Of course not Edward. You would take care of her better than I could imagine. Just make sure it's what she wants as well," she smiled at him. "I will sleep better knowing you're with her." Sam said to Edward.

He leaned over and lightly kissed her. "I am going to miss you. I have gotten used to having you around." he said.

Sam looked at Eva and sighed. "I am going to miss both of you." she said. Eva ran over and jumped in between them. Sam lay back on the blanket and held Eva in her arms. Edward lay next to them and smiled. The three lay there and enjoyed the warm Erebus sun.

A tone sounded bringing Sam back from her reverie. That was her alarm alerting her she was due on the bridge in a few moments. She stepped out of her room and over to the command lift. The bridge officers' quarters were directly above the bridge on deck six and took only seconds to access. It was extremely convenient. She left the lift and walked through the massive hatch of the main bridge.

Easily three times the size of the *Hypnos* Bridge the *Nyx* boasted a full combat crew of seventeen plus the Admiral. It could get very hectic. To the port was the semicircle of the combat systems team and their three crew members. Just forward of them lay the domain of Lieutenant Binici and her two navigators with their large holo screens and flowing data.

On the opposite side to starboard sat the large semicircle station of engineering. It was bustling with activity as they came and went checking data lines. Forward of the engineers was the large consoles of tactical and the imposing figure of Asteria Hypnea. Asteria calmly directed her crew with efficiency and ease.

Between the four stations lay the large command holo where the command team directs the ship. Currently the ships status floated surrounded by several overlays of navigation and tactical data.

Just in front of the command holo was Major Kane's pilot station and Chief Santiago's communication station.

Sam stared out the front of the ship. The bridge was located directly under the large shovel shaped nose of the ship. It had the first actual windows of any ship she had been on. Recent improvements in nano-fabrication created by Commander Dower were being implemented all over the ship. Those windows were one of the more impressive creations. Right now the massive blast shields were retracted and she could see the dry dock sitting only a few hundred meters away. She looked to her left and could see Acheron off in the distance. A sudden pang of home sickness stabbed at her. She took a deep breath and looked down at the holo.

She took another breath and looked up, "All right ladies and gentlemen let's get her up to speed. All stations report by the numbers and perform a full up systems check," Sam said.

The Bridge came alive as the crew activated their consoles and began systems checks and diagnostics. Tones alerted everyone that Captain Adam Stuart had arrived on the Bridge.

Sam turned and smiled at him, "Afternoon Boss, systems coming online now."

"Excellent! It's been a long three months." he said eagerly.

They both watched as holos blanked and flickered then booted up and ran through diagnostic settings. A Petty Officer from Navigation looked up at an Engineering technician.

"Blown data circuit on Navigation console thirteen point eight delta." he said.

"Stand by." The technician said as he popped a cover and crawled into the deck under the console. He wiggled and squirmed and then crawled back out.

"Give it a try now." he said putting the cover back on.

"Aye, thanks sparky." the Petty Officer said.

Sam smiled and leaned over to the Captain, "They have been calling the engineers sparky, as in one of Sparks' team…" she said to him.

He smiled and chuckled, "Well it does seem to fit." he said.

After several minutes Chief Warrant Officer Kila Zucco stepped in front of the Captain. "Sir, all systems check out and are operational. Chief Engineer is requesting permission to detach from dockside power and load all circuits." she said smiling.

Kila was another of the original *Hypnos* crew. She was the lead Bridge Engineer and the best ship structural engineer in the fleet. She could figure out which single beam to cut that would ruin and entire dreadnaught.

Adam nodded, "Permission granted Kila, load the systems and bring up the reactors."

He activated the ships com, "All stations, prepare for internal power switchover. Monitor and report all issues promptly." he called.

There was a slight momentary dimming of the lights and a resonating hum filled the deck as the incredibly powerful reactors powered up.

"Sir, two hundred sixty-four minor faults and one conduit failure have been logged. One com substation failure, and two thruster nodes have overloaded. Shield deterioration on the port aft quarter due to emitter failure." Kila reported.

Sam looked surprised, "That's all?"

Helen appeared on the port holo. "Sir the ship is stable,

all systems are operational and status is classified green, although the shield is not where it should be." she said frowning.

"Helen, you have done absolutely extraordinary work. You and the build team are amazing." Adam said to her.

Helen smiled, "Thank you sir, we will have her at one hundred percent in time to depart."

Admiral Lune stepped into the Bridge, "Congratulations Helen."

"Admiral, thank you." she said.

Coline walked over and stood next to Adam casually. "Looks like it's almost time to leave Adam…"

"Yes, I would have to agree Coline." he said.

Commander Helen Dower
Deck Two, Main Engineering
Light Destroyer Nyx, Dry Dock
Asphodel Fields, Tartarus System
191.0188 FCUDT 16:41:42

"You're sandbagging Ben… you know I don't pay by the hour don't you," Helen said grinning at Marine Chief Warrant Officer Ben Coso in the big holo of the Engineering center.

"Awe shucks Ma'am, this is hard work, and you know I love getting all nauseas for you out here in zero-G…"

Ben was leading a team of engineers out on the hull of the ship repairing the shield emitters. He was an old hand at external repairs and was the head of the electrical engineering section.

Helen laughed at him, "Hurry up! Dinner is getting cold." she said making an inside joke about the old dinners the crew used to have before the *Nyx*.

"Tell Gunny I want spaghetti!" he laughed. "We are clear, go ahead and power up the grid."

The engineering staff ran through the power up sequence and the system went live. There was a bright flash off to the left outside the visual pickup and alarms went off on the console.

"Stars, Tony clip in and go get her, Susie back him up will ya," Ben ordered his team. "Sparks emitter thirty-four blew out, took specialist Conroy out into low orbit. Recovering now, we're going to need medical at airlock delta seven." he said.

"Roger Ben, they will be there when you arrive. What else do you need?" she asked.

"We're good now boss, Tony has her and we are headed direct to the airlock." Ben said.

Helen nodded and called the Bridge, "XO, we have an accident with one crewman injury on the hull outside airlock delta seven." she reported,

Sam looked concerned, "What's happened Helen?" she asked.

"We repaired the emitters that were malfunctioning and when we activated the grid a new emitter overloaded. I will have it removed and brought in for inspection; it should not have done that." she said upset.

"Okay, let me know if you need anything, I will inform the Captain." Sam said.

Helen disconnected and got up, "Jacob you have the section, I am going to run up there and check on them." she said looking at Naval Lieutenant Jacob Lavagnino.

"Aye Ma'am, I will take care of it." he said to her as she nodded at him.

A few minutes later she saw the medics rushing the crewmen down the passage into medical. She saw Brynn and her second in charge take over and start diagnostics. Ben walked up next to her.

"I figured you'd be here," he said as he walked up. "It didn't look so bad but she was unconscious and nonresponsive," he indicated Specialist Conroy.

They watched awhile until Brynn sealed the Specialist into a white capsule so she could rapid heal. She walked out after sterilizing her suit and looked at Helen and Ben.

"Well, she won't suffer any permanent damage. The blast basically ruptured several of her organs and knocked her unconscious. She will require several days in medical stasis to complete the re-growth," she looked at Helen and smiled, "Maybe a look at the safety procedures, she was obviously far too close the emitters."

"Yea, I think that would be prudent. Thank you Brynn. Let me know if something changes." Helen said.

Several hours later Helen walked back into a much less populated engineering section. Jacob and another engineer were standing next to a destroyed emitter. Jacob saw her and motioned for her to join him. He dismissed the other engineer and looked at Helen as she walked up.

"This is the faulty emitter," he waved his hand at the burned device next to him. "We have completed the inspection; the results are… unusual."

She raised an eyebrow at him, "What do you mean, 'unusual,' how?" she asked.

"This emitter did not malfunction, Helen it could not have overloaded like it did." he said seriously.

She looked confused, "Your saying it did something it could not have done… That's not possible. Unless…" her face went wide with surprise. "You think…?"

He looked blankly at her, "Helen I don't know, all I know is that it could not do what it did. Beyond that I can only speculate."

Helen pulled her tablet out and activated her com.

Sam looked back at her from the tablet, "Helen, you're up late, what's wrong?"

"Sam I need your and Asteria's help with something potentially serious," she said evenly, "Can you get down here now?"

Sam immediately looked concerned, "Of course I will be there in a few minutes, and do I need to alert anyone?"

Helen shook her head, "Not yet, I will need your assessment to decide what to do next." she said.

Asteria appeared in the tablet next to Sam, "I am on my

41

way as well Helen. Is this in reference to today's accident?" she asked.

"Yes Astie, data file three forty-seven dash sixty-two bravo." Helen said reading the file header.

"We will be there in a minute, standby." Sam said as she disconnected.

A few minutes later the four of them were in an engineering planning room to the starboard of main engineering. Helen looked grim as Sam reviewed the data.

Asteria looked up from the technical scans of the emitter. "Your evaluation is accurate; this was not a possible outcome unless outside interference occurred."

Sam looked at them, "If the technical data is correct the analysis is also correct. It seems someone deliberately caused this emitter to malfunction. We need to initiate a scan on all installed and surplus emitters."

Jacob looked confused, "Why sabotage a single emitter; it would gain you nothing except maybe hurting one or two people."

Asteria shook her head, "We know nothing about this and it would be pure speculation to try to guess. It could be the beginning of something more contrived or a spurned paramour…"

Sam frowned at the table, "I'm going to put security on the critical systems and mandate stringent safety protocols until we figure this out."

"Just to be clear, we're saying there could be a saboteur aboard." Helen said.

Sam nodded, "Yes."

Lieutenant Simay Binici
Deck Thirteen, Forward Eight Twelve Four
Light Destroyer Nyx, Dry Dock
Asphodel Fields, Tartarus System
194.0188 FCUDT 05:27:00

The light came on as Simay called out loudly, "Good

morning Midshipmen! It is now zero five twenty-seven and you have three minutes to be ready for training. Fall in!"

At the sound of her first words chaos erupted in the bay. Two Midshipmen were sprawled on the floor trying to hurry. Simay noticed that Miss Carroll was wearing level three armor as she jumped from her berth. She observed the chaos for three minutes.

"Your three minutes are up! Get in line now!" she ordered.

The group hurried into a single rank along the white line on the deck. Simay walked slowly down the line. Mr. Bailey and Perez were disheveled but nearly completely dressed. Miss Worley was nude from the waist up and Mr. Gustafson was from the waist down. Mr. Scott was missing shoes and finally Miss Carroll was in her Marine pressure suit.

"You will be ready for training in three minutes or you will train as you are at that time. You are not allowed to sleep in your training uniform. You will have your level three uniform ready by your berth at all times unless you're wearing it! An emergency could happen at any time and you shall be ready!" She looked at them seriously, "Am I understood?"

They all responded in chorus, "Yes Ma'am!"

"Excellent, we will now run to the training hall and do our daily workout. Follow me." Simay turned and ran out the hatch. The group quickly followed behind. Simay ran them down the outside of the ships passageway all the way down to the base of the enlisted crew quarters across to the port and back up to the nose of the ship. The route is closed to foot traffic during the hours of training to allow for running. It forms a track of one half kilometer in length. She took them on four laps. They attracted a bit of attention in their unusual state of dress.

An hour later she stood in front of them in their quarters. "Alright, it is now zero six thirty you have thirty minutes for personal hygiene before breakfast in the Officers mess. You will be at breakfast. It is an important part of an officer's day to socialize with the other officers every morning. You will need food to maintain your strength and vitality," she looked at them. Miss Worley was obviously displeased and Mr. Perez was not paying attention.

"I highly suggest you all figure out a way to be ready for training. In five days you will be required to dress as the least ready person in the group is dressed. If you do not want to embarrass yourselves and run in front of the entire crew naked I suggest you make a plan," she said grinning at them, "Dismissed."

The Midshipmen turned and began gathering their things to shower and prepare for the day. Simay left the room and headed for the lift. In minutes she was in and out of the sonic shower and dressed a few minutes after that. Brynn smiled at her as she stepped out of the small bathroom.

"Are you coming to breakfast with me?" Simay asked her hopeful.

Brynn looked at her with a slight grin, "Ok, I just don't want to disrupt your schedule."

"I need to maintain my personal welfare as well as my professional," Simay said in a mocking tone.

Brynn was well known for her sage advice similar to her teasing words. Brynn feigned shock at Simay. They laughed as they walked out toward the Officers mess.

"How was your first training day?" Brynn asked her.

Simay rolled her eyes in frustration, "I'm pretty sure Jennifer Worley would kill me if I gave her a chance. I am positive Katherine Carroll could..."

"The Marine?" Brynn said raising her eyebrows. "Why do you think that?"

Simay shrugged, "I am really intimidated by the Fleet commandos, they are tough and focused. The Cadet did her whole workout today in her level three armor and didn't break a sweat."

Brynn nodded understanding, "Yes, they *are* tough.

They are also smart, honest, and extremely loyal," she said.

"The last time I met extremely loyal Soldiers they threw me in a cell and nearly beat me to death," she said quietly.

Brynn placed her hand on Simay's arm, "That was different, commandos are not indoctrinated they think for themselves," she said carefully. "You do not have to fear them."

Master Chief Shia O'Connell
Deck Thirteen, Ships Mess
Light Destroyer Nyx, Dry Dock
Asphodel Fields, Tartarus System
195.0188 FCUDT 07:10:34

Shia stepped away from the food dispenser and surveyed the room for a place to sit. Near the back a young lady sat alone staring at her plate. As Shia approached she sized up the pensive sailor. She had auburn red hair tied back tightly exposing her high cheekbones and sharp chin. She saw the small silver circle of Marine Cadet rank on her forearm as she paused at the table.

"Mind if I join you Ma'am?" Shia said smiling.

She looked up suddenly, "Um, of course Master Chief!"

Shia nodded, "Thank you, Cadet...?"

"Carroll, Katherine Carroll." she replied.

"And I'm Shia O'Connell. Nice to meet you Miss Carroll."

Katherine's eyes widened, "The security chief?"

Shia chuckled, "Yes, but don't worry I'm really a nice person and it you looked like you could use some company."

Katherine's head dropped a bit, "Is it that obvious Chief?"

Shia looked over the top of her coffee cup and saw Katherine's stunning silver eyes carefully looking back at her. "Call me Shia and no it's not that obvious, I just have some experience in the 'not fitting in' arena." Shia saw a tiny bit of relief in Katherine's face as she relaxed. They ate in silence for a minute before Shia looked at Katherine again.

"So, what's the problem?" she asked.

Katherine grimaced for a second and looked at her plate.

Shia cocked her head at Katherine, "You know a few months ago I was a civilian. I spent years on tiny ships and freighters as a security specialist. This is the first time I've ever been on such a big ship; it took me a week to figure out how to get from the bridge to engineering. There's fifty times the number of people on this ship than I'm used to." She sipped her coffee slowly, "Is this your first time on a big ship?"

"Yes," Katherine said to her breakfast, "It's my second time in space... besides the month of training around Hades."

"Is that what's bothering you?" Shia asked.

"No... I'm just having trouble fitting in. I'll be ok." Katherine said looking up at her.

Shia nodded, "I'm sure you will."

"Hello ladies!" Josephine said sitting down, "Another beautiful morning."

Shia laughed, "Hey Joe, have you met Miss Katherine Carroll?"

Joe smiled brightly at Katherine, "Only in passing, it's nice to meet you Katherine."

"Nice to meet you Mrs. Santiago," Katherine said quietly.

"Oh call me Joe, the mess hall is the only place I can relax around here," she grinned back at her, "You two looked like you're in deep conversation, so I thought I would lighten it up!"

"Always sunny eh Joe?" Shia said.

"Of course, otherwise I would go nuts and start painting murals with the condiments..." she giggled.

"See Katherine? The trick is to find one or two friends who are insane and ignore the rest. Keeps you on your toes," Shia poked her tongue out at Joe.

Katherine smiled at the exchange.

"Well it's settled, we're officially friends!" Joe said to Katherine.

"I think you can do better... Joe's really unstable," Simay said sitting next to Katherine.

Joe feigned shock at the sudden arrival of Simay.

Katherine went rigid at the sound of her senior Lieutenant's voice. Simay looked at Katherine, "Relax Katherine, I'm not really that bad."

Shia leaned over to Katherine and whispered loudly, "Simay is a little bit crazier than Joe, just so you know," she leaned back and winked at her.

Katherine let out a snort at the comment and tried to hide her smile.

"Hey what did you just tell her!" Simay demanded playfully.

"Only the truth dear Simay, only the truth," Shia teased. She watched Katherine slowly relax and after a few minutes joined the groups' small talk and rumor telling.

As the small group of ladies separated and headed for their daily duties Simay stepped up next to Shia.

"I haven't seen Katherine that outgoing ever, she seems to like you," Simay said, "Thank you for that."

"She looked like she needed a friend, and I'm a friendly person," Shia said.

"Sure..." Simay said mocking her as she headed through the mess hatch.

"What?" Shia said in defense as Simay disappeared.

Cadet Katherine Carroll
Deck Thirteen, Officers Mess
Light Destroyer Nyx, Dry Dock
Asphodel Fields, Tartarus System
196.0188 FCUDT 07:06:04

The mess hall for breakfast yet again... Katherine's brain was trying to create an equation out of the chaotic pattern of her breakfast of scrambled yellow protein. She had been studying so much she couldn't focus on anything. She had fallen asleep studying in the simulation lab last night after Marine physical training that evening. Luckily a concerned Petty Officer had woken her up in the early hours of the morning. The ancient battle she was studying had been playing for hours while she slept through it.

She had been assigned to adapt ancient battle strategies into modern space tactics. She had to first decipher the strategy then attempt to apply it and formulate an algorithm that would simulate it. She wanted to sleep, not eat. Another day of trying to understand the mind of an ancient warrior who used wooden stakes to fight was going to kill her.

"Hello Miss Carroll," Major Callis Kane said as he sat across from her, "You look distracted."

She frowned, "Sorry Sir, I have eight-thousand-year old battle strategies running amok in my head."

Joe laughed as she sat down, "A little light breakfast thinking..."

Katherine smiled at Joe, "Morning Joe."

"Sounds like Asteria is running you hard in Tactical," Callis said.

Katherine looked up at him blankly for a second before she replied, "Um, yes Sir." She looked at the wall and saw the ships clock. "Oh! I have to get to work, excuse me Sir," she said hurriedly.

"You didn't eat," Joe said looking at Katherine's plate.

She looked down and frowned, "Oh... well I'm ok, I will grab something in a bit," she said as she stood to leave.

"Miss Carroll," Callis said as she moved to leave but didn't seem to hear him. "Cadet!" he said louder.

She turned and looked at him, "I'm sorry, yes sir?" she said quickly.

He placed a meal bar on her tray and looked her in the eye, "You are to eat that on the way to duty. Do you understand?" he said seriously.

She looked at him suddenly incredibly intimidated, "Yes sir!" she said.

He nodded and she hurried off to dispose of her tray. As she entered the small alcove where the recycler was she suddenly sprawled out onto the floor in a clattering heap. As she sat up on the floor in horrid embarrassment she spotted Midshipmen Worley standing near the wall.

"You really should watch where you going, you almost splashed me with your stupidity," she hissed.

"You tripped me!" Katherine said quietly.

A smirk crossed her face and she walked away laughing under her breath. Katherine picked up her tray as an orderly stepped over to help her clean up.

"I've got it Ma'am, don't worry it happens from time to time," he nodded to her. "You've got some on your uniform."

She wiped off the remains of her breakfast and fought to hold back tears as her face turned red.

"Ma'am?" the orderly said as she started to turn to leave.

She looked back at him and he was holding out the meal bar. "Oh, thank you?" she said quietly.

"Crewman Harris," he said smiling.

"Thank you Harris, I'm sorry about this," she responded and hurried away.

She stepped into the passageway with the bar in her hand. She ripped it open and shoved it into her mouth. She hurried down the passage toward the lifts as she chewed the bar. The sudden taste made her stomach grumble in hunger pains. She jumped into the lift before the doors closed.

"Breakfast must be terrible today if you're eating that…" a young crewman said looking at her.

She looked at him as she took another mouthful and shrugged. The door opened and she hurried off down the passageway.

An hour later Katherine sat on the floor of a simulation room as a young general from earth history lead an army through a beautiful valley. He faced terrible odds and was outnumbered but pushed on. She began to recognize little things like the timing of certain orders and the path of certain groups.

This really is beautiful when you just observe she thought. She had on a whim, set the computer to high detail, and what appeared in front of her was unbelievable. She was in the battle. She sat on the grass next to the General's table and watched him write orders to his Captains. She had stood on the line as Soldiers fired ancient chemical guns at each other without cover. She followed the flow of the battle and suddenly she understood.

She jumped up and opened four simulation windows. She asked for four specific battles she had seen in the past days and rapidly advanced them to certain points. In a few minutes she had it. All five battles had similar tactics even though they were hundreds of years apart.

The door slid open and Commander Hypnea walked in. She looked at Katherine, "What did you discover Miss Carroll?" she asked.

Katherine stared at her in disbelief. She had walked in at the precise moment she had figured it out.

"Um, Ma'am, I believe the tactics used in these five battles I am studying are the same even though they are completely separate," she said hesitantly.

Asteria walked over and looked at the windows. "Very good Miss Carroll, you recognized that in a very short time. These battles are all in a tactic called oblique order. It is quite variable and difficult to recognize," she looked at Katherine. "The first step in defeating an enemy is recognizing how they are attacking you and then countering it. Marines are taught to attack and win but you must be more, especially when you order those who attack."

She walked around the simulation and stared at the General. "Why did you play this one in high definition?" Asteria asked.

"It was just an impulsive decision at the time I began it. I believe it helped me understand though," Katherine said.

"Maybe… watching the General make decisions that ended the lives of men caused you to connect somehow," she turned and walked to Katherine. "You are done here for today, come with me to the Bridge we are about to depart dry-dock and I want you to be there," Asteria said.

Katherine smiled happily, "Yes Ma'am!"

They walked out of Tactical and down to deck five. As they approached the Bridge hatch a Marine in level two armor saluted them. Katherine smiled at him as she passed.

She stopped dead as she entered the Bridge. Star struck she stared at the sight in awe. It was far larger than she thought it would be. There were several separate workstations and a large holo in the center. She felt that there was an electricity in the air. Asteria turned and motioned for her to follow. She stopped at the commander's chair and came to attention. Katherine quickly did the same and her breath caught as she saw who was in the chair.

"Commander Hypnea and Cadet Commando Carroll reporting for duty, Ma'am," Asteria said as she crisply saluted.

Admiral Coline Lune smiled at them. She saluted back, "Welcome to the Bridge Miss Carroll, you must have made an impression on the Commander to be here today."

Asteria dropped her salute and headed for the tactical consoles. Katherine tried to hurry after her.

Asteria looked at Katherine, "Sit here next to me, place your hand on the console and sign in. This will be your station while you're in Tactical. You are to monitor the ships traffic and orbital data network," she said as she sat down.

Katherine sat and went through the process of registering the console to her codes. Katherine looked around the Bridge. She saw Lieutenant Binici on the port side facing her and Major Kane up front next to Warrant Officer Santiago. She turned to see Major Delaney in the rear of the Bridge.

She looked behind her and froze. Commander Dower looked up and smiled happily at her. Katherine couldn't believe she was looking at the most famous engineer in history. Commander Dower went about her tasks as Katherine tried not to stare at her. She returned her attention to the console in front of her.

"All right ladies and gentlemen… and Callis," Captain Stuart said as he walked in. "Let's get our lady out and stretch her legs a little," he said as he sat next to Admiral Lune. "I want an all up beginning with engineering."

Helen smiled, "Engineering is in the green!" she said proudly. "We have full thrusters, shields, and reactors are at one hundred percent."

"Combat is all up Captain," Lieutenant Commander Volkov said.

Asteria laid a tablet on the desk in front of Katherine. She read it and her eyes went wide.

Captain Stuart looked over.

"Sir, Tactical is all up. Plot is clear and orbital net is online," Katherine said and swallowed hard.

He smiled at her and looked at Lieutenant Binici, "Navigation is all up. We have course information for high orbit plotted sir!" she said with confidence.

"Helm up at your command," Major Kane said.

"Com is all up, we have confirmation for departure from dock control and ready for handoff to orbital traffic control," Chief Santiago said.

Captain Stuart looked around, "Natalia, how about we pull back our armor and use those pretty new windows."

"Aye sir," she replied.

Katherine looked up startled as the lights dimmed and bright light pierced the Bridge from the front of the room. She stared in amazement as the shields retracted and directly in front of them was the dry dock. Actual windows! The perfect blue and white sphere of Acheron sat just beyond the end of the dock struts. Small ships silently glided through the view surrounded by deep black of local space.

It took Katherine's entire will to tear her eyes from the magnificent view.

"Callis, take us out," Captain Stuart said.

"Aye sir!" he responded, "Sequence initiated."

The ship began to slowly slide out into space. "Seventy-five meters to the end of the dock," Asteria announced. "Fifty meters. Twenty. Clear!"

The com chirped, "FCS *Nyx* you are clear for orbital entry proceed on manual," the dock master said.

"Manual control established, course locked and initiating," Callis called out.

Outside the dry dock slipped off to the starboard and the ship accelerated out between several small stations.

"Good job ladies and gentlemen, begin rotation of shifts. We anticipate exit approval in twenty-four hours," Admiral Lune said as she stood and headed for the command lift.

Asteria looked at Katherine, "Excellent Cadet, you are on first watch. It is from zero eight to noon at which point you are to complete your shift in Tactical. You are dismissed, see you tomorrow."

"Yes Ma'am," she signed off the console and stood. As she walked out she remembered she had level one commando training today. Excited she hurried off to the hell hold.

"Were you guarding the hatch to the Bridge...?" a familiar voice said.

Katherine looked up to see Midshipmen Worley. She had successfully avoided the Midshipmen thus far except in their quarters.

"I mean that's what Marines do, right. What else would you be doing on deck five?" she rolled her eyes at Katherine as she laughed and walked away.

Katherine retreated into the lift with her head down. Her excitement all but disappeared.

A short while later Katherine stood in the armory staring

at the impossible machine that applied level one armor.

"It's simple, you just step in and it suits you up," Master Sergeant Goody said smiling. He typed in a command and motioned her onto the platform.

Katherine stood in a super thin plain suit that served as the base for the heavy commando armor. She took a deep breath and stepped up into the machine. Bright green light flowed around her and she took a sharp breath as she realized it was a graviton field. The field lifted her body gently off the platform and began to hum. Above her hatches opened and the armor slid down surrounding her in the air.

"Ok here it goes." Master Sergeant Goody said as he activated the console.

Massive plates closed in and snapped to her legs sealing to her body like puzzle pieces. In seconds she was cocooned in reactive metal. The heavy helmet was the last piece to snap closed sealing her into darkness. She took a tentative breath inside the suit.

"Can you hear me?" he asked.

"Yes, it's dark. What do I do?" she asked beginning to feel claustrophobic.

"Standby, I am powering you up," he replied.

She could feel a warm tingle as the suit connected to her neuro implant and suddenly she could see again. Streams of data ran past her vision and a piercing electric shock ran down her spine. Then she realized she could feel the gentle flow of air across her body.

"I can feel the outside of the suit!" she blurted out surprised.

"Good that means you're fully connected. The suits sensors are feeding your brain data. You have full tactile sensation in this suit," Sergeant Goody said from his console.

Katherine looked at him suddenly scared, "Can I feel pain?" she asked concerned.

Sergeant Goody laughed, "No... well yes but it won't

hurt. It feels like pressure on you skin," he said to her slight relief. "You can step down but do it slowly, your suit is configured to delay right now so you can't hurt yourself."

She carefully moved her arm and it snapped up to her face.

"Slow!" he said alarmed.

"I'm trying!" Katherine replied scared. Forcing herself to be precise and slow she moved one leg at a time and stepped to the deck. She stopped and looked at Sergeant Goody trying to stay as still as possible.

Three hours later Katherine was flying through the air after a combat drone with fierce anger in her mind. She snatched it just before she hit the ground and placed it between her and the deck. She jammed her suits thumbs into its control circuits and rolled with perfect fluid grace back up into a crouch. She twitched threw the drone, it flew across the room and collided with the last active drone. They blew apart into pieces.

The lights flashed and came to full intensity. Katherine's face shield slid fluidly back into her helmet. Commando armor was the most advanced suit in the colonies. It looked organic, like it was grown from her body. In a way it was, the material actually interfaced with her body underneath. The suit was mated to her nervous system. She wasn't alerted that her weapon was out of ammunition, she felt it, like it was another arm. Katherine absolutely loved it.

Master Sergeant Goody stepped into the room smiling. "You Miss Carroll are a natural. Watching you fight is like watching a symphony back on Acheron. You have received a perfect score, the second on the ship! Congratulations."

She turned and looked at him, Thank you Goody."

"I checked your file, you don't have a call sign?" he said.

"No I don't. I never had the opportunity to need one," she said.

"Well, we found one for you. The boys think you attack with the vengeance of a dragon and venom of a snake...

55

You have been named, Miss Carroll. Wyvern."

She felt her armor react. A long scaled two legged dragon appeared stretching from her left leg to her left shoulder. It had wings that reached out and touched her right shoulder. It was both regal and terrifying. Her helmet altered to show two white fangs stretching down from above her forehead in the symbol of the Marine unit.

"Welcome to the Vampyres Wyvern," he said.

Katherine grinned back at him proudly.

Lieutenant Simay Binici
Deck Ten, Aft Port Training Bay
Light Destroyer Nyx, Dry Dock
Asphodel Fields, Tartarus System
197.0188 FCUDT 20:07:50

Simay grunted with effort as Sergeant James Colfax increased the gravity on the training mat. "Getting soft Binici..." he said grinning.

"No!" she gasped as she fought to stay upright in the staggering gravity well.

"Good now we're going to run through the katas," he said stepping heavily onto the mat in front of her. "Remember, focus on your center, move slowly through each iteration and breathe."

They took up the initial pose and together began to slowly move to each fighting position in rhythmical precision. After several minutes Simay felt her heart settle into a steady beat and her sweating slowed. Her breathing was deep and calm. She had been working on these ancient warrior training exercises for the past week. James had suggested it after realizing she was so stressed out. Against her initial judgment it was actually working quite well and she now enjoyed these sessions very much.

"Is this one point five gravities?" she asked slowly.

"Ha, you wish. Two gravities. You'll be a mean lean Marine machine in no time," he said quietly.

Simay studied him out of the corner of her eye. "Are all Marines so driven and confident?"

He looked at her carefully, "Well we're all different but our training does give us some of that, yes."

"Sailors are different; they don't lack for confidence usually but it's far more obvious with the Marines," she said flowing into the next pose.

"You're confident and driven, and a sailor," he pointed out.

She grunted, "Different, I wasn't trained by the Federation. Ottoman's are aggressive and vicious because of fear. They are not confident. You want to do good because you love your nation and leaders and they in turn treat you well. Ottoman's do well because if they do not they will be executed."

James was one of the few people aboard Simay had confided in about her past. She openly talked about it with him and trusted his judgment. He in turn had learned to trust her and know she would not lie.

"But the effect is the same is it not. Both have strong traits that get the job done. Fear is powerful it is just as powerful as love," he said philosophically.

"So you think there is no difference?" she said casually.

"You tell me; would you rather be here or there," he said quietly.

"Yes there is a distinct difference. I know that for a fact. I would even counter your argument and say that the Federation system, our system is far more powerful than theirs," she said strongly.

He smiled, "Oh do tell Binici."

She looked at him. "I would willingly give my life for each of you because I believe. I would not ever quit if you needed me because I know you wouldn't either. That is a product of the environment we are in. As an Ottoman I would have willingly sacrificed all around me but not myself unless it was the last resort and failure was assured. In the Federation failure is not death, it is forgiveness. I may fail but the compassion given to me will steel me to not fail again," she said strongly, "We are more powerful."

James smiled, "You answered your own question."

"What do you mean?" she asked him confused.

"Marines are confident and driven because we will never fail to help each other. We believe in each other. That trust enables us to be far more than a single person. There is no fear or uncertainty; as long as another Marine breathes I am not alone," he said seriously.

They finished their exercise routine and sat down to meditate. Simay processed all that they had discussed while not moving a muscle. Finally, the timer ran down and the gravity slowly returned to normal. She opened her eyes and looked at him.

"How do I teach that to someone?" she asked.

"Normally it's done organically, through training Marines learn that they cannot complete tasks without help. The only help is other Marines. Camaraderie is built through practice and solidified in shared mutual experience," he explained.

"That doesn't explain how I came to it," she said plainly.

He shook his head, "No, you experienced severe trauma. Essentially you assimilated into it but it still took time and shared mutual experience on the *Hypnos*."

She sat quietly thinking for a minute. "So I cannot teach it, I can only help someone by being the example," she said slightly defeated.

He reached down and helped her stand up, "Don't worry your Cadet will be fine. She has an excellent Senior Lieutenant and many fine Marines to show her the way."

Simay looked at him suspiciously.

He grinned, "Marines are also very intuitive..." he said as he headed for the shower room. "See you in twenty-four hours Binici. And you need to work on the foot placements in kata six."

She slowly shook her head as he walked away. Sometimes he could be so frustrating she thought.

Katherine floated in the graviton field and deactivated her neural link from her armor. The plates vibrated and burst apart around her. They silently glided up and into the storage bay above her head. Her left arm burned and tingled as she flexed it worriedly. I can't feel my left foot at all she thought concerned. She looked up as Sergeant Goody spoke.

"Good training session Wyvern, but your reaction and control dropped twenty percent. Is something wrong?" he said stepping out of the graviton field across from her.

She looked at him blankly, "Um. I think I hurt my arm, it sort of burns," she said unsure.

He helped her out of the graviton field and looked at her seriously. "We've been training hard you should go get some rest. Sometimes armor takes time to get used to," he said watching her.

"Yea I think... I'm just tired," she said walking toward the hatch.

"What's on your schedule for the rest of the day?" he asked her.

"Nothing, I just have physical training with Major Delaney tonight," she said as she paused at the hatch.

Goody nodded slowly.

A half hour later Katherine stood in the small brightly lit personal hygiene room. She squeezed her eyes shut to block out the blinding glare from the glassy white walls. Falling forward into the shower and leaning against the cold metal wall she stared at her hands in the hot water. They would shake and jerk periodically. What's wrong with me she thought? Suddenly her stomach clenched and her mouth began to water uncontrollably. Katherine burst out of the shower through the frosted glass door diving for the latrine across wet slippery floors. She gripped the edge of the cold metal and heaved convulsively, emptying her stomach in several painful thrusts.

"Stars! Are you ok?" Midshipman Jennifer Worley said as she came into the room.

Katherine looked up passively at her from the floor. "What do you want?"

Jennifer squatted next to her and grimaced, "Do you need help. I can call the medics," she said concerned.

"No I'm..." She was interrupted by a chocking dry heave.

"Come on, don't be stupid and let me help you." Jennifer said softly. She reached down and helped Katherine to her feet.

Katherine looked at her uneasily, "I just need to rest. I'll be fine."

Jennifer looked at her carefully, "Ok, come on I'll help you to your berth," She guided Katherine out and down the row of berths. The cold air drifted across her wet skin and she shivered again.

As Katherine lay down she looked at Jennifer. "Why are you being nice?"

Jennifer looked at the deck and shrugged. She looked back at Katherine and for a moment there was a different woman in her eyes. Sad almost. Then it vanished. "I can't just let you die while I'm in the room, which would be difficult to explain," she said as she stalked out of the bay.

The ship began to get quieter and quieter as the crew entered stasis for the month and a half long voyage to the engine test location. Sooner than she would have liked Katherine found herself in medical.

She shivered a bit as she stood nude in front of her stasis pod. She stared at her reflection in the pods cover. Her physique was quite well defined. Strong shoulders, neck and chest framed her upper body. She smirked at the fact that her breasts had reduced in size, they were already somewhat undersized to begin with. Her legs were streaked with muscle. Her body fat was well below the norm for women. She routinely defeated the Master Sergeant in suit combat now. Unfortunately, there had been a few issues. Lately there had been jitters and interruptions in her suit control and twice now she couldn't stop her hands from shaking.

"Good morning Miss Carroll," Brynn said as she walked up interrupting Katherine's thoughts.

"Good Morning Colonel," she answered quietly.

"First time in stasis?" Brynn asked her.

"Yes Ma'am, first time," Katherine answered.

"Well it's not difficult. You step in and close your eyes, and then you will open them and be released. It's that fast," she said smiling, "Turn your head so I can insert the stasis drugs in your implant port."

Katherine turned her head to the right exposing the medical and neuro implant port behind her left ear. Hers glowed the dark green of commando branch. It stood out brilliantly on her pale skin as it crawled up her spine around her ear and along her chin. Several branches extended from her neck running down her left arm and up into her skull. At the base of her spine it continued past her left hip and down her left leg to her toes. Her left eye glowed green from the implant inside.

Brynn carefully inserted the drugs and stepped back. "You're in excellent health Miss Carroll, you could use a bit more vitamins and you're showing signs of severe mental stress," she frowned. "There is some irregularity in your neural connections. You seem to be experiencing stripping similar to someone with cybernetic implants... This is extremely unusual," she typed on her tablet for several seconds.

"Oh my... You seem to be connecting to your commando suit at an unprecedented level. The data flow is damaging your physical neural connections," she looked at

Katherine seriously.

"What do you mean, will I have to stop using my skin!" Katherine asked suddenly frightened.

Brynn looked at Katherine for a second. "If I could reinforce your neural connections you would choose that over reducing suit use?" she asked seriously, "Even if it meant adding cybernetics to your brain."

"To keep my skin... yes Ma'am," Katherine said instantly.

"I will see what I can do while you're in stasis and we'll discuss it when you wake up," she said, "Step in here please."

Katherine stepped into the pod. Brynn reached in and connected several cables and tubes to her implant. Katherine noticed she smelled like flowers of some type.

"Lean back and be calm," she said to her.

The stasis pod door slid shut and restraints slid easily in place holding her gently in the pod. She looked down and saw thick pink fluid filling into the pod. It made its way up her body tickling torturously. Just as she thought she couldn't take it anymore a serene calm settled over her. She watched happily as the fluid reached her chin and flowed up around her face. She had a slight thought of drowning as the fluid poured down into her mouth and filled her lungs. Then she just tumbled away.

Commander Samantha Leeane
Deck Six, Officers Mess
Light Destroyer Nyx, Dry Dock
Asphodel Fields, Tartarus System
203.0188 FCUDT 15:10:22

Sam sat with Asteria and Dr. Driscoll in the empty mess hall sipping her steaming coffee and waiting for Captain Stuart to arrive. She looked up at them and grinned. "Just like the good old days," she said.

"Technically that was only several months ago..." Brynn

said, "But I agree. It's nice to get some space."

Asteria looked at them curiously, "Humans are so interesting. You cannot survive without each other but are constantly trying to find your own space."

Brynn laughed, "Well, when you put in that perspective."

Adam and Coline walked in and paused at the three of them smiling at each other. "Interrupting anything?" he asked.

"No sir, just remembering the 'good ole days'..." Sam said lightly.

The two new arrivals sat and grabbed hot drinks. After sipping his coffee Adam looked at Brynn. "So we have an issue with Cadet Carroll?" he said looking at Sam and Brynn.

Bryn set her cup down and activated the small holo on the table. "Yes, I discovered this when I scanned her befor stasis Sergeant Goody had forwarded a request for the scan due to unusual readings from her armor." A three dimensional view of Katherine's brain floated above the table and slowly rotated. Several red points flashed within.

"What you see here is neural damage. It is the byproduct of direct linkage to neural networks on a higher level than normal. The Cadet seems to have a propensity for massive data flow into her brain. It's what makes her such an excellent candidate for commando armor use. Unfortunately, human technology has exceeded the ability of the human body to cope with the interfaces and limiters were installed to prevent overloads. The Cadets physiology is fighting the limiter and the result is brain damage."

Coline looked alarmed, "Is she suffering any effects?"

"Not yet, this is quite pronounced but relatively minor. On the other hand, it happened exceptionally fast. At this rate she will lose function in three or four months."

Adam stared at Brynn, "Three to four months! This kind of damage takes decades in most cases."

"Yes normally, but like I said Katherine is exceptional," Brynn said seriously.

Sam looked at the two officers, "Typically in these cases we have only one option. Cease use of armor and reassign the Marine."

Adam nodded, "But since we're talking about it I assume you have another."

"Yes sir," Brynn said and nodded at Asteria.

"There is the option of implanting a micro quantum processor to take over the processing and linkage between her brain and the suit. We have two such processors onboard. This would in effect buffer her command signals to and from the suit and eliminate the possibility of damage. I suggested this because of her extraordinary skill and unique ability to control the suit on a fundamental level. It poses an opportunity to further the research into expanding the human technology interface," Asteria said to them.

Coline frowned, "So she would be a research subject?"

"Ma'am, it would be completely voluntary and the process for implanting is well established. You yourself have a very similar processor to control your cybernetics. It is much smaller though. Commander Dower is working on nanite body suit interfaces that would only be possible with these types of modifications. We also have a mandate from Federated Medical Command to expand our knowledge in this area of technology," Brynn explained, "Of course it's ultimately your call Ma'am and I feel you're well qualified to make that decision."

Coline sighed and looked at her cybernetic arm, "If I hadn't met you Brynn I would emphatically say no. The interface provided to me in Hades was not enjoyable. Your modifications have allowed me to expand beyond all possibilities." She flexed her cybernetic fingers and looked at the others. "Assuming I say yes what are the risks?"

"Same as with any physical surgical procedures. We need to open her skull and place the core, which has its inherent risks. Beyond that... rejection and her ability to control the device. Worst case is she cannot access the core and it goes inert, or we damage her brain during surgery."

Sam nodded at them, "Or we give her the opportunity to be an excellent Commando operator with cutting edge technology and a skill set nobody but Asteria has."

Coline sighed again, "Very well, I would be a hypocrite to deny her this. I leave the ultimate decision to Katherine although I am sure I already know what her answer will be."

Cadet Katherine Carroll
Deck Four, Medical Bay
Light Destroyer Nyx, Forward Frontier
267.0188 FCUDT 10:27:54

Falling her brain screamed! Katherine managed to rip open her eyes just as she was dumped out of the stasis pod. She went to her knees as the fluid poured down the grating around her. Then she realized she couldn't breathe. She leaned forward and simultaneously coughed and gagged disgusting pink fluid out of her body.

"It's all right Miss Carroll, just focus on breathing," a voice said to her.

She continued to heave and gag. Then finally she took a ragged breath and began coughing. Several seconds later she seemed to have the act of breathing back under control. She looked up and saw a man dressed in medical burgundy. Thick pink slime dripped off her kneeling form in slow motion.

"Miss Carroll, I'm Doctor Gallant. You have been brought back a few days early. I believe Doctor Driscoll will inform you of the reason. Right now I will take you to get cleaned up, ok?"

She couldn't manage to talk without another bout of coughing so she just nodded.

An hour later she sat on a table in main medical as Brynn walked in with Asteria and smiled.

"Miss Carroll, we have a solution for your neural difficulties. It will require your acknowledgement and consent to perform," Brynn said.

"Yes, do it," Katherine said decisively.

"Let me explain it first. We will need to open your skull and insert a micro quantum processor. It cannot be built with nanites we must physically place it and then let the nanites wire it in to your brain. Once active it will act as a buffer and controller to the input output signals from your brain. In effect you're getting cybernetic implants without the implants. Your cybernetics are your suit," she said, "There is always severe risk with physical surgical operations. You must be aware that damage or death could occur."

Katherine looked at her, "Ok, go ahead."

Asteria stepped up to her, "If you're going to insist on this you will receive the only device we know that works. It is a highly modified nonstandard cybernetic device. You will have several modified abilities that we cannot remove or deactivate. You may find them disturbing at first."

Katherine felt the first twinges of fear as Asteria said that. She looked at Asteria, "You designed it?" she asked.

"Yes."

"Then I have no problem with the modifications. Do it," Katherine said.

"Katherine, you're aware of the social stigma? People with cybernetics are looked upon as incomplete or damaged. You may experience some amount of friction in your life because of this," Asteria said calmly. "It's uncommon and still experimental for people to have cybernetics."

"But, there are two on this ship and you're fully cybernetic?" Katherine said looking at the two Officers.

"Yes, the Commander had no choice without her cybernetics she would be unable to function, the Admiral chose to be modified so she could retain the use of her body. You would be choosing to modify based on a non-critical need," Brynn replied.

Asteria nodded, "I was 'born' this way. Fully cybernetic and have faced rather severe discrimination from both humans and artificial intelligence," she said sadly, "This is a choice you should not take lightly. Take some time to consider it."

Katherine looked up at Asteria, "I don't need time Ma'am, I agree to the procedure. Losing the suit is not an option for me."

Asteria nodded and placed her hand on Katherine's arm, "Okay," She said calmly.

An hour later two doctors walked in with equipment and began setting up around her.

"Lean back on the table and relax," Brynn said.

She leaned back into a sitting position as the table folded up to support her. A large warm blanket was placed over her.

Doctor Gallant walked up with a hair removal device and looked at her. "Sorry, for this one, you're losing your hair. You want part or all of it cut?" he asked giving her a hopeful smile.

She sighed and looked at him, "Take it all…"

In a few short minutes her head was bald. She dreaded what she looked like.

"Ok, you're going to feel unusual. You're receiving a neural block which will paralyze you from the neck down and deaden all your nerves. Just stay relaxed and focus on my voice," Brynn said.

Her body went cold and it actually felt like her head had been removed from her body. A device extended from the table and encircled her head locking it into place.

Asteria stepped in front of her and held a small box. "Would you like to see the micro core?" she asked.

Katherine's eyes widened, "Yes."

Asteria opened the box and inside was a brightly glowing blue square that twinkled and shimmered.

"It's amazing!" Katherine said.

Asteria closed the box and handed it to the Doctor. She walked up and stood next to Katherine's shoulder. "I will be right here for you," she said calmly.

"All right Katherine here we go," Brynn said.

Katherine heard the doctors working behind her and could see them next to her but felt nothing for many minutes. Then she saw Dr. Gallant take the core out of the box and hand it to Dr. Driscoll. Seconds later Katherine saw brilliant flashes of light all around her and then slowly everything faded away to darkness. "Katherine!" she barely heard them call her as she slipped away.

Commander Samantha Leeane
Deck Four, Medical Bay
Light Destroyer Nyx, Forward Frontier
267.0188 FCUDT 11:41:53

Parts of stasis tubes littered the deck around her. The smell of burning stasis fluid burned her nose and made her eyes water.

"How many did we lose?" Adam asked behind her. She turned and saw Brynn look at him pale.

"Five, five innocent souls," she said calmly. "Six if we can't wake up Miss Carroll," she said sadly.

Sam closed her eyes in mental pain. She opened them to see Asteria stand up from the debris.

"This is definitely the work of malicious intent," she said, "If we needed conclusive proof someone was sabotaging systems this is it."

Adam took a deep breath, "How do you think we should proceed. I don't think interrogating the entire crew will be an effective strategy."

"I will begin to build a profile. The person must have specific skills because we cannot pin down a time frame it was carried out. The pods obviously were not wired before they were filled otherwise it would have been detected," Asteria said.

"We already have guards on sensitive areas. That may well be the reason the ship didn't have a reactor meltdown instead of this," Sam said.

"Dammit, we need this stopped before it gets any further!" Adam said frustrated.

"Adam, maybe we should delay bringing any more crew out for a few days while we work on possibilities," Sam said seriously.

He nodded, "Get Shia and Tameria out and up to speed. They will have ideas on how to work this," He said to Brynn.

She nodded, "No problem, I can have them up in an hour."

Sam looked in the window to surgical. "How is Carroll?"

"She is stable. Her vitals are all in the green and she is in all practical sense fine. She is just… gone. Her cybernetic implant is impairing our ability to scan her brain appropriately. She could wake up in a few seconds or not for years. The explosion was incredibly bad timing. I think the EMP wave caused some kind of interaction in the core and… turned her off," Brynn said sadly.

"Once her brain heals from the surgery Asteria will attempt a neural connection and see if she is there."

Sam nodded, "Let's hope she finds her way back."

"I can't help but feel guilty looking at her," Adam said staring through the med bay glass.

"It's not your fault Adam." Brynn said, "If the explosion hadn't happened she would be fine."

"Yes, but I supported the decision, I just wanted her to succeed. Her combat scores are incredible, second only to Shia." He said sadly.

Sam looked at Adam, "She'll recover, and she's strong."

Shia became aware of the ache in her body before the tube opened. Relief flooded through her mind as she recognized that she was coming out of stasis. Ever since the incident eleven years ago she felt this way. She still got cold chills remembering getting into that tube without knowing she would wake up.

The tube opened and she dropped to the grate heaving the stasis fluid out of her lungs.

"You're a pro Shia." Sam said as Shia stood and wiped the fluid from her face.

"Been in a tube a few times…" Shia said through damp vocal chords.

Sam smiled, "Got something for you when you're ready, you're up a few days early."

Shia nodded, "Shower and coffee first," she grumbled.

"And a checkup…" Brynn said walking in.

"Aye, Aye Ma'am," she mumbled again as Sam laughed at them.

An hour later Shia stood in the stasis bay cup of coffee in hand looking at Sam incredulous.

"Five people!" Shia said shocked.

"Plus Cadet Carroll by association," Sam said nodding. "Five killed and two seriously injured. I need you Shia, you and Tameria have the experience for this."

Shia involuntarily grimaced at the mention of Katherine's injury. "Has anyone contaminated the scene?" she asked refocusing her mind on the topic.

"Only the Captain, Asteria, and I have been in this room. Also Brynn responded but I don't believe she entered."

Shia nodded, "I need a detailed forensic scan and all the ships data from the last month, especially right before we began stasis," she said looking around.

The walls on this side were scorched and pitted. Five empty stasis tubes lay in various states of debris. Shia frowned at the brown blood stains splashed across the floor.

"At least they didn't feel it," she said sadly.

They left the room and stood in the passageway outside the surgical bay.

"How is Katherine doing? Was she in stasis nearby?" Shia asked concerned.

"She is unresponsive but stable. Brynn was performing a surgical procedure on her when the explosion occurred. Something about the electromagnetic spike put her in a coma," Sam said looking at Katherine through the window.

"Oh no... you think it was just chance? You don't think she was a target?" Shia asked concerned.

"No, the procedure wasn't planned until this morning when we woke her. Her tube was in the port holding bay. Just bad luck," Sam said.

Shia didn't know why that relieved her to hear but it did.

The next day Shia sat in the security office with four holo screens open around her. Complex video algorithms scanned holo footage as she watched. Another holo ran through the forensic scan for the third time. The console rang and a red message flashed across the field.

"Damn!" Shia said angrily. "How can the forensic scan be negative?" she said to herself.

The security com activated and Asteria appeared. "There is nothing wrong with the ships sensors Shia," Asteria said.

Shia looked at her, "Sometimes you scare me Asteria... I didn't even say that it was the ship's fault."

"You were thinking it..." she grinned, "Human behavior is sometimes predictable."

Shia shook her head slowly, "Have you found anything?"

"Possibly, I found a DNA profile in the ventilation shaft

that does not match any on record. It does match someone from the construction crews," she said tilting her head.

"Well that is easy to explain, why is it significant?" Shia asked.

"It is significant because the medical bay ventilation was installed after he was killed in an accident in the cargo bay..." she replied.

Shia thought a moment. "He couldn't have had contact with the materials before installation?"

"No, they were in storage on Acheron."

Shia looked interested, "You think he is alive. Living as a stowaway or something?"

Asteria shrugged, "Maybe but doubtful. The ship would pick up his vital signs, it is more likely he is impersonating a crewman. The accident requires more investigation but it is a lead" Asteria said.

Shia leaned forward forgetting the holo footage, "What do you want me to do?" she said menacingly.

CHAPTER 3
Saboteur

"Has there been any progress?" Brynn asked Sam.

"Asteria has found a lead that points to the construction crews but it is still not solid. We're going to have to get the crew up soon," Sam said frowning.

Brynn nodded slowly and sipped her tea. "You don't think the construction of the ship was impaired, do you?"

"No nothing like that, thank the stars. The theory is that an accident was initiated to cover up the replacement of a crew member. Like I said it's still unfounded at the moment," she stretched her arms and sighed.

Quite suddenly soft insistent alarms sounded. Brynn looked up startled. "Dammit! Sam help me out!" she said as she jumped up and hurried into the surgical bay.

Sam followed her in and saw Katherine laying on the medical table. Brynn turned off the alarms and grabbed a long tube from a locker.

"She has stopped breathing, connect this to the port over there and activate it when I tell you," she handed the other end of the tube to Sam as she worked.

Dr. Gallant came in and quickly began assisting Brynn. Another tone sounded urgently and Katherine began convulsing on the table. Sam looked down at her helpless.

"Sam hold her on table so she doesn't fall off," Brynn said.

Sam hesitated and then braced her body against the table while holding Katherine's hips. Katherine's body twisted and jumped as her spine went decorticate.

"It's her nervous system Dr. Driscoll. It's trying to

compensate," Dr. Gallant said looking at the scan of her brain.

"Give her the anticonvulsants and see if we can get it back in control so I can get her breathing again," Brynn said.

He activated several controls and in seconds Katherine settled down. Brynn went to insert the tube in her throat and paused.

"She is breathing again," Brynn said watching the monitor.

Suddenly Katherine let out with a piercing scream. Sam nearly fell into the medical equipment behind her when she jumped away startled. Brynn and Dr. Gallant stepped back shocked for a second. Then Katherine was quiet and still again.

"Well… that was interesting," Brynn said quietly. She looked at the scan of Katherine's brain. "I think that this young lady is fighting as hard as she can to stay with us. Her brain activity is off the charts."

They stood there for several minutes watching.

Commander Helen Dower
Deck Two, Chief Engineers Quarters
Light Destroyer Nyx, Deep Space
279.0188 FCUDT 19:19:19

"How many pilots have you passed on the flight evaluations?" Helen asked as Xander removed the terminal connector from his neuro implant.

"Counting today's tests… one." he smiled.

Helen eyed him analytically. "Callis doesn't count," she said.

"Oh, well then none." he said as he stood to get a drink. "It's not my fault, Callis said to make it hard to pass and Astie helped me program the situation," he said in response to her frown.

Helen felt an incredible sense of fear for a second and she broke out in cold bumps as she shivered.

Xander looked at her for a second. "Are you ok, you have an odd look on your face?" he asked.

She looked at him, "I had this crazy moment of fear," she said concerned.

He set a cup of tea down for her and started to sit.

"Help me!"

She stood up and looked around, "Did you hear that?"

Xander looked confused, "Hear what?" he stood and walked over to her, "Seriously are you ok?"

She looked at him confused. "I need to go to medical" she said abruptly and grabbed the hatch. She hurried out in a rush with Xander standing there shocked at her departure.

In a short few minutes she stepped into the medical bay to see Asteria entering from the other side. Asteria stopped and looked at Helen.

She walked up to meet Helen outside the recovery bay. "Tell me you know why I am here," Helen said to her.

"Likely the same reason I am here," Coline said entering medical behind Helen, "I was compelled to come here like something forced me."

"Did you hear that?" Helen asked suddenly. All three looked through the window to the left and saw Brynn staring at them from Katherine's bedside.

They entered the room and stepped over to Katherine's side.

Brynn looked at the three of them. "Her brain activity spiked about five minutes ago. I was afraid she would have another convulsion."

"Brynn I think she called us," Helen said, "We are the only three on the ship that have the same hardware. It's too much to be a coincidence."

Asteria held her hand over Katherine's head for a second. "Her neural rig is completely constructed. It went active several minutes ago," she said, "I believe I can create a connection."

Brynn looked at her, "If you think it's safe, go ahead and try."

Asteria looked at Helen and Coline, "Be careful, don't touch her left side or you may be pulled into her mind accidently."

"Why can I hear her?" Helen said.

"She is in effect screaming across the quantum connection. You are hearing the disturbances caused by that," Asteria said. She looked down and carefully placed her hand on Katherine's left shoulder.

Cadet Katherine Carroll
Deck Four, Medical Bay
Light Destroyer Nyx, Deep Space
279.0188 FCUDT 19:37:01

Cold waves splashed against her chest as she protected her face. She looked out confused at the expansive body of water in front of her. She tried to move but her legs refused to move correctly. The harder she tried the more violent the waves were until she looked up just as a wave crashed over her.

She floated free in the cold water. As she opened her eyes she was not in water, she realized, she was in zero gee training again. Below her floated the beautiful blue and green planet of Hades. As she stared at the beautiful planet she realized it was growing larger. She was hurtling towards it. Fear and panic gripped her mind. She flailed her arms and legs wildly trying to do something to slow down. Just as she started to feel the first wisps of the atmosphere her fear got the better of her and she released a primal scream. She curled into a fetal position and hugged her legs tightly.

Everything stilled and she felt the floor beneath her feet. She stood and looked around. She was in her parent's kitchen on the planet Styx back in Tartarus. Her birth mother walked in and put dishes in the sink. She looked out the window and sighed.

"Mom are you ok?" Katherine asked her.

Her mom didn't seem to hear her. Katherine walked

over and placed her hand on her mom's arm to get her attention. Before she touched her she simply disappeared. She looked around for her and saw Asteria standing in the back yard. Katherine was confused at the sight of Asteria in such an unusual place as her home. She walked out the back door and stopped.

"Where are we?" Asteria asked her.

"This is my home on Styx Commander," she replied.

"Are you sure?"

Katherine looked around and frowned, "No, I think I may be dreaming or something."

"Yes, something."

"Am I losing my mind Commander?" Katherine asked concerned.

Asteria smiled at her, "No, you're finding it actually."

Katherine frowned, "I don't understand. Why won't you tell me?" she said irritated.

In the sky a ship entered the atmosphere and began approach. It was suddenly late afternoon as the sun shifted in the sky.

"I'm sorry Commander, I didn't mean to yell," she said suddenly embarrassed by her outburst.

Above them the incoming ship started smoking and flames trailed behind it.

"How will I know if I find my mind?"

Asteria looked up at the ship coming at them, "You already have. You just need to see it yourself. Only you can stop this."

Katherine looked up and saw the ship looming above them. She could hear it thundering down from above.

"I don't know how; I don't have the knowledge or tools I need!" she said emphatically.

"Yes you do. Katherine what is the last thing you remember before this."

She looked up at the ship worried. "I was falling toward Hades from orbit," she said scared.

"No, that was not real. If it were you would be dead."

"I remember being cold!" she yelled over the tremendous sound of the ship above them. "I couldn't move, I was afraid!"

All around them parts of the ship began crashing down. The house exploded in flames and flashes of impacts went off everywhere.

"You need to go back there Katherine," Asteria said calmly.

"No! I can't... I'm afraid," she said as tears ran down her face. She turned and saw her parents standing at the door. Katherine ran over to them, "Please tell me I don't have to go! Please... I don't think I can do it this time, I can't."

Both her Mother and Father looked at her with sad eyes. Katherine closed her eyes and dropped her head in defeat.

"Please..." -she pleaded quietly. She turned around and the world was burning. Fifty-meter-high flames surrounded her and Asteria.

"I don't know the way..." Katherine said.

"Yes you do," Asteria said, "You must go back."

Katherine closed her eyes and thought of the cold. She swallowed her fear and concentrated on the feeling. Suddenly she remembered. The operation on her brain, the cold feeling was because of the operation. She pictured the room and the sound of Dr. Driscoll's voice. Voice! Dr. Driscoll had said to focus on her voice and she would be ok.

Katherine stopped and stood perfectly still. She listened intently for that voice. The sound of the flames and crackling of the fire receded into silence. She thought she heard electronic noises, and then faintly, off in the distance, voices. She forced herself to focus on the voices and they slowly grew louder. There! She thought and her eyes popped open. Blinding light flooded into her eyes.

"She's back!" Brynn's voice said.

Katherine choked and gagged on tubes in her throat as she tried to talk.

"Don't try to talk Katherine, you have been gone awhile. It's ok, relax," Brynn said quietly.

She coughed and choked as the tubes were carefully removed. She blinked and looked around. Her head was immobilized so she could only move her eyes. She saw the Admiral and Commander Dower standing by her. She stared at them amazed.

"Welcome back Miss Carroll, I knew you could do it," Admiral Lune said smiling.

Tears ran down Katherine's cheeks. Commander Dower reached out and carefully wiped her face. As soon as she touched her left cheek an intense emotional wave of pride and serenity washed through her. Katherine was shocked to realize the emotions came from the Commander.

"I'm giving you a relaxant Katherine you still need to heal," Brynn said.

Her eyes grew heavy and she slowly drifted asleep.

Cadet Katherine Carroll
Deck Four, Medical Bay
Light Destroyer Nyx, Deep Space
292.0188 FCUDT 18:39:41

She opened her eyes and looked at the mirror. Her red hair was only a centimeter long. Her face looked puffy and she had dark circles around her eyes from the swelling in her brain. She slowly turned her head and saw the bright red twenty centimeter scar that formed a jagged crescent on the back of her skull. Dr. Driscoll had told her they could remove the scar in a few months.

"Are you ready?" Dr. Driscoll asked from behind her.

"Yes Ma'am, I am ready," Katherine replied. This morning she was being released from the medical bay.

"You are not cleared for duty yet. You can move freely through the ship on your own for a few days then I will consider releasing you," she said, "Light duty only, understood?"

"Yes Ma'am, I understand," Katherine nodded slowly.

"Ok, off you go then," Brynn said smiling.

She walked out of the medical bay and found herself walking toward the Hell Hold. She paused outside the door and wondered why she came here. She stepped through and casually walked over to Master Sergeant Goody's office. He looked up as she entered and grinned widely.

"Well, look who isn't dead!" he stood up and walked over to her. "I take that back, you kind of look dead Ma'am..." he said winking at her.

She laughed sadly at that.

He guided her into a chair and sat across from her. "How are you doing Wyvern?"

She sighed and looked at him. "I am alive, and no longer completely human. How should I be doing?"

"Are you feeling bad for yourself?" he said looking at her. "You don't forget why you did this. You never were human you've always been one hundred percent Marine."

"I was weak. I almost didn't make it," she said frowning.

"Ma'am, what I saw in that medical bay was the most amazing recovery I have ever seen in my entire career. No one would have made it, but you did. You have it, whatever it is, it's in you," he said seriously.

She was surprised. She didn't know he came to see her. She nodded at him.

He stood, "Now, off with you, you don't need to be in here. Come back when you can train," he said standing.

She stood and walked to his door. "Thank you Sergeant Goody."

"It's what I'm here for... kick you in the pants remind you who you are," he said, "Night Wyvern."

Twenty minutes later Katherine was laying in her bunk. She felt empty of everything. Like the past month had sucked all her emotions away.

The hatch popped open and the Midshipmen came in. "Well, well. Look who came back. I thought they left you in stasis because you're not needed" Midshipmen Worley said, "Love the new haircut…"

She just stared at them as they went about their business.

"Wow! That's an amazing scar," Midshipmen Bailey said as he noticed her head.

Worley laughed, "They removed your brain so you could be a more effective Marine Officer!"

Katherine turned red and looked at Miss Worley. She instantly stopped laughing and quickly walked to the shower room.

Katherine lay down and tried to relax.

"She went to see you twice a day, you know?" Midshipman Perez said quietly from the bunk next to Katherine.

"Who did?" Katherine asked sarcastically.

"Worley…" he said casually as he headed to the shower. "Glad you ok Carroll."

She scrunched up her face confused at his comment and leaned back in her bunk. She could not sleep on her left side anymore. It just felt wrong somehow. Eventually she drifted off into a fitful sleep.

Commander Samantha Leeane
Deck Five, Conference Room
Light Destroyer Nyx, Deep Space
293.0188 FCUDT 09:19:41

Asteria activated the holo and data flowed across the table. "As you can see the amount of data is substantial. I have analyzed the situation and come to the general conclusion that this is what happened," she said to Captain Stuart.

"Please go ahead and explain," he said.

"On date one fifty one there was an accident recorded where two individuals were killed. Both were contract dock workers working on the reactor installation. They were between the reactor and the wall when the crane released prematurely and crushed them. I believe what actually happened was a dock worker and a crewman were intentionally trapped in between the wall and the reactor when the crane released. Another dock worker switched credentials with the dead crewman and took his place," she said.

"Is that possible?" Sam said.

"Yes, it would require high level access to the computers but it is possible to alter the readings to match your own," Asteria said.

"Do we know who this is yet?" Sam said eagerly.

"No, the data was corrupt and I am working to reconstruct it. Until we know who the crewman is we are still stuck," she said to Sam.

"What if we find out who was on that deck at the time of the accident and check all of them. That's better than the whole ship," Shia said.

"Yes that may work," Asteria said, "Let me work on it."

"How much longer until we're ready to depart?" Adam looked at Sam.

"We were planning another ten days."

He nodded, "I would like this to be resolved before we head out."

"I will do my best sir," Asteria said.

Cadet Katherine Carroll
Deck Seven, Tactical
Light Destroyer Nyx, Deep Space
293.0188 FCUDT 13:10:58

Katherine peered into Tactical from the edge of the hatch. She saw several crewmen working quietly at the consoles across the room. She didn't see Commander Hypnea anywhere. She stepped back just in time to see Asteria turn the corner.

"Miss Carroll, you are not cleared for duty yet," Asteria said stopping in front of her.

"Yes, Ma'am... I just wanted to... well, can I use a simulation room to watch more battles? I didn't think it would really count as work, and I can't lay in that berth any longer!" she said pleadingly.

Asteria cocked her head at Katherine. "Yes you can watch simulations but not in the simulation room. Come in I will give you something to keep you occupied that has to happen before you return to duty," Asteria walked into Tactical and headed for her personal office. She motioned Katherine inside and closed the hatch.

The room was fairly dark and had a large multipurpose console along the back wall. Beyond that the room was relatively empty. There was another hatch to her left she noticed as Asteria reached for it. She ushered Katherine inside and a large gray cat stood in the middle of the room. It meowed loudly at the sight of Katherine.

"Royal, this is Cadet Carroll she's allowed in here," Asteria said to the cat. "Miss Carroll meet by roommate Royal."

Katherine was shocked. "You have a cat!"

"Yes, my status allows me some flexibility in the Fleet rules," she said as she bent over and rubbed his head. "Please have a seat in that chair and lean back," she pointed to an odd looking chair.

Katherine stepped over and sat carefully down. Royal immediately leaped into her lap and sniffed at her. He looked at her and meowed. Katherine was unsure what to do as she looked at the large fuzzy gray animal. Royal bent his head and rubbed his face down her arm. She reached up and petted him carefully. His chest rumbled as he purred.

Asteria came over after typing on her console for a few minutes and looked at them. "He is a busybody..." she said. "If you pet him he will love you for life," she reached down and picked up Royal placing him on the ground. He looked up at her and protested the removal of his attention.

"I am going to activate your cybernetic core. This will

enable all the functions at once. It may be a bit overwhelming for a second," she said calmly.

"It isn't active... I thought it was already," she said surprised.

"No only system management functions are active. We believe the system triggered from the blast in medical and that is what put you in a coma. We decided to leave it deactivated until your brain recovered from the trauma."

Katherine nodded, "What is going to happen?"

"You will have expanded access to all electronic systems. You will also be able to see electromagnetic waves and communicate via wireless and physical links to other cybernetics. This communication is all encompassing, it will seem as if you can read their mind and feel their emotions."

"Really!" she said scared.

"Don't worry the others have adapted to it quickly," she said, "Lean back and place your arms on the ports."

Katherine looked at Asteria for a second and then leaned back. She looked at the unusual ports. They were like channels for her arms to lay in and they were lined with a black fuzzy coating. She carefully lowered her arms into them and settled. As she watched the fuzzy covering grew out towards her flesh and touched. They then continued into her arms like fine tree roots in soil. She looked at Asteria in alarm.

"It's ok, you are establishing a direct connection to the ship. Try to relax you mind."

She took a deep breath and looked up. She blinked and the room changed. It was no longer a dull gray room, it had brightly colored glowing walls. All around her data streamed across the bright walls. There was a hologram of the ship floating in the middle of the room. "Stars! It's beautiful," she said.

"Your core is active and functioning perfectly. Your link to the ship is solid. You are seeing advanced oculographic interfaces. That's your brains interpretation of the raw data within the ship's network. Whenever you're in range of the ship you will automatically link. It will give you all the computing power of the onboard core," she said smiling.

Katherine thought about the ship core and was instantly connected to it. It was massive, like a yawning black hole in her mind. She felt an intense feeling that it would swallow her up. She started sweating and shaking as she fought to keep from falling in.

"Miss Carroll, it is only in your mind, you have control. Control your thoughts, look at your fear, and realize what it is," Asteria said.

Katherine's heart was slamming in her chest. She was imagining being pulled into the dark, vividly remembering being in her coma. She was drenched in sweat as she fought it. She heard Asteria say something. Something about fear. Focus she thought I need to focus. She forced herself to take a deep breath and then she just relaxed and let go.

She didn't fall. Data burst out of the dark in front of her. It flowed all around her in glorious shimmering patterns like crystalline rain drops. She was overwhelmed from sensory input. She stood and staggered forward a few steps before collapsing to the deck.

"Miss Carroll, you must focus," Kneeling next to her Asteria said sternly.

Katherine tried to focus on a single strand of data. Her body was fighting to stay in control. Waves of nausea crashed over her and she gagged. She heard Master Sergeant Goody's voice in the data stream around her. She focused on the Marines voice with all her strength. Suddenly she was in the Hell Hold.

"I want that deck to shine like the stars themselves!" Sergeant Goody said to three Lance Corporals.

"Yes Sergeant!" they replied in unison.

The vision shook and shuddered then stabilized again. Katherine looked down and saw straight through the deck at the reactors below. They thrummed and vibrated.

"Miss Carroll,." Asteria's voice came to her.

The scene faded and Katherine found herself looking up

from the deck at Commander Asteria. She stood up shakily and looked at her. "Ma'am," -sweat ran down her face in streaks and her stomach clenched.

"You got the hang of it at the end. You need to keep practicing and you will have control," she said.

"Yes Ma'am."

"I need to return to work, I suggest you return to your quarters and rest," Asteria said.

Master Chief Petty Officer Shia O'Connell
Deck Nine, Aft Passageways
Light Destroyer Nyx, Deep Space
296.0188 FCUDT 09:10:05

Security Chief Shia O'Connell waited at the intersection of compartment ten on deck nine trying to look inconspicuous. Her previous life as a Hades System Law Ranger had prepared her for life as a security chief but not for the realities of Military life. She had worked long and hard to integrate into the crew. She still wasn't sure what inconspicuous was supposed to look like...

"You're sure he is headed this way?" she asked on her com.

"Yes Shia, he is coming through compartment nine now," Asteria replied from tactical, "He is in passage four, start walking now."

Shia stepped into the passage that would take her to the intersection where the crewmen would pass. She casually looked at her tablet as she walked.

"Slower, he is ten meters from crossing," Asteria said in her com.

Just as Shia approached the intersection a middle aged crewmen strolled by. He was roughly five foot six with black close cut hair and walked in an assured manner. He crossed the intersection without a moment's hesitation and continued down the passageway.

Shia absently turned in a few feet behind him and

followed. "Got him, in pursuit," she said quietly in her com.

They walked through compartment eleven and twelve headed for the engineering spaces in the aft of the ship. He drifted a bit farther ahead of Shia and turned right into compartment thirteen.

"Something's wrong, I lost his signal," Asteria said.

Shia hurried up to the intersection and peered around the corner. The passageway was deserted. Two more security crewmen walked up behind her and positioned themselves for cover.

"Lost him, I'm moving forward to check it out," Shia said. She pulled her sidearm and motioned for the crewmen to follow her.

She stepped out and walked along the wall down the passage. Ten meters down the passage split one going left the other continuing another ten meters ahead. Shia motioned for the crewmen to take the left passage and she continued forward.

She reached the end of the passage where it turned left and she paused. Swallowing to control a surge of adrenaline she turned the corner. The passage was empty.

Suddenly a rumbling boom and rush of air thundered around her.

"Alpha team report!" she said in her com.

"Shia, there has been an explosion in the passage to your left, what's happening," Asteria said in her com.

"I'm on my way to find out," she said as she scrambled to her feet and hurried back down the passageway. As she turned the corner she saw her two crewmen on the deck surrounded by bent and scarred metal from the left wall.

"Medical! I need a medical team in thirteen five now!" Shia said in her com.

"They are on the way Shia, what's happening?" Captain Stuart asked from the Bridge.

"Sir I have two security crewmen down from an apparent explosion in passage five. I am securing the area for secondary explosives," she said, "The target is not among the injured, he must have gotten away."

"Dammit!" Shia said as she slammed her fist against the wall. She watched as the corpsman pushed the stretcher quickly down the passageway.

"Calm down Shia," Master Chief Tameria Heyerdahl said as she walked up, "We're doing everything we can."

Shia looked at her hotly, "I shouldn't have lost him… how could we lose his signal!"

Tameria looked at her, "Shia you know better than that. This happens sometimes," Tameria placed her hand on her friend's shoulder.

"Tam this isn't your ordinary subterranean city with dark alleys! It's a Fleet warship, this isn't supposed to happen."

"You're right, it's a Fleet ship with Soldiers aboard… Shia, we'll find him," She said leading her down the passageway.

Shia looked at the deck, "You're right… I'm just upset," She said. Shia looked at the burned walls and deck plates. I won't rest until I find you she thought angrily.

Cadet Katherine Carroll
Deck Seven, Tactical
Light Destroyer Nyx, Deep Space
296.0188 FCUDT 11:30:15

Katherine stood outside the main engineering hatch. She was beginning to think that the feeling of overwhelming fear and trepidation was all she would know anymore. Taking a breath and fighting the acid burning in her stomach she opened the hatch and stepped inside.

Two and a half days ago she had stumbled onto the flight simulations in her exploration of the ships systems. She discovered she could now simply access them with her cybernetics. It was not difficult as long as she stayed away from the core. That massive black hole was terrifying. Katherine had spent the entire time laying in her berth flying. She had managed to earn her basic and advanced flight qualifications in a matter of days. She reveled in the freedom of flying ships.

Unfortunately, even that was not enough to take her away from the seemingly never ending teasing from her fellow roommates. Midshipmen Worley had sunk to ever deeper lows in her verbal abuse. Katherine was now being regularly harassed. She was deeply depressed by it.

This morning Katherine had reported and been cleared for duty by Dr. Driscoll. After a brief meeting with Major Delaney, Katherine had been informed of her new rotation to Engineering.

As she walked across the large compartment she fought the instinct to turn around and go back to the simulations. Stepping into Commander Dower's entry Katherine knocked on the open hatch.

Commander Helen Dower looked up from her large console. "Hello Cadet Carroll. Are here to be my minion...?" she said smiling.

Katherine was caught off guard by Helen's jovial attitude, "Um, yes Ma'am?"

Helen smiled a little more at her response. She stepped around the console and closed the hatch. The room suddenly got very quiet. As Helen stepped by, Katherine couldn't help notice Helen's cybernetics. Remembering Asteria's comment about physical contact Katherine stayed clear of Helen. The last thing Katherine wanted was to reveal her fear to a Fleet Commander.

Helen looked at Katherine for a second. "Have you been cleared by Dr. Driscoll?" she asked.

"Yes Ma'am. This morning," Katherine said.

"What do you know about engineering?"

Katherine looked at the deck, "Very little Ma'am. My education was more physical than mental."

Helen chuckled, "Well if what Asteria says is true you have quite a natural ability in the mental arena," Helen looked at Katherine and seemed to come to some conclusion. "How about a tour to start off with," she said as she headed for the hatch, "Come on Katherine."

An hour later Katherine was beginning to feel much better about her tour in engineering. Meeting the Warrant Officers had been quite an episode. Ben and Kila were very likable. Katherine followed Helen up to a hatch on the port side.

"Saved the best for last," Helen said to her as they stepped inside, "Welcome to the cybernetics lab," Helen said smiling.

Katherine froze as data streamed around her. She had not accessed her core, it had accessed on its own as she entered the lab.

Helen looked at her and smiled, "I never get tired of seeing it, isn't it beautiful."

Katherine realized she could feel Helen. She was sharing the connection with her. Helen radiated confidence. Katherine focused on the room and what was in it. She saw an unusual data stream from the work bench. It flowed and moved like an organic being. Waves of green and blue flowed around the bench in magnificent displays.

"That's the current prototype nanite combat suit," Helen said noticing Katherine's gaze. "It can only be utilized by those of us who have implants right now but hopefully I can get it to integrate with standard implants soon."

"What does it do?" Katherine asked walking up to it. The green and blue waves responded to her proximity and washed over the two of them.

"It senses and responds to threats. Your implant can tell the suit how to react in response to your intended actions. Say you get attacked from the left, it could create thicker armor on your shoulder if you cannot respond fast enough."

"That would be amazingly helpful!" Katherine said.

"Exactly..." Helen responded, "Why don't you try it out?"

"What! Really I can try it," Katherine said amazed.

"Well you're the only one with an implant that is certified to use commando armor…. I guess it's made for you," Helen said.

Katherine reached out and touched the material. It instantly connected with her mind and she suddenly realized she could feel the workbench beneath the suit. She carefully pulled her hand away and stared at Helen in amazement.

Cadet Katherine Carroll
Deck Seven, Tactical
Light Destroyer Nyx, Deep Space
299.0188 FCUDT 17:28:12

Katherine hurried down the passageway as fast as she could without running. She was going to be late for her gunnery lessons with Mr. Petrokov.

Her first day in engineering had been amazing, working on the new nano tech with Commander Dower was incredible. Unfortunately, that was not how the last three days had been. She had been assigned to work with Lieutenant Lavagnino on the reactors. He had her literally crawl into number four today and identify parts with him. She had quickly come to the conclusion that engineers were insane. She had activated her core in there and saw the walls radiate residual gravitons. She nearly passed out in shock until the Lieutenant assured her they were harmless.

Turning the corner and jumping through the hatch into the Gunnery section she skidded to a stop in front of Master Chief Warrant Officer Harold 'Gunny' Petrokov.

"Right on time Ma'am!" he said in his boisterous manner.

"Sorry Chief Petrokov, Lieutenant Lavagnino kept me late today," she said hurriedly.

"I told ya to call me Gunny Ma'am," he said slapping her on the shoulder.

Technically she outranked the old Chief Warrant Officer because of the way the rank structure worked. Warrants were above crewmen but under all regular officers. Technically she was the lowest regular officer... Out of respect for their position and knowledge most regular officers would never attempt to throw their rank at warrant officers.

"Yes, Gunny, I will," she said.

He smiled broadly at her and pointed at the big eighty millimeter cannon nearby. "Go hop in the eighty and begin the startup, I'll send Sergeant Hopper over to be your crewmen. Ten credits say you qualify today," he said as he walked off toward the gunnery consoles, "Hopper! Get your butt over and crew for this little lady. Maybe you'll learn something from her superior skills."

Katherine jogged over to the gun and climbed up into it.

Sergeant Hopper jogged up behind her. "Evening Ma'am, ready to defend against the evil drones?" he asked smiling.

"They will never see their end coming!" she said as she climbed into the gunners' seat.

Master Chief Petty Officer Shia O'Connell
Deck Four, Medical Bay Morgue
Light Destroyer Nyx, Deep Space
299.0188 FCUDT 18:00:05

Shia walked up to the polished white tube and looked down at it. Sam stood just behind her with a grim expression.

"I should have been there," Shia said.

"Shia you know better than that. Don't second guess yourself," Sam said to her.

"Still, this shouldn't have happened," she said.

Sam walked up and put her hand on Shia's shoulder. "I know you have lost people before, why is this bothering you so much. What's wrong?"

Shia looked at Sam then back at the tube. "I think I had my guard down. You know, I wasn't thinking this could happen. I feel like I let my team down," Shia said.

She placed her hand on the tube as the realities of the Military life crashed down around her. She didn't have the benefit of Military Basic training to set her in the right frame of mind. Her and most of the command crew had been civilians just months ago. She had signed the contract with the expectation that it would be the same as it was on the *Hypnos*. It wasn't, and she has already lost someone she was responsible for.

"I'm sorry Shia," Sam said, "I know this hit you close to home..."

Shia's face turned pale, "Sam please. I've tried very hard to forget what happened."

Sam was the only person on the crew who knew Shia's history, from the time before she began running security on long haul deep space freighters. Shia was an up and coming Federal Ranger when she was trapped on a damaged freighter with her team. The only way to survive was to sleep away the years drifting through interstellar space in failing stasis tubes. When they were finally recovered only two of her original seven-person team lived. Sixty years had passed her by and left her completely alone. She was plagued by guilt every day since.

"It's alright, I will be fine. I just didn't expect this," she said, "Do we have any leads on this guy?" she asked changing topics.

Sam shook her head, "We're sure he is on the ship still but he is avoiding detection quite well."

Shia turned and looked at Sam, "Let me know as soon as we find him, I have a score to even out..."

Katherine's body buzzed with anticipation. She was going to test Commander Dower's new suit this morning with her level one commando armor. She almost ran to the cybernetics lab when she stepped through the main engineering hatch.

As she entered the lab she saw the two techs drinking coffee. "Morning Specialists," she said to them.

"Morning Ma'am, the suit is prepped and ready for you," One of them said nodding to the bench.

She walked over and looked down at it. She had been using her cybernetics almost constantly for the past several days especially in gunnery training and didn't even notice the activation as she entered the lab. Of course she didn't access the core, which still caused her great difficulty.

One of the Specialists stepped out and the other came over to Katherine. "I can help you suit up if you like Ma'am," she said.

"Thank you," she said to her as she deactivated her standard suit and slipped out of it. Picking up the generation two nanosuit she felt it connect to her cybernetics. As she slipped it on she felt the suit join with her skin. It cycled through its initiation and activated. It crawled up and around her neck to her jaw and halfway up the back of her head.

Katherine looked at herself in the mirror smooth wall. The suit covered her body like a second skin. She looked like someone painted her nude form forest green, you could even see her bright silver medical and neuro implant through the suit.

"Looks perfect," Helen said as she walked in.

Katherine turned and grinned at Helen, "It's fully functional Ma'am."

Helen walked up and looked at her approvingly, "Activate the internal armor," she said.

Katherine looked down and the suit seemed to go fluid for a brief instant then there were plates covering her. They seemed to shift and move as she did. As she raised her arm the shoulder plate slid back and down providing continuous coverage.

"It's excellent, Ma'am!" Katherine said.

"Good, this one is yours. You're the only one who can use it. Gen three should be out soon."

"What! I can have this one... Ma'am, really?" Katherine was shocked.

"Yes Katherine, it's yours. Now let's go give it a real test," she said smiling.

Several minutes later they entered the training hall in the Hell Hold. Katherine stood wide eyed as she saw Major Delaney and Captain Stuart in commando armor.

"Am I going to fight them?" she said to Helen surprised.

"You're going to crush them!" Master Sergeant Goody said behind her.

Katherine swallowed hard and looked at the room. Master Sergeant Goody walked over and stood in the observation room with Lieutenant Sheffield. Major Delaney and Captain Stuart walked up to her and Helen.

"Mrs. Carroll, time to impress me," Adam said, "Major Delaney and I have thirty years of experience so don't hold back... we won't," he said winking at her.

The training buzzer went off and they took to their sides. Katherine forced herself to focus and connected with her armor. Her new suit slid up and surrounded her face and her commando helmet closed. Data streamed around her.

Suddenly the lights went off and the room filled with metallic dust and smoke. Her sensors went blind. She crouched low. I'm blind! She thought. She heard a scrape to her left and suddenly a crashing blow sent her reeling off into the right side wall.

She instinctually created a view of the room from

memory and positioned it over her vision. Where are they...? I heard him first. She thought. Heard him... She instructed her suit to broadcast an ultrasonic ping. Instantly she had a real time view of the room. She dove forward and rolled away from the impending attack. Turning she swept the legs out from the nearest target. She pirouetted on one arm and swung her legs up and out at the other target catching him in the chest. She hit the wall and shoved off into the smoke filled room. She came to a crouch in the center of the room and watched them.

The two stood and began to circle the room. She became aware of two more targets entering the room from the other side.

"Cheating I see..." she said to herself. She jumped straight up and grabbed a pipe that ran along the length of the room. Her suit grew hooks that she clipped onto the pipe and slid toward the two new targets.

She looked down at them below her and swung her legs down. The clips released and she dropped behind them. In a blinding flash she pushed one dropping him to the ground and picked up the other and threw him at the first two targets. He flew across the room and struck them.

She became aware of the fourth target as her suit reacted and grew a vertical plate from her shoulder that protected her face from impact. A solid metal pipe struck her with a powerful smash. Her suit absorbed all the kinetic energy. She stood and grabbed the pipe from the attacker and threw it across the room.

She leapt at the wall and rebounded into target number four sending him sprawling out into the room.

She dove right and rolled as flashes of plasma splashed around her in beautiful waves. Two on the other side of the room were firing at her. She ran straight at them diving and jumping over and under their shots. She full body tackled them both smashing them into the wall.

The training buzzer sounded and the room vented.

Captain Stuart retracted his helmet and looked at

Katherine, "Amazing..."

"I'm sorry Sir, it took me awhile to figure out how to compensate for the loss of sensors," she said apologetically.

"Awhile...? Cadet how long do you think this session lasted?" the Captain asked.

Katherine looked at him not understanding, "Maybe ten minutes..."

Major Delaney walked up, "It was ten seconds Ms. Carroll."

She just stared at him.

"Well done Cadet," Captain Stuart said to her.

The other Marines stared at her in awe as she walked out of the training room in her new suit.

Lieutenant Simay Binici
Deck Four, Medical Bay
Light Destroyer Nyx, Deep Space
300.0188 FCUDT 13:19:08

Simay sat at a holo console with Dr. Driscoll and Commander Leeane watching Katherine test the new nanosuit.

"Her neural scans are fine, far faster than normal but the striping is nearly gone. She isn't using the cybernetic core at its potential but it is doing what we intended," Brynn said happily.

"What capacity is she using it?" Sam said astonished.

"Something around twelve percent," Brynn said looking at them.

"Stars! She can do more than what we just saw?" Sam said.

"Yes, far more. For some reason she isn't accessing the deeper functions. She has only used peripheral functions and the autonomous reflexes. I believe the trauma has scared her from accessing the ship's core and thus limited her ability to use the cybernetics," Brynn said looking at the data on her console.

"She has been having a hard time with things especially the other Midshipmen," Simay said, "That combined with traumatic stress caused by the core in her head... I can understand her fear."

Sam looked at Brynn, "What's your assessment?"

"She is fully functional and obviously combat capable. Her emotional state is another matter," Brynn said frowning.

"Well she will just have to learn. We can't teach her to be confident and assertive," Sam said.

Simay looked at Sam, "What do you want me to do?"

"Nothing, let her sort out the other Midshipmen" Sam said frowning.

"Yes Ma'am," Simay said.

Commander Helen Dower
Command Deck, Bridge
Light Destroyer Nyx, Deep Space
303.0188 FCUDT 10:41:09

"Sir, Higgs is charged and ready at your command," Helen said standing at the engineering console. Katherine and Kila sat in front of her operating the complex systems while she monitored.

"Course is plotted and locked in Sir," Simay said from Navigation.

Helen saw the Captain activate the ships address system. "All stations, we will transit in thirty seconds, lock and secure."

Adam looked around the Bridge for a second. "Well let's be about it. Commander Dower take us out."

"Aye Sir," she said. Looking down at Katherine Helen nodded. Katherine typed in a series of commands and the Higgs sprang to life.

One kilometer in front the ship an invisible field formed, fed by the emitters mounted on the bow. The aft rods vibrated as invisible energy from the center of the field expelled out behind the ship in a dizzying display of blue. As the energy readings dropped below the threshold the superconducting accelerators fired concentrated gravimetric particles from the reactors directly into the center of the void.

The gravimetric particles began to spin into a vortex faster and faster forming a torus. As the torus stabilized the third stage initiated. The CoNeE drives created a graviton spike that drove right into the center of the torus.

As the graviton spike was fired a blue circle formed expanding to sixty meters in diameter. The huge release of energy burst from the outer edges of the circle. Super charged particles discharged perpendicular from the blue ring in a brilliant iridescent shower beginning blue and moving through the spectrum as they burned out in their second-long lifespan. As they dissipated a pencil thin blue line enclosed a fisheye lens that shined back at them. The bridge was bathed in cool blue color.

"Navigation course confirmed, gravity bubble collapsing," Helen announced. The ship was propelled forward by the narrowing gravity well behind them. They slid past the event horizon and into another form of space. In a matter of seconds, they exited the other side smoothly passing the event horizon into regular space now ten light years from their starting point.

"Sir transit complete, recharge in twenty seconds," Helen announced, "All systems check out."

"Position confirmed, we are exactly at predetermined coordinates Sir," Simay said from the Navigation console.

"Tactical is clear Sir, Asteria said.

Helen breathed a silent sigh of relief. She had worked tirelessly to ensure that the ship was ready. She couldn't be more proud as all the systems performed flawlessly.

"Excellent, good job everybody," Adam said, "Commander Dower when you're ready I think we can move to Clare."

"Yes Sir, initiation in ten seconds," she said.

"Course to Clare system is locked in Sir," Simay said.

"Activating," Helen said as Katherine initiated the sequence.

CHAPTER FOUR
Clew Bay

Clare System, Independently Governed Space
48.2 Light Years from Home System
303.0187 FCUDT 11:27:10

Hovering nearly fifty light years forward and down the Orion Cygnus arm from Federated Colonial home system lies Clare. Most of Clare's past includes violent battles, wars, strife, and finally occupation by the most feared pirates in the local bubble.

There is little in the way resources around the beautiful red class four star. Three damaged planets and a ring of debris are scattered about. The large star refracts off all the scattered debris and casts a red glow across hundreds of light years. That coupled with the terrible fighting in the system has garnered it quite the mythical reputation.

The primary hub of activity in the system is the massive orbital station known as Clew Bay. Originally a mining station on a medium sized asteroid it has since been expanded into a thriving community. The asteroid has been hollowed and colonized. Massive metal girders extend above and below the dull grey rock for hundreds of meters. The interior is so massive it has its own weather and seems to nearly always rain at the lowest levels.

Despite being a bastion for pirates and criminals it is secure, orderly, and well governed. Grace O'Malley the leader of the largest pirate fleet this side of Orion Cygnus teamed up with the Federated Colonies during the war and became a privateer against the Briton systems. In a bold move she led the fight to capture and hold Clare as a foothold for attacks into Briton space. Under the tutelage of then Lieutenant Adam Stuart, Grace O'Malley became an exceptional leader.

Unfortunately, Lieutenant Stuart was forced to return to Federated Space at the closing of the war. The separation of Adam and Grace fueled a fire that burned for decades between the two. The course of the Hypnos led them to Clare and a reunited Adam and

101

Grace for a short time relieving the tension between them.

After the war Grace found life as the de facto ruler of Clare to be quite fulfilling and settled into the role. Nowadays she spends her time negotiating security contracts and assembling a proper government. Her close contacts to Adam have allowed her to potentially get Clare recognized as a sovereign Nation.

Cadet Katherine Carroll
Deck Thirteen, Passageways
Light Destroyer Nyx, Clare System
304.0188 FCUDT 05:40:21

The *Nyx* flashed into the beautiful red light of Clare system without fanfare. Unfortunately, Katherine missed it. She was running after Lieutenant Binici along the passageways of the crew deck in their morning torture. At least they had finally managed to all get dressed this morning.

Katherine brought up the rear of the little formation as usual to avoid the taunting of Midshipmen Jennifer Worley. She breathed deeply and tried to focus. She was watching their formation run on the ships camera network.

Three days ago she had learned to limit accessing her cybernetics while running. She had focused a little too much on the data and run straight into the bulkhead. As distressing as it was, Jennifer had made it much worse.

She saw something odd on the camera up ahead. In an instant Katherine was sprinting to the front of the formation.

"Watch it drone!" Jennifer spit as Katherine shoved past her.

Just as Katherine reached Lieutenant Binici a plasma bolt flashed out at them. Just grazing Simay on her left shoulder as Katherine tackled her to the deck.

"Ottoman traitor!" The attacker screamed and fired another shot at them. Alarms blared and the man turned and ran down the passageway.

A Marine sentry came sprinting up the passage.

"Wyvern, are you injured?" the Corporal asked her as he quickly approached.

"Were fine, he went that way. Alert the Bridge and pursue," Katherine ordered the Corporal.

"Aye, Ma'am," he replied and headed off.

Katherine stood and looked down at Simay.

"Thank you for that," Simay said as Katherine helped her up.

"Lieutenant!" Midshipmen Gustafson called out.

Katherine turned and saw Midshipmen Aaron Bailey had taken a plasma bolt in his right leg. He was laying on the deck unconscious with Jennifer holding his head.

Two more Marines ran up and one tossed a plasma rifle to Katherine as he ran past her.

"Hold your position Ma'am," he said as he continued down the passage.

She activated her cybernetics and scanned the passageway with the ships sensors. She was secure for the moment. Several seconds later two medics ran up with Commander Leeane behind them.

"Simay!" Sam said as she approached.

"Ma'am, we're fine. Middy Bailey needs medical attention but he looks stable," Simay said.

Sam reached out to Simay's shoulder raising her eyebrow.

"It's nothing, Brynn will fix it. I'm ok," Simay said to her, "Katherine saved me, somehow she saw it coming."

Katherine turned as a commando approached in badly scarred and burned armor. The helmet retracted and she was surprised to see it was Master Chief O'Connell.

She looked at Sam and shook her head, "He ghosted again. No trace," Shia said in disgust.

Three hours later Katherine found herself on the Bridge with Chief Warrant Officer Kila Zucco. She stared out the Bridge windows at the amazing view. Clew Bay was just a twinkling red dot to the port and Clare burned bright red in the center of the view. The watch shift went by slowly and they got ever closer to Clew Bay. Near the end of her watch Major Kane approached her.

"Cadet Carroll, I reviewed your flight simulations. You appear to have completed the shuttle qualifications adequately. I would like you to assist in the upcoming shuttle flights as a pilot trainee," he said to her.

"Yes Sir!" she said surprised.

"Very good, tomorrow morning report to the flight deck," he said smiling as he headed off the Bridge.

Lieutenant Simay Demir Binici
Deck Four, Medical Bay
Light Destroyer Nyx, Clare System
304.0188 FCUDT 12:32:58

"He tried to kill me," Simay said to Brynn.

"He was unsuccessful, we'll catch him," Brynn said softly. She carefully injected accelerator into Simay's shoulder.

"I probably won't be safe until the Empire is defeated," She said sadly.

"Hmpff, this is the safest place you can be. I think he attacked you as a last resort. We have him cornered and he is getting desperate, Brynn said.

Simay looked up at Brynn, "You're not making me feel better..."

"My job is to heal you not placate you..." she said smiling.

She turned her head and looked at Midshipmen Bailey through the window in the next room. "How is he?"

"Oh, he'll be fine. A day in the tube to regenerate his muscles. He is young and resilient," Brynn said, "He will have a war story to tell his friends," she chuckled.

"You're not worried?" Simay asked Brynn.

She looked down into Simay's eyes. "There is always worry on warships. I think you can handle it and I trust the

Marine that has been assigned to accompany you..." she said, "Now stop moping and get back to work Lieutenant. I have rounds to make."

She sat up and sealed her suit, "Yes Colonel, right away," she said grinning.

Master Chief Petty Officer Shia O'Connell
Deck Eleven, Senior Petty Officers Quarters
Light Destroyer Nyx, Clare System
305.0188 FCUDT 03:57:01

An obscene alert was sounding in Shia's quarters. She rolled over and activated her com. "Yes?" she said in a sleepy voice.

Tameria Heyerdahl's dark skin and blue eyes stared out at her. Tameria was Shia's counterpart for the night shift and one of her best friends of many years.

"Wake up grumpy, I got our guy accessing an airlock on deck six," she said to her.

Shia sat straight up in her berth, "I'm on the way!"

"Meet the crew at airlock nineteen on your deck, you're going to have to chase him outside," Tameria said.

Shia jumped across the small room and quickly climbed into her commando armor. I got you this time she thought to herself.

She swung open her hatch and stepped into the passageway. "Coming through! Make a hole!" she hollered as she stormed down through the small space. Crew jumped out of her way to avoid being smashed by her bulky armor. She saw the other security crew as she quickly approached airlock nineteen.

"Shia, we're tracking him. He just left the airlock in route to the surface of the station," Lieutenant Commander Volkov Delaney said in her com.

"Thanks Natalia, I am at the airlock now we are entering," Shia said.

A crewmen handed her a pulse rifle and she slung it to

her armor. She walked into the waiting airlock with the four crew.

"Everybody connect your tethers and link your suits to mine. Nobody goes solo. We want this guy breathing so he can answer questions and then I am going to beat the life out of him," she looked at them in cramped space, "Understand?"

"Yes Chief," they answered.

The airlock cycled and the door slid open. Black space yawned out before them in a soul crushing abyss. The station stood looming just above them glowing pink in Clare's red glare.

"I have a link to your suit bringing up tactical graphics," Asteria said to her over the com.

A series of lines and icons popped up in her vision. A steady red triangle just above and left caught her attention.

"Got him on my display. We're departing the ship in pursuit," Shia said. She took a deep breath and leaned out into the abyss. It was similar to jumping into water you knew was freezing. The mind just can't accept that you're not going to fall forever. Too many years of evolution on solid planets with down being your feet.

Her suit registered the others connection and she triggered the maneuvering unit on their backs. Her suit plotted an intercept course and they rocketed off in a delta shaped formation. Shia watched her displayed relative speed as it climbed to several hundred meters per second. If they hit something now they would be turned into a puddle of organic goo.

She saw the red icon stop gaining distance and slowly begin to draw closer. The station began to grow in her vision as they speed closer. It covered her entire field of vision in seconds and it was still several thousand meters away.

"Shia, hold on. I am altering your vector for collision avoidance," Asteria said.

Her suit thrusters fired and she rolled right then left.

Her vision tunneled and she saw stars as the inertia tore at her body. She saw a light flash and something gray ripped past them on their left. Her course stabilized and her vision cleared.

"Let's not do that again..." she said to Asteria.

A green flash popped past above them causing Shia to jump. Then three more flashed around them.

"Asteria can you tighten us up we are receiving plasma fire. He is way too far away for anything but a lucky hit," she said.

The four crew drifted in closer together and they pulled their weapons out.

"Station security has been alerted. Without a more localized location they cannot do much. The station is just too big. They do have several fighters in route to the area," Natalia said from the Bridge.

Shia's heart began to pound as they rapidly approached the surface of the station at full speed. She couldn't keep the image of her body being pulped as it hurtled into the rock. Beads of sweat formed on her forehead as she forced the fear out of her mind.

Just as she thought she couldn't take it anymore her suit began deceleration and vectored to parallel the surface.

Flashes of plasma flickered all around them as they leveled out.

"I brought you down early to avoid the plasma fire. You are directly behind him. Still no idea where he is headed, there are hundreds of airlocks and hanger bays on his heading," Asteria said.

"Copy, detach the crew into teams of two and keep us on pursuit," Shia said to Asteria.

Behind her the four crew split into two teams and separated to her left and right flanks.

"You're free to engage on low power settings when you have a clear shot," Shia ordered her team.

They rolled and turned as they pursued the saboteur across the surface of the meteor. It was pocketed with ridges, hills and sharp valleys. They flashed past a large smooth gray hanger door. There were black scorch marks as plasma impacted around her on the metal door.

An alert icon flared to life, "Chief! Team one has to break off. He managed to wing our thruster control unit. I got us stabilized but only barely."

"Copy, fall back and await pickup," she said marking their position, "*Nyx* I need a pickup on these coordinates!" she said transmitting the data.

"Copy Shia, Callis is on the way with the shuttle," Natalia said.

The three sped across the surface. Green light reflected off the canyon walls as Shia took shots at the fleeing prey. He took a sharp left turn and disappeared around a hilltop. Shia gritted her teeth as she whipped around the after him. She spotted him on the other side of an open hanger bay door and increased her speed.

Just as she cleared the edge of the door the nose of a massive ship thrust out in front of her. Her suit went into emergency deceleration to avoid collision. Her vision dropped to pinpoint and her head throbbed from the inertial pressure. She snapped her eyes shut trying to avoid letting them hemorrhage. She felt her forehead touch her helmet visor and somewhere in her mind she hoped her spine wouldn't snap.

She curved up and over the ship narrowly missing a com tower as she passed the ships Bridge. She was completely immobilized inside the suit as it decelerated and came to rest on the dock inside the hanger. Behind her the two remaining crew landed.

As she came to rest she dropped to her knees and tried to recover from the massive inertial shock. She could taste coppery blood in her mouth. One crewman ran up to her and checked on her vitals as the other ran after the suspect.

"G... Go with him!" Shia croaked pointing at the other crewman. He ran off after his teammate.

A few seconds later Shia stood and stumbled after them

recovering with each step.

"Shia, you need to stand down. You're going to be laid up for a week if you keep going," Natalia said to her.

"I'm fine," she said spraying blood on her visor with her words.

She followed the security team down the deserted dock toward a hatch. She staggered up to the hatch and the two crewmen turned toward her.

"Chief, the hatch is welded, we will have to cut through. He's gone Chief."

Shia dropped to her knee and coughed up blood.

"Dammit!" she screamed as she pounded the deck with her plasma rifle. She threw the bent and broken rifle against the wall.

"Shia! Your vitals are unstable. You need to get to medical," Natalia said concerned.

Shia stood and began to sway then collapsed to the deck unconscious.

Cadet Katherine Carroll
Deck Thirteen, Midshipmen Quarters
Light Destroyer Nyx, Clare System
305.0188 FCUDT 04:15:51

Katherine lay awake in her berth connected to the ships system. She watched as Chief O'Connell rocketed away from the ship in pursuit of someone. She was riveted to the sensor data as the events unfolded.

Suddenly her com activated. Major Kane appeared.

"Cadet since your awake report to the hanger for flight duty immediately. Level two armor," he said to her and disconnected.

She leapt out of her berth and flung open her locker.

Midshipmen William Scott nearly fell out of bed as she startled him, "Stars! Carroll what are you doing."

"Sorry William, I have been ordered to the flight deck for an emergency," she said as she quickly got dressed.

"Shut up! Trying to sleep over here..." Midshipmen Worley said angrily.

Katherine activated her new nanosuit and triggered level two. Plates grew out and solidified. She slammed her locker a bit harder than she intended and hurried toward the door. A boot crashed into the wall next to the hatch as she passed.

"Don't come back drone!" Jennifer yelled.

Katherine hurried down the nearly deserted passage for the lift to deck five and the flight control center.

Minutes later she hurried into the flight control room. Major Kane looked up from the console near the main holoscreen.

"Cadet, good timing. Shuttle one is prepped and loaded down on the deck," he said nodding to the holo. He turned and picked up a duffel- "This is your flight gear put it on and follow me."

She grabbed the duffel and opened it. In a few seconds she had on her flight systems harness and helmet designed to integrate her into the cockpit controls. Her nano suit began to integrate the control of the new gear into its functions as she hurried after Callis.

"Your sim scores were excellent, it's time to do it for real," he said over his shoulder, "Just remember it's exactly the same, your body knows how to do it just don't let your brain get in the way," he said chuckling.

They crossed the hanger and into the sleek little shuttle. Callis closed and sealed the shuttle door after two rescue crewmen entered and began stowing gear in the rear of the shuttle.

"We're good to go Major," they said as he passed them.

"Copy, strap in and hold on," he said.

Katherine followed him to the cockpit and he pointed to the pilots' seat.

"That's your seat. Your call sign is Wyvern?" he asked.

"Yes Sir, Wyvern," she said.

"Good, mine is Zero. Strap in and cycle it up. Our mission is crew pick up from combat damage down on the station's surface. Be ready for anything though they are still in pursuit," he said as she sat down and began power up.

In a few seconds she looked over, "Systems up and green," she said.

"Good, it's all yours, call control and get us out of here," he said.

She nodded and took a breath, "*Nyx* flight, shuttle one green for exit, request departure clearance," she said.

"Shuttle one clear for immediate departure, vector clear for cross ship exit. Contact Clew traffic upon exit," control said.

Katherine activated the shuttle thrusters and the shuttle lifted off the deck a few meters. She eased the controls forward and the shuttle began to slip forward.

Callis looked at her, "Give it a good push... this is combat speed. If it doesn't scare, you you're doing it wrong," he said.

Katherine swallowed and pushed the controls. The shuttle leapt out of the hanger and rushed off into space in a flash. She banked the shuttle to the starboard and saw the stations loom ahead. She suddenly realized she was flying a space craft, a real actual space craft! She looked around through the thick clear view ports surrounding her and saw *Nyx* to her right. Her heart soared.

"We have the best life in the universe don't we?" Callis said.

She noticed he was looking at the scenery as well, "Yes Sir!"

"Don't forget to call Clew traffic." He said.

"Oh...!" She activated the com, "Clew flight this is shuttle *Nyx* Alpha on vector for personnel recovery sector thirteen delta."

"*Nyx* Alpha, radar contact, proceed on vector. Traffic in vicinity four phoenix fighters, call tally," Clew control said.

"Copy will call tally on traffic," she answered.

"Tactical data is up," Callis announced.

Katherine saw a green icon appear off to her right a bit and as she turned she saw a red icon some distance farther off being pursued by Chief O'Connell.

"Bravo team this is shuttle one inbound to your position, thirty-five hundred meters out. Five minutes," Callis called on com.

"Copy shuttle one, we're secure and waiting," they replied.

A com alert sounded in the cabin. "Zero Shia is injured in hanger deck two sixteen I need you to divert and retrieve her!" Natalia called

"Nat, I copy we're in route," Callis answered. He looked at Katherine, "Expedite to that hanger Chief O'Connell needs us."

"Yes Sir!" she quickly inputted a course to the hanger and accelerated at max speed. The shuttle streaked through a parabolic curve and headed into the hanger. There were four massive ships inside blocking the docks. Her cybernetics connected to hanger control and she evaluated the scene. Katherine looked at the space available and she decided she could fit between the two top ships. She continued to head in at speed.

Sweat beaded on her face. At the last second she twisted the shuttle on axis and slipped between the massive hulls. She rolled and turned into a hockey stop decelerating hard. The bottom of the shuttle went parallel to the wall and used it to increase the power of the thrusters. It scorched the metal as it came to a stop. Katherine rolled off the wall and swooped down the last seventy meters to set down gently on the dock next to the waiting crew.

Callis drew a deep breath, "Well... your test flight is complete," he said as he let go his death grip on the seats armrests.

I'm in trouble, he looks upset she thought to herself. Her stomach rolled over and she swallowed trying to relax.

The pararescue jumped from the shuttle and helped carry Shia on board. They put her on a stretcher and secured her.

"We're secure Major!" they called.

"Ok Wyvern let's get the chief to medical," he said.

A few minutes later they were approaching *Nyx's* hanger.

"*Nyx* control shuttle one on approach request priority landing for medical emergency," she called.

"Shuttle one your clear for immediate landing your choice," they replied.

She glided the shuttle in past the graviton curtain and settled as far up the deck as she could to get near the lifts.

"Down and secure, your clear to exit," she called to the rescue team.

Callis looked at her, "How did you know you would fit between those ships?" he asked.

She looked at him nervously, "There was a continuous span of six and a half meters between them with enough room past the engines to turn and decelerate. This special operations shuttle is five meters at its widest point," she said.

"How did you know it was six and a half meters?" he said incredulous.

"I calculated it from the hanger control sensors on the station," she said.

"The hanger... you accessed the station's computer!" he said, "How?"

"Yes from the shuttle's com. It extended my cybernetic range," she said, "I didn't mean to do it... I just did," she said ashamed.

He looked at her amazed, "Cadet you passed your ratings. You're approved to pilot shuttles. Now since were refueled let's go get Bravo team."

"Aye Sir," she said a bit confused by the conversation.

The clamor of the Hanger bay was always relaxing Sam thought. Crew hurried about moving cargo and parts. Flight crew tinkered with the shuttles. Maybe it was because it was also the largest open space on the ship she thought. She looked over and saw Cadet Carroll in flight gear headed for the shuttle.

"Good morning Cadet Carroll," she said as she approached.

"Good morning Ma'am," she replied.

"Are you going on this mission with us?" Sam asked.

"She is your pilot today," Callis said walking up behind Sam.

"You've gained your rating! Congratulations Ms. Carroll."

"Thank you Ma'am," Katherine replied a bit embarrassed.

"Good Morning all," Captain Stuart said as he, Admiral Lune, and Major Delaney approached. "Are we ready to go?" Adam asked looking at Callis.

Callis nodded at Katherine.

"Sir, shuttle one is prepped and ready at your command," she said.

Adam smiled at her, "Excellent! Let's be about it."

Sam followed Michael Delaney into the small shuttle and took a seat behind Captain Stuart.

Michael leaned over to Sam, "We should take Carroll with us, good training for her and she is a juggernaut..."

Sam smiled, "I agree."

Callis sealed the hatch and stepped into the cockpit.

"Standby for departure, all crew confirm secure," Katherine's voice floated through the shuttle.

Minutes later the shuttle glided into their designated hanger and Sam poked her head into the cockpit.

"Ms. Carroll I would like you to accompany us on our visit," she said.

Katherine looked up at her, "Aye Ma'am."

Katherine followed her out into the shuttle cabin as everybody was exiting.

"Stick to me and the XO like glue, keep your ears open and remember you're a Marine commando," Sam heard Michael say to Cadet Carroll.

"Yes Sir," she answered.

As they stepped onto the dock and tall muscular man in green level two armor stepped forward. "Good morning, Ma'am. It's good to see you again Sir. Welcome to Clew Bay."

"Donnelly! I like the new uniform. Colonel suits you," Adam said, "Coline, Colonel Donnelly here is the field chief of security for the station."

"Nice to meet you Colonel," she said.

"If you would follow me I will escort you to Governor O'Malley," he said smiling.

Two Soldiers led the way and Donnelly stepped up next to Michael.

"Well looks like I finally out rank you Mickey..." he said smiling.

"Go ahead push it a little more," Michael said joking.

"Falcon, nice to see your back in one piece," Donnelly said to Sam.

She nodded, "I hope you have improved your security..." She said wincing at the memory of being abducted last time she was here.

"Probably not," Michael said eyeing Donnelly.

Donnelly nodded at Katherine, "Who's the new officer?"

"She's off limits that's who she is," he said noticing Katherine peeking over her shoulder at him. "Remember I know you from when you were disreputable..." he said in a

115

mock serious tone.

"Oh come on... I didn't know you liked her and that was a long time ago!" Donnelly said laughing as they arrived at the conference room. He stepped out and activated the hatch leading inside.

Master Chief Petty Officer Shia O'Connell
Deck Four, Medical Bay Emergency suite
Light Destroyer Nyx, Clare System
305.0188 FCUDT 19:38:49

Shia awoke with a start. She was confused for a minute and didn't know where she was. Joe stepped up and looked down at her.

"Shia, you're in medical on the ship," she said to her.

Shia visibly relaxed. Then suddenly remembered losing the suspect again. Her vitals spiked as her anger surged.

Brynn walked in and looked at Shia, "You need to relax or I am going to put you back to sleep."

She nodded and looked down at herself. There was a rather large tube sticking out of her chest. She tried to ask what was wrong and realized she couldn't talk.

"Relax, you are temporarily paralyzed from the neck down to allow your body to rebuild. The inertia caused multiple failures in your organs and most of the vessels in your lungs hemorrhaged. You're lucky, it could have been much worse," Brynn said, "I will have you out of here in a day or two. Your unique physiology has had to work overtime so take it easy."

Shia activated her neuro com. *Is there any progress on finding the saboteur?* she asked Joe silently.

"Not yet but the Admiral and Captain are on the station with Mrs. O'Malley. I am sure they will discuss it," Joe said.

I need to get back over there...

"Shia, rest. You need to get better. Then you can continue," Joe said to her quietly.

Senior Captain Mercan
Deck Nine, Passageway Four
Interstellar Space
308.0188 FCUDT 06:32:12

The passageways glowed in the violet light that signified the ship was traveling in graviton induced space as Senior Captain Mercan quietly walked through his ship. He valued the time before the crew was awakened and tried to spend it collecting his thoughts on several daily walks around the ship. Technically these were 'inspections' but he knew his crew well and the ship was always held in perfect readiness. Nearing the end of his stroll he turned and stepped into the spartan Medical bay.

"Doctor, are we on schedule?" he asked sternly.

A thin gaunt man looked up at him from a computer terminal, "Greetings Senior Captain. The crew is being prepped and schedule will be met."

Their eyes met for a second and Captain Mercan sensed nothing but compliance from the ship's doctor. 'Good' he thought, 'my crew knows their place.' He nodded looked at the computer screen seeing the stasis tube blinking their ready activation status. Turning sharply, he stepped out of Medical and walked confidently down the passageway toward the bridge. As he entered he heard the gruff voice of the AI announce his presence to the few crew who immediately stood at attention. Ignoring them he walked over and sat in the vacated command chair. He activated the computer and looked up impatiently at Sub Captain Kosta, his Executive Officer.

"Sir, twenty-seven hours until translation for the enemy system. Crew are being awakened now and the ship is at one hundred percent," Kosta said evenly.

Mercan nodded and scrolled through the data on his computer. He was slightly incensed at being diverted from the impending fleet action and simultaneously pleased that he had been selected to lead this small force. A simple system capture and fortification was perfect to add to his record and if god smiled on him then so would the Emperor. "Kosta when the crew is awake I want drills run to ensure perfection."

"Yes Senior Captain. I will inform the department heads," he replied.

Senior Captain Mercan stood and walked into his ready room not even noticing that three crew were still standing at attention.

Cadet Katherine Carroll
Deck Seventeen, Conference Room Alpha
Clew Bay Station, Clare System
308.0188 FCUDT 16:52:47

Three days! She had been sitting through these conferences for three days. There has been talking, yelling, threats, and promises. They didn't seem to be any closer to an agreement than the day they walked in here.

Admiral Lune had offered to make Clare a territory of the Federated Colonies, not a colony. That gave them the right to protection by the colonies and the freedom to travel in all Federated Territory without immigration fees.

It didn't allow them representation or the ability to vote in congress. But they could petition for full membership in the future.

All this was contingent on a few things... Clare must have a functioning government based on the Federated standard. They also must have civil services, and participate in Military recruiting efforts. They would be subject to a very minimum taxation due to the restricted privileges. They must also have the same set standards of law as the Federated Colonies.

It was really not much Katherine thought but apparently Mrs. O'Malley thought differently. She was apparently not so happy with the lack of representation portion.

Katherine had heard the XO say that Mrs. O'Malley

would eventually sign but had to put up resistance to maintain her standing in the eyes of her population. That same population were known pirates... Katherine thought she would never understand this circus.

On a brighter side apparently Katherine had been named the semiofficial shuttle pilot for the duration. Anything that got her flight time was a good thing she thought.

Katherine looked up as the lights brightened. They must be finished for the day.

"Thank the lord their done for today," Simay said quietly next to her.

Lieutenant Binici had accompanied the group for the last two days and Katherine had gotten to know her pretty well.

"I would rather fight them all with a fork than bicker over a treaty like this," Katherine said back.

Simay chuckled, "A short while ago I would have just shot her and taken over the station..." she smiled.

"Well she may be facing that if she doesn't align with the Colonies..." Katherine said not quite sure what Simay meant. She stood and stretched.

Simay stood and looked at Katherine, "Come on maybe we can get back in time for dinner."

Sam walked up to them, "Simay, we are staying to have dinner with Grace. You two are welcome to eat on the station. There is a really nice place on deck seventy-four."

Simay looked at Katherine and raised her eyebrows. "Sounds like a plan Ma'am," she said.

"Good, meet us here at twenty hundred to return to the ship," Sam said and smiled, "Stay out of trouble..." -she winked.

Katherine and Simay stepped off the crowded lift and flowed with the crowd out into the main chamber. They both froze in awe. It was easily a hundred seventy levels tall and nearly a kilometer across. There were suspended platforms on various levels and catwalks stretched all the way across on some.

They walked to the railing and looked at it in awe. There were clouds drifting around above them and the air was humid and cool. All around them there were stalls selling fruits and vegetables. Katherine had never seen such a place.

"Where did all this come from?" Katherine asked.

"Do you think it's all stolen?" Simay said quietly.

Katherine admired a large variety on one of the stalls. She picked up a bright red fruit and looked at the lady who stood nearby.

"Where does this come from?" she asked.

The lady smiled, "Oh that comes from Alesia, child."

"Ruth you're not supposed to tell them that!" an old man said from behind her.

"Oh quiet, she's a Fed, we'll all be Feds soon enough," she said to him.

"Alesia?" Simay asked.

"It's the Clare homeworld," she said smiling.

Master Chief Petty Officer Shia O'Connell
Shuttle Two
Light Destroyer Nyx, Clare System
308.0188 FCUDT 18:02:21

Shia stood in the back of the shuttle brooding quietly. She had laid in bed for three days making a plan on how to find her prey. An hour ago she had received a message from the station Security Chief Calvin Flanagan. He wanted to meet with her and discuss a possible lead. She had immediately jumped on the scheduled shuttle.

She walked down the gangway and onto the dock seconds after the shuttle landed. She was met by a security officer who escorted her to Calvin's office.

"Shia it's good to see you!" the large happy man said as he grabbed her had. "I would give you a hug but in that armor it would be unfulfilling..." he said laughing.

"It's nice to see you too Calvin," she said.

"All business today aren't you lass," he looked at her seriously. "Well come on, I'll show you what we have so far."

He led her out onto the main floor and up to a series of holoscreens. He activated one and data flashed up on the screen.

"Most of our merchants are nice respectable folk. Even the ones who don't appear to be," he said absently, "They report suspicious clients because they are actually afraid that the Ottoman Empire is going to slag us all."

Shia raised her eyebrows at him.

"Yea tell me about it. The most infamous pirates in the arm are scared and want to join the good guys," he said laughing, "Never thought I would live to see something hokey like this. Anyway, we got a report about someone buying unusual items and tracked him. He has been in and out of the resident level and spotted walking through engineering," -he brought up an image of the individual.

Shia stood straighter as soon as she saw it. "That's him," she said angrily, "Where is he now?"

"Relax, he dropped off our grid but we'll pick him back up," he said looking at her. "You want to join our trackers?" he asked.

She looked up at him with predatory eyes, "Absolutely."

He grinned, "Thought you would, but Shia, don't go doing something crazy. I know deep down your just a good ole Ranger, I need that person. Not the one standing here right now," he said seriously.

Shia looked at the deck- "Ok, I will keep in check."

He nodded...

Twenty minutes later Shia was on the lower resident level. She found a dark alleyway a distance from the suspected residence that had a good view. She settled down in some trash and pulled out her plasma rifle to wait in the darkness.

"I got you this time..." she whispered to herself.

Sam watched Katherine and Simay hurry up to the shuttle with several bags of fruit in their arms.

"XO I found oranges!" Katherine said excited.

Sam just shook her head. The two were so excited she didn't have the heart to scold them for being late.

"Come on you two you can tell me about it later. We need to get going," Sam said to them as they shuffled aboard and stowed their bags.

Katherine turned and looked at Sam, "Ma'am, we found out about a planet here in Clare that is habitable," she said hurriedly.

Sam gave her a disbelieving look, "That's impossible. This system was destroyed years ago. You saw it when we arrived," she said beginning to get frustrated with the young officers.

"Ma'am, we looked it up, it's on the far side. A planet called Alesia. This fruit comes from there," she said as she put her flight gear on.

"We did look it up Ma'am," Simay confirmed as she strapped into her seat.

Katherine nodded as she disappeared into the cockpit.

Sam turned and looked at Adam and Coline raising an eyebrow. "Alesia...You think?" she said to them.

"It would be the most likely planet..." Adam activated his com, "Asteria, could you scan the far side and let me know if there is a viable planet out there. Maybe hiding from us?" he said.

"Aye Sir, tasking now," she replied.

He leaned back and looked at them, "If it's there she will find it."

Alesia was legendary, once a beautiful lush world in the green belt of Clare it was reduced to ash during the multiple battles on this system. There were stories of verdant fields of tall grasses, crystal clear oceans, and dense forests. Myths of strange and wonderful native life. It was the reason the Britons claimed this system. It was also the reason for many of the battles. It was long believed to have been totally destroyed several decades ago. It wasn't even a consideration twenty years ago when Adam had helped to finally wrestle this system from Britons grasp.

"A viable planet would change everything out here," Coline said verbalizing about the implications, "Especially if it's Alesia..."

As they approached the hanger bay for landing on *Nyx* Adam's com alerted.

"Captain, I dispatched a remote to scan the system. It has just cleared the bend in the orbit. I am reading a single planet with viable atmosphere. It is point nine-nine earth gravity and has minimal ship traffic. It matches the database records for the orbit of a planet named Alesia," Asteria said, "Would you like me to continue scanning?"

Adam looked at Coline, "Yes Asteria, please continue, we will be on the Bridge in a few minutes."

"Why wouldn't she tell us about Alesia, it would have given her a far bigger bargaining chip?" Coline said.

Since expanding into the galaxy humanity has realized there are far fewer viable planets than they expected. There are hundreds of colonized worlds known to humanity but when placed next to a list of stars in the Orion arm it quickly becomes a very small number indeed. The ever expanding reach of mankind has placed natural viable planets as the number one commodity. Naturally this would vault Clare into a precarious position between several powerful entities.

"Target spotted heading in station on street fourteen," a station security officer said quietly on the com. "Chief Shia, he's headed your direction."

Shia immediately became alert. She stiffened and gripped her rifle a little tighter, "Copy, I am in position."

"Shia, hold and observe. We are bringing a team down," Calvin said to her.

She sighed, "Aye, Calvin."

A few seconds later she spotted the target heading for the door to the residence. He paused and thumbed the door then entered.

"Target has entered the residence," Shia reported.

She switched to infrared vision and settled in to wait.

She sat there in the light rain and looked up at the massive city towering up the walls of the station above her. It was nearly the antithesis of her home town of Derwin on Ixion. Derwin was a subterranean warren of tunnels like a massive human anthill. This was a beautiful humming open beehive of activity. Where Derwin was closed and claustrophobic, Clew was open and airy. Shia didn't particularly like Clew. Every time she had visited had resulted in a bitter firefight. Shia snorted at the thought, I get into bitter fights on every place I visit...

Her thoughts were interrupted as she noticed movement across the way. Her suspect stepped out of the residence and made to move off.

"Alert, suspect is on the move. I am in covert pursuit," Shia said on her com. She quietly stepped out and moved silently along the wall toward the road he had walked down.

She saw him a hundred meters away and casually stepped out to follow him. She visually tagged him so her suits computer would continue to track him.

They wound up through the terraces of the lower levels and he stopped to purchase a lift pass. He stepped under cover of the light rain and waited with a small crowd. Shia wandered up and purchased a lift pass as well then moved off a short distance nearby to watch and wait.

"We are at the east lift access station. Still in pursuit," she said.

"Copy Shia, we have an additional coming up behind you," Calvin said.

Several minutes later the lift arrived and the crowd jostled up to the entrance while the outgoing passengers disembarked. Shia helped an older woman in a faded purple dress up onto the ramp and stepped aboard behind her.

"Thank you miss; this rain really makes my bones ache," the lady said to her.

Shia just smiled at her and nodded as she kept her awareness on the tracking tab in her visual.

The lift started and stopped at its various programmed access points and people came and went. Shia noticed that the higher they went up the station the healthier the population seemed. After several minutes and dozens of stops she noticed the suspect step forward preparing to exit. Shia waited so she wouldn't draw any attention.

As the lift stopped she merged with the crowd and followed the suspect off and into the passageways. She looked at the locator as she passed it on the wall.

"We are on level two fourteen. Anything important on this level?" Shia asked.

"Hmm, that's the small craft docks and the lower entrance to engineering. He could be there for either," Calvin said.

She let a bit of distance build between them as she walked around the rotunda. She saw him making his way toward a large bulge in the rock wall. She increased her pace as he approached the main hatch for engineering.

"Looks like engineering," Shia reported.

She hurried past several people and quickly stepped up

through the hatch trying not to lose him. She breathed a sigh of relief as saw him walking down the central corridor.

Silently she followed.

The glaring red com alert flashed angrily above Helen's head. She swatted at it trying to make it go away. Suddenly she jumped up realizing what it was and startled Xander awake. She activated the com and Captain Stuart smiled at her from the holo.

"Morning Helen," he said happily.

"Humph," Helen said and looked at him.

"Yes, there seems to be an issue with the stations reactors. Shia has tracked our little friend to the engineering decks and thinks he may have tampered with them," he said

"That could be bad!" she said as her head cleared.

"Grace O'Malley mentioned you could be of help since I believe you father built the reactors..."

"Yes sir, he told me about that a few months ago. That he worked with you during the early occupation of Clew Bay," she said running her hands through her hair, "I would be happy to help them check out the reactors."

"Good, meet us at the shuttle in an hour. I will assign Cadet Carroll to assist you," he said and disconnected.

Helen looked at Xander who sleepily looked up at her.

"I've got to go to work lover," Helen said to him as she kissed him.

"Be careful," he said.

She smiled happily at him, "I have a Marine escort so don't worry."

An hour later Helen jogged across the bay floor in her level two armor carrying two heavy packs. Katherine met her halfway to the shuttle.

"Morning Ma'am, let me take one of those packs," Katherine said shouldering one of the two gear packs Helen was carrying.

"Thank you Katherine. I hear your going with me this morning," Helen said smiling.

"Yes Ma'am. I am more than happy to assist you today," Katherine replied.

Helen eyed her suspiciously as they stowed the gear bags.

"The colonial deliberations have been enlightening..." Katherine said quietly.

Helen laughed as she took her seat. She looked up as eight marines in commando armor entered and made their way to the rear of the shuttle. One paused at the entrance and looked at Katherine.

"Your skin in the port locker Ma'am," he said.

"Thank you Master Sergeant," Katherine replied.

Commando Lieutenant Sheffield entered and nodded to Helen as he disappeared onto the flight deck.

"The Captain has been delayed, we have been cleared for departure. Please secure for lift in five seconds," Katherine announced over the com.

Helen leaned back and relaxed as the shuttle lifted and headed across the cold expanse to the station. She let her thoughts drift through her conversation with her father now a few months in the past. I get to work on your reactors design she thought. The chime of the docking alert brought her back to the present.

As the shuttle settled Helen made her way to the hatch. Two commandos grabbed her gear and she followed them off the shuttle. As the group neared the main entrance Helen saw a large team of station security gathered.

There was a slight tremble in the deck. Helen stopped suddenly and looked at the others.

"Did you feel that?" she asked Katherine startled.

Katherine stopped and looked at Helen- "No..."

A deep rumbling shutter rolled across the deck. Bits of

regolith and dust rained down off the walls nearby.

Katherine stared at Helen, "Ma'am...?"

"It's the reactors, their out of sync," Helen said calmly. "We need to get inside and shut them down now."

Master Chief Petty Officer Shia O'Connell
Deck Two Forty-Nine, Engineering
Clew Bay Station, Clare System
309.0188 FCUDT 07:28:56

Shia watched the man enter a room outside reactor control. As she stepped in a second later a plasma shot flashed past her face. Shia dove back out of the room and took cover.

"Calvin, you see where I am? Is there another way in or out of this room?" she asked on com.

"No, that's the main core coolant center for the reactors. You're at the only access point," he replied.

Three more security crew came up and took positions across from her.

"Ma'am, what do we have?" one of them asked. As he peered inside a plasma bolt struck him in the face. He fell to the deck with his head a smoking wreck.

Shia looked at him and shook her head- "Calvin, one down."

"Why has he suddenly taken position and started firing at you?" Calvin asked, "In a room with no exits..."

"It's defensible for a last stand?" Shia quipped back.

"Doubtful. Something's up here we can't see," Calvin said, "Your engineer, Dower, is on her way to check out the systems. She is bringing some Marines."

Shia raised her eyebrow- "Well that might be helpful."

Her com buzzed and squealed. Shia instinctively dove for cover as the passageway was suddenly engulfed in flame and collapsing rock from the walls. The air was crushed out of her as several hundred pounds of rock slid down around her.

Helen worked at the console pulling up different controls. Nearly every reading Katherine saw was not good. She could hear Lieutenant Sheffield over the com ordering the commandos into search patterns.

"Katherine, access that panel over there and bring up the schematics for the reactor control lines," Helen pointed across the room.

She stepped to the console and brought up the diagrams. They were all red and flashing.

"Um, Ma'am..." Katherine said looking at Helen.

"Damn, that's what I thought," -Helen looked at Katherine with a worried look- "The cooling system is hard wired. The whole core is building to overload and I can't do a thing to stop it," -she slammed her fist into the desk.

Helen walked over to the holo that displayed the whole system map. She looked at it for a few seconds.

"Lieutenant, I need access to that cooling control room immediately," Helen said as she motioned for Katherine to join her.

"Ma'am, it's been blown to pieces. There are a few tons of rock blocking the way," he replied, "Maybe we can cut through the wall from the next room?"

"Negative, it would take far too long," -she stopped in front of a com station and looked worried. She activated the com and called Captain Stuart.

"Helen, how is it going?" he said as soon as he saw her.

Katherine noticed he had a worried look on his face that matched Helen's.

"Sir, I suggest you evacuate the station," she said gravely.

"It's that good huh," Grace O'Malley's face appeared next to his.

"Ma'am, the cooling system is hard wired and shutoffs

are disabled. The system is not supplying enough coolant and the reactors are heating up. The saboteur knew the exact weak point and sealed the room. I cannot stop this without blasting into the room but that may set it off sooner," Helen said.

"How much time...?" Grace asked concerned.

"Hour, two on the outside," she answered.

Grace and Captain Stuart just stared at Helen.

"Dear stars!" Grace said in shock.

Katherine's com went off. She stepped away and activated it.

"Cadet Carroll, are you in contact with Master Chief O'Connell?" Natalia asked.

"No Ma'am. We haven't seen her. We assumed she was with the security team," Katherine said.

"Our last contact was near the coolant control room," Natalia said.

Katherine looked at Helen and back to Natalia with a shocked look- "Ma'am, that passageway is buried under debris!" Katherine said as she ran out of the room headed for the passageway. She sprinted down the passageway and called for the Lieutenant.

"Sir, Chief O'Connell may be buried in the coolant control passageway," she said.

"Understood Cadet, I have four commandos on their way right behind you," he replied.

She skidded up to a stop in front of the rubble and accessed the stations monitors. There was a faint reading just inside the edge of the debris. She started digging and hurling rocks out of the way. In a matter of seconds, she had Shia's head uncovered.

"Chief! Can you hear me? Shia!" Katherine yelled.

The other Commandos came running up. She looked at them, "She's here, help me uncover her but be careful it's unstable," she said.

"Yes Ma'am," they said as they moved in to help.

"Cadet Carroll, we just picked up her bio signs again.

She is unstable and deteriorating," Natalia said.

"Yes Ma'am, we have her here but she is buried in rock. We are digging her out now," Katherine said.

A frantic hour later Katherine pulled Shia's limp form from the rubble as the walls and deck rattled around them. Her vital signs were critical and she was suffering from severe shock. Katherine activated Shia's stasis injections and put her body into mild hibernation. The deck rumbled and shook under their feet in heavy convulsions.

"Commander we have the Chief. What is your status?" Katherine said on her com.

"I'm still in reactor control trying to give the evacuation as much time as possible," she replied with stress in her voice.

"Sergeant take the Master Chief to the shuttle, I'm going to make sure the Commander gets out," Katherine said to the Commandos.

"Aye Ma'am," he replied as they lifted Shia on a trauma board.

Katherine hurried down the passage as the deck thundered and the walls rained rock debris on her. Somewhere outside she heard a siren start wailing. Trying to hold on to the wall she stumbled into the reactor control room.

"Ma'am, we need to go!" Katherine said to Helen as she approached.

"No I can buy us some more time. I just need to get this compensator readjusted," Helen said.

"Commander... Please!" Katherine pleaded.

Helen stepped back looking at the main holo, "No!" They looked in terror as the conduits leading to the reactors went critical. The deck buckled and huge crack formed on the left wall as the conduit exploded. Part of the exterior wall of the station vaporized and atmosphere began venting.

Katherine's com went off, "Ma'am we can't delay any longer, the hanger is coming apart. Where are you?" Master Sergeant Goody said.

"We're headed out of engineering now!" she replied.

As they turned the corner to the main hatch Katherine saw it was collapsed.

"Master Sergeant, the hatch is collapsed, we're not going to be able to get to the hanger from here," Katherine said.

"There's another exit a hundred meters that way," Helen said looking at a map on a console.

Katherine nodded, "Sergeant Goody we're headed for the south exit.

"Ma'am, were leaving the hanger, we will try to swing around to the south side," He said.

Another blast shook the station and the lights flickered. The console Helen was using sparked and popped.

"Come on, we're out of time," Helen said sadly as they hurried down the passageway.

They stepped out of the south hatch and stopped cold. The station was deserted and dark. Clare's red light shone in through massive stress cracks in the walls. The effect was stunning.

"Sergeant Goody we're out of engineering, what's the plan," Katherine said on her com.

"Ma'am, we found a bay not far from you two hundred twenty meters to your south and up a level," he said.

"Ok, I have the waypoint we're on the way," she said.

As they crossed the deck to the stair a station alert went off on her cybernetics. She looked at Helen and saw the fear in her face.

"The reactor... We're not going to make it," Katherine said scared.

"Yes we are. Run!" Helen said.

They sprinted across the deck for the stair as the station quaked and rattled. They tumbled to the ground and bounced off the stairs.

Helen grabbed her elbow and rolled onto her back.

"Ma'am! Come on," Katherine helped Helen up. They ran toward the waypoint in Katherine's vision.

The hatch opened and they sprinted up into the shuttle.

"Welcome aboard Ma'am," Sergeant Goody said as they scrambled up the gangway.

Katherine pushed onto the cockpit and sat down next to Lieutenant Sheffield, "Let's go Sir!" she said.

The shuttle lifted off the deck and turned to exit. The station's reactors went critical and the first one went nova. Katherine watched in horror as the bay door crashed down into the deck sealing them inside.

"Stars! Maybe we can blow it..." Sheffield said hopefully.

"We're way too close it would blow us to bits," Helen said from the hatch.

Katherine looked out the viewport as the ship slowly turned in the disintegrating bay. Another explosion rocked the station as the second reactor went nova.

"Sir, I have an idea. Ma'am, you might want to strap in," Katherine said grinning.

She grabbed the controls and turned the shuttle to face the hatch they entered. Taking a deep breath linked her cybernetics to the shuttle, slammed the thrusters on full and rocketed at the wall.

"Cadet!" Sheffield yelled.

The shuttle crashed through the weakened wall and streaked into the interior of the station. Catwalks and chunks of signs cascaded down from the upper levels. Katherine twisted and rolled around the debris. She saw the last two reactors overload on her link to the station. Turning the shuttle, she flew a parabola around the interior and headed for the spot in the wall that they could see the light of Clare shine through before. As they flashed through the station the reactors went nova below them. The walls blew apart and the shuttle hurtled out in front of the expanding explosion.

"You have got to be kidding me!" Lieutenant Sheffield said as the sped away from the destroyed station.

The com activated, "*Nyx* to shuttle one."

"Shuttle one clear of station go ahead *Nyx*," Katherine said.

CHAPTER FIVE
Imperial Assertion

Commander Samantha Leeane
Command Deck, Bridge
Light Destroyer Nyx, Clare System
309.0188 FCUDT 09:24:18

Sam watched horrified as the station came apart in a blinding flash. The link from shuttle one dropped out seconds ago when the bay had collapsed. She looked at Captain Stuart hoping this was all a cruel joke.

"I've got a signal!" Joe said excitedly.

"Shuttle one clear of station go ahead *Nyx,*" Katherine said on com.

Sam nearly dropped to the deck in relief as she heard the com.

"Shuttle one, intercept at one forty-three, up three degrees... What's your crew status?" Admiral Lune said to them.

Katherine looked back at them from the com, "Ma'am, six commandos, Lieutenant Sheffield, Commander Dower, Master Chief O'Connell, and myself," she replied, "Chief O'Connell is in medical stasis with critical damage."

"Will she make the intercept?" the Admiral asked.

"Yes Ma'am. She is stable for now," Katherine answered.

Admiral Lune nodded- "See you there," she said firmly.

Sam transferred Katherine's transmission to her console. "Shia?" Sam asked quietly.

"Ma'am, Shia suffered trauma to her lower body. Broken right femur, left tibia and fibula, shattered her left knee and possibly ruptured a kidney," Katherine said gravely, "She is currently in a medical coma."

Sam nodded silently with her eyes squeezed shut. "Take care of her... I am going to leave your connection open to monitor on my console notify me if you have any changes."

"Aye Ma'am," Katherine said.

Sam looked at the main holo that displayed the evacuation ships as they made for Alesia.

"Sam how many didn't make it?" Captain Stuart asked solemnly.

"The reports are coming in sporadically, looks like twenty-four thousand made it off. Approximately... Eight hundred on seven ships... Didn't get clear..." she said swallowing hard.

"Admiral, Mrs. O'Malley is on the com for you," Joe announced.

Coline nodded and Grace appeared on the holo.

"Admiral, I have just signed the colonial agreement," she said, "I would like to make an official request for assistance. The Clare system and Alesia are not capable of dealing with this alone," she said gravely.

"I will make the request to the Federated Congress immediately. Until then we are at your service... Governor O'Malley," Admiral Lune said.

"One of our ships is experiencing reactor difficulty, the *Barregos*, can you assist?" Grace asked.

Sam checked the holo. "Admiral shuttle one it twelve hundred kilometers from their position," she announced.

Coline nodded- "Governor Commander Dower is nearby I will divert her to the ships location to assist."

"Thank you Admiral, I'll be in touch," Grace said and disconnected.

Sam looked down at her open connection to Katherine and saw her concentrating on her duties, "Katherine, we need you to take Commander Dower to assist a ship. It is reporting reactor difficulties."

"Aye Ma'am, I saw its transmission a minute ago," Katherine replied.

"Please have a Marine detailed to Commander Dower at all times for her protection, is that clear?" Sam said straight faced.

"Perfectly clear Ma'am," Katherine replied, "We are

routing to the *Barregos*."

"Admiral shuttle one is in route to the *Barregos*," Sam said.

"Thank you Commander," Coline replied.

All around her the bridge hummed with activity. Voices raised and lowered like a waves on the ocean. A rhythm began to settle onto the crew as they performed their duties.

Sam zoomed the holo out so she could see the entire system. *Nyx* was just outside the expanding debris field of Clew Bay behind the mass exodus of evacuation ships. Ships were scattered across the ecliptic headed for the least time transit to Alesia. Sam walked over to her command chair and sat heavily. This is going to be a long day she thought.

Commander Helen Dower
Passenger Compartment
Nyx Shuttle One, Clare System
309.0188 FCUDT 09:43:06

Reactor readings streamed across Helen's tablet in a furious red streak. "It doesn't look that bad actually," she said out loud.

Master Sergeant Goody stepped up from the crew compartment, "Well the quicker you get it fixed the quicker we can get back to the ship, Ma'am," he said looking down at her.

Helen looked up at the large sergeant and smiled. "I really won't know until I get to the reactor."

Sergeant Goody nodded, "Well I am assigning Lance Corporal Farr to be you're..." he searched for the right word.

"It's ok Sergeant, I'm used to having Marine sentries with me. Thank you I'm sure we will be just fine," she said grinning.

He nodded understanding, "We will enter and asses the status of the ship and its safety. Once we clear it you can come aboard and begin repairs. The Lance Corporal will have a standard ship repair package with him. If you need anything else call us and we will get it there for you."

"Thank you Master Sergeant," she said nodding. She stood and made her way through the passage into the crew compartment. She sat down and secured her harness absently thinking about Xander. He was undoubtedly worried about her. She smiled at the thought of him fretting at his control console. She typed out a quick message to him and transmitted it to reassure him.

Lieutenant Sheffield's voice came on over the com, "On approach to target thirty seconds out, Commandos at the ready" he said. Five heavily armored men and women stood and clipped into the ceiling rails. They walked down the length of the compartment and stood idly waiting. It looked like they could just as easily been waiting for an elevator or transit tube back on Acheron. They were joking and laughing as they stood there jostling back and forth.

"Are they always like that?" she asked Corporal Farr who was standing to her side.

"Aye Ma'am, the more dangerous the board the dirtier the jokes and the meaner the teasing is," he said smiling at her, "This is pretty light..."

"Oh my!" she exclaimed at the thought.

"Ok Ma'am, we will be right back to get you," Master Sergeant Goody said as he passed and stopped in front of the Marines. "Ten seconds, I want good dispersal this time," he looked at them seriously, "These people just lost their homes, they are scared, they need help, and I expect the highest honor and morality of a Federated Marine!" he said proudly.

The light above the hatch turned amber signaling all clear as the nearest Commando popped the hatch and disappeared into the boarding tunnel. The hatch was dogged closed and the light switched red as the Marines swarmed through in seconds.

"Commander Dower could you come up to the cockpit

please?" Lieutenant Sheffield said over the ship com.

She hopped up and a few moments later was sitting down next to Katherine, "What's up Lieutenant?" she asked.

"Ma'am, another ship is calling on distress, were the closest to assist. *Nyx* has dispatched the fighters and shuttles to assist others," he said displaying the current situation on his holo display.

The com interrupted him as Master Sergeant Goody's face appeared, "Sir, every thing's good over here, just scared families and cargo. We're going to run a complete scan should be clear in about five minutes," he said crisply.

"Very good Master Sergeant. We may have another assignment as soon as your done so let me know what you find," Lieutenant Sheffield replied.

Helen looked at the holo displaying the data on the ship requesting help. It seemed to be a minor issue with their life support. "It looks like several of these ships were not prepared to fly. That one won't even be able to enter the planet's atmosphere, it has no heat shield," she said pointing it out.

"Yes Ma'am, they say that they just jumped on whatever was available that could hold air and clear the blast zone," Katherine said sadly.

"At least they bought enough time for recovery but it's going to be long and painful for a few," Sheffield said.

"Well you could leave me and my escort here to fix the reactor and go help that ship. You should be able to get it going and get back for me without much trouble" Helen said.

Katherine looked at her with one eye for a second. Helen knew Katherine was considering the implication of losing her. "Don't worry this ship appears to be benign. It's full of families, women and children. One Commando should be able to hold them off," she said smiling.

"I would like to run it past the command if you don't mind Ma'am," Sheffield said.

Helen nodded and headed back to the crew compartment to prepare her gear. "Let me know Lieutenant," she said.

An hour later Helen was up to her waist in a reactor access port as the shuttle disconnected and began to pull away. Lance Corporal Farr stood off to the side watching the hatch. She sighed and settled into the task of changing out several burned out conduits. Hopefully this wouldn't take too long and they would soon be on the way to the next crisis.

Commander Samantha Leeane
Command Deck, Bridge
Light Destroyer Nyx, Clare System
309.0188 FCUDT 10:10:54

The bridge was quieter now that the crew had settled into the routine. Sam watched as shuttle one approached the second ship in distress. She fretted a little about allowing Helen to stay behind but Helen had assured her that the little ship was safe.

She sipped her coffee and relaxed a little. There was a little commotion over in tactical and suddenly the alarms sounded.

Asteria looked over at Sam and Captain Stuart, "We have multiple graviton waves on the edge of the system," she said calmly.

Captain Stuart looked at her, "Multiple?" he asked raising an eyebrow.

"Yes Sir, either thirty very large ships just translated or the Empire has arrived in force," she said, "We have several hours until visual confirmation. Location is one eighty-seven, up ten degrees."

Lieutenant Binici stared at the data, "Sir, graviton waves are consistent with two combat divisions of the Imperial fleet. Two Frigates, six Barques, and twelve Brigantines are typically in those formations."

Sam took a deep breath slowly, "This is bad," she said to Captain Stuart.

He sat there a few seconds thinking, "Ok, we can't afford to hope that Heliocorp just flashed in with thirty freighters... Let's alert the governor and make an all ship broadcast to hurry along the recovery. Asteria please begin making plans to confront our visitors with the available warships in the system."

Sam could feel the tension creep up as the tempo increased. She looked at the flashing icons representing the unknown arrivals. Why would the Empire be here, she thought? Why now. She turned to Adam, "You think this is the beginning?" she asked quietly.

"I don't know, it's a bit less aggressive compared to what they did at Hades," he said, "It's likely they didn't expect us to be here."

"It would be relatively easy to take the system with what they brought had we not been here. Even with us here..." she didn't finish the thought out loud. Adam just nodded in understanding. They stood bad odds against that much tonnage.

"Lieutenant Binici could you assist Commander Hypnea in possible tactics of the Imperial ships please," Captain Stuart said to her.

"Of course Sir," she replied.

"Let's set a briefing for thirty minutes after visual confirmation in the conference room. Alert the department chiefs please," Adam said to Sam.

"Aye boss, what about Helen?" she said.

"Get shuttle one to expedite and pick her up as soon as they can," he replied looking at the holo.

Sam nodded and activated the com connecting to Katherine on shuttle one.

"Ma'am?" Katherine answered.

"We have unexpected visitors inbound arrival in about ten hours. We need you to expedite your assistance to the ship you're attending and go get Commander Dower.

Return to *Nyx* as soon as possible," she said.

Katherine looked at her worried, "Yes Ma'am, I will let you know our status as soon as we assess the ship condition," she answered.

"Thank you Cadet," Sam said and signed off.

Several hours later Sam found herself seated at the main conference table waiting for the update brief to start. She had passed the tense time by trying to eat and relax but it just didn't happen. Space combat was tedious and stressful. Hours of watching your enemy head toward you knowing that a battle would take place but unable to act. Planning and drilling possible tactics would help but you still had so much time to ponder the coming threat. Like watching an avalanche coming downhill at you in slow motion.

They had finally gotten sensor data and confirmed that there were two divisions of Imperial fleet ships burning in system. It looked like there was going to be a fight in the next few hours or so. It looked like it was going to be nasty.

The department heads were all at the table reviewing last minute data as Captain Stuart and Admiral Lune entered. The Admiral's tones sounded and Sam rose to attention with everyone else.

"Thank you, please be seated," the Admiral said as she made her way to her seat. "I appreciate everyone's hard work," -she sat carefully and looked around the table. "I will start by updating you on the position of the Federated Government. Congress has been apprised of the new status for Clare and has ratified the treaty. Clare is now a protectorate of the Colonies and will be treated as such. Governor O'Malley requested military assistance but the distance and time frame is such that no help is forthcoming. As you know we are the only ship currently in possession of the Dower drive. Also the focus for the Colonies is to protect the forward frontier of which we know the Empire is staging an attack. The fleet believes as do I that this is an attempt to disrupt and possibly gain an anchor head in the flanks of our territory. Our mission is to defend Clare and prevent that anchor head from being established. Governor O'Malley has turned over control of her small fleet to me for immediate deployment." -she looked to see they all understood the current political situation- "Commander Hypnea would you please appraise us of the current tactical situation."

"Ma'am, there is two divisions inbound headed for the inner system. It appears they are vectored for the planet. We're looking at two Frigates of battle cruiser size, six Barques of destroyer size, and twelve Brigantines of corvette size. Armor and weapons of similar power to our own," Asteria said, "Lieutenant Binici believes they will attempt to enter and control the inner systems through a singular path. If that fails, they will attempt to blockade and attrite through minor actions."

Captain Stuart looked and Simay, "Is that typical of the Empire?" he asked.

"Yes Sir, standard siege tactics apply when faced with uneven odds. Nearly all actions I have been involved with happened that way. Although fighting is second nature to the Ottomans and they will throw their lives away on attacking when need be, if they want an anchor head they will hold back to preserve the structure of the system. Eventually everyone surrenders," she said grimly.

"So they need the infrastructure and its inhabitants," he said calmly, "What about the possibility of them transiting into the inner system like they did at Hades?"

"Sir when the carrier came out of graviton drive in the inner system it destabilized the star, Clare is much larger than Hades. The risk of supernova is considerable. Also Imperial ships must be specially rigged and crewed to stand up to the incredible stress of the transit. It is doubtful that any of these ships are so rigged," she answered.

"Well that's good news," he said shaking his head.

Asteria looked up at the holo, "Offensively we have thirteen ships of destroyer size and smaller. I have sketched out a deployment plan in response to the initial attack and follow on siege positions. The inner system orbital defense platforms software has all been upgraded and are online. We have a solid defense that should hold them off," she said.

Sam looked at the Captain, "We're planning to hold not defeat?" she asked him.

"Currently that is our only option. We don't have the capability to openly attack. The Clare fleet is a big unknown in terms of capability and crew. I believe taking up defense is really our only feasible option right now," he said.

Sam nodded slowly.

Adam looked at Michael, "Major what's the status of the evacuation fleet?"

"Sir, most of the ships have entered the final vector for planetary orbit. There is a handful still powering in but they should be clear in three hours. Commander Dower has repaired the *Barregos* and it is headed for the planet. Shuttle one has had to evacuate the stricken ship and is dispersing the refugees to other ships. They should be able to pick up the Commander and return in a few hours," he reported.

Adam nodded. "Excellent let's get it done," he said.

Everyone stood and hurried away to their assigned tasks. As the hatch sealed Adam turned and looked at Coline. "What do you think?" he asked her.

She looked at him for a second with a sad expression. "It's a damn mess. That's what I think. Congressman Valentine wants to negotiate with them but the Senate is blocking because they believe that the ships here don't have the authority."

"They do have FTL communications..." Adam said frowning.

"Yea, that's part of the mess back home. Congress and the Senate are at loggerheads over this so our orders stand. Fleet headquarters doesn't want to tie us down, we're to attempt peaceful communication but not allow hostile action against Clare."

Adam raised his eyebrow, "That doesn't sound like

authority to preemptively attack..."

"You're right, it doesn't," she said evasively.

The violet light reflected off the various consoles below the command dais Senior Captain Mercan sat upon. He studied the crew carefully as they went about routine duties before translating out of graviton space. Satisfied they were performing adequately he turned his attention to the tactical readouts. It would be tricky maneuvering in system he thought there are many defense platforms scattered about. The most current readings were from Captain Teriyaki's Barque *Praxia* and had been uploaded from before they departed the main fleet. His thoughts were interrupted as the Navigation officer approached him.

"Sir, three minutes until translation," he stated.

Mercan nodded and opened a status screen on his computer. It blinked blankly as it awaited data from the small fleet. He took a deep breath and waited impatiently for the translation.

"Translating now," the navigation officer announced after several minutes.

The status screen slowly began to fill as the other ships exited graviton space. Two frigates, six Barques, and twelve brigantines all reported ready. Mercan switched to the tactical display and studied it carefully.

"Sir coded message inbound. It was set to transmit upon arrival of an Imperial ship," communications called.

He activated his communication console and looked at it with curiosity. A message from a loyalist he thought. He sabotaged the station reactor intending to weaken them. Very good.

"Tactical, give me scans on the station in this system,"

he demanded.

"Sir, I'm unable to locate the station. There is the remains of a very large explosion and preliminary scans indicate a blown reactor core where the station was last reported."

"That fool, he destroyed the entire station!" Mercan hissed, "Find me something of value here, now!" he demanded.

"Sir I'm reading many small ships headed for the other side of the system and a seven hundred and fifty ton Barque sized vessel that doesn't match any known designation," Tactical celled out.

"A warship? Do you think they destroyed the station?" he asked quickly.

"Sir it appears to be assisting the smaller ships. Reading a Federated transponder," he replied.

He looked up surprised, "Is it the ship were looking for?"

"Sir all I can read from here is a Federated ship of unknown class," Tactical replied evenly.

The bridge hatch opened and Chief of Security Senior Captain Kartal walked in. "Senior Captain. A word with you please," he said curtly.

Mercan looked at him intently and slowly nodded. Kartal was the political officer on board and was the only person who could order him around. He could also relieve him and kill him for any suspected treason, at any time. Mercan rose and stepped down, "Please, we can talk in my ready room," he said as he led the way across the bridge.

They entered the room and Mercan stepped over to the coffee dispenser, "Coffee Kartal?" he asked as he poured himself a cup. He has always maintained a decent relationship with the dark political officer and despite their differences usually got along.

"No thank you," he said stopping in the center of the room. "What do you make of this unknown ship?" Kartal asked flatly.

"I was contemplating the possibility that it was the ship Teriyaki encountered here a while ago," Mercan replied evenly.

"It is not the same ship," Kartal said, "The scans do not match and it is flying different colors."

Mercan nodded, "Transponders are easy to come by in these rogue systems," he sipped his coffee, "Possibly a new class of ship. Should we not capture it just in case?"

Kartal nodded, "The Empire agrees with you. New orders are for us to secure that ship at any cost," he said flatly, "The ship that Teriyaki encountered possessed new engine technology that the Emperor wants. You will get it for him."

Mercan swallowed and nodded, "Yes Senior Captain." he said carefully. Kartal had never before forcefully ordered him to do anything. This was decidedly serious Mercan thought to himself.

Kartal turned and departed leaving Mercan in the room alone. He set his coffee down carefully and tried to put the conversation out of his mind. Orders from the Empire? He thought. We've only just entered normal space there's no way Kartal spoke with his superiors before coming in here. The first hints of suspicion began to curl into his brain before he shook it off. "Nonsense," he muttered.

A few seconds later he strode back into the bridge confidently. "Tactical transmit plan beta three to the rest of the fleet. Com get *Distania's* Captain on the line," he said dourly.

Sitting at his command seat his com panel alerted him of the connecting call.

"Senior Fleet Captain," a brooding Captain said from the screen.

Mercan looked down at him, "Captain, plan beta three is in effect. Get you units in and force the enemy inside the graviton limit. The Federated ship is a priority capture so do not engage. Am I understood?"

"Yes Sir," he replied.

Mercan terminated the connection and looked up. Threat alerts sprang up as Clare's system defense platforms activated. "Take out those annoying platforms and get us in position," he ordered.

Cadet Katherine Carroll
Cockpit
Nyx Shuttle One, Clare System
309.0188 FCUDT 14:17:36

"Master Sergeant! We have to go now!" Lieutenant Sheffield yelled into the com. "Carroll what's the status of the hostiles?"

"Two Barques and five brigs decelerating hard for orbit. There is a frigate coming right at us. The rest are setting up on *Nyx* trying to protect the ships headed for the planet" she said flatly. Her stomach was knotted and she swallowed hard. The image of the massive ship burning straight at them made her heart slam in her chest.

"Damn! These ships are going to get slagged," the Lieutenant said.

The com alert sounded, "We're sealed and ready to go," Master Sergeant Goody said.

Katherine grabbed the controls and activated the engines.

"Oh my stars..." Sheffield said startled. The collision alarms began screaming and alerts flashed across the consoles.

Katherine looked at the tactical data just as the first missiles impacted the freighter they were departing. The large freighter split in two and seemed to shudder. Katherine had a moment to think that maybe that was all that would happen. Just as suddenly an expanding ball of fire and antimatter slammed into the shuttle as it desperately tried to escape.

"Hang on!" Sheffield yelled into the com.

Katherine yanked the acceleration to maximum. The

ship bounced and shook as the wave slammed into them. The power flickered, the ship went dark and the engines shut down. They were slammed into the starboard side as Katherine saw fire and sparks shoot through the cockpit. Her suit snapped shut as the atmosphere vented and everything slowed down.

She watched wide eyed as sparks floated slowly across the cockpit. Her eyes followed the sparks to the source at the main console. There was a jagged metal spike slowly ripping its way into the room. Flames boiled in through the jagged rip forming beautiful billowing waves. They looked like flowers blooming. Burning, searing, advancing, and lethal flowers.

Katherine turned and saw Lieutenant Sheffield frozen in slow motion. She watched in horror as the metal spike advanced toward him. Trying to leap out of her chair she realized she couldn't move. Her body reacted like it was stuck in thick heavy fluid. She had barely moved as she watched the spike dive into Lieutenant Sheffield's chest. The billowing flames flowed around her engulfing the small space.

Time returned to Katherine as she slammed into the aft bulkhead from centrifugal force of the tumbling shuttle. The flames flashed out as the remaining air was consumed. Katherine gasped in a breath and passed out from the intense centrifugal force.

"Cadet Carroll can you hear me?" Katherine barely heard in her com. She coughed and blinked. She realized she was floating in the cockpit. "I... I read you. I'm ok," she replied.

"We're resetting the reactor you should have control in a minute," Master Sergeant Goody said over the com.

Katherine carefully made her way to her seat and strapped in. She purposefully avoided looking at Lieutenant Sheffield's body.

Katherine gripped the controls as the power flickered

back on. She looked at the tactical holo as it cycled back online. The surrounding space was a mess of debris and expanding gas. The single remaining forward view screen blinked on lighting up the dark cockpit. Looming just above them was the massive frigate and the proximity alarms sounded.

"Ma'am thrusters are back up at half power," Sergeant Goody said over the com.

"Good, the hostile is right on top of us. I'm going to try to get us away. Hold on!" Katherine replied.

She activated the thrusters and slowly moved away. The tactical alarms sounded as the frigate targeted the shuttle. Katherine immediately shut down the engines. Holding her breath, she stared at the console willing the targeting lasers to shut off. After a long minute the alarms quieted.

"Sergeant Goody we're too close, the automated targeting keys in on our thrusters. We're dead in the water until they move off. The shuttle is caught in the gravity well we're drifting toward the planet. I may be able to get us away as we separate from them," Katherine said.

"Roger Ma'am, we're going to keep working on the systems back here."

Katherine sat back and stared at the planet as it slowly grew in the view screen. We just need to make it back to the ship she thought, please let us make it...

Commander Samantha Leeane
Command Deck, Bridge
Light Destroyer Nyx, Clare System
309.0188 FCUDT 14:11:24

Sam and Simay watched silently as an Ottoman frigate thundered into the small group of ships around shuttle one.

"They are initiating thrusters," Simay said quietly.

"They're going to make it" Sam said with more confidence than she felt.

The tactical plot lit up with missile icons and Simay took

in a quick breath. The thrust vector grew as the shuttle began to move. They both watched as the missiles impacted the freighters and the tactical screen lost resolution from the expanding explosions.

"Oh stars!" Simay said in horror.

Sam looked at Simay with concern, "There's still a chance they got clear. We'll have to wait to find out."

All around them the bridge was busy. Admiral Lune was directing the Clare fleet ships into blocking positions and Captain Stuart was directing *Nyx* in a pursuit of another frigate. The ship rumbled as missiles impacted the aft quarter.

"Natalia transfer power to our aft shield projectors!" Captain Stuart called out.

"Aye Sir transferring," she replied.

The com activated, "Captain we're maxed out on reactor power, I need Commander Dower to do any better." Lieutenant Lavagnino said from engineering.

"XO what's the status of Commander Dower?" Adam said as she walked up to him.

"It's a mess out there but we have a fighter picking her up now," Sam said, "Twenty minutes to return."

Adam nodded and looked at her in question.

"Shuttle one may have been lost... We lost contact with them after a frigate struck a freighter as they were departing," She looked at Simay and leaned closer to him. "It doesn't look good," she said quietly.

Adam closed his eyes a second and nodded, "Keep me informed."

"Admiral three Barques are headed for the planet at full power," Tactical announced.

Admiral Lune looked at the holo plot. "Miss Santiago dispatch those three ships in sector four to intercept. We have to keep them away while the final evacuees enter orbit," she replied to them.

"Natalia we're turning in on the frigate hit them with the graser as we come inline," Adam announced.

As they passed the back of the frigate the forward graser unleashed a massive blast. The topsides of the frigate ripped apart as the graviton beam slashed across it.

"Good hit! Graser recharging twenty minutes!" Natalia said grinning.

"Sir, frigate is running for the outer sector," Tactical announced

"Damn! The frigate pulled us out of position. Com connect me with the Governor," Admiral Lune said.

The holo screen flashed up and Grace O'Malley looked back at them.

"Governor there are several ships headed your way. Doing our best to stop them but they might get through. How is your defense shaping up?" Coline said.

"Admiral we're working on it but it's slow. These people are farmers and merchants. Do what you can and some help down here would be nice," she said, obviously stressed.

Coline nodded in understanding, "I'll try to get some Marines to you somehow," she said hopeful.

"Thank you for the heads up Admiral," Grace said and disconnected.

Adam stepped over to her and brought up the status of shuttle one. "Our Marines have been involved in a scuffle, their status is unknown at the moment but the shuttle is about to enter the atmosphere..."

Cadet Katherine Carroll
Cockpit
Nyx Shuttle One, Clare System
309.0188 FCUDT 15:47:36

The shuttle rattled and vibrated as it collided with the upper atmosphere. Katherine could feel the heat as it built up below her feet and sweat began to bead on her forehead. She gripped the flight controls tightly and tried to ignore the lifeless body of Lieutenant Sheffield sitting next to her. Alarms began sounding as the shuttle jerked violently off course and Katherine fought to regain control.

I don't know what to do, Katherine thought as she fought off the memory of the attack. Fear gripped her mind as the heat built dangerously around the shuttles hull.

After what seemed like hours but was only seconds the temperature stabilized and she nosed the shuttle over into the upper atmosphere of the planet. She jabbed the only operating console and it began to scan for a landing site. It flashed quickly that there were no suitable sites.

"Damn!" she exclaimed as she looked at the data. The shuttle was barely operating. She fired the port thrusters and began a spiral that would air brake the shuttle.

"How bad is it?" Master Sergeant Goody asked as he stumbled into the cockpit.

Katherine looked at him then over at the body of the Lieutenant.

"Damn, hang on," he said as he grabbed the body and hauled him out the hatch. "He will have to wait, more important things to do..." he said sitting down next to Katherine.

"Find us place to set down, quickly!" Katherine said to him as she fought the shuttle for control.

"Got a beacon at two-zero-two, coming around now. It looks too far to land but maybe we can get close," he said as he scrolled through the data.

"Got it, just over those mountains," she replied as the shuttle leveled and streaked toward the ground. The hull shrieked and groaned as it bled off heat from its entry. As they neared the crest of the mountains Katherine shook her head, "Not going to make it over..."

She tensed and gripped the controls as adrenaline burned through her blood. At the last second she yanked back and brought the shuttles nose up. The ruined engines on the rear of the shuttle struck the rocky ground and tore off in a fantastic explosion. She shoved the controls forward and the shuttle continued down the slope of the mountain only meters off the ground. For a single second she thought maybe they would glide down to the floor of the valley in front of them, then the shuttle struck the ground. She fired the thrusters in an attempt to stop their forward motion and they exploded against the hull. The power flickered and failed leaving them in total darkness. Katherine was slammed into the console in front of her and everything seemed to again slow down. The last thing Katherine thought before fading into unconsciousness was that she had failed to save the lives of her Marines.

Sometime later a light flittered in front of her and she realized her eyes were open. She leaned back in her seat and felt around for the restraint release in the dark. She thumbed the lock and it popped open loudly.

"That you Ma'am?" she heard the Master Sergeant ask.

"Yea, how are you doing?" she asked him.

"Got a bit of a headache but I am in one piece. That was a good bit of flying," he said.

"Hardly, we crashed in case you have memory loss," she said sarcastically.

The cockpit suddenly flared with light as her suit came back online and the lights activated. She carefully stood up and checked her medical implant status. "Looks like I'm good to go," she said.

"Good, help me get this console off my legs…" he said as she stepped over to him.

He was pinned under a bit of wreckage from the flight console and it was sitting on his legs. She activated his medical implant and saw his suit had protected him from any damage. She reached out and pried the console up and away from his legs.

"Ouch…" he said as the metal crumpled away from his legs.

Katherine helped him to his feet and looked at him seriously.

"Come on Ma'am let's go check on the squad," Sergeant Goody said as he limped to the hatch leading into the crew compartment.

A few hours later as the sun began setting, the squad had the beginning of a camp in place. The Marines hurried about under the eyes of the Master Sergeant. Katherine sat inside the ruined shuttle compartment next to Master Chief O'Connell's stasis tube. The readout indicated her injuries had been repaired as best the tube could manage. She would wake from stasis soon but likely not be physically capable of much.

Katherine had a deep sense of guilt and hopelessness over the current situation. She leaned back and ran her hand over her very short hair trying to forget the past hours. Closing her eyes, she fought back tears.

There was a bang on the hull and a Lance Corporal stuck his head inside. "Ma'am we got the emergency communication terminal up. Call coming in from *Nyx*," he said.

She cleared her throat and looked at him. "Good, thank you," she said as she stood up. She stepped out of the shuttle and looked up into the darkening sky. Off on the horizon she saw flashes out near the ecliptic.

"Ma'am, com is active," the corporal said as Master Sergeant Goody walked over to join them.

She sat in front of the terminal and activated it, "*Nyx* control this is Cadet Carroll on emergency channel."

The com buzzed then activated, "Cadet Carroll good to hear you, standby transferring to the Captain," Chief Santiago said.

Captain Stuart and Commander Leeane appeared on the screen. "Cadet thank the stars! We thought we lost you when we saw the shuttle burning through the atmosphere. We are receiving the shuttles flight data now what's your status?" Captain Stuart said with some relief.

"Sir..." Katherine began with difficulty. "We... I managed to set us down mostly in one piece. Only superficial injuries from the landing. The shuttle is a total loss; we seem to be quite some distance from a settlement of some type," she hesitated for a second, "Lieutenant Sheffield, Sir, he was killed when some debris collided with the shuttle."

Captain Stuart nodded in understanding. He looked at her intently through the com link, "Cadet, I am putting you in command of the Marines down there. We have a few Ottoman ships that slipped through the defense network. The settlement you mentioned is the only one on the planet currently. I want you to get to the settlement and run the defense until we can get you some help," he said watching her, "Can you do that?"

"Yes Sir, we will move to the settlement and provide defense," she said numbly.

"Contact them on com channel two seven alpha. Governor Grace O'Malley is there she will help you, she's done this before," he said smiling.

Katherine nodded acknowledgement.

Commander Leeane leaned forward, "What's Master Chief O'Connell's status?" she asked quietly.

Katherine looked at the Commander, "Ma'am, the tube has repaired her enough to wake her but she needs further care. I am worried she may suffer permanent damage."

Sam nodded, "She might surprise you, and Shia is one of the toughest people I ever met."

"Ok, we have to go. Good luck Miss Carroll I already know you'll do us proud," Captain Stuart said before the com deactivated.

Katherine let out breath and sagged. Oh stars what have I gotten into, she thought. The Corporal sat quietly next to her. She looked at him and nodded, "Connect us to the settlement," she said to him knowing he had monitored the conversation. He typed on the console a second and it flashed to life.

"This is Federated Colonial Marine commando commander Katherine Carroll; I need to speak to the Governor," she said officially.

The man on the screen looked at her wide eyed, "One second Commander I will connect you," he said hurriedly.

Grace O'Malley appeared on the screen as confident as ever, "Miss Carroll it's good to see you again. I understand you have your squad and happen to need a job..." she said smirking.

"So it would seem Ma'am," Katherine said.

A minute later Katherine stumbled over to the bench next to Chief O'Connell's stasis tube and collapsed into it. She didn't even notice that the tube was empty until Shia spoke.

"You look like you could use a day off..." Shia said shakily.

Katherine jumped back- "Shia! You scared the life out of me," she said, "How did you get out of stasis?"

Shia looked at her and shrugged, "The tube opened and I got out," she looked around at the twisted compartment. "This doesn't look like Clew Bay... what happened?"

Katherine sat back down and looked at the deck. "The stations reactors went critical, it's gone. We managed to dig you out of a collapsed tunnel before it went up. You were... are severely injured."

"That would explain why I am so sore. How did we end up on a planet?" she said

Katherine looked at her, "Once we were clear we began assisting evacuees. We dropped off Commander Dower and went to help a freighter. While there the Ottoman Empire arrived. They destroyed the freighter and our shuttle was damaged on the escape, this little spot of dirt is the best I could do..." Tears welled up in her eyes, "The Lieutenant was killed... it was my fault."

Shia looked at Katherine, "Your shuttle was attacked, I hardly think that was your fault. What about the *Nyx*?"

Katherine wiped her face, "They are holding off the main attack. I have been assigned to stop the Ottoman forces on the planet from attacking the primary settlement,"

Shia looked intently at Katherine, "How strong is the Ottoman force?" she asked.

"Unknown as of yet," she said carefully.

Shia leaned back and sighed, "How many Marines do you have?"

"Eight," Katherine said.

After catching Shia up on current events and taking her to the corpsman Katherine sat in front of the emergency electronics suite reading the scans from Grace O'Malley. How am I going to protect these people she thought? She closed her eyes and sat there silently. Her personal com went off and she jumped up startled. She stared at the holo as it activated and Lieutenant Binici appeared.

"Cadet Carroll," Simay said when she saw her.

"Ma'am!" Katherine said unsure.

"Katherine I wanted to talk to you before you began your mission. I read the brief from Governor O'Malley and I know she is tasking you to defend against the Imperial Soldiers. I have information you will find valuable," Simay said sympathetically.

Katherine sat back down and looked at her, "Ma'am, any information would be helpful."

"Do you remember the attack on me in the passageway, when you saved me?" she asked.

"Yes Ma'am. The saboteur took a shot down the hall," she said, not understanding the change in topic.

"That shot was meant for me. He yelled 'Ottoman traitor'," she swallowed remembering it, "I am going to tell you something that is deeply classified but you need to know so you will understand and believe what I am telling you."

Katherine looked at Simay and faintly nodded.

Simay looked down for a second to collect her thoughts then began. "A little less than a year ago I was a sub captain executive officer on an Ottoman destroyer. We discovered the *Hypnos* out on the frontier and pursued them. The

Captain wanted desperately to obtain the Dower drive and was bested by Captain Stuart twice. During the chase it was discovered that I went behind the Captain's back and arranged the kidnapping of Commander Leeane at Clare. I was placed in the brig aboard. For more than a month I was nearly continuously tortured by my fellow Ottomans until I was no longer mentally or physically recognizable.

By luck Captain Stuart was captured and placed in the brig with me. I assisted him in escaping to the *Hypnos* and was taken aboard. I further assisted him in locating and obtaining vital intelligence from within the Ottoman home system," Simay finished and looked at Katherine.

"You're not from the colonies? You're Ottoman," Katherine said hesitantly.

Simay nodded, "Yes I was born on an Ottoman controlled world. I prefer not to consider myself Ottoman, I am a Federated Colonial Officer and loyal to the colonial citizens."

"I didn't mean to imply you weren't Ma'am," Katherine said quickly.

Simay smiled, "Its ok, I didn't think you were. Now the reason I told you all that. Your about to face the most ruthless enemy you're ever encountered so listen close..."

Lieutenant Simay Binici
Bridge Communications Station
Nyx, Clare System
309.0188 FCUDT 17:18:05

Simay closed the connection to Katherine and looked up at Chief Josephine Santiago.

"She'll be fine," Joe reassured her, "She's a strong leader."

Simay nodded, "I just hope she realizes it."

Alarms sounded on the bridge and a distant rumble shuddered through the deck plating.

"Simay I need you at the tactical console," Captain Stuart

called to her.

"Aye Sir," she said as she jumped up and hurried back to the station.

She studied the readouts for a minute then turned to Captain Stuart, "Sir it looks like the blocking action has succeeded. The Ottoman fleet is headed out of the inner system. Tactical is predicting blockade positions based on the enemy fleets outbound vectors."

"Sir based on those predictions I have programmed the defense platforms for efficient coverage," Asteria added.

"Excellent," replied Adam, "All stations go to level two alert, get some food and rest," he said as he studied the tactical holo.

Simay sat watching the scans of the planet as the ship slowly moved away leaving Katherine and her Marines behind. Good luck she thought silently.

Cadet Katherine Carroll
Eastern Mountains
Alesia, Clare System
309.0188 FCUDT 18:18:05

Katherine sat alone on a rocky ridge a short distance from the shuttle crash site. The darkening sky stretched out before her mimicking her mood. She thought about the information Lieutenant Binici had told her.

The Ottoman Soldiers are tough and severe. They will never stop, Simay had said. That is their weakness, you must break their will, make them think they cannot beat you.

"How am I supposed to do that?" she asked out loud.

"Katherine are you ok?" -she jumped and looked to see Chief O'Connell approaching.

"No," Katherine replied glumly.

Shia walked up and sat nearby, "What's wrong?" -she frowned- "Sorry I'm probably not supposed to ask you that. This Military thing is new to me but you look like you need me again."

"It's ok, it's new to me too," she said looking out at the horizon. After a few moments she looked back at Shia, "I don't know what to do, I'm scared and I think something is wrong with my implant," she said sadly.

Shia looked concerned, "Well the first two I can help with but what's wrong with your implant?"

"I keep having these episodes, like time slows and I can't move. If I could have moved I could have saved Sheffield," she said in a rush.

"When does it happen?" Shia asked.

Katherine shrugged, "Right at the worst possible time. Once during training, twice when I was flying and then during the attack and crash."

Shia thought for a moment, "So when you're stressed and need more time you go into slow motion... Sounds like a good thing," she said.

"But I can't move, what good is it if I can't move," she said frustrated.

"You were in your armor when it happened right, the suits have inhibitors that prevent us from injury. You should check you suits records and see if that's what happened," Shia said.

Katherine snapped her visor closed and called up her suit diagnostics. In seconds she saw that her inhibitor was nearly constantly active. She slid her visor open and looked at Shia. "What happens if I turn it off?" she asked.

Shia shrugged, "I don't know. I have heard stories of Marines ripping muscles and breaking their backs. The suit moves faster than the brain can tell the organics to move." Shia looked at Katherine questioningly, "Why did you use the suits optics to check the systems, you can access it with your cybernetics..."

Katherine looked away embarrassed, "I don't use it much.... It's like being drowned in a freezing ocean when I try to use it."

"Well you'll never get past this if you don't try to overcome your fear," she said seriously.

"Lieutenant Binici said fear was a tool, I should focus it and drive it into that which I fear," Katherine said frowning.

"That's good advice, especially from someone who knows a thing or two about overcoming fear," Shia said.

Katherine looked at Shia surprised that she knew about Simay.

"I was there when we found her," Shia said seeing Katherine's surprise.

"Oh, I forgot you were original crew! I'm sorry," Katherine said frowning.

"It's ok, there is so many crew onboard now I forget that they all weren't there with us," Shia said smiling, "If you need to talk Katherine please feel free. I've been where you are in a way. Alone, alien world, in charge of people you barely know... Old hat for this old lady."

"Sounds like you should be in charge," Katherine said looking at the ground.

Shia shook her head, "Not at all, you have so much more training than I ever did and I not in great shape. These Marines have great confidence in you, you just need to see it yourself."

Commander Helen Dower
Multi-Role Star Fighter Aegis
Nyx, Clare System
309.0188 FCUDT 20:41:45

Helen took a ragged breath as she was pressed into the back of the seat. The fighter accelerated out past the pursuing Ottoman ships in a blaze of gravimetric particles. Helen slammed into the port side of the tiny cockpit as the pilot spun the tiny ship starboard barely evading a missile.

"Ma'am how are you doing back there?" the pilot yelled back at her.

"I'm fine Breaker, just get us there in one piece!" she grunted back at him.

"I'm taking us into that debris cloud, should shake those

cursed smart missiles they keep shooting at us," he said as the ship spun again and accelerated.

Helen could barely focus on the holo in front of her as the graviton field tore at her mercilessly. As the ship stabilized her vision snapped back into focus. Her breath caught as she saw the debris field he was headed into.

"Stars! The radiation levels are off the charts in there!" Helen blurted out.

"Yes Ma'am, we will only be exposed for a minute or two... we'll make it," he said stoically.

Before she could open her mouth to protest the small fighter flashed into the cloud. The holo in front of her fuzzed out into blurry static. Chimes activated in the cockpit and Helens suit visor began flashing angry red warnings at her. She imagined she could feel the intense radiation pummeling into her and her cells burst apart inside her body. A cold sweat beaded on her face and nausea started to boil in her stomach.

"We're almost through hang in their Ma'am!" Breaker said over the insistent chimes of the ship.

She focused on the holo and suddenly the systems popped back online and they rocketed out of the irradiated debris field. A shuddering sigh of relief escaped Helen as she saw the *Nyx* appear on the tactical holo.

Helen leaned back in the seat and stared at the holo as the *Nyx* slowly grew closer.

"*Nyx* flight, this is Aegis inbound with precious cargo," Breaker said on the com.

"Aegis fighter, this is *Nyx* control we have you on approach, alert condition two combat landings required, proceed via standard approach," the flight officer nodded at them on the holo, "Welcome back Aegis."

Breaker twisted and looked at Helen through his strange flight helmet. "Are you ready?" he asked quietly.

Helen swallowed and tried to nod but the bulky organic flight suit only let her wiggle a bit. "Uh yes," she replied shakily.

Although intimately familiar with the mechanics and engineering of how a fighter lands in the flight deck Helen had never actually been in a combat landing. It involved a high speed approach into an access hatch only slightly larger than the fighter. It would then collide with a graviton curtain that enveloped the ship and stopped all motion in an instant. If any part failed, they would smash into the hanger wall at hundreds of meters per second.

Staring wide eyed at the forward holoscreen she watched the approaching *Nyx* rapidly grow in size. Forcing herself to keep her eyes open she gripped the armrests until her hands ached. She frantically searched the holoscreen for the hanger bay access. A sudden alarming fear splashed across her mind as she imagined they forgot to open the bay.

"On vector," the computer quietly announced.

Just as she was about to ask about the bay doors she saw them on the looming massive dark grey hull. The computer chimed and the world went black instantly as the ship screamed through the bay doors and collided with the graviton curtain.

Her vision narrowed and stars popped all around her as the inertia heaved her forward into her safety harness. Just as suddenly they were floating across the bay and gently set on a cradle.

"Welcome home Ma'am," Breaker said.

Nearly unable to move from the violent and rigorous flight Helen could only sigh loudly in response.

The top of the fighter hissed and popped then the cockpit roof slid back into the body of the craft. Bright light of the hanger bay poured into the ship and a cheery face of a crew chief appeared above her.

"Welcome aboard Ma'am, you're free to exit the ship," she announced. She reached in and activated Helen's flight suit.

The suit unsealed and disconnected from Helen's implants. The flight helmet melted back off her chin and the dark face shield crawled back over her forehead.

Helen looked up at the chief, "I think I'll take a minute..." she said in a shaky voice.

The chief smiled and nodded, "I'm going to connect the fighter to the main power conduit, take a minute or two, I'll be back to help you out. Ok?"

Helen leaned back in the seat again... "Thank you chief," she replied taking a deep breath.

A moment later Sam's smiling face appeared above Helen. "How's it going Sparks? Nice to have you back in one piece," she said happily.

"Oh stars Sam I feel terrible! That was the only time I'm riding in one of these," Helen replied looking up at Sam.

Sam grimaced in response. "Here let me help you out of this thing," she said as she reached down for Helen's shoulder. Helen carefully disengaged from the tangle of the flight gear around her and let Sam pull her into a standing position. Balancing herself on the cockpit seals she looked around at the chaos of the flight deck.

"Looks like it's been busy," Helen said.

"Yea, pushing off the initial attack was touch and go but we came off in great shape," Sam said.

"Are you ready to exit Ma'am?" The crew chief said as she walked up next to Sam.

Helen nodded, "Got too eventually," Helen said in resignation.

Sam and the Chief hauled Helen out of the fighter with as much respect as they could muster but basically dragged her over the side and dumped her on the deck. Helen stood there shakily and looked at Sam.

"I think you should visit Brynn, come on Sparks," Sam said putting her arm around Helen and led her off to the lift tubes.

"Thanks Sam," Helen said quietly.

"For you, no problem. Besides I need you to fix the reactors again..." she said giggling.

"You broke them again..." Helen said smiling.

Sitting in her cabin Sam finished her daily letter to her daughter Eva and sighed happily. Her letters were a bright spot in her day and loved them as much as Eva loved receiving them. As she sent it to the queue to transmit she saw it send immediately. The faster than light com must be active she thought. Then a message popped into her inbox. Opening it she saw it was from Eva's father and immediately read the short note.

*'Falcon, heard through the grapevine you're having a good time…
I'll give the little one your love.'*

Strange she thought. Eva's father Edward Windsor is the attaché to the Briton government. An ex-spy. Eva lives with him on the Federated home world so of course he would see her. The message, she thought, how did he find out about Clare and calling Eva little one is unusual. Little one… Sam suddenly remembered something from her time on the Briton home world. Of course she thought!

Sam walked onto the Bridge with her customary coffee in hand and headed for Simay's console. As she approached Simay nodded a good morning and brought up the current situational display.

"Morning Simay, how is the day shaping up?" Sam asked looking at the display.

"It's just as we predicted Ma'am, the Imperial ships have formed into a blockade around the system just outside the graviton limit. This could go on for a quite a long time…"

Sam nodded noting the position of the ships, "And any news of the planet or our Marines status?"

Simay frowned, "No, we are out of position and the Marine com link is inactive. The colony transmitter is too low power to reach us."

Sam sighed, "Well we just have to hope for the best then," Sam looked around the Bridge, "Seen the Captain or the Admiral yet this morning?"

"No Ma'am, they are in a com session with home system upstairs," Simay said motioning above her head.

Sam nodded and walked toward the command lift as she passed Asteria she smiled, "You have the Bridge Astie, I'm going to see what the boss is up to."

"Aye XO, they have been in there for thirty-two minutes," Asteria said happily.

Sam could hear Admiral Lune's raised voice before she even activated the hatch leading into the faster than light com room. Pausing a second to collect her thoughts she pushed into the room.

"Admiral please! You must reconsider. We are in a very precarious situation here. The Imperial ships have us locked in for the duration and without aid were going to lose this system!" Coline Lune protested loudly.

Admiral Tabitha Matthews stared hotly back at them from the com holo, "Coline, I am perfectly aware of your situation," she said angrily, "regardless my hands are tied by the Government we both swore to obey. Your standing orders are to hold as long as you can, defeat if possible but under no circumstance are you to allow that ship to be destroyed or captured. Allowing the Ottoman Empire to obtain the technology onboard the *Nyx* would put the entire Federated Colonies in a... how did you put it, precarious situation. The loss of Clare is nothing compared to the loss of the entire Colony."

Coline stared back at Admiral Matthews, "Yes Ma'am," she replied defeated.

"Coline, I'm sorry. There was a reason we put both of you on that ship, you're the best improvising officer in the fleet. You'll figure this out, I have faith in you and your crew," Admiral Matthews said easily, "HQ Fleet out."

The holo went blank and the dim lights activated. Sam

stepped up to the two of them and shook her head.

"So no help for us today?" she said jokingly.

Coline looked up at Sam and smiled sarcastically, "Not from Admiral Matthews… I don't blame them; they couldn't get here with any force to help in less than six months."

"They could use the *Hypnos*," Adam said shrugging.

Coline scrolled through the data downloaded from Fleet headquarters. "No they have it completely disassembled. It wouldn't be space worthy for months and it's doubtful that it would supply enough firepower to help."

Sam looked the two Officers, "I got a message from Edward," she said slowly.

Adam looked at her carefully, "How is the old General?" he asked casually.

"He made reference to our difficulty and that he was going to contact an old friend in the spy network. Short note nothing to cause suspicion or elaborate," Sam said.

"You're saying he is asking the Briton government to help us?" Coline said suspiciously.

"No the contact is in the Federated Colonial Fleet. It's a long shot at best but the best option for him to pursue," Sam hesitated, "It's what I would do in his place."

Adam looked at Coline, "Well let's keep this off the books for now, if it pans out or he needs our help we can address it at that time," he said as Coline nodded.

"Thank you Sam for telling us," Coline said

They walked through the hatch together and sealed the com room. "What's the status downstairs?" Adam asked.

"Imperial ships have positioned themselves for long term blockade, we positioned for long term blockade, and no contact with the planet or our Marines," Sam said less than hopeful.

Adam nodded as they walked to the lift leading to the bridge. "Well looks like we need to review our supply status then. Place the fabricators on restriction."

Coline looked at her tea and sighed, "Guess I can resort

to drinking hot water instead of tea."

"Never!" Sam said teasing her.

Coline gave Sam a ferocious grin, "Let's see how you fair without that coffee you're so fond of XO…"

Sam looked at her cup still steaming in her hand and gave a mock frightened look as they stepped out of the lift onto the command deck.

CHAPTER SIX
Blockade

Cadet Katherine Carroll
Eastern Mountains
Alesia, Clare System
312.0188 FCUDT 09:21:00

The Marines all paused in front of a line of towering trees and stared into the darkness beneath the blue green foliage. They had marched down the rocky rubble strewn slopes for two days without seeing more than small brush and grasses. The sight of one-hundred-meter-tall trees was shocking to see. As was the slight twinge of hypervigilant fear at the nearly total darkness beneath those limbs.

"Take a break and check your gear!" Master Sergeant Goody called out at the Marines. He stalked over next to Katherine, "Well that's a mighty creepy place," he said as he approached.

"You're not afraid of the dark are you Goody?" Shia teased, "Thought you were a space Marine or something."

"Well, let me tell you... stars only know what kind of animals prowl this forest. I am not afraid of no man, but, huge reptiles with poison fangs are totally different."

"What makes you think that's what's in there?" Katherine asked smiling.

Goody looked at her seriously, "What makes you think there isn't?"

Katherine's smile faded, "Now I don't want to go in there. Thanks for that Master Sergeant."

Goody smiled broadly, "That's what I'm here for. Keeping you on your toes Ma'am!" -he strode off toward the Marines- "Alright that's enough resting! I want enviro shields up and two by two formations. One with infrared and one with ultraviolet. We got no idea what kind of creepy crawly things are out here and I don't like being surprised," he hollered at the Marines.

As they entered the towering forest Katherine peered around from the middle of the small group. Her suit picked up the background noise of the vegetation and light breeze. The things Goody said about alien creatures gnawed at the back of her mind. "This is silly," Katherine said aloud.

"What's silly?" Shia asked next to her.

Katherine looked at the dark silhouette of Shia next to her- "Sorry, thinking out loud. It's silly to be afraid of things unknown."

"Creatures in the dark... Well silly to be afraid but I agree it's a possibility we need to be aware of," Shia said, "I wouldn't have thought about it I'm from an underground city. The forests of Hades are well manicured."

Katherine nodded, "Me too, only parks and houses where I grew up."

Shia raised her eyebrows, "You're from a station?"

Katherine shook her head- "No I was born on the planet Styx in Tartarus."

"I've never been there. It didn't have any forests or anything?" Shia asked.

"Well, there is a section dedicated to vegetation but I was never allowed to visit. My parents were not really into the outdoor kind of thing. We tried to camp once in the back yard..." Katherine said laughing silently, "Did you ever go camping?" she asked Shia.

"I can't really remember growing up," She replied casually, "It's been a long time."

Katherine hesitated and looked at Shia confused.

"I'm older than I look. Long story," Shia said more carefully as she walked past Katherine.

They marched on silently through the dark woods as the sun silently marched across the sky.

Helen looked up from the engineering console with a concerned look, "Sir, the ship wasn't designed for this, it was designed to cross interstellar space not lay motionless inside the graviton limit. These are the most advanced reactors in human history but they still have limits like the need for fuel," Helen said apologetically.

Adam looked morose on the holo screen, "I know the ship needs fuel but it has never been an issue before," he said.

"Well usually we get our fill crossing space and it's a marvel of efficiency. Also we usually don't have to make parts for other ships and fight battles… this is not something that was ever planned for," Helen explained.

"How do stations get fuel? There has to be a way like that," Sam said from behind Helen.

Helen looked at Sam and shook her head. "Stations take excess fuel from ships before they depart. The Station AI calculates the ships requirement and leaves them enough to get into space. That's the real reason for stasis of the crew, to allow for the ship to build up its reserves," Helen said pulling up their fuel status, "We were full up when we arrived in Clare and fortunately didn't dock with the station. That would leave us enough to last months but there is only one other ship left that can fabricate parts for the system."

"So we're burning all our fuel making parts for the other ships," Adam said.

Helen nodded, "Yes and making combat maneuvers, fighting, and supporting our awake crew," Helen pulled up her projections, "At this rate our normal supply will be exhausted in less than a month."

Admiral Lune looked alarmed, "At what point will we lose the ability to use the Higgs drive?"

Helen frowned at the Admiral and pointed to her projection, "I programmed the computer to project that, it's going to happen soon, shortly after we will lose the CoNeE as well."

"Adam this is a serious problem," Coline said.

"Ma'am, I suggest we start moving around the system, it won't solve the issue but it will prolong the fuel reserves," Helen said flatly.

"Unfortunately that is not possible. If we leave this position the Empire will have an opportunity to attack," Coline said unhappily.

"I'm sorry to be blunt Ma'am but in three weeks that won't matter anymore," Helen said.

"Helen can we get fuel from other ships?" Sam asked.

Helen nodded, "Yes but that would leave them nearly useless."

Sam thought for a second, "What if we have the rest of the fleet maneuver around and collect fuel? Then in intervals come to top us off."

They all looked at Helen expectantly. "I would have to run the numbers. It would be limited because inside the graviton limit the particles are higher in energy and harder to collect, it's slower. I can say it would prolong our supply but by how much is pretty much a guess," Helen said as she typed on the console.

Adam looked at Helen, "Your guess Helen is better than my guarantee. Let me know as soon as you can and we will work out the tactics. Thank you Helen I know you'll figure it out."

"Yes Sir," she replied stoically.

The holo of Admiral Lune and Captain Stuart disconnected.

"That was a good idea Sam," Helen said turning to Sam.

Sam smiled, "I have my moments. I just thought why couldn't we steal that fuel back like the stations do?"

Helen nodded as she typed on the console, "Have you heard form Eva?"

Sam smiled broadly, "Yes a few days ago. She is starting basic academy this week! Edward said she is very excited and is going to wear the dress I bought her before we left."

Helen looked at Sam smiling, "Awe, that's so sweet. You sound very proud."

Sam nodded, "You'll see as soon as you and Xander have one for yourself."

Helen looked wide eyed at Sam, "Oh my! Don't say that, it scares me to death!"

"Why, Xander and you would be amazing parents!" Sam said.

"Oh I think we be ok and Xander is all for it but the responsibility, Sam, I don't know how you do it," Helen said.

"Helen, you're the chief engineer on an experimental interstellar ship and you're afraid of responsibility!" Sam said laughing.

"It's different!" Helen protested.

Sam put her hand on Helen's arm, "No Helen it's not different it's just better," Sam stood up and smiled, "I've got to get to the Bridge before Adam and Coline do something rash."

Helen laughed, "You're the best Sam, thank you."

Cadet Katherine Carroll
Eastern Mountains
Alesia, Clare System
313.0188 FCUDT 22:41:06

Trees bigger than any Katherine had ever seen shot straight up into the jet black sky around her. Most were nearly ten meters in diameter and covered in thick red bark. She stared up at the tree she was resting against. No single branch in sight, it was amazing how tall they were. This place sent shivers down her spine, it felt wrong somehow.

Katherine caught herself staring at Shia's face as she slept next to her. Shia jerked and twitched in her sleep then suddenly woke up.

"Bad dreams?" Katherine asked quietly.

Shia looked up at her in the dark- "They are always bad these days."

Katherine snorted, "That's ominous, and seems a bit dramatic for you."

Shia sat up and slid back to lean against the tree with Katherine. "Yea maybe. I think it's just the forest getting to me. It's too quiet, seems unnatural."

Katherine smiled to herself, "I was just thinking that. I thought it was just my unfamiliarity with these kinds of places. The last time I was in the field was on Ixion and this is nothing like that. First of all, there are no bugs."

Shia laughed, "Are you referring to the fire beetle?"

"That's right! I forgot what they were called. Nasty big armored bugs. They were everywhere."

Shia nodded, "They were something of a nuisance on Derwin when I was there. I even had one in my bed once. I seem to remember someone once telling me you could eat them."

Katherine stared at Shia, "Why would you ever want to do that?"

Shia just laughed at Katherine's disgust. They sat in silence for a bit before Shia spoke again.

"I miss our morning breakfasts with Simay."

Katherine looked down at the tube of protein she had been trying to eat all night, "Tell me about it, what I would give for some fried bread."

"You don't have to tell me; you steal mine every morning," Shia accused.

Katherine feigned being hurt, "You said I could have it, beside you can't deny a simple Cadet who needs those calories... nor can you deny my charming personality"

Shia shook her head laughing at Katherine, "How do you think Simay is doing?"

Katherine looked back up into the dark canopy above them- "Lieutenant Binici is a very strong woman, I'm sure she is fine."

Katherine tried not to think too much about it. If the *Nyx* couldn't send any supplies or support, then things were likely quite bad. She saw Shia look at her and knew she was thinking the same thing.

"You're right I'm sure they're fine," she said not quite believable.

Off in the distance a loud cracking noise followed by a flash and ground shaking boom roared through their camp. In seconds the Marines were alert and scanning the area.

"Lidar contact eight hundred meters at two nine six degrees. No movement, got it on infrared, it's hot," Goody called out, "Cole, you and Corporal James go check it out."

"Moving Sergeant," Cole answered.

"The rest of you keep your eyes on and scan the perimeter. Commander I'm headed to your position," Goody called out.

Katherine and Shia lay prone facing the direction Goody had called out. Katherine could see heat blooms dancing around in a dust cloud that appeared to be small fires. She tracked the Marines as they moved closer to the disturbance. Sergeant Goody arrived and joined them in their position.

"Ma'am, what do you got," he asked.

Katherine activated her cybernetics and joined with Staff Sergeant Colfax's armor. She transmitted the feed to both Goody and Shia.

"Whoa, is that what you see?" Shia said startled.

Goody stared at Katherine shocked for a second then concentrated on the data she was sending them.

On the feed Cole was approaching a fallen tree. It towered above him even lying on its side. With a heave he jumped and barely scrambled to the top of it. From the top of the fallen tree he scanned the immediate area.

"Doesn't look like weapons fire, looks kinetic," Goody said quietly.

"Goody, there's something metallic in the bottom of the crater. The suit is picking up radiation, the kind we have from orbital drops. This isn't a drop though looks like wreckage from a ship," Cole explained.

Katherine's cybernetics analyzed the data from his suit and confirmed his theory. "He's right. Must be a ton of this stuff in orbit or the battle up there is getting fierce," she said to the group.

Goody nodded, "Cole, place some remotes to monitor and come back."

"Aye Master Sergeant," he replied.

Shia sat up and looked at them. "Eight hundred meters, that's awful close."

"Coincidence has to be. There's no way anybody could have been aiming for us. We barely know where we are," Goody said sarcastically.

"Great, another thing to worry about. Getting randomly annihilated by space garbage in a scary forest on an alien planet..." Shia said smiling.

Katherine smacked her hands together, "Boom! Master Chief pancake..." she said laughing, "Maybe you get hit by latrine!"

Goody just shook his head at the two in exasperation and walked away.

Shia leaned close to Katherine, "That data was incredible, is that what you see all the time?"

Katherine looked down embarrassed, "I sent you the data in a visual feed. That's not what I see. I don't really see it at all," she said quietly.

"Katherine, really, it was amazing," Shia said seeing Katherine's reaction, "What do you mean you don't see it?"

She looked at Shia and relaxed when she saw the look of concern on her face, "It's more like I know it and feel it."

Shia gave her a confused look.

"When you close your eyes and face a fire you feel the heat, or you know the wind is blowing. It's like that. I don't see it. It's just there in my mind" Katherine said slowly.

Shia put her hand on Katherine's shoulder- "You're amazing you know that."

Katherine snorted, "You're delirious for lack of sleep Shia. I feel like a total freak."

Admiral Edward Windsor
Prime City Market District
Planet Acheron, Tartarus System
314.0188 FCUDT 09:26:10

The double sun of Tartarus shone down on the pedestrian street as the chief Briton attaché Edward Windsor strolled along happily. He admired the wonderful prosperity of the city market and smiled to himself. Quite amazing he thought for this wonderful colony to have come so far in only a hundred years. His attitude was quite a paradigm shift considering he fought for the Britons in the closing of the war for independence. He was always a bit too progressive for the House of Windsor which as events turned out placed him here. He checked the time and quickened his pace.

As he walked his thought once again turned to the series of events that were unfolding out in space. Sam what have you gotten into this time thought. Smiling again he recognized that his love for her was tied to her propensity to stir up trouble. Always the excitement and adventure seeker he thought. Well I shall support you as I am sure you would me Sam, he thought.

Turning into a quiet walk leading to a sheltered café he spotted his contact sitting in a shady spot. He casually walked over and sat down.

"It's been awhile, it's nice to see you again," Edward said.

"Indeed Edward, it has been awhile," Chief Ranger Jeffery Dumont said smiling from under his fancy wide brimmed hat.

"Thank you for meeting me, this is a nice café," Edward said looking around.

"It serves me well when I'm in town. Nice and quiet,"

he leaned forward, "I assume you're aware of the situation in space. Last I heard congress can't spare any help for our people," Dumont said casually.

"I heard the same. What's your interest in this, you normally don't get involved in extrasolar 'situations'? Are you expanding your operations area?" Edward asked quietly.

"No this is personal. I have a friend on that ship who just happens to be the best Ranger in the Colonies," Dumont squinted at him, "I want her back."

"Ok fair enough. What's your plan, the Colonies can't spare a ship and I can't get my people involved. You thinking of going rouge or something?"

Dumont leaned back and grinned, "Sort of, got a line on a fancy ship that would do the trick. Only problem is we need someone who can fly her and that is where the other party comes in."

Edward looked at him alarmed, "Other party? I don't like the sound of that."

"Relax Edward it's nothing nefarious…" someone said from behind him.

Edward was on his feet in seconds and face to face with the owner of the voice. "Samuel Leeane! What are you doing here?" Edward demanded.

"Same as you. Trying save my sister," Samuel smiled, "Good to see you Edward," he said as he took a seat at the table.

Edward stood for a second staring at the two of them then slowly sat back down. "I feel a bit out of the loop here," he said carefully.

"Well it isn't exactly easy to communicate with you nowadays…" Samuel said.

Edward shrugged in answer, "So what's the situation?"

Dumont tilted his head to the side in thought, "Well you are probably aware of the political turn in Clare, they went and made it a protectorate. Shortly after the *Nyx* arrived Clew bay was destroyed, but O'Malley being sneaky had a hidden planet that they escaped to."

"Yep, and either through excellent timing or pure coincidence the Empire arrived right on time to muck it all up. Captain Stuart and Admiral Lune managed to fend off the initial attack but are now in a blockade standoff." Samuel said.

Edward nodded, "That matches most of what we have been able to dig up as well," he leaned forward, "I don't have to tell you how Briton feels about Clare being in the Fed... but they want the Empire there even less. If Clare falls to them Briton will have to dedicate forces to their frontier. That would keep them from coming to your aid if you come under attack."

Dumont nodded in agreement, "Our congress is taking the advice of the Defense committee and bolstering our forces toward the Perseus Transit but holding a large reserve here. They are willing to sacrifice Clare to protect the core systems. I hate to admit it but it's a solid move. We still don't know enough about what's going on."

"That was the *Nyx's* mission, to find out. Meanwhile the Fleet is working their hardest to get Dower Drives built and installed. It's extremely complicated work and we're likely to be deep in this fight before that comes to fruition," Samuel said.

"What's the Admirals take on this?" Edward asked.

"Strictly toeing the line for congress. After sending the *Hypnos* out to stop the fight they are on a short leash," Samuel smiled broadly, "But... I have been promoted to the Fleet special operations section. The Chairman of the special operations committee has authorized a covert mission to assist Clare."

"So you're working for Admiral Thomas? Not Admiral Matthews?" Edward sat back thinking.

Dumont sipped his coffee and looked at Edward, "So, we've gone and committed treason by telling you this. What's your motivation in helping us?"

Edward leaned forward and stared at the two Federated

Colonial Officers- "Well, I would say it's completely benign but you two wouldn't believe that. I have the primary concern to help Sam... I want her to come home to me. That said I also want Sam back because the *Nyx* wouldn't be in Clare and it is in the best interest of Briton to have as few Federated warships on the frontier as possible," He looked at them carefully, "You know I support your independent nation wholeheartedly, but I will look out for Briton's interests in this."

Samuel smiled, "Thanks for being straight with us. What I need from you is back up in Clare from your Military. But, before that I need you to get Briton to recognize Clare's protectorate status. You will be welcome to station ships there as well as us, jointly, but Clare system Governor has the final say."

Edward frowned, "You're not making this easy are you!" Edward put his head in his hands and sighed. After a moment he looked up at them, "Ok, I agree that academically that sounds like the best course of action, it would be a boon for Briton to have ships back in Clare. I will try to do what I can, just remember I'm not the most popular guy in the family."

The two nodded at his comment.

"You know that it's eight months one way for communications... I don't think Sam can wait that long," Edward said frowning.

"What if I could get you home in a few days?" Samuel said.

Edward laughed, "What? I thought *Hypnos* was scrap metal. How could you possibly..." he suddenly remembered Dumont's comment about a ship, "You said you were a long way from retrofitted Dower drive ships!"

Samuel grinned, "Yes we're at least a year out for warships... but there is one small ship ready that we cannot use for Fleet operations. You can probably guess which one."

Edward thought for a few minutes then his eyes grew

wide, "You're talking about *Revenge!*" he said surprised.

Samuel nodded, "Yes, the very ship you helped bring back from Port Royal. Just happens to be a Fleet special operations project, my project."

"And I have the crew in custody at the Federal holding facility," Dumont said.

Edward smiled and reached for his coffee, "Gentleman I think we may have a deal…"

Senior Captain Mercan
Deck Four, Main Bridge
Ottoman Frigate, Interstellar Space
322.0188 FCUDT 10:21:18

Data scrolled by as the tactical display updated and Captain Mercan stopped on the section showing the planetary information. He brought up the visuals of the blue green world and frowned. This simple planet was what they were fighting for. It was barley populated and had little to no industrial capacity. This system was a total wreck. Why would they fight so hard for it he thought? Well he'll make them fight for it if that's what they want. He leaned back in thought and a few seconds later his alert chimed.

"Sir, activity with the Federated ship," his Tactical officer announced.

"On my way," he said curtly.

He deactivated the terminal and walked out onto the darkened bridge, "Update!" he ordered as he approached the command dais.

"Sir the Federated ship is docking with anther slightly smaller vessel," Tactical answered quickly.

He looked at the tactical display and zoomed out observing the positions of the remaining vessels. He quickly activated his com panel opening a connection to the Frigate *Distania.*

"Yes Senior Fleet Captain?" the *Distania's* Captain answered.

"Take two Barques and immediately head toward the planet. Drop off all your ground troops with orders to destroy and occupy. I want you to reinforce to the ground commander that I want that planet and they shouldn't bother to return otherwise…" he growled.

The Captain grinned wolfishly, "I understand Senior Captain. We are on the way," the com deactivated and Senior Captain Kartal appeared in his place.

"Mercan what are toying with?" he demanded.

"Captain Kartal, the enemy is protecting the planet with all they possess here in the system. I plan on dropping heavy ground forces and taking the planet and its resources for our Emperor! It will also serve to weaken our enemy by forcing a battle on two fronts," he explained hurriedly.

Kartal nodded slowly, "I'm going along with this for now Mercan but remember you're betting your life on this… literally," he said harshly and deactivated the communication link.

Commander Samantha Leeane
Bridge
Nyx, Clare System
322.0188 FCUDT 10:33:20

The bridge hummed with activity around Sam as she watched the delicate movements of ships in the tactical display. Her stomach rumbled uncomfortably and she put the thought of food out of her mind. Two weeks of minimal rations was wearing on the crew and taking a toll on her as well. Sam turned as Captain Stuart walked onto the bridge with Admiral Lune.

"Ok people let's go to alert one," he said happily, "Time to get some much needed fuel."

Sam smiled, "It's been two days since I had any coffee," she said frowning at Admiral Lune's sarcastic smile.

"Coffee's on me XO," Admiral Lune said.

"Sir, the Clare ship *Crusader* is on final approach for

docking on our starboard side," announced Asteria from the tactical console.

"Thank you, please proceed," Adam said.

Sam watched as the destroyer sized ship carefully slid up next to *Nyx* and extended an umbilical. In a few short seconds the console registered fuel transfer in progress. She glanced at the full tactical display and saw two Ottoman ships suddenly alter vector.

"Captain, movement in sector four. A Barque and a frigate just rapidly altered course," Sam called out.

"Figures... Engineering how much time for transfer?" Adam asked.

"At least fifteen minutes Captain. We need this fuel." Helen said from the holodisplay.

Adam nodded studying the tactical plot, "Launch our fighters and prepare intercept course. The second we're done with the transfer initiate course. Have the *Crusader* fall in formation with us."

"Captain Ottoman course is confirmed; they are headed for the planet," Simay called out, "Intercept course plotted, weapons range is confirmed at two hundred kilometers."

"Stars! We can't get to them any sooner? They are going to be awful close to the planet," Sam said.

"Ma'am, it's highly probable they intend to launch shuttles and land troops on the surface," Simay said glancing at Asteria.

"That assumption is mine as well," Asteria confirmed.

Admiral Lune looked up from the holo, "Have all Clare ships stand up to Alert one and look for incursions. Tell them to hold position in accordance to plan bravo three."

"Aye Ma'am," Chief Santiago replied.

"Five minutes remaining on fuel transfer," Helen announced.

Adam tapped his com, "Gun deck, load and prepare for ship to ship combat."

"Aye Cap," Gunny answered, "Three minutes to condition green."

185

"Sir, Ottoman ships just opened their shuttle bay doors," called Asteria.

"Joe, alert Governor O'Malley she is about to have unwelcomed guest," Adam said unhappily, "It looks like it's going to be up to them to hold."

Sam looked up, "Any way to alert Carroll on the planet?"

"Not at this time Ma'am, still no com signal from her Marines," answered Joe.

Sam looked at Adam and frowned- "They're going to get surprised."

Adam shook his head- "Can't avoid that now. She's going to have to be ready."

Cadet Katherine Carroll
Eastern Forest Edge
Alesia, Clare System
322.0188 FCUDT 10:33:50

An eerie glow cut rays through the thick undergrowth of the dark forest around them as the Marines slowly pushed forward. For the last five days they have been making painfully slow progress. The undergrowth in the forest constantly dragged at them and hid holes and drop offs in their path. Twice a Marine fell in to a mossy pit disappearing without as much as a yell.

"Ma'am, the brush is thinning up here. I can see the edge of the forest up ahead," the Lance Corporal on point said quietly in her com.

"At last, take up position at the edge and hold for the squad to assemble," she replied.

As she approached the bright edge of the forest she felt an intense relief wash over her. She hadn't been aware how stressful the last few days had been. Kneeling at the edge next to Sergeant Goody she looked at his scanner as it swept the open fields in front of them. Gentle rolling hills covered in tall blue green grass waved in the breeze in front of them.

"Nothing on the scanner except a small power reading

about three kilometers to the northeast. Small building of some type," Goody said pointing.

"Well maybe somebody's home. We could use a power source, we're dangerously low" Katherine said.

"I could use a real place to relax for an hour…" Shia said kneeling down next to them.

"Yea, two weeks in the suit…" Goody said.

Katherine nodded, "Ok let's go see what we can see."

Goody stood up, "Move out Marines, standard formation. Three kilometers to point delta, recon and hold."

The Marines silently moved together as if they were one person. Two weeks of this has made us a seamless team Katherine thought as she watched them. Stepping out into the sun she raised her face shield and marveled at the feeling of the warmth. Sighing she fell into the middle of the formation and quietly stepped through the tall grass.

Katherine lay prone as the grass waved around her on the edge of a small clearing. A medium sized square building sat a few hundred meters away in the brilliant afternoon sun. Sergeant Goody was just off to her left searching the area with the suite of electronics built into their suits.

"Quiet place," Katherine mumbled.

"Yes Ma'am, no signs of activity within several kilometers. Want me to send the recon team to enter the structure?" Goody asked.

Katherine sighed, "Yea, send them in. Be nice we need friends."

"Aye, I'll send team one, they are at least clean…" Goody snickered.

Katherine watched as the pair of recon Marines moved silently across the open area and positioned next to the door. On the go signal they popped the door and slid inside with textbook precision. Katherine monitored them with her cybernetics, virtually seeing through their eyes. It was definitely a home. Soft chairs and family photos were scattered about, an obvious cooking area and storage room led off the rear of the room. The Marines checked four more rooms, sleeping chambers and a study of sorts, before they signaled an all clear.

Katherine was up and moving before the signal registered. "Goody, find the power source and get the com set up, post a security and search the immediate area. When we're sure it's clear rotate out for some real rest, at least partially out of suits."

"Aye Ma'am," Goody responded.

Katherine stepped up onto the porch of the building and turned to watch the squad head off on their respective assignments. Shia stepped up and smiled at Katherine.

"What?" Katherine asked her.

"You. You are really fitting into command. It suits you," Shia said as her eyes shined back at Katherine.

As the sun settled in the sky Katherine sat watching it from the front of the building. Most of the Marines were resting in various rooms and it was eerily quiet. Her com chimed and brought her attention back.

"Ma'am, the com relay is up. Traffic for you coming in," the Lance Corporal said.

"Thank you, on my way," she quickly replied as she stepped out the door. Walking into the storehouse she saw Goody and the Lance Corporal studying the data.

"What do we have?" Katherine asked walking up to them.

"Ma'am looks like their fighting up there, got the *Nyx* on line for you," Goody said as Katherine sat down at the com terminal.

"*Nyx* this is Marine Unit Commander Alesia how do you copy," she said quickly.

"Commander Carroll, standby for *Nyx* actual. Good to hear from you," Chief Santiago replied.

A few seconds later Captain Stuart appeared, "Carroll,

finally. What's your situation down there?" he asked concerned.

"Sir, difficult terrain and power issues but we are recharging. We were delayed but making progress toward the settlement now. Our status is green and with open ground I expect to be at the settlement within four days," she reported.

Adam nodded, "I see your current position. There are inbound Ottoman shuttles headed your way. Two ships broke through and are going to drop. Keep your eyes open and be ready. Sending you the data now. I'm sorry but we don't have any support for you. You're on your own Carroll."

The data downloaded and Katherine nodded, "Yes Sir I understand. We'll do our best."

The holo blinked off and they were staring at the tactical data.

Commander Helen Dower
Engineering Command Deck
Nyx, Clare System
322.0188 FCUDT 18:41:03

The engineering console rattled in front Helen as the engines maxed out at one hundred fourteen percent. She watched the readouts intently as they all began to blink warnings.

"Captain were maxed out, too much of this and I'll be rebuilding engines for the next two weeks," she said on the com.

"Ok, we're nearly there, keep it up as long as you can Sparks," he replied.

Helen nodded. He only called her Sparks when it was serious. "Jacob reroute cooling line twelve!" she called out.

Pressure fittings began to pop on the charging line leading to the reaction chambers. The temperature in engineering was noticeably hotter as the cooling systems began to be over worked. Alarms sounded and Helen looked at Adam on the holo, "Sir, that's all I can do. I have to back down to ninety percent," she said pleading to him.

He looked at her for a second then nodded, "Down to ninety Sparks."

Helen reduced the output and the engines readouts stabilized. Loud pops and clicks sounded throughout the engineering deck from the contraction of the metals cooling.

Alert alarms sounded and Helen looked at the small tactical display on her console. The Ottoman Frigate turned to face *Nyx* and was dropping shuttles for orbital insertion. In a flash the two ships passed firing devastating weapons at each other. Helen gripped the edge of the console anticipating the imminent damage alarms.

Her console flashed red just as a massive boom thundered into the engineering space. Heavy shields smashed down around her as she watched purple and red waves of plasma wash across vaporizing the deck and walls of engineering layer by layer. Billows of steam jetted out from ruptured conduits and small flashes of fire popped up.

Helen stared wide eyed as fifteen of her engineers working not meters from her a second ago were struck by the cascading waves of plasma. They died in a matter of seconds. Horrified Helen stared as plasma collided with the crew transferring its energy into their bodies. They flashed to dust as their particles broke their bonds and accelerated away. The super-heated plasma burned straight through them.

"Commander! We have to get out of here!" Lieutenant Jacob Lavagnino yelled over the blaring alarms.

Helen stared at the chaos in front of her in shock as her people died around her.

Jacob grabbed Helen and yanked her to her feet. She just went limp in his arms- "Ben! Help me get the Commander out of here, Kila, get everybody up to the auxiliary engineering control center," Jacob ordered.

Chief Ben Coso ran up to help, "Jake what about our people?" he said alarmed.

Jacob looked around, "It's too late Ben, the plasma conduits breached. Nothing could survive that and if we don't get it locked down it will eat through the hull. Now let's go!"

Helen looked around in a daze as they carried her to the lift. The ship rumbled and shook as the battle continued.

Jacob looked at Helen as they rode the lift- "Helen we need you, come on. Snap out of it... Sparks!"

Her eyes rolled back and she collapsed in their arms.

Commander Samantha Leeane
Bridge Command Deck
Nyx, Clare System
322.0188 FCUDT 19:01:53

A single missile arced across the black of space as it erupted from the tubes of the Ottoman Frigate. Its electronic sensors switched on and quickly spun to avoid the Federated counter measures. As it accelerated the electronics became useless from relativistic time dilation. Purely by chance it redirected at the last millisecond and missed the point defense cannon fire by millimeters.

The thundering missile slammed into *Nyx's* hull at nearly light speed. Its anti-matter warhead blew forward and in less than single human heartbeat breached *Nyx's* engineering spaces.

Sam watched in horror as the missile struck. The ship's sensors flared red in engineering then went off line. Nearly the entire engineering deck went off line in seconds.

"Captain! Engineering has been disabled," Sam called out.

She looked at the Bridge engineering crewman at his console.

The engineering crewman looked back at them pale, "Sir... I think, the engineering control room was destroyed… Auxiliary control is standing up, reactors are stable," he stammered.

Captain Stuart nodded, "Send damage and emergency crews, stay focused people this isn't over yet."

Turning back to the tactical holo Sam watched the Ottoman ships flee toward the safety of their comrades.

The Clare ship *Crusader* engaged the fleeing Barque. Missiles erupted and beams of deadly light lashed out at the ship. The Ottoman ship began to rotate as debris showered off its port side.

"Got him!" Sam said in a deadly voice.

"Sir, orbital defense platforms are engaging the shuttles. Our fighters are perusing as well," Asteria called out.

On the display Sam saw the shuttles twisting and rolling to avoid the deadly platforms. Multiple hits were recording on the shuttles but so far none were stopped.

"Those shuttles are really tough," Sam murmured.

"Yes but we seem to have managed to keep them from landing anywhere near the settlement," Adam said.

"Sir! Another volley from the Frigate," called a tactical crewman.

"Helm come to two-six-three, roll ten degrees!" Adam called.

"Sir, their missiles are targeting the Barque!" Asteria said confused.

The watched as the Ottoman Frigate destroyed its own Barque. As the Frigate retreated and the shuttles streaked across the atmosphere *Nyx* was left chasing an expanding cloud of debris from the Barque.

Sam brought up the damage control data and gasped. "Sir, request permission to assist in engineering!"

Adam looked at the data, "Granted, see who's in charge down there and get us back online," he said concern in his tone.

Sam hurried off the bridge and as soon as she entered the companion way she broke into a run. Stepping off the lift she entered instant chaos. Heavy clear blast shields were down across the entire room. She could only barely make out a blackened charred smoke filled room on the other side. Her breath caught as she recognized a few things in there.

"XO, Ma'am, we're over here," Chief Kila Zucco called out.

Sam hurried past several people who seemed to be in shock and saw Kila working with several others on access hatches in the floor, "Kila what happened?"

"XO, a missile blew the plasma conduits as it cut into the engineering deck. The plasma flooded into the bay and before the shields could drop it ate through most of engineering. As you can see we can only access the control center but it's totally burned out. We still don't know if any shields dropped anywhere else inside. There could be people trapped," Kila blurted out.

Sam nodded, "How many were in there?"

Kila looked down at the deck, "Fifteen, maybe more. Jacob and Ben carried the Chief out pretty quickly but she was not in good shape."

Sam's heart skipped a beat at the description of Helen, "Very good, what do you need?" Sam managed to say.

"Medical to get these people out of way, and time to vent and access this compartment. Jacob should be up in Aux control getting the ship in order," she said.

"Done, let me know if you need anything else," Sam said as she headed for the lifts and medical.

Turning she looked at the eerie sight of engineering one last time before the lift doors closed.

Sam quietly walked into medical and saw Brynn in the examination room. Brynn looked up and motioned for Sam to enter.

"Brynn, could use a few more hands in engineering," Sam said quietly as she approached.

Brynn nodded and looked down at Helen, "Of course, they should be on the way now."

"How is she?" Sam asked.

"In shock, but otherwise unhurt. Could you stay with her for a moment?" Brynn asked.

"Of course," Sam said stepping to Helens side.

Helen twitched and looked up at Sam. She instantly broke into tears as Sam reached down to hug her.

"Sam! There all dead because of me!" Helen cried.

"Helen that's not true, we were attacked. You couldn't have stopped that," Sam said seriously.

"I watched them die, they were only meters away Sam!" Helen cried out.

"Helen it'll be ok," Sam said as they stood alone in the medical bay.

Cadet Katherine Carroll
Eastern Prairie
Alesia, Clare System
322.0188 FCUDT 19:57:51

"Ma'am you should see this," the Lance Corporal said from the door.

Katherine stepped away from the tactical data and out onto the grass in front of the building. The Lance Corporal pointed to the sky in the south.

Trying to see what he was indicating she scanned the horizon with her enhanced vision. Small flares sparkled brightly in long streaks across the sky. Her cybernetics scanned through known identifications in seconds. The only response was 'unidentified shuttle'.

Goody stepped up next to her, "What is it?" he asked.

"Shuttles entering the atmosphere, hundred maybe hundred fifty kilometers out due south," she said quietly studying the contrails.

"Looks like they're here then," Goody said.

"Yep, looks like it. Let's call the Governor," Katherine said turning back to the building.

Grace O'Malley looked back at Katherine from the holo

with a tired expression- "Yes we see them, in fact there are three different formations coming in. Thankfully the orbital platforms caused them to enter the atmosphere on trajectories that place them several hundred kilometers out from the settlement," Grace said grimacing.

"How are your preparations coming Governor?" Katherine asked.

Grace frowned, "Not well, my people are spacers and farmers. Most are overly stressed just being trapped on the planet. We are fortifying the settlement as best we can but it is slow."

Katherine looked down at the tactical data as it updated from the settlements scans. Three distinct formations of Ottoman Soldiers appeared on her map. The nearest was a hundred thirty-five kilometers to her south. Estimated strength of four hundred...

"Commander, if we're going to survive this I'm going to need your help. We can maybe stop one formation but all three will walk in and take over," she frowned and looked down, "I don't want to ask you to do this Commander."

"It's ok Madame Governor you don't have to ask. I will stop the Ottoman forces from reaching the settlement," Katherine said.

Grace stared at Katherine for a moment, "Thank you Commander Carroll. Good luck."

"With respect Ma'am, Federated Marines don't believe in luck, they believe in training," Katherine said, "Vampyres out," the holo disconnected as Katherine exhaled heavily.

Katherine sat outside the little building staring at the night sky. She was running simulations in her cybernetic core trying to find a tactic that would work for their current situation. She sighed heavily as she focused her eyes back to area around her and saw Shia sitting next to her.

"Didn't want to bother you, you looked preoccupied," Shia said seeing Katherine notice her.

"I was running simulations trying to come up with a

tactic," Katherine said shrugging, "Nothing comes out well. I just don't know how to stop them all."

"Stop them all?" Shia said in question, "We'll be lucky to survive contact with one of the groups," she said sarcastically.

Katherine frowned at her comment and started to say something but hesitated. Survive one group, she thought.

"Shia! You're brilliant… I got it," Katherine said excited.

Commander Samantha Leeane
Aux Engineering Command Deck
Nyx, Clare System
323.0188 FCUDT 03:19:27

Sam ducked under a bundle of cables that hung across the passageway as she picked her way to the auxiliary engineering control room. The ship was a mess of control cables and conduits snaking through the passages connecting damaged systems. Having most of the engineering deck destroyed was a massive blow to the operation of the ship. It contained hubs for every major system. Now those hubs were bundles and tangles of cables laying on the deck throughout the ship.

She looked into the control room and saw Lieutenant Lavagnino directing the remaining engineering crew with confidence. On the wall behind him the local tactical plot showed the ship moving back into position.

Jacob saw her at the hatch and stepped over to her, "XO everything is coming together. We have control of the ships systems here and fortunately took very little damage to critical systems."

Sam nodded, "Just wanted to see how it was going and update you on Helen."

Jacob frowned, "I need her back bad."

"Hopefully soon, she was pretty shaken up but otherwise healthy. Brynn is monitoring her tonight."

He nodded, "XO our fuel situation is not good. Those maneuvers used a lot of fuel. Quick calculations give us maybe two to two and a half weeks... Then we have to leave," he said seriously.

Admiral Edward Windsor
Prime City Shuttle Port
Planet Acheron, Tartarus System
323.0188 FCUDT 04:10:56

Sun streamed in through the clear dome of Acheron's shuttle port and danced across the polished floor of the boarding area. People sat around in circular sections waiting patiently for their scheduled shuttles. Children laughed as they played brightly lit holo games nearby. Edward smiled to himself thinking about Eva as he passed the children and headed for the military shuttle boarding area.

Sitting on the shuttle he stared out the holoport at the beautiful planet below. He suddenly realized how much he didn't want to leave. He has a wonderful family here, a bit unusual but wonderful nonetheless. He sighed and relaxed as the small predatory ship grew in front of the shuttle.

Chief Ranger Dumont smiled at him as he stepped out of the shuttles hatch. "Welcome aboard Edward," Dumont said.

"Thank you Jeffery," Edward replied.

"You have everything you need?" Dumont asked him as they walked down the passageway.

"I believe so, yes. It's going to cause a stir when we arrive," he said blithely.

"That is not in doubt my friend..." -laughed Dumont as they entered the Bridge.

Senior Fleet Captain Kelli Anne Vellius turned toward them as they entered. Smiling she extended her hand, "General Windsor, it's a pleasure to meet you," she said.

"Captain Vellius, pleasures mine. Thank you for giving me a ride," Edward said shaking her hand.

"We're about ready to depart, couple of hours out to the system limit then we will power up the Dower and jump to your home system," she said indicating the tactical holo.

"Wonderful. Thank you again Captain," he said.

Standing quietly in the back of the Bridge he watched as the ex-Ottoman Barque glided out across the system toward the Dower limit. I'm on my way Sam hang on, he thought. The sleek black space ship now fitted with the four long rods that symbolize the faster than light engines plunged in deep space and disappeared.

Cadet Katherine Carroll
Eastern Prairie
Alesia, Clare System
325.0188 FCUDT 04:22:11

"Ma'am, everything's ready. The settlement's reactor is set and the Ottoman force is headed straight for us," the Sergeant said.

"Very good, thank you. I want you to depart to the north and hold," she said to him.

"Aye Ma'am, exiting no," he replied.

"Are you sure about this?" Shia asked coming up behind Katherine.

"Shia, I thought I told you to go with Goody…" Katherine said surprised, "I can't have you exposed to this much risk," she said concerned.

"Yep and I told you no. I'm not leaving you here alone to face this without me," she said back.

Katherine sighed in resignation. "Fine," they stood there looking out to the south at the approaching enemy. After several minutes Katherine looked at Shia, "Thanks for staying."

Shia smiled, "I'll be right by your side Katherine."

Katherine's com toned quietly, "Ma'am the enemy is approaching our position. They will be arriving at your position in a few minutes. Sending you updated scans now," Sergeant Goody said quietly.

"Confirmed, thank you Goody, see you soon," Katherine replied.

"Please be safe Ma'am," Goody said then signed off before she could respond.

Katherine and Shia turned and walked inside the little home and quietly waited.

Several silent hovering drones floated in overhead as Katherine and Shia stood motionless inside the building. Shortly behind the drones the Ottoman force arrived at the small clearing right on schedule. Three large six wheeled vehicles lead the way. Looking like squat black reptiles the wheels crushed the blue green grass and sank into the fertile soil. A large cannon that most likely was some type of kinetic launcher sat atop on a turret. Behind them were roughly ninety Ottoman Soldiers on foot in medium non-powered armor. Katherine's implant quickly informed her that they were no match for the Marines Commando armor. The main column split and formed a half circle around the settlement. Dust floated across the field kicked up in the gentle breeze and reflecting in the rising sun. It was eerily quiet for a few seconds as Katherine and Shia stood motionless waiting.

Knots twisted in Katherine's stomach and her legs turned wooden as she stared at the data flowing through her cybernetics. Her vision narrowed and she saw stars twinkle in her peripherals. Katherine mentally nodded and despite the fear and trepidation she felt, she forced herself to step out the door followed by Shia. She looked at the force in front of her, dropped her visor and smiled.

"Greetings, I am Federated Colonial Marine Commander Carroll and this planet is a protectorate of the Federated Colonial Government. You have illegally landed. As a representative of my Government I request you depart immediately," Katherine said smiling.

The Ottoman Soldiers stood motionless in front of her.

A hatch popped open and a rather well dressed officer rose out of an armored vehicle.

He smiled and laughed slightly, "So the mighty Federated Colonial Marines send a woman to warn us off... Miss Carroll, I don't think you realize the strength of the force in front of you. I will neither recognize your claim to this planet nor depart as you requested," he looked at his force and smiled.

Katherine pointed at him, "You're making a mistake, and I will give you one more chance..."

The Ottoman Officer laughed, "Detain them!" he ordered.

Four Soldiers quickly approached Katherine and Shia. As the lead Soldier approached Katherine and Shia's armor triggered into combat mode. Five micro-drones popped off their left arm and hovered in a cloud around them. The collar on the armor raised and closed around their necks and chins. Their armor plates slid forward and locked into place in rapid succession. The already imposing figures of the Marines was suddenly much more predatory.

The first Soldier hesitantly reached out to grab Katherine, Shia suddenly moved in a blur around her and with one arm snatched the Soldier up and hurled him into the small building behind them. At the same time Katherine dove into the second Soldier crushing him beneath her then rising up with her fist so hard it sent the third Soldier sailing through the air up over the shocked Ottoman line.

Katherine mentally triggered the preset reactor behind the small home as the two sprinted straight at the Ottoman Officers armored vehicle. In milliseconds they smashed into it head on. The armored carrier heaved up and rolled over on its side smashing several Soldiers that were not fast enough to avoid the attack. As the vehicle crashed down in front of her Katherine realized her path was blocked.

"Shia, run!" Katherine said.

At the last second, in desperation she leapt straight up. The reactor overloaded and in a blinding flash erupted causing a massive fireball to envelope the area. The concussive blast caught Katherine in mid-jump and sent her hurling through the air. She smashed into the edge of the armored vehicle with tremendous force. A strange heaving crushing pain barely registered as she tumbled through the air. She plowed into the ground a hundred meters away from the smoking wreckage.

"Goody now!" she heard Shia call on the com.

Purple plasma and the scream of kinetic rounds howled in the Alesian air above Katherine then suddenly it was quiet.

Katherine's vision swarmed as she lay on her side. Bright red alerts covered her suits visor but she couldn't read them. Her eyes watered uncontrollably and pain ripped up the back of her jaw. I'm hurt badly, Katherine thought as she tried to asses.

Master Sergeant, I'm not getting any vitals from the Commander…" The Corpsman announced on the com.

"Must be suit damage, I just talked to her. Commander what's your status?" Goody called on his com.

Katherine didn't know her status. She couldn't feel her body or move. She could barely see straight. Panic began to build in her mind- "Goody, I think something is wrong," she tried to say but only managed to choke.

"Master Sergeant! Found her, I need the medic now!" Shia called out.

Katherine was slowly rolled over onto her back and bright sunlight streamed into her eyes until Shia's worried face came into her view.

"Katherine! Can you hear me!"

Shia stared down at Katherine with intense concern- "Katherine, hold on! We're here."

The Corpsman ran up and quickly scanned her. Shia gasped as she saw the readout, it wasn't good.

"Sergeant, she has multiple system trauma and her spine is severed. Her vitals are rapidly deteriorating," the Corpsman said to them as Goody ran up.

Katherine tried to speak but only managed to gasp and choke.

"She can't breathe; move back I need to get her an airway!" the medic said quickly.

Shia moved over to the opposite side to give him some room. She watched horrified as the medic popped open Katherine's neck piece and stabbed a metal tube into her throat. As soon as it blinked green Katherine stopped choking.

Shia looked into Katherine's eyes- "It'll be ok, you'll be fine," -Katherine looked back at her and Shia saw the fear and confusion in her eyes. Tears silently rolled down Katherine's face. Shia shook off her armored glove and carefully wiped Katherine's cheek. As she gently touched her face Shia felt Katherine's jaw relax a little.

Shia... it's bad, I'm hurt bad... Katherine sent to her via neuro com.

Katherine you're going to be ok. Shia sent back.

Shia... I'm sorry. Katherine sent.

Shia's went rigid, "No, don't you say that! You're going to be fine," Shia said forcefully.

The Medic looked at her surprised, "Uh... I've done what I can Chief. We will have to wait and see, she needs time." He said looking at her.

A secondary explosion went off nearby and Shia leaned

over Katherine defensively.

Goody looked at her, "We need to move. We can't stay here," he said quietly, "Corpsman get the Commander on a stretcher."

Shia ran her hand gently across Katherine's cheek again, *Don't you dare give up,* she sent to Katherine.

The Marines gently lifted Katherine and put her in the combat stretcher. They eased her up and prepared to head West away from the engagement area.

Commander Samantha Leeane
Chief Engineers Quarters, Engineering Deck
Nyx, Clare System
327.0188 FCUDT 10:44:07

Commander Samantha Leeane stepped into Helen's quarters quietly. Data chips and tablets lay strewn across the floor haphazardly. The lights were on full intensity and her counter was littered with cups. Sam stepped into the center of the room and looked around- "Helen, are you here?" she called out. Asteria had told her Helen was in her room but Sam was announcing her presence. She stepped over to the doorway leading to her bedroom and looked in.

"Helen can I come in?" Sam asked seeing Helen curled up in the corner of her bed with her knees tightly held to her chest.

Helen shrugged and grunted quietly.

Sam walked carefully over and sat on the edge of the bed- "How are you Helen?"

Helen looked at Sam and shrugged again.

"Jacob said you came into engineering this morning for a bit. He was happy to see you," Sam said casually.

"They all looked at me like I was sick. I couldn't stay," Helen responded quietly.

"Have you been sleeping?" Sam asked her diving straight into the heart of why she came.

"I can't," Helen said flatly.

Sam sighed softly, "You need sleep Helen. Brynn can help you with that."

Tears silently ran down Helen's pale cheek, "I see it over and over when I sleep. My people dying right in front of me. I can't do it."

Sam stared at Helen carefully, "It wasn't your fault. We're at war with the ones who are responsible. The rest of your people need you, the ones that survived."

"They are my responsibility, working in a ship I designed. My carelessness killed them," she cried, "I see their faces when I close my eyes, hear their cries…"

Sam moved over and put her arm around Helen.

"Not just the ones in engineering, the ones on Clew Bay and all those lost running away!" she said softly.

"Clew wasn't your fault either Helen, that was an Ottoman spy. You can't shoulder all this for yourself," Sam said surprised.

"Everything's falling apart. What did I do wrong?" Helen cried into Sam's shoulder.

"Nothing Helen, you did nothing wrong," Sam replied softly. Sam sat silently with Helen and eventually Helen fell into a fitful sleep curled up next to her. Sam stroked Helen's hair and chided herself for not seeing this coming. Helen was so young and unprepared. Everybody just saw the brilliant engineer who always smiled and never noticed she was so young. The realities of this war were all too real even though there wasn't actually a war yet.

Sam sat in the forward briefing room studying the tactical plot Asteria had displayed, "What are they doing?"

"I believe they are preparing to attack the orbital defense platforms. The Ottoman ships orbit slightly closer to the line with each revolution and as you can see they are firing drones inward to force the defense platforms to reveal their positions. The platforms have excellent range but with precise tactics they can be beaten," Asteria explained.

Captain Stuart leaned forward, "This looks more like

brute force. Do they have any weapons that can range our platforms?"

Simay looked up from the display, "None that I know of could touch them. Other than simply saturating the area with missiles and hoping for a lucky shot through the electronic countermeasures."

"They could time the graser recharge and possibly get a fighter within range but it would be suicide for the pilots. Also they would need many fighters to layer the attack knowing the success of the final relied on the death of the ones before it," Asteria said sadly, "A tactic we would never consider."

Simay nodded, "But one the Ottoman Commander definitely would..."

Sam looked wide eyed, "That's insane!"

Asteria nodded, "To us it would be, but logically the lives of a few to secure success is a sound tactic however inhumane it is."

Captain Stuart sighed, "She's right historical records are rife with brave Soldiers on suicide missions fighting to save the masses."

Admiral Lune frowned, "All these centuries of human progress and we still just throw away lives to gain a few more centimeters," Coline sat back and thought for a moment. "Alright, think of as many tactics regardless of how insane and get me a counter that can best secure our platforms. Those little buggers are really all that's keeping them from running us to ground."

Everyone nodded and rose from the table.

Master Chief Shia O'Connell
Eastern Prairie
Alesia, Clare System
327.0188 FCUDT 18:22:11

Blue green grass moved in great waves from a gentle southern wind as Shia stared across the wide plain in front of her. Facing west she saw great mountains thrusting up from the ground reaching far into the sky forming an impassable barrier. Behind her the crumbling rocky hills rolled into the forest. Smoke drifted up signaling the spot they had stopped the Ottoman Soldiers. Sighing quietly to calm down she walked over to where Master Sergeant Goody was kneeling.

"What's the good news?" she asked despondently.

"Can't see them yet, but scans show them moving this way. A hundred and twenty Soldiers with thirty armored vehicles," he said looking at his tablet.

"You still want to try to get to that mountain range? It's a long way," she replied looking north east toward the advancing enemy position and thinking about Katherine.

"Yes. This open plain is no place to fight a fortified column of troops. At least we can get above them, maybe find some cover up there," he said standing up and looking at her.

They both stood in the mesmerizing grass silently. Shia didn't want to bring up the situation with Katherine again. The look on Goody's face said all that needed to be said. After finding Katherine's body in that burned out hole Goody's mood had changed significantly. She refused to give up hope that Katherine would recover from her trauma. As soon as they were out of hearing range of the other Marines Goody had asked her about the rationality of taking Katherine with them. Her reply was short, final, and angry.

"We'll just have to move fast and stop less," he said in response to her comment about how far it was.

Shia nodded and watched him head back to the small group of Marines. She looked at the mountains they were headed for and sighed again. Walking back to the group she stopped and sat next to the corpsman.

"Go eat something, I'll sit with her," Shia said tapping him on the arm.

He nodded, "Thank you Master Chief."

Shia silently looked at the small group and then down at Katherine. Her armor was burned and scored making it look almost as if it was made of stone. There were numerous thumb sized divots all across her left side from plasma rifle hits. She looked in Katherine's eyes and smiled.

I'm slowing you down too much, Katherine sent to her.

"No you're not. We're fine," Shia said to her softly.

Shia, I'm not going to get better. I've been hurt too badly. The respirator is for short term emergency use; it will fail soon. You can't get me to a stasis pod. You have to know that, Katherine sent to her.

Shia closed her eyes, "You're wrong. You're going to be fine."

My spine is severed. My body is already shutting down.

Shia looked at her with a pained expression, "Not yet, don't give up yet. Please try to get better Katherine," -As she stared at her Katherine gagged and blood ran slowly out the corner of her mouth.

"Corpsman!" Shia called anxiously.

He came running up in seconds, "Ma'am hold on!" He said as she yanked open his medical kit.

"What's wrong?" Shia asked scared.

"She's developed edema in her lungs, there must be some internal bleeding that's backing up in her lungs," he said as he placed a tube in Katherine's mouth that began to remove the blood. "This will clear it out for now."

At the words 'for now' a pit formed in Shia's stomach and acid burned her throat.

"She's stable again," the Corpsman said to Shia and Goody.

"Will she get better?" Shia asked the Corpsman.

He looked back at her gravely.

Goody looked at Shia with a serious expression. "We need to carry on; we need to move Shia."

Shia looked down at Katherine feeling like they should do more but knew there simply was nothing to do. "Yea we can't stay here."

Goody nodded and stood up, "All right Marines pack up and head out. Point; keep your eyes on the sky no telling what kind of automatics they have out here."

The Marines snapped into action and in moments Shia watched them deftly lift Katherine up and the small group stepped toward the looming mountains in the west.

Several hours later the Marines were resting in a hollow as the sun set behind them. Goody paced along the small rise restlessly watching the eastern horizon.

Katherine slowly opened her eyes as Shia sat quietly next to her in the grass. She looked up at her with a slight smile.

Shia the Ottoman are getting close, Katherine sent to her.

Goody walked over and kneeled down.

Goody, you need to move. You can't fight them here, Katherine sent to him.

He nodded and reached for the combat stretcher.

No. I am only slowing you down. Leave me here for them. I can still use my cybernetics to slow them down. I don't have much time left, She sent.

"No!" Shia said shocked, "We won't leave you here for the Ottoman. Don't be ridiculous Katherine."

Katherine looked at Shia, *I'm dying Shia, that can't be helped. Please, you have to go on without me. Let me help in the only way I can.*

Goody stepped away to give them some space as Shia took off her gloves and held Katherine's face softly. "No, I won't let you. I never got to tell you... I wanted to..." a tear ran down her chin.

I know Shia, you don't have to say it. It's ok. You'll be ok, she sent to her.

As the first twinkling stars began to pop out in the sky above Shia and Katherine the Marines armor sounded an alert. Goody dove to the ground as a sleek black drone screamed past missing him by a meter.

"Incoming!" he yelled as the Marines instantly reacted.

He rolled back up and began to scan the sky for the deadly machine.

Shia reflexively leaned over and covered Katherine. She looked down and pressed her forehead against Katherine's- "This conversation isn't over," she sat up and activated Katherine's helmet.

Jumping up Shia activated her weapons and ran to Goody's side.

"It's got stealth. I'm only getting intermittent readings on it," Cole said hurriedly.

"Yea, I think there may be two of the nasty little things out there," he replied calmly.

Suddenly a flash lit up the night sky as a rocket exploded meters away from the Marine line. Dirt and rocks rained down on them. The drone flashed past again and was immediately lost in the darkness.

"Damn, we can't stay here there's no cover. We have to move," he said.

Two more rockets screeched in followed by plasma fire. The Marines suit network was working furiously trying to locate the drone. A target popped up and the Marines opened fire. Shia could see the drone hovering only twenty meters away as the plasma lit up the area. The drone immediately returned fire and streaked off.

Goody was hunched over his tablet searching the satellite map. "There," he pointed, "There is a small bluff with some cover, Marines, move out. Heading one eight seven, three second over watch, in twos, move!" Goody yelled at them as four more rockets landed ever closer.

Shia turned and looked back at Katherine lying peacefully in the tall grass- "We have to get Katherine!" Shia said.

"She wants us to leave her," Goody said over the noise. Rockets flashed in and impacted between Katherine's body and them. The ground shook and rumbled, grass began to catch fire and smoke choked the area. Shia made to run toward Katherine and Goody grabbed her, "If we don't move we're all going to die. I'm sorry."

Shia stared back at him in anger, "I can't leave her," she said as bright purple light flittered all around them and rocket impacts showered the area.

He hauled Shia up and out of the hollow, "We have a mission, we have to move on!" he yelled at her, "Shia!" Goody dragged Shia behind him forcefully as the Marines evaded the incoming drone fire.

Shia fought against his pulling, "Katherine, Katherine!" she yelled into the darkness.

Sergeant Goody whipped her around and looked into her faceplate, "Shia we have to go."

"No, I will not leave her!" Shai said forcefully as she yanked free of Master Sergeant Goody's grasp.

Sprinting back across the grass she slid to a stop next to Katherine's body as rockets impacted all around her. She rolled Katherine's body up onto her shoulders and heaved her up. Shia staggered under the incredibly heavy combat armor as she headed after the other Marines.

Cadet Katherine Carroll
Eastern Prairie
Alesia, Clare System
327.0188 FCUDT 19:17:01

The ground shook under Katherine as the rockets impacted nearby. She stared up at the night sky as a deep panic settled over her.

I don't want to die she thought fiercely. This can't be the end. Telling Shia to leave her was the hardest thing she had ever had to do. She wanted to scream for her to come back, to not leave her here alone.

I cannot, she forced herself to think. Closing her eyes she steeled herself. I will do this she thought. Taking a mental sigh, she opened her quantum core and after a second she plunged into the data.

In an instant her body vanished from her awareness as

she let her mind be carried away. Great waves of data flowed around in magnificent dancing patterns. As she passed through them incredible sensations flooded into her. She floated from stream to stream in seconds she no longer remembered her body, all that mattered was the dazzling and infinite fields of data. She didn't even notice when Shia heaved her up and carried her away.

CHAPTER SEVEN
Posturing Politic

Senior Fleet Captain Kelli Anne Vellius
FedCon Special Operations Ship Revenge
Outer Limits, Tartarus System
323.0188 FCUDT 08:49:20

The oddly shaped bridge stretched out down below the raised dais upon which newly appointed special operations senior fleet captain Kelli Anne Vellius now sat. She grimaced at the funky controls of the holotablet affixed to her command chair and looked down at her executive officer.

"This holo is still glitching," she quipped.

Commander Tristan Reese looked back up at her with a wry smile, "Probably operator error… Ma'am"

"Seriously! If this bucket survives our first jump, I'll be amazed," she grunted in anger and gave up looking for the data. "Engineering what's our time of arrival for the jump coordinates."

"Cap, two hours fifteen minutes," the Petty Officer responded from below her.

Kelli nodded and sat back, "This is weird you know. I feel like I am lording over the bridge up here. I can see every station."

"Well I would have thought you to enjoy that your highness," a heavy male voice said from the bridge hatch.

Kelli turned and looked at the owner of the voice, "Well you know me too well so I'll just have you keep your trap closed," she said smiling as the imposing figure of Lieutenant Colonel Josh Tammerlane strolled into the bridge.

"My Marines are all buttoned up in aft hold. After seeing the crew quarters, they appreciated the situation better," he said smiling.

"I can imagine, those little three meter by two meter

tubes are rough. Speaking of I am so glad I had them turn my ready room into quarters," she said smiling at him.

"Oh me too," he winked at her.

It was well known now that the Captain and the Colonel were an item after being assigned together for several years. Colonel Tammerlane had secured the *Hypnos* when it arrived back home and subsequently quarantined by fleet intelligence. Being a security risk he was eventually assigned to the *Revenge*; a ship with the same technology. Captain Vellius received the same fate and in light of her exemplary combat record was truly the first and only choice for this assignment. Kelli was more than happy to accept a command that complimented her relaxed style and rough demeanor, especially if it included one Josh Tammerlane.

"So Tristan is the high queen giving you any trouble?" Josh asked the XO.

The XO laughed, "Keeping me on my toes Colonel, that's for sure."

"Hey you stay out of this!" Kelli pouted at Josh, "Did you ever see the security office before we ripped it out?"

Josh nodded, "Yea it was a whole bridge. Seems the Ottomans had trust issues."

"From what I hear the Political officer ran herd on the Captain from security and could take control anytime they suspected disloyalty," she rolled her eyes, "Imagine having a senator questioning your every move with orders to shoot you if they felt like it."

"I cannot imagine. That's why we can't let them win," he said passionately, "So what's the plan for our little visit to Briton?" he asked changing topic easily.

Kelli shrugged, "We jump in outside the limit and scream diplomatic mission. Hopefully they won't blow us out of space."

Josh rolled his eyes, "Great plan... Maybe we can get adjoining cells."

"Well popping out of a wormhole in an Ottoman ship flying Federated colors with a Briton diplomat who happens to be a royal wasn't exactly in the Fleet doctrine," she said guiltily, "doing my best here."

"Wouldn't want any other at the wheel love. I'm at you ready," he said smiling at her.

"Excuse me Cap, we're one hour out from the limit," the engineering PO said.

"Thank you Engines," she reached out and tapped the ships com, "All hands prepare for Dower initiation ETA one hour. Standby stations and be prepared," she announced.

The sleek black destroyer glided silently through space toward the Heliopause of the Tartarus system. It was a tiny spot of humanity in a vast expanse of space. It carried the hopes and dreams of many lives. It was headed for inevitable combat. Kelli Anne Vellius was determined to see it through and come home.

"All right ladies and gentleman, prepare yourselves," Kelli announced as she stood on the raised dais. To her left Jeffery Dumont and Edward Windsor stood observing and Colonel Tammerlane stood quietly to her right.

"Engineering please initiate the Dower drive," Kelli announced.

"Ay Cap, initiating now," the P.O. replied.

At the rear of the sleek black ship the massive graviton reactors began building power. Super accelerators mounted along the forward section of engineering spooled up and prepared for the massive surge. Suddenly the reactor conduit valves opened and flooded the Higgs reactors with tremendous energies and they hummed with activity. Out in front of the ship a field began to form slowly. The now charged accelerators connected to the massive molybdenum rods that jutted out in front of the ship. As the Higgs field contacted the rods, energy discharged into them and flooded the graviton reactors instantly bringing them back to full power. In seconds the energy levels in the Higgs field was null and frame dragging began to form an invisible hurricane of spinning space. The graviton engines built up and fired straight into the throat of the wildly spinning space inside the Higgs field. The graviton blast accelerated through the field reached out and connected deep into interstellar space.

Kelli was transfixed by the sight in front of the ship. At first there was nothing then a point of light burst into existence that grew into a sphere twice as big as the ship. It began to clear in the center and move outward toward the edges. Suddenly the sphere radiated a burst of color outward away from the now clear wormhole. Beautiful particles flashed away beginning red and changing through the colors of the spectrum as they expended their energies in a brief glorious life.

"Oh my stars!" Kelli exclaimed, "That was quite a show."

"Cap, the graviton well is collapsing contact with the event horizon in thirty seconds," the engineering PO called out.

There was a brief shimmer as the ship slid into the wormhole and disappeared.

Kelli looked at the navigator, "Transit time?"

"Cap, eleven hours. We're going a long way," he said smiling sarcastically.

Kelli snorted, "A hundred light years in eleven hours! I almost can't believe it."

Ambassador Edward Windsor
FedCon Special Operations Ship Revenge
Wormhole Transit
323.0188 FCUDT 13:27:52

Edward stepped into the cramped conference room behind Jeffery Dumont and nodded to the Officers already present. Cables and holo emitters were clamped to the bulkheads betraying the hurried retrofit of the ship. He carefully found a seat along the back wall and sat down just as Captain Vellius entered the small room wearing the black pressure suit with gold piping of a Senior Fleet Officer.

"Greetings everyone, thanks for being here. Ambassador Windsor the show is all yours," she said to Edward.

"Thank you Captain," he said nodding to her, "It's difficult knowing where to begin so I will start by saying that this will be more difficult than you assume."

Jeffery laughed, "You're the King's brother right. It couldn't be that difficult."

Edward frowned, "Yes and no. Actually I do not have the ability to simply walk in and have a chat with the King and he couldn't give us what we want anyway."

"What do you mean? He can't or won't?" Samuel Leeane asked carefully.

"Your belief that the Sovereign rules everything is incorrect. He maintains appointment and veto power but doesn't enact policy. The power comes from the two political bodies and the Prime Minister," he said carefully, "It's a checks and balance. Power is decentralized by the three ruling bodies. There is the House of Civilians, the House of Nobles, and the Sovereign."

"Something like our Senate, Congress, and President?" Samuel said.

Edward nodded, "Yes quite similar although only the House of Civilians and some Nobles are elected. The rest of the Nobles and the Sovereign have hereditary peerage that gives them the right to rule."

"This is wonderful but what does it have to do with our visit?" Samuel asked.

Edward took a deep breath and looked at Samuel. "Because my brother is the Sovereign he inherited the peerage of my family, which means according to Briton law I inherited the second title of Marques of Amesbury. I am only a lord in the House of Nobles. In Briton treaties can only be entered into through the House of Civilians. As ambassador I can sponsor a foreign diplomat onto the floor

217

of the House but cannot introduce the treaty myself."

"So we need you to get the treaty into the House of Civilians?" Jeffery asked.

"Yes also I will help you navigate the political situation. I really don't see any difficulty with the House of Civilians, they will be easy to convince as long as they are aware of the threat the Empire poses."

"By political situation you mean exactly what then?" Samuel asked.

Edward frowned again- "It's the House of Nobles that will be a very real problem. They are concerned about profit more than security and I can tell you that Clare will be an expense in more ways than one. I know this because I am a Noble and my gut reaction was to say no. Clare has cost us dearly in the past and there was immense relief when we finally let it go."

"Maybe I'm not following but we're going to cruise in and call your government through this House of Civilians who will pass it to the House of Nobles then to the King. After all this we go save Admiral Lune," Kelli said carefully, "Doesn't sound too hard."

Edward looked at Kelli with trepidation, "It has to be done in person."

Kelli laughed, "Well we're short one Federated diplomat!" she slowly stopped laughing and looked at Edward.

"Madam Captain, according to interstellar law you're the only one here with authority to speak for and enter into political terms for your government," Edward said carefully.

Colonel Tammerlane laughed loudly, "Didn't think about that when you said yes to this assignment did you!"

Kelli looked back at them in mild shock, "Ok, how bad could it be?"

"You will have to address both the Houses in open session. First you will address the Civilian by describing the terms of the treaty. You will then have to listen to the government and the opposition and rebuke their arguments defending your position. They will then vote by voice which you must refute and ask for physical voting. By vote the treaty will pass, fail, or require alterations. If the alterations are acceptable it will move to the Nobles. Once it is in the Nobles you will face a panel led by the House Lord, Majority leader and Minority leader. After this open debate and agreement, they will vote. It will pass or fail," he said evenly.

Samuel shook his head. "How long do you expect this to take?"

Edward shook his head, "The lower house should be a day, two at most. The Nobles can hold it in debate for up to a year."

Kelli looked up again in shock, "A year! We can't wait that long."

Edward nodded, "I agree. That's why I am here. I know the Nobles and their ways. With my help we will get them to pass it. It's up to you though to provide the profit that they will require."

Kelli looked at Edward seriously, "Because of the Leeane's I'm choosing to trust you but this 'profit' thing sounds tricky."

"I understand Captain. By profit I don't mean money although that would be incredibly simple. I mean that there are a few individuals whom the power flows through. It's those individuals that need to see the benefit of the treaty to themselves or their planets. The others will follow them based on the idea that if it's good for the few it will somehow benefit them," Edward said slowly watching Kelli relax slightly.

"Ok so what do we do first?" Samuel asked.

"Well assuming we are allowed to land, the first thing we will do is talk to the King," Edward said smiling at the reactions of the small group.

A holodisplay on the port side wall of the Captain's quarters displayed the strange and beautiful world outside the ship. Dazzling waves of colors rippled along perpendicular to the ship giving the illusion of movement. Every so often it would shimmer like a stone tossed in a puddle causing the waves of color to stop ever so slightly. Kelli stared at it mesmerized.

"Supposedly that's hyper accelerated gravitons shearing through space-time," Josh said from next to her.

She looked at him a second then back to the display, "Where did you hear that?"

He shrugged, "That crazy engineer that installed the reactors was going on about it. It was more complicated than what I said but that's what I remember."

Kelli smiled at his comment, "Kind of romantic isn't it, falling through a rainbow."

Josh rolled his eyes, "Sometimes you really surprise me. Little miss death dealer likes rainbows and kitties!"

"And big guns!" She laughed as she squeezed his biceps.

They sat for another few moments and Kelli sighed, "Well back to work. The stars only know what the Britons are going to do when we show up," she leaned over his muscular arm and kissed him on the cheek.

He stood up and reached down for her, then lifted her clean into the air in a strong embrace- "I'll be with the Marines in case you need me love," -he lightly set her on her feet and smiled widely as he stepped out the hatch.

Kelli brushed at her skintight pressure suit out of habit and stepped out onto the bridge.

Edward and Commander Leeane were already seated by the bridge hatch as she calmly walked over to the command chair.

"Evening Cap, ten minutes until event horizon," the navigator announced.

"Thank you. Tactical please ensure all offensive weapons and shields are in standby and offline. I want a brief scan for immediate collision avoidance then passive only."

"Aye Cap," Tactical responded.

"Event Horizon!" Navigation called out.

There was a brief shutter in the deck plates and the holo displays popped up with a normal view of space.

"Cap clean exit we're inbound to the London system at point four light. Position is point one four seven gigameters from the limit of the system," the navigator called out.

"Negative for collision passive sensors are collecting. Two ships in range at two-four-seven up three degrees," Tactical called.

"Excellent. Com broadcast our presence please," Kelli asked.

"Signal out Cap," Com answered.

Kelli turned to Edward and Samuel, "Well now we wait," she said wryly.

They sat watching the displays slowly update as the passive sensors collected data over the next hour and tried not to feel the building pressure.

"Cap got movement. The Briton battle cruiser and its destroyer just went to full burn headed this way," Tactical called.

"Finally!" she grimaced, "This is the first time I have ever wanted to be noticed... feels so weird."

"Course plotted, intercept with inbound ships in two hours twenty-four minutes," Tactical announced.

"Cap inbound message, reads 'Hold course, deactivate weapons and shields, do not cross fourteen AU line or you will be fired upon' end of message," Com announced.

Kelli smirked, "Well that's mighty accommodating of them. Not even a visual?" she looked at tactical, "Will we intercept before the fourteen?"

"Aye Cap, intercept at twenty-six AU from the primary," she replied.

Kelli stood and stretched, "Tristan you have the bridge, I'll be in my quarters. I have a feeling it's going to be a long night and I have to read all about the Briton government," she said in a discouraging tone.

Commander Reese grinned at her, "Thank the stars I'm just the XO…" he said blissfully.

"Don't tempt me," she mock threatened him as she walked by.

Ambassador Edward Windsor
FedCon Special Operations Ship Revenge
Outer Limits, London System
323.0188 FCUDT 23:39:50

Edward was stretching his back as Captain Vellius walked back into the bridge. He nodded at her as she walked up.

"Seems about that time Lord Windsor," she said mildly.

Edward laughed, "You've been studying."

She nodded lightly and he followed her to the base of the dais. "What's the situation, we should be able to see the color of their paint by now," she asked the crew.

"Aye Cap, a battlecruiser and a destroyer breaking at twenty-five hundred kilometers off our starboard. Two additional battlecruisers burning in from the fourteen AU line," Tactical answered, "They have missiles armed and shields up."

Captain Vellius stopped and looked at Edward, "Well shall we call them?" she said smiling.

Edward nodded, "I suppose so."

"Com hail the Britons please," Kelli said tipping her head.

"Coming up on screen Cap," Com answered.

A tall well-built man wearing the maroon and white of a Briton fleet officer appeared with a stern face, "Unidentified ship, come to zero velocity and prepare to be boarded," he announced.

Kelli straightened up, "Greetings, I am Federated Fleet Captain Vellius. We are here on a diplomatic mission with the Briton ambassador to the Federated Colonies," she said smiling.

The Briton officer looked at them with suspicion. "You are in Briton space in an unidentified class of ship, you are to do as I say or you will be engaged," he said curtly.

Edward stepped closer and looked at the Officer- "I am Lord General Edward Windsor identification one six bravo three sierra six two," he said evenly.

The Briton looked at Edward and then off screen for a second- "Code in… omega three," he said evenly.

Edward nodded, "Blue sky."

The officer looked off screen again for a few seconds then back at Edward, "Lord General I have your location as Federation planet Acheron. Please explain this unorthodox situation."

"I am here to introduce a Federated diplomat to the bicameral house in order to secure the terms for an accord. Under the interstellar law section one twenty-two of the Federated peace treaty this ship claims diplomatic status. I request that you allow us to enter standard orbit to facilitate that request," he stated officially.

The officer was reading something off screen, "I am required to ask who your diplomat is My Lord as it cannot be you."

Kelli stepped up next to Edward, "I am that diplomat. Federated Fleet Senior Captain Kelli Anne Vellius, commander of this vessel identification command code alpha seven two three one delta," she said clearly and confidently.

The Officer looked at her quizzically then down at his holo screen- "Is this… accord a military matter?" he asked.

"Yes it has direct consequence to the security of both of our system," Edward said calmly.

After several seconds the Officer looked back at them, "I am willing to concede the boarding action until I receive clarification from the admiralty, however you are to reduce velocity to zero at the fourteen AU line and shut down to station holding thrusters only. I emphasize that if at any time I read something I construe as offensive I will engage instantly," he said in a warning tone.

Edward looked at Kelli with a questioning look.

Kelli nodded and looked the helmsman, "Helm take us to zero at fourteen astronomical units' station keeping only," she ordered.

"Aye Cap, decelerating in twenty-seven minutes," Helm answered.

The Briton Officer nodded and disconnected.

Kelli looked at Edward and smirked, "Well he was cordial."

Edward shrugged, "It is a bit of a stretch of the treaty terms for us to be asking for this so I don't blame him for being put off."

"He's probably asking for an Admiral to be flown out here as quickly as possible so he can be done with us!" Dumont said from the hatch.

Several hours after coming to a full stop at the fourteen AU line Edward, Jeffery Dumont and Captain Vellius stood at the command holographic screen watching the busy system traffic move about the primary planet. They were surrounded by three Briton battlecruisers and every so often the computer would alert them of targeting scans.

"Well they seem to be taking their time," Kelli said leaning on her elbows.

As if on cue the com petty officer turned to them, "Ma'am, incoming message."

Kelli stood up straight and nodded, "Up on screen please."

A rather proper woman in the Briton maroon and white uniform with four thick braided gold stripes on her arm appeared. "Greetings Lord General Windsor, Fleet Captain, I'm System Admiral Tabbitha Dunkirk. I want to thank you for being so patient and complying with our requests."

Kelli smiled, "It's a pleasure Admiral and I understand our appearance is unorthodox, I am sorry for the disruption we caused."

"I appreciate that Captain. The government of Briton has decided to allow your request for diplomatic status. It is under certain conditions though," she said smiling.

"That's good news Ma'am, thank you," Kelli replied, "What are your conditions?"

Admiral Dunkirk leaned over and transmitted a file, "Captain, you are permitted to enter orbit around Amesbury at the predefined coordinates I just transmitted. You will be accompanied by two Briton cruisers at all times. Further you will at no time activate offensive systems or actively scan the planet surface. You will be allowed to land a single shuttle at the spaceport of Thames for diplomatic processing. That shuttle will not contain any offensive weapons beyond what is allowed by law for personal security. You will be met at Thames by the Federated Colonial Ambassador and briefed on procedures. I have included a brief description of what and whom you may take with you on your first visit in the file I transmitted," she explained clearly.

Kelli briefly looked at the file, "This all seems agreeable Ma'am."

She smiled, "Excellent. I do have one question if I may?"

"Of course Ma'am, what can I do for you?" Kelli said.

Admiral Dunkirk leaned forward, "Can you tell me, are you commanding an Ottoman ship? I have never seen such a design."

Kelli grinned widely, "I'm not certain I can tell you Ma'am, but it sure would be an insult to the Ottoman Empire if we did capture one of their ships and convert it for our use…"

Admiral Dunkirk raised an eyebrow as she smiled, "Yes, yes it would certainly be quite an insult," she said understanding, "Thank you for your candor Captain and any request you have concerning system issues forward to me. I hope to speak to you again soon. General Windsor, welcome home."

"Why thank you Admiral Dunkirk, it's lovely to be home," Edward said smiling.

Senior Fleet Captain Kelli Anne Vellius
FedCon Shuttle Ship Revenge
Planet Amesbury, Thames Spaceport
325.0188 FCUDT 08:10:50

The sleek black shuttle gently touched the ground with a slight shutter and the thrusters suddenly quieted. Kelli stood up and smoothed her immaculate dress uniform as she sighed internally.

"You look great Cap," Colonel Tammerlane smiled at her.

"I can't believe this was in the ships stores actually… it's almost as if someone knew I would need it," she smirked at Samuel.

Samuel feigned ignorance with a wide eyed shrug. Kelli shook her head and stepped up to the shuttle's hatch. Looking back along the isle of grey canvas grav seats she saw the four others getting ready. Edward nodded at her silently. She activated the holopanel and it flashed green. In front of her the heavy airlock door hissed and slid open. Colonel Tammerlane stepped up behind her and they stepped out into the bright sunlight of New London.

Several hours later she stood alone outside massive wooden doors that led into the chamber of the Civilian House. Her face burned hot from adrenaline and sweat slowly ran down her back. Kelli swallowed hard trying to stifle the knots in her stomach. Doubt overwhelmed her mind as she stared at the pale brown doors in front of her. The floor began spinning and she snapped her hand out to keep from falling.

"Easy there!" Jeffery Dumont said grabbing her carefully.

Kelli held onto him tightly and looked up at him. "I can't do this," she said quietly.

Dumont grinned, "Ma'am, you have faced overwhelming enemy forces in the most hostile environment known to humans and despite the odds, you're still here," he nodded at the doors, "You can't tell me you're afraid of a bunch of old men whose only weapons are hot air."

She closed her eyes tightly and lowered her head- "You make it sound like it doesn't matter. This could mean winning the opening battle of the war or losing an entire system."

Dumont lifted her face to look in her eyes. "Regardless of their decision, we're going to Clare and we're going to win. Don't you forget that. You're the one, Fleet Captain, you were chosen because you can do this."

A gentle tone sounded and the doors began to open. Kelli looked at Dumont and breathed deeply.

He let her go and nodded- "One battle at a time."

The doors swung open in front of her and revealed a cavernous room. To her left and right were rows of stadium seats filled with people twenty levels high stretching hundreds of meters into the room. At the far end of a long walkway were three occupied chairs. Kelli looked up at the distant glass ceiling and marveled at the detailed stained glass above.

"Madam Ambassador, the dais is yours," the royal guard said officially.

She looked up the walkway and saw a circular dais rise up with a podium in the center of the room. She nodded and strode to the dais with as much confidence as she could.

Edward sat in the plush sofa chairs in a small alcove of the office of the King of Briton. Soft sunlight filtered in through nearby windows making the small space feel warm and comfortable. Edward felt very uncomfortable. Across from him sat his brother King Henry Windsor who carefully sipped steaming tea.

Henry placed his cup back on the saucer and sighed-"Edward, you've always been rash but this... it's pushing the limits Edward," Henry slowly shook his head, "The Admiralty is expressing concern about you, not to mention the Prime Minister who wants you locked down planet side."

Edward snorted and looked out the window silently.

"It took a lot to get you posted to the colonies. I did it for your own good. To keep you out of the line of fire," Henry sighed again.

"So you only have my interests at heart and not your own when you exiled me," Edward said curtly.

"Don't be so simple minded Edward! You ran off on that crusade to find some phantom enemy and never returned dammit!" he said quickly.

Edward turned and looked at his brother, "Considering the state of affairs in our galactic arm it's a good thing I did!" he said hotly.

"Yes, you found the Ottoman Empire. Stars only know whether they would be a threat if you hadn't exposed them. There are some in the Admiralty who think you caused this!"

"What! You think I caused the largest fleet in the galaxy to attack us! Those ships that are on their way to the colony border were under way months before I left," Edward replied hotly.

"Edward, relax. You know I believe you. I am simply bringing up all the viewpoints currently out there," Henry said leaning back in his chair, "What's going on with you, you're different Edward."

Edward stared angrily at the floor, "Things have changed. That's all," he said after a moment.

"Well great. I can't go to the Prime Minister with 'things have changed," Henry said sarcastically.

Edward slammed his fist on the arm of the chair and looked up quickly- "I have a daughter Henry! She is all I care about now!" he blurted out in anger.

Henry stared back at him stunned- "Wh... What? Where is she? Who is the mother...?" Henry stared at Edward, "Sam? It's Sam isn't it?" he said quickly.

Edward stood up and stepped to the window staring outside- "Yes, that's why Samantha left so quickly," he said hesitantly.

"How long have you known about this?" Henry asked.

"A few months," Edward replied.

The two remained silent for several minutes in the sun bathed room. Henry stared at his now forgotten tea as it sat on the table between them.

"Ok so this explains why your acting so unusual but why Clare? What does a treaty over Clare have to do with your daughter?" Henry asked confused. He stood picked up his tea and stopped- "Stars Edward... is your daughter in Clare?" he asked seriously.

After a quiet second Edward shook his head, "No, Samantha is."

Henry's head dropped, "Ah, the issue is illuminated,"- he stepped over and placed his cold tea on the serving platter. "I cannot keep cleaning up after your little episodes. I'm sorry Samantha is in danger but this Edward is something that will directly impact Briton."

Edward turned and faced his brother, "Well then I'm sorry to have bothered you, it won't happen again," he said vehemently as he turned a stalked to the large doors.

"Edward! For the love of the stars I meant it's not up to me this time!" Henry said loudly.

Edward paused at the door looking down at the handle, "Your niece's name is Eva Victoria Leeane. Named after Mother," Edward said quietly, "Goodbye brother."

Senior Fleet Captain Kelli Anne Vellius
FedCon Shuttle Ship Revenge
Planet Amesbury, Planetary Orbit
327.0188 FCUDT 17:50:43

Kelli arrived at the hatch of the massive dreadnaught and paused brushing off her formal pressure suit. The hatch cycled and a Soldier crisply saluted her.

"Good evening Ma'am, if you will follow me I will escort you to the Admiral's quarters," he said officially.

Returning his salute Kelli smiled, "Thank you Staff Sergeant."

She followed him down the passageway for several minutes and arrived at hatch guarded by another Soldier. He saluted then activated the door chime. The hatch cycled and she followed the Staff Sergeant inside.

"Ma'am, Senior Fleet Captain Kelli Vellius," he announced.

Admiral Dunkirk rose and approached them, "Thank you Sergeant, dismissed," she said to him.

As he departed and sealed the hatch the Admiral offered her hand, "Captain Vellius thank you for joining me for dinner."

Kelli returned the hand shake and smiled, "Thank you for the invitation Admiral."

She motioned to several plush chairs, "Please have a seat, and call me Tabbitha. I would prefer this be a more personal dinner than formal relations between two system nations. I would like to get to know you a little bit."

Kelli walked over and sat, "In that case please call me Kelli."

Kelli studied the Admiral as she carefully settled into the chair. Tabbitha Dunkirk appeared graceful and confident as she moved to her seat. Her silver and white hair was tied back in a braid then coiled into a bun. Her clear pale skin and green eyes stood out in contrast with her dark maroon Briton uniform. As far as Kelli could tell her appearance was flawless and Kelli felt a twinge of intimidation.

A steward entered from a side hatch placing two drinks out for them. Kelli nodded her thanks and he quietly departed. Tabbitha sipped her drink and smiled.

"Briton brandy, I hope you like it," she said savoring the flavor.

"It's very nice, much smoother than the version we have," Kelli said tasting it.

Tabbitha leaned back, "I've been following your progress closely in the House, and I have to say I'm impressed. You have an elegance in your diplomatic skills."

"Well it certainly hasn't been easy. The process is quite different back home. Here it is much more formal with factions and houses," Kelli said carefully.

Tabbitha laughed lightly, "Oh rest assured Kelli I have no affiliation to the parties. Unlike most of the Admirals in the Fleet I rose from the rank and file. I am simply a commoner that survived a few brutal battles in the colonial war," sensing Kelli's anxiety she smiled, "There's no ill will Kelli, we were and are simply doing our jobs. Besides you must have been very young during the war."

Relaxing a bit Kelli nodded, "Yes I didn't join the Fleet until several years after the war ended."

"And you're a Senior Captain. You have risen quickly, and demonstrated you can handle yourself I might add."

"I do my best," Kelli said sipping her brandy, "If I may, what do you think of the situation?"

Tabbitha tipped her head back for a moment in thought, "Before I answer that I would like to ask you a question," she said casually, "Are you truly offering joint control of the system or simply asking for assistance in fending off the

Empire?"

"What I am offering is sincere. Joint military control of the Clare system," she said earnestly.

"What you are offering," she repeated, "You're implying your government may have different thoughts?"

Kelli snorted, "I can't speak for their intentions, only mine. I can tell you if I have any say on the matter then it will be what I have offered. It will also have already been agreed upon."

Tabbitha nodded, "I believe you," she remained silent for several seconds looking at Kelli. "To answer your question I have to freely admit that my intentions are not purely innocent. I do agree that in the defense of my home we should move forward with this. I support your treaty wholeheartedly. You should know I have petitioned the Admiralty for consideration as the senior officer to be assigned to Clare should this become reality."

Kelli raised an eyebrow, "You want to be a combatant commander? Isn't the London system Admiral a prestigious position?" Kelli looked up, "I'm sorry I didn't mean to be rude."

Tabbitha shook her head, "Nonsense, your speaking your mind," she replied easily, "I feel that should this happen it could go two ways. One, we don't get along and fresh infighting begins over control of Clare. Or second, the first ever joint military command is successful. Whomever the commander is would be in a fine place to lead future joint relations," she said smiling brightly.

Kelli nodded in understanding, "You have motivation to make it succeed."

"Personal motivation aside, I believe it is morally right as well. Do you know who may command the Federation side?"

Kelli shrugged slightly, "Admiral Coline Lune is in system now. She would be provisional at least for the near future."

"And do you trust her?" Tabbitha asked carefully.

"I certainly do, she has placed her life and career at risk for the protection of Clare. She also played a key role in stopping the hostilities over the recent misunderstanding between our governments," Kelli said easily, "She is also a good friend of mine. I trust her with my life."

"Ah but can I trust her with mine?" Tabbitha said coyly.

Kelli looked at her questioningly.

Tabbitha laughed, "Its ok I was being rhetorical," she stood and motioned to the table, "Let's move to dinner shall we, my steward is an excellent cook!"

Kelli rose and followed her to the table, "I have to say, you're not what I expected."

"Oh I'm sure I can meet those expectations, just give me time," she laughed.

After a lovely dinner and general small talk about the similarities of the two nations Kelli sat quietly across from Tabbitha in the large sitting room. Tabbitha leaned over and carefully set her drink down as she looked up at Kelli.

"So with the civilian house passed you will be facing the jackals in the house of nobles," she said seriously, "Are you ready for them?" she asked blithely.

Kelli raised her eyes at the change in topic. "Edward Windsor has briefed me on the procedures... and some of its members," she said with trepidation.

Tabbitha nodded, "You're going to need all the help you can get. If you want the least amount of friction, you'll need to appease a few."

Kelli relaxed a bit and nodded, "Edward said as much. He hasn't mentioned exactly whom I need to get through to though."

Tabbitha smiled at Kelli's comment, "Something you should know about General Lord Edward Windsor is that his loyalty lies with himself only. Fortunately, his path and Britons has been aligned but there is talk among the Admiralty that this has changed. We certainly don't believe he is aligned with the colonies but his interest doesn't seem to be Briton either."

"Are you trying to tell me I can't trust him?" Kelli asked quietly.

"No. From what I know of him he won't lie to you, instead he simply won't tell you all you need to know. That's simply my advice to you, do what you will with it," Tabbitha reached out and handed a small data chip to Kelli, "That is all the data I can give you on the House of Nobles. Pay attention to the section on Lord Smythe of Cygnus. He seems a tiny player but in actuality his vote will win you the House."

Kelli retrieved the chip, "Thank you. How do I get a meeting with him?"

Tabbitha grinned widely, "Oh don't worry that will happen without your even trying."

Senior Fleet Captain Kelli Anne Vellius
FedCon Ship Revenge
Planet Amesbury, Thames Spaceport
328.0188 FCUDT 06:00:56

Kelli sprinted down the track as her lungs burned and her pulse hammered in her ears. Colonel Tammerlane further increased his distance in front of her as she forced herself to ignore the pain building in her legs. How can such a large man run so damned fast she cursed silently. As she rounded the corner she saw him casually leaning against the bulkhead waiting for her.

"Getting slow old woman!" he chided her as she staggered up to him.

Unable to catch her breath she dropped to the deck and made a rude gesture at the large Marine.

"Oh yea," he said in response to her, "Maybe we should run another lap?"

She carefully stood back up and kissed him on the cheek. Then placed her forehead on his chest leaning on him as she quickly recovered.

He laughed heavily and lifted her chin to look at her face-"Come on before the crew sees their Captain pass out," he said as he guided her into the officer's locker room.

Kelli popped open her personal locker just as her com alert sounded. Taking a deep breath, she activated it-"Captain Vellius," she announced.

"Ma'am, message from Amesbury. You're requested to contact the House Representative at your earliest convenience," the Com Officer announced.

Kelli slouched at the news, "Thank you com, on my way shortly," she deactivated the com and looked at Josh. "Sorry looks like I can't enjoy my shower today," she said grinning at his overly exaggerated pouting.

"Well, next time you really need to run faster..."

Kelli stepped onto the bridge as the shift change finished up and quietly waited for everyone to hand off their consoles. "Good morning Ma'am," her XO said walking over to her, "Everything's nice and quiet. Standard traffic and shipping, engineering fixed that glitch in the lift and we're at one hundred percent."

"Excellent, thank you XO," she said happily, "I need to make some official calls so hang out and enjoy the scenery."

"Aye Ma'am," he nodded as Kelli walked over to the com section.

"Com, contact the Royal House Representative, please," Kelli said to the Petty Officer as she approached.

The holo flashed and the secretary to the representative appeared, "Good morning Ambassador, please hold while I connect the Representative," she said happily.

A second later the round face of the Representative appeared, "Ah, good morning Madam Ambassador. I'm sorry for contacting you so early."

"Good morning Mr. Representative, I'm at your service at any time," she said with more pleasantness than she actually felt.

"Oh, that's kind of you to say. I wanted to tell you that

during a closed session last night the Civilian House passed the treaty to the House of Nobles by a majority vote," he said pleasantly.

Kelli nodded- "That's great news Sir, thank you."

He nodded, "Yes, excellent news," he looked off screen a second and back to her, "Moving forward from here the treaty will be introduced to the House of Nobles within forty-eight hours as is standard procedure. Further you are invited to attend an informal dinner with select Noble representatives this evening. I am sending you the details now. Do you have any questions I may address at this time Madam Ambassador?"

Kelli smiled knowing his question was only a formality and that he could not and would not answer any of her questions. "No Mr. Representative, thank you for the information I look forward to future contact," she said feeling her stomach tighten at the very thought of having to talk to this bureaucrat again.

He nodded politely and the holo blinked off. Before Kelli could even turn around the com P.O. called to her, "Ma'am, incoming message for the Dreadnaught *Bastion*."

Kelli stopped and took a deep breath, "Put it on screen please," she said.

Admiral Tabbitha Dunkirk appeared on the holo.

"Good morning Admiral. What can the *Revenge* do for you today?" Kelli said smiling.

"Morning Captain Vellius, I wanted to congratulate you on the passing of your resolution," Admiral Dunkirk said smiling.

Kelli grinned back, "My, word travels quickly out here."

"Well us Admirals have to gossip about something. Enjoy your dinner tonight I believe the conversation won't be as enlightening as last night but important just the same," she said lightly.

Kelli tilted her head in understanding as she remembered Tabbitha's comment about meeting Smythe, "Thank you Admiral I am sure it will be enjoyable."

"Good day Captain," Admiral Dunkirk said, and then paused, "By the way. The press has discovered your story and the passing of it through the House. Wear your best shoes when you arrive in Thames today," she said with a fierce twinkle in her eye and disappeared as the holo blinked off.

Kelli put her head in her hands and groaned, "The press..." she said in resignation.

Kelli wandered down the passageway on her way to the shuttle bay and paused at the hatch to Edwards's quarters. She thumbed the controls and received the entry signal. Edward looked up as she slid back the hatch, "Afternoon Captain," Edward said quietly.

"Lord Windsor, our shuttle waits to take us planetside," she said smiling.

"Yes, um, I think I should stay aboard this evening. If you don't mind Captain," he said glumly.

Kelli blinked at him, "Are you feeling well, do I need to call the Doc?"

"No nothing like that. I'm afraid my presence may not do you any good, quite the opposite in fact," he looked up at her and half smiled, "It seems my reputation is suffering a bit. I'm sorry Captain," he said sadly.

"I'm sorry to hear that Edward, I hope it's not because of what we're doing," she said seriously.

After a moment he took a deep breath and settled a bit. "Unfortunately this has been coming for some time for me. It is entirely my doing. After Samantha left I had some difficulty personally and my motives are now in question. I fear my presence will detract from our current mission," he looked up at her, "I'm frankly surprised you haven't heard any of that yet."

Kelli nodded, "Actually Admiral Dunkirk mentioned something vaguely. I figured it would come out eventually if it mattered."

Edward nodded, "Thank you for giving me the time to

bring it up."

"I'll leave it to you to do what you think is best," Kelli said moving to leave.

"Captain?" he said as she turned, "I want you to know I'm fully vested in this. Sam and Eva are all I have now."

Kelli nodded, "I understand, thank you Edward. We will save her, I promise that."

Kelli closed his hatch and strode down the passageway trying to stifle the twinge of anger she felt. She thought he was somehow taking the easy way out. Feeling sorry for himself and hiding from the issue. Her gut instinct from years of Military training made her think he was weak and it angered her. Stop! She told herself, I don't know the whole story and I being selfish. I will give him the benefit of the doubt for now she decided. Taking a deep breath, she pushed the situation out of her mind and stepped into the shuttle bay.

Senior Fleet Captain Kelli Anne Vellius
FedCon Ship Shuttle Revenge
Planet Amesbury, Thames Spaceport
328.0188 FCUDT 17:03:56

As the shuttle gently settled on the Thames spaceport shuttle pad the shuttle pilot came on over the com. "Ma'am, it has been requested we remain aboard until the Briton security forces arrive to escort us," he announced.

"Security forces? What's going on?" Colonel Tammerlane asked.

"Sir, there is a rather large group outside, apparently waiting for our arrival," the pilot responded.

"It's the press," Kelli said unhappily.

"I thought this was supposed to be all under wraps, why is the press here," Samuel said suspiciously.

Kelli leaned back and sighed, "Admiral Dunkirk mentioned that the story got out this morning."

"Got out..." he said more suspiciously.

"Ma'am, Royal Marine Lieutenant Colonel Gerry requests permission to enter the shuttle," the pilot announced.

"Granted," she said in response and ignoring Samuel's questioning looks.

The hatch slid back and a large well-built Royal Marine wearing burgundy and black utility dress uniform stepped inside. He snapped to attention and crisply saluted Kelli.

"Ma'am, Lieutenant Colonel Gerry reporting," he said confidently.

"Greetings Lieutenant Colonel. What brings you to us this evening?" Kelli said returning his salute crisply snapping her hand down.

"I have been charged with providing you additional security during your stay as the risk assessment has increased due to the public announcement of your mission," he said officially.

"Well that sounds ominous," she said.

Gerry smiled, "Basically Ma'am the press has gone wacky and we're going to keep them from holding you up. Plus, the Nobles want to show that we're on good terms," he shrugged, "If I may put it bluntly Ma'am."

Kelli grinned, "Yes you may Lieutenant Colonel," she said laughing. She stepped aside and nodded to Josh, "This is Lieutenant Colonel Tammerlane my head of security. I think you two will get along just fine."

"Please call me Daniel Ma'am, nice to meet all of you, I have your itinerary," Lieutenant Colonel Gerry said offering his hand.

"I'm Josh, lead the way Daniel," Colonel Tammerlane said shaking his hand.

The ground car moved swiftly out of the city and into lovely wooded parks dotted with large houses. In minutes they were turning onto a long drive that led to a particularly large house. As they turned she spotted the throngs of press waiting near the gates outside.

"Don't mind them. They are restricted to the outside grounds," Daniel said frowning at them.

"Small miracles," Kelli muttered as the car pulled up to the front of the house.

The door opened and Josh climbed out first then helped Kelli, "Into the fire we go," he said quietly to her.

"Stars this is a huge house," she said in awe and gripped his arm tightly.

"I'll be right next to you all night," he said calmly.

She pulled him closer and looked up at him smiling, "Thank you."

Standing at the massive wooden doors something suddenly caught her attention. A flash of light from the gates out by the main road. A camera she thought maybe a flood light. She felt the air knocked out of her and barely registered being slammed into the granite pillar next to the door as most of the wall erupted into chunks of rock and blue red plasma. She collapsed to the ground and was engulfed in smoke and debris as the massive blast thundered around her. Her vision sparkled and tunneled as she began to lose consciousness. Through sheer mental effort she stayed alert in the choking cloud.

Colonel Gerry staggered up the stair and dropped to his knees next to Kelli- "Ma'am, are you hurt?" he choked through the dust. Heavy gray soot stuck to his face where he had a large laceration that looked like a large black crack.

Kelli tried to move but could only barely turn her head, "Josh," she croaked.

Daniel looked at her seriously, "We'll find him, and help is on the way. Stay still Ma'am."

As he reached down and moved a large piece of rock off her legs pain ripped up her body. She let out a guttural shriek and everything faded to a blur as she passed out.

Jeffery Dumont stood looking down at Captain Kelli Vellius as she slept on the white sheets of the hospital bed. It had taken two days to regrow the bones in the left side of her body. Left arm, eight ribs, left femur and her whole left foot, he thought as he looked at her. Stars she's lucky to be here. Anger tickled at his mind. How could this have happened? An entire dammed company of Briton Marines and they nearly killed her right in front of them. He sighed loudly and looked up as the door opened.

"Samuel, you should be resting," Dumont said as Samuel walked in.

"Nonsense, I'm fine," he said walking up to the bedside. "How is she?" he asked.

Dumont looked back down at her- "Better, doc said she'll be awake anytime now."

"She's a fighter. Can't imagine how she survived. Daniel said she was awake when he got to her," Samuel said.

Dumont grunted at the mention of Lieutenant Colonel Gerry.

"It's not his fault Dumont. Let it go. If the situation was reversed what would you have done differently?" Samuel said somberly.

Dumont gritted his teeth and looked at the floor- "I'm willing to admit academically that your right but I need to blame someone. Josh is dead dammit and she nearly joined him!" he looked at Samuel. They both avoided speaking out loud that it was going to be difficult to tell her about Josh when she woke. Pure coincidence had placed Josh in the line of fire as he had leaned over to talk to her in those final moments. The pain of losing a friend paled to what Kelli would feel having lost her lover despite him saving her life.

Dumont believed it had to have been a Briton citizen

241

that attacked them. So far they had been kept in the dark about what was going on. Dumont had gone so far as to have ship security track Edward aboard. It had not escaped him that Edward stayed in orbit the day it happened. Suspicion plagued his mind every second. The sooner Captain Vellius woke up the sooner they could get her back aboard the *Revenge* and safe. This was turning into a disaster quickly.

"Excuse me," Colonel Gerry said from the door.

"Colonel, please come in," Samuel said politely.

Dumont glared at him a second then returned his attention to the floor.

"How is the Captain?" Daniel asked quietly as he approached.

"Better, waking up soon we're told," Samuel said, "Mostly thanks to you getting to her so quickly, thank you again by the way," Samuel said.

Daniel looked down at the floor, "Please that's not necessary, I feel responsible for this. It happened on my watch."

Dumont shifted uneasily- "Who did this?" he said quietly.

Daniel cleared his throat and looked at Dumont- "I have been informed you will be briefed as soon as the Captain is able to attend," he said uncomfortably, "It's bigger than we thought initially."

Dumont looked at Daniel and a sinking feeling settled in his stomach, "Doesn't sound good," he said.

Daniel's jaw tensed, "It isn't."

Captain Kelli Anne Vellius
Briton Royal Thames Hospital
Planet Amesbury, Thames
331.0188 FCUDT 11:17:32

Kelli sat on the edge of the hospital bed and tried to focus on sealing her formal uniform jacket. Her hand tingled and felt numb as she fumbled the seal again. "Dammit!" she cursed and shook her hand violently back and forth.

"It's takes a while for the nerves to reconnect," Admiral Dunkirk said from the door.

Kelli looked up quickly at the sound of her voice. "Admiral, I didn't hear you come in," she said trying to stand up formally.

Tabbitha waved Kelli back to her seat, "Relax Kelli, you've earned some informality," she said stepping up to her. She reached down and sealed Kelli's uniform with a smile.

Kelli grimaced as Tabbitha sealed her uniform.

"Kelli, needing help once in a while doesn't mean you're helpless."

"I know. I'm just having a hard time dealing with..." Kelli stopped herself before she said his name.

Tabbitha nodded, "Yes, I heard. I'm very sorry for the loss. From your reaction I assume he was more than your security officer."

Kelli's chest tightened and pain stabbed at her. She could only nod back in assent. She fought back the sudden water pooling in her eyes.

Tabbitha stepped over the counter and poured a glass of water. She waited a second for Kelli to regain control of herself and handed the water to her carefully.

"Thank you Tabbitha," she said sipping the water. They stayed in silence for a few moments before Tabbitha crossed her arms and looked at Kelli.

"Are you ready for this?" Tabbitha asked with concern.

Kelli stood and took a deep breath, "Yes Ma'am. As ready as I can be."

Tabbitha nodded, "Let's be about it then. We will be meeting with the Admiralty board and the King of Briton. Best to not be tardy."

Kelli stepped out of the armored ground car and into

tremendous chaos of the press. Four Briton soldiers quickly came up to her side and motioned her forward through the heaving mass of people. Reporters yelled and hollered questions trying to see past the Soldiers escorting her. She unconsciously hunched over and placed her hand on the Soldiers back in front of her as they moved forward to the door. After what seemed like minutes they finally reached the glass doors and entered the building.

"You sure make an entrance Ma'am," Samuel said in the sudden silence of the large foyer.

"Samuel, this is crazy!" she said wide eyed and fighting off an anxiety attack.

"Yes Ma'am," he said as they followed Admiral Dunkirk to the lifts.

On the ride up Kelli focused on breathing to slow her racing heart. In a few moments she would be facing the entire Briton Admiralty likely in the most unsettled emotional condition she had ever been in. All too soon the doors chimed and silently slid open. She took a final deep breath and stepped out behind Admiral Tabbitha Dunkirk.

Four Admirals rose to their feet as the small group entered the room.

"Senior Captain Vellius, thank you for meeting us so soon after this terrible incident," the closest Admiral said as they approached, "I am Fleet Admiral Sir Geoffrey Younger. These three are Admirals Blunte, Waller, and Sifford," he introduced his companions.

"It's a pleasure to meet you all, this is Commander Samuel Leeane," she motioned to them.

"It's pleasure to meet you Commander. I believe I know you sister Samantha," Sir Geoffrey said nodding to Samuel. "Admiral Dunkirk," he said nodding to Tabbitha, "Please have a seat all of you, would anyone like tea?"

They all found seats and took cups of tea from the steward as Sir Geoffrey cleared his throat.

"I'll get right to it Captain so not to waste your time, I assume you have lots of questions so I'll try to be concise.

Over the past three days' things have continued to get worse here so I apologize for the secrecy," he said sitting down.

Kelli nodded thinking about the news reports she had seen in the hospital.

"You may have seen the public news but if you haven't then I'll briefly cover what's happened. At approximately the same time as the attack you were involved in three other separate attacks occurred. Thames was thrown into utter chaos. Two hundred people were killed or injured that night in similar plasma explosions. Three of our Nobles were killed," he frowned and shook his head.

"Due to Colonel Gerry's quick reaction his Soldiers managed to capture several of the perpetrators involved in the attack on you. Subsequent interrogation revealed that the party involved was the Ottoman Empire. Our intelligence division managed to track down their rather sizable terrorist organization before they went dark. It spans several worlds and systems throughout Briton space. In fact, in the days preceding the initial attack thirty-seven more incidents have occurred across our systems," he said sadly.

"Thirty-seven!" Kelli exclaimed, "How many casualties?"

"Too many," Admiral Sifford said quietly.

Sir Geoffrey nodded and leaned back. "As you can imagine the public demanded answers and in a press release late last night we informed them of what was happening. There was an equally demanding pressure for us to do something after that press briefing. Early this morning the House of Nobles passed your treaty as a step toward securing our Nations. After suffering such extreme acts of terrorism it was obvious we needed to act. We also believe we haven't seen the last of the attacks"- The door opened behind them and the Master at Arms stepped inside.

"Sir, Your Royal Highness King Henry Matthew Windsor and the Royal Prime Minister Dame Bethany Scott," he said crisply.

The group stood quickly and snapped to attention.

Kelli instantly recognized the resemblance of King Henry to Edward. He stood tall and confident as he walked over to the group. She took mental note of the tired appearance in his eyes. He seemed a man who had not slept well in several days. He walked straight to Kelli and extended his hand.

"Senior Captain Vellius, my most sincere apologies for the tragic incidents that have occurred on Briton soil. I am sorry for our first meeting to have been under this trying circumstance. Regardless it is my pleasure to meet you and hope your treatment has met your needs," he said with deep sincerity.

"Thank you your Majesty, Briton hospitality has been wonderful. It's a pleasure to meet you as well. I'm very sorry for the events that have occurred to your people. I hope we can help each other through this," she said shaking his hand.

"Indeed I believe that together we can confront this threat strongly. Beginning with securing Clare from the Ottoman Empire," he said motioning everyone to sit.

"Your Highness, I have briefed the Senior Captain on events to date," Sir Geoffrey said.

"Excellent, then moving on to the future I want to discuss logistics," he said nodding at Sir Geoffrey.

Sir Geoffrey cleared his throat and glanced at a data pad. "Captain Vellius, the Admiralty has decided to assign Admiral Dunkirk to the Joint Combatant Command of Clare. According to your report one Admiral Coline Amélie Lune is currently the ranking officer in system?"

Kelli nodded, "Yes Admiral. She is aboard the destroyer *Nyx* currently assigned to the system."

"Excellent, provisionally we accept her future assignment as Admiral Dunkirk's Federated Colonial equivalent Joint Commander. Until that time, we accept you as the Acting Joint Commander. Is that acceptable?" Sir Geoffrey asked.

"Completely acceptable. I have had the opportunity to get to know Admiral Dunkirk and believe Admiral Lune will work very well with her as will I," Kelli said smiling at Tabbitha.

Henry leaned forward, "Unfortunately Captain it will take months to get our task force to Clare. What do you expect to find when we arrive?"

Kelli grinned, "Well your Highness that's the thing. I can tell you that I can get one of your destroyers, two corvettes, and ten fighters to Clare much faster than several months."

Henry raised an eyebrow, "Really... How?"

"I'm sorry but I'm not allowed to tell you how. It's pushing the limits for me to tell you at all," she said pensively.

Henry was quiet for a minute, "You can't give me anything? I have to take this on faith?"

Kelli leaned back and looked at him, "I can't give you anything about the travel... but I do have something that may make up for that," Kelli reached in and pulled out a simple data pad. She activated it and set it on the table between them.

"On that data pad are the schematics for a device that will allow you to communicate instantly between two points... regardless of distance," she said. They stared at her and the data pad in disbelief- "Also, I can give you a working transceiver that is paired with a clone I am prepared to install aboard Admiral Dunkirk's command ship. It would allow you instant information flow from the battlefield in Clare," Kelli leaned back and looked at Henry, "Hopefully your Highness that increases your willingness to have that faith you asked about."

Henry looked at the Prime Minister and then at the Admirals. Finally, he returned his gaze on Kelli, "We have an agreement Captain. By the end of today you will have a destroyer, two corvettes, and ten fighters at your disposal. Admiral Dunkirk, take a squad of legionaries with air support and depart with Acting Joint Commander Vellius."

"Yes Milord," Admiral Dunkirk said smiling.

Henry rose to his feet, "One final thing Captain if you would," he offered his hand to help her to her feet.

Kelli stood at attention in front of Henry wondering what he was doing. He reached out and took a leather case from the Prime Minister. He held it out in front of his chest at waist level and opened it. Inside was a hand scanner surrounded by gilded scrollwork of gold and silver. He looked at Kelli and smiled.

"Senior Captain, I would like to offer you hereditary peerage on behalf of the people and civilians of the nation of Briton. It was voted upon and approved by the House of Nobles in conjunction with the treaty last night. As the person responsible for the acquisition of new territory it falls to you as the representation of such territory. It only seems fitting that as joint territory a foreign noble is appointed."

Kelli was immediately taken off guard. She was completely speechless for a moment. Then suddenly very embarrassed.

"I don't know what to say, I don't think I'm the right person. I don't deserve this," she stammered.

Henry smiled, "On the contrary Captain you're the only person who deserves this. You have paid more than any of the other nobles have to obtain their peerage. Please, I am sincere."

Kelli looked at the beautiful scrollwork for a moment then up at Henry- "What do I do?"

Henry looked at the Prime Minister, "Bethany if you would please."

Bethany stood straight and the Admirals all snapped to attention. "To all who are present and viewing, know that in accordance to Briton law, heraldry, and constitution the House of Civilians and Nobles with the approval of His Royal Highness Henry Michael Edward crown ruler of the nation of Briton does hereby bequeath the official hereditary peerage of jointly controlled territory known as the system of Clare to Federated Senior Fleet Captain Kelli Anne Vellius," Prime Minister Bethany Scott announced crisply.

"Captain if you would place your hand on the scan pad please," Henry said.

Kelli suddenly realizing she was being recorded felt intensely self-conscious. She carefully reached out and laid her hand on the scanner. It activated and pale blue light illuminated. Her hand tingled warmly and she knew nanites were working their way through her skin. The glow dissipated and Henry nodded.

"Ladies and gentleman may I introduce Federated Senior Fleet Captain Lady Baroness Kelli Anne Vellius of Clare," Henry said out loud.

Two hours later after extensive planning with the Admirals and their teams Kelli stood quietly looking out over the city of Thames from the high tower of the Admiralty building. She felt numb inside. So much has happened in the past days she just couldn't wrap her mind around it. She consciously avoided any thought of Josh and the painful empty hole she felt in her chest.

Outside the noon sun shone off the beautiful façade of the Ministry of Defense building. Briton Soldiers stood guard at newly erected road blocks on either side of the street preventing traffic from passing in front of the two buildings.

"I never thought I see Soldiers guarding the streets of Thames in my lifetime," Admiral Dunkirk said quietly walking up next to Kelli.

Kelli looked up at her, "I was thinking something similar," Kelli looked back at the street below, "We need take the same measures on Acheron."

"How do we fight this threat?" Tabbitha said frowning.

Kelli turned and looked at her with her face solidly set, "Together," she said confidently.

CHAPTER EIGHT
Winter War

Commander Samantha Leeane
Command Conference Room, Command Deck
Nyx, Clare System
331.0188 FCUDT 06:55:09

The quantum com system disconnected as Sam walked into Admiral Lune's ready room with Captain Stuart. Coline took a deep breath and stared up at the bulkhead.

"Ma'am, looks like you need some tea," Sam said setting down a steaming cup.

"Thank you Sam," Coline said smiling, "Things are rapidly getting complicated."

Sam and Adam sat down at the small conference table and waited for Coline to relax a little. After a few moments she brought up the holo and nodded at it.

"So we have heard from several systems concerning the Ottoman hostilities," Coline said looking at them.

Sam leaned forward and stared at the data, "The Federated Prussian Systems and the Republic of Milan?"

"Yes, and it's not good. The Prussians signed a treaty with the Ottoman Empire to secure their borders a decade ago. It binds them into supporting them in any endeavors that do not endanger their territories. If they openly oppose the Ottomans, then the treaty is void. Mainly fearing that their fleet is not capable of defeating open Ottoman invasion and the economic impact would destabilize the entire region. Their main supply trade routes travel through Ottoman space," Coline said dully, "In response the senate has placed an embargo on the floor of congress to eliminate trade with them in totality. There is the belief that the embargo will be ratified by the allied systems."

Adam took a sharp breath, "That will surely result in a declaration of war from the Prussians."

Sam nodded in agreement, "They are not known for

level headed actions."

Coline frowned, "Yes that is the consensus of the fleet Admirals. In light of these actions the fleet has redoubled the recruiting and building efforts."

"And the Republic's stance?" Adam asked.

"Better than Prussia. The Republic believes the Ottoman to be of little threat to them due to their distance from the boarders. They are also buffered by the Madrigal system which lies between them and the Prussians. Madrigal has also claimed neutrality," Coline said bringing up the system maps, "The Republic has offered humanitarian aid in the event that hostilities begin but will not assist in warfare."

"Great. So at the moment we're standing alone," Sam said exasperated.

"Well, the government still doesn't fully believe the Ottoman Empire is going to attack us directly. They have admitted that the events here are troubling but amount to no more than two nations bickering over territory," Coline explained.

"Tell that to the residents of Clare!" Sam said incensed, "And our Marines fighting for their lives down there."

"Fortunately Briton seems open to talks of support. That may only be because they don't want the Empire sitting on their borders and know it would only be a matter of time before they came looking for a fight," Coline continued not acknowledging Sam remarks.

"So all eyes are on us," Adam said, "They must be waiting to see which direction Clare falls. If the Ottoman succeed here, then… what? Briton has no option but to dedicate a substantial force to defensive positions. The Federation will be pinned between flanking positions with two noncommittal systems to their rear. The threat of a combined Prussian – Ottoman force would send us into a cold war that could last for who knows how long."

Sam put her head in her hands, "At least we have the Perseus Rift. The five hundred odd light years between the

Orion-Cygnus and the Perseus will slow them down considerably and really stress their supply routes."

"As long as we keep the Dower to ourselves you mean," Coline said quietly.

Adam nodded, "If the any other Ottoman allied system obtains the Dower we will be in serious trouble."

Coline brought up another holo, "This is the official diplomatic transmission from the Ottoman Emperor," she said to them, "It outlines his 'request' to our government. Basically he says if we give him the ship that violated the borders of the empire he will ensure a peaceful resolution to the current situation. He also included detailed scans and holo recordings of the event. He knows the ship has technologically advanced drive systems," Coline activated the holo recording and an image of the Hypnos floated in front of them.

"Well it was bound to happen. We were in quite a hurry to get away from that station. They surely saw us depart through the wormhole," Adam said reluctantly.

Coline nodded silently, "The Admirals were displeased to say the least," she looked up at Sam, "Any word from Edward?"

"Not since his message about Eva going to visit my parents," Sam said lightly, "Anything from home about it?" she asked.

Coline shook her head sadly, "No. Whatever is going on it's well below the line. Admiral Matthews implied help was on the way but did not directly say it was."

"Well there's a reason the Chief of special operations and the Chief of intelligence are different people. Maybe Admiral Thomas is playing it close to the chest," Sam said shrugging.

Later that morning Sam sat looking at the tactical plot as yet another system defense platform or SDP blinked out of existence. She sighed and unconsciously reached for her coffee before remembering there wasn't any. She carefully placed her hand on the table and closed her eyes.

"We're down to one hundred ten SDP's, I am closing the gap in coverage but at this rate there will be insufficient platforms in seventy-two hours," Commander Asteria Hypnos said from across the table.

"Doesn't matter, by then we will be nearly out of reaction material and unable to maintain the system," Lieutenant Lavagnino said quietly, "In forty-eight hours we will be unable to initiate the Dower Drive."

Samantha gave Lieutenant Lavagnino a hard stare, "Let's not focus on the negative," she said with more edge to her voice than she intended. "What's the status on current issues?" she asked in an easier tone.

"I'm sorry Ma'am. As of this morning we have full control of the ships systems. Nearly every system has had to be bypassed and hard wired into the auxiliary engineering control center. The hull is repaired and the main beams are at full strength. Repairs to main engineering will have to wait until we can get more reactor mass to produce the required components," Lieutenant Lavagnino reported.

"Thank you Jacob, please tell your crew they have done an excellent job," Sam said, "Tactical?"

Asteria looked up, "Ma'am, the Ottoman fleet continues to maintain position. We have been able to get complete and detailed scans on each vessel and are currently locating weaknesses in their physical structure. Unfortunately, they seem to have defeated our SDP stealth quite effectively. That is to be expected given the amount of time they had to study it."

Sam nodded and looked at Colonel Driscoll, "Brynn how is Medical?"

Colonel Brynn Driscoll activated the holo screen and motioned at it, "Supplies are fine. We anticipated needing quantities so we are stocked for a good bit. So far I have seen forty-three crew with symptoms of exhaustion. Less than I would have anticipated but it will only worsen. Minor injuries are on the rise and we have two serious accident cases now. One was a fall from the main beams in the hanger. Simple lack of awareness issue. The other is a plasma burn from the repairs on the hull. Beyond that we are one hundred percent. I have stimulators ready in case we need to go on alert but I have a responsibility to tell you that extended use causes serious problems. Everyone that takes them will require significant down time to recover."

"How much down time?" Sam asked her.

"At least two times the length of use. Stims for a day requires two to recover," Brynn said seriously.

Major Callis Kane nodded, "I remember stim training in flight school, after two missions I could barely function without them. I can't even remember the week following."

Sam typed on her tablet and looked up, "Does anyone else have anything?"

Warrant Officer Josephine Santiago cleared her throat.

Sam looked at her, "Yes Joe?"

"Ma'am, still no report from the Marines planetside," she said carefully, "The extended com buoy will be in place soon."

Sam looked at Lieutenant Binici for a second to see her reaction. She looked tired, eyes bloodshot and dark. Sam knew she had been working tirelessly trying to find anything she could do to help Cadet Carroll on the surface. Looking back at the whole table Sam nodded to Captain Stuart.

"One month. This has been going on for one month. We have held a superior force at bay that whole time. They have had to resort to pecking away at us bit by bit but we're still here. I am confident we will find a way to continue," Captain Adam Stuart said coolly. "I know you're all tired and stressed. I know you want coffee and hot food. But I need you to be the officers I know you are. I need you to find me options. No matter how crazy the option is, I want to hear it. You have one day," he rose and looked at them, "Make me proud people. Dismissed."

The group all rose and headed out of the conference room somberly. Samantha ran her hand through her hair and grimaced at how greasy it was. Power rations were taking a toll on everybody. She looked up at Adam.

"Good speech," she said as she stood up.

Adam looked at her carefully, "They needed it. Moral is falling, they need strength. Besides I believe in them, in us."

"Always the optimist," she said sarcastically. She stood in front of him and studied his face, "Do you think they will make it in time?"

Adam stayed quiet for several minutes. Finally, he sighed, "They have to," he said and he stepped out of the conference room.

Sam sat back down and put her head in her hands on the table. She thought of Edward and Eva. So far away, will I ever see you again, she thought. It was getting harder every day to look at the crew and keep a stoic face. We're going to die out here she thought despondently. The lights in the conference room flickered and went out. Power saving programs only allowed the lights to be active for set amounts of time. She rose and straightened her pressure suit then stepped out of the dark room to start her day.

Commander Helen Dower
Main Engineering, Engineering Deck
Nyx, Clare System
331.0188 FCUDT 07:13:22

Darkness was all around her, she lay on the floor, cold metal pressed on her back. Something moved beyond her vision. The floor rumbled and vibrated for a moment. She looked down at her feet and bright light flashed momentarily. Her heart froze in terror as she saw the thing that moved slowly towards her in that brief flash. It was black and amorphous. Crawling towards her. She could hear it getting closer in the darkness. Helen couldn't move. She was frozen in terror. Slowly the creature emerged from the darkness less than a meter away from her feet. Helen involuntarily convulsed at the sight of it. It slowly reached out for her. Just before it touched her Helen let out piercing scream.

The Engineering bay appeared around Helen as she lurched awake. She stared at her feet where the creature was only moments before. She closed her eyes and wiped her sweat drenched face. It was a dream she told herself over and over.

Helen stood in the center of the burned out Engineering bay. Black charred metal and plasma burn scars rippled the deck and hull around the room. A large silver metal cable coiled around her and terminated in hundreds of micro filaments that snaked into her cybernetic arm. In the center of the room stood a jumble of particle accelerators and superconducting coils. Wires ran everywhere through dozens of computer nodes and into the accelerators. Helen stood staring at the pile of machines and equations raced through mind as she connected to the ship through her cybernetics via that metal cable.

She climbed up on the makeshift coil and pulled out a wrench to adjust the settings. She was only slightly aware as Commander Samantha Leeane overrode the lock on the bay and stepped inside.

"Helen, I need to talk to you," Sam said to her.

Helen paused for a second then turned back to the machine ignoring Sam.

Sam walked up to the machine and stared at it, "Helen I want you to go to medical with me. We're all worried about you," Sam looked up at her, "Xander is worried about you. Please Helen."

Helen shivered and kept working, "Not yet," she said shakily.

Sam squinted up at her, "What do you mean Helen? You're not ready to go to medical?"

Helen climbed down and activated a nearby computer node. Data streamed through her mind as system diagnostics programs checked the status of her machine. As the checks all came back she relaxed and began to shake.

Her hands trembled and knees went weak. She collapsed onto the deck in a violent seizure. Before she lost consciousness she vaguely heard Sam yell out to her.

Commander Samantha Leeane
Deck Four Passageway, Deck Four
Nyx, Clare System
331.0188 FCUDT 08:17:48

The medical stretcher bounced against the bulkhead as the corpsman tried to guide it down the passage. Helen was thrashing and shaking in a grand mal seizure making it difficult to maneuver.

"Careful her feet broke the restraint straps!" Sam said alarmed. She grabbed the end of the stretcher and turned it into the Medical Bay.

"Over here quickly!" Brynn said as they entered, "Sam, what happened?"

"Jacob said she was acting strange; I went to check on her in the damaged engineering section. She was completely unaware of my presence and talking to herself. She just suddenly dropped and started doing this," Sam said quickly.

Brynn quickly checked Helen as they put her on the medical table, "Grand mal, Major Gallant, get me the anticonvulsants. Sam what happened to her arm?" Brynn said examining the remains of Helen's cybernetics.

"She had it hardwired to the ship with data cables. We had to act quickly so I removed her arm. I'm sorry Brynn. I figured we could repair it later," Sam said sadly.

"It's ok, there doesn't appear to be any physical damage. You did what was necessary," -Brynn injected the anti-convulsion drugs and Helen slowly calmed and lay still. "Activate the scanner Major. Let's see what's got her having seizures," Brynn called to Doctor Gallant. The long white tube slid silently around Helen's body and began to hum quietly.

"Helen!" Warrant Officer Xander Beaumont said

alarmed as he hurried through the hatch.

Sam grabbed him as he rushed inside, "Xander its ok, she's stable for now."

"What's wrong, what happened?" he said concerned.

"She had a seizure. We're scanning her now to find out why," Brynn said walking up to him and placing her hand on his shoulder. "Have you noticed anything about her recently that appeared unusual?" Brynn asked.

Xander stared at Brynn, "Other than her being depressed, not sleeping or eating, not talking to me and locking herself in engineering?" he said sarcastically.

Brynn frowned, "Yes, I'm sorry Xander. Has she not been taking her medication?"

"I can't be sure. I thought she was but maybe not," he said looking at the floor, "She has been so distant; I couldn't help her."

"It's ok Xander. Posttraumatic stress doesn't cause seizures. This is not your fault. We'll figure this out," Brynn said soothingly.

"Colonel the scan is coming up," -Major Gallant called over.

Brynn turned and stepped over to Helen. A holographic image of Helen appeared above her body. Brynn began switching between modes and a soft tissue image came up- "There," Brynn pointed out.

Major Gallant nodded, "Blastoma, in the left hemisphere of her brain. But what caused it? She has no genetic markers for cancer."

The holo flipped to cellular diagnostic. Red flares popped up all over the scan. Brynn looked up, "Severe radiation damage. Looks to be nearly a month ago she took a lethal dose. How did we not catch this?" she asked Major Gallant.

He frowned, "Nothing indicates she needed a deep scan according to her records," he said scanning her files, "Maybe something that happened on the mission before when the station went critical?"

Sam looked alarmed, "The Marines were in armor, and they would have been protected. We didn't get a mission profile because they haven't been returned to the ship."

Brynn nodded, "Yes that could be it. Regardless, Helen needs immediate treatment. We can get rid of the blastoma in a few days. The radiation will take much longer. I'm confident you'll have Helen back good as new Xander," Brynn said comforting him.

Senior Captain Mercan
Deck Four, Main Bridge
Ottoman Frigate, Interstellar Space
331.0188 FCUDT 10:21:18

"How many of my Soldiers have you lost Colonel?" Captain Mercan hissed at the com screen, "These people are settlers and pirates! You're telling me they killed over one hundred Soldiers in twenty minutes" -his face red in anger.

A pale faced Ottoman Colonel looked back with a squinted glare, "Fleet Captain, Second Battalion encountered Federated Marines. They are all outfitted in very powerful combat armor. They were lured into an improvised explosive trap."

Mercan stared back at him, "Really, how do you know they were Federated Marines and what are you doing about it?" he challenged.

The Colonel nodded and a video popped up. It showed two massively armored women. As it began playback one of the women explained that they were Federated Marines protecting the planet. The video stopped and the Colonel looked back at Mercan.

"Fleet Captain we are in pursuit of the Marines. Approximately four days ago we attacked them via drone and managed to eliminate one," he said boastfully.

Mercan cocked his head, "One?"

"Yes Fleet Captain, as far as we can tell. These Soldiers are using massively enhanced armor. They are very difficult to eliminate," he smirked back.

Mercan leaned back in his chair in the dark bridge and thought for a moment. Finally, he leaned back and looked at the Colonel, "I expect you to capture the settlement and eliminate the Federated presence at all cost..." he stared at him, "Don't bother to return if you fail either of those tasks." He disconnected before the Colonel could respond.

He stood up and looked at his bridge crew, "What's the status of our penetration through the defense perimeter?" he demanded.

"Sir, one more platform down. At the current rate we should have an entry vector in three days," the Tactical Officer replied immediately.

He shook his head in frustration as he walked off the bridge. As he reached the hatch he spotted Captain Kartal silently watching.

"Kartal," he said in greeting.

Kartal simply nodded curtly and stared at the bridge crew.

Master Chief Shia O'Connell
Western Barrier Mountains
Alesia, Clare System
332.0188 FCUDT 05:01:01

Great white fluffy snowflakes lazily drifted down all around Master Chief Shia O'Connell. *We've marched across these horrid plains for four days* Shia thought. *Those evil drones won't give us a minute of rest. Having to hide during the night has cost us dearly.*

She stared at the holo in front of her.

"How far out are they?" Goody asked as he walked up.

Shia looked up at him, "A day. Two at most. Depends on if they stop for the night," she signaled the Marine's tiny drones to circle and return to their position.

"Looks like they are getting ready to launch another drone," Goody said watching the footage, "How many of those creepy things do they have?" he asked rhetorically.

Shia watched him walk away to check on the Marines. Anger and accusation washed across her mind. Stop she told herself, it's not his fault, I let Katherine get injured, it was my fault she scolded herself.

Shia held out her hand and caught a snowflake. Its delicate arms and patterns clearly visible through her suits optics. She absently flexed her knee as the cold invaded through the deteriorating seals. She ignored the soft tone chiming in her helmet alerting her of the dwindling power supply.

As the sun set Shia dropped into the tree covered defilade she shared with Staff Sergeant Colfax and settled in. Within minutes they heard the drone pass overhead looking for them.

Leaning back, she looked up through a gap in the top of the small bunker. The clouds were dissipating and unfamiliar stars winked back at her. Her mind turned to *Nyx* and she wondered how they were doing. It seemed like years since she left the ship.

"Why did you join the Fleet Chief? You'd have been an excellent Marine," Cole asked softly from the other side of the bunker.

Shia looked back down at him, "Wasn't given the option. I was handed a contract and put on a shuttle. I got off the shuttle a Master Chief Petty Officer," she replied.

"You're one of the twelve!" he said surprised, "That explains a lot."

"What's that supposed to mean?" Shia asked defensively.

"It explains why you're so good. The original crew is all exceptional," he said seriously.

Shia relaxed, "I just have a lot of experience fighting. It's all I have ever done."

"You obviously have had a lot of training. You even repair your own armor."

Shia grunted, "I first learned in the alpha model, it was

much simpler. Had these weird errors all the time, guess I got good at fixing them."

Cole looked at her surprised, "Alpha? Those were fielded seventy years ago. I grew up looking at them in the Fleet museum. Why did you train in one, and where, because I want to try it."

Shia grimaced and scolded herself internally. That info had slipped out accidentally.

Whatever I'm going to die here anyway, she thought morosely.

"Sorry Cole, I didn't mean to say that. I am objectively very old. It's a long story," she said pensively.

He sat there for a minute in silence, "You're more than a hundred years old..." he said in awe, "That means you were around before the war!"

Shia leaned back and looked up at the stars, "Yes, yes I was," she said moodily

"What's wrong Chief?" Staff Sergeant Colfax asked her quietly.

She sighed and looked at him, "Nothing," she lied.

"Doesn't look like nothing," he said sheepishly.

"Fine, you want to know? It's eating me up inside that I left Katherine's side. I swore I would stay by her side and not an hour later I left her and she... she..." Shia couldn't even say it. She fought the lump in her throat, "I can't close my eyes without seeing her."

Cole sat there and waited for her to continue.

She lay her head in her hands, "Damn Goody, he wouldn't let me get her any help. I can't even look at him without getting angry even though it's not his fault! What's worse is that I know he was right," she blurted, "I wish I had been killed next to her, Cole, I miss her so much!" Shia scrunched her face up tightly. "I can't believe I just said that!" she said in shock.

"You obviously cared about her," Cole replied casually, "You shouldn't be embarrassed about it."

She looked up at him sadly, "It shouldn't have happened,

wasn't supposed to happen... What am I saying, nothing did happen."

Cole raised an eyebrow at her in mock confusion.

"I've been around a long time. This has never happened to me and I having a little crisis," Shia said, "I'm sorry, I shouldn't have said anything."

Cole smiled, "It's ok Chief, we all need to get it out sometimes," -they sat quietly for a while. Finally, he looked up, "By the way after all your years, you couldn't have chosen a more deserving person than Commander Carroll. It was obvious she had feelings for you."

Tears silently ran down Shia's face.

"Try to get some sleep Chief, I'll take first watch," Staff Sergeant Colfax said to her.

Shia nodded, "Thank you Cole," she said halfheartedly. She let her thoughts drift and shortly her thoughts returned to Katherine who lay in shallow defilade only meters away. It had been days since the breathing tube failed and Katherine's vitals had ceased. Shia refused to let her go hoping that bringing her home would stifle her guilt and heartache.

Cadet Katherine Carroll
Western Barrier Mountains
Alesia, Clare System
332.0188 FCUDT 05:00:00

Time no longer existed. The incredible open expanse allowed her consciousness to stretch out everywhere. The hundreds of computer nodes allowed her to think dozens of thoughts simultaneously. It was total freedom. Data flowed around Katherine as a remote part of her awareness connected to another source. This one felt vaguely familiar. As she moved on part of her kept returning to that data. She felt like there was something important she was supposed to remember.

Withdrawing a dozen processes and concentrating she

returned to the data and examined it. It shined like a brilliant silver thread. A face flashed through her mind. It was of a woman with dark auburn hair, deep gray eyes, and sharp chin.

Katherine followed the flow of data towards the source trying to remember more. As she neared the source of the local data the ambiguous forms reconfigured into an open plane with points on it. The amazing silver thread terminated into the plane near seven other thin threads. This is important she considered. The image of that smiling face passed through her mind again and Katherine felt something. It came from somewhere nearby.

Slowly she withdrew more of her consciousness from the vast fields of data and concentrated on remembering. That face haunted her. "Katherine where are you?" She heard faintly. Shia! She suddenly remembered. Alesia, I'm on Alesia she thought. I died on Alesia... Wait I felt something, something real. She scanned the data field and found where the feeling came from. As she neared it she opened the data and stared at it.

Her body lay surrounded by bright green and silver waves of electromagnetic data. She studied it carefully trying to figure out what it was. Her body beneath the waves had no vital signs but there was intense activity in her brain. She suddenly recognized the green waves. Nanites she thought, that's the nanite suit. A thought occurred to her. Nanites...

Reaching out to the vast data network she focused on the nanites and connected to them. After a few minutes the bright green and silver waves began to flow in beautiful ribbons and waves as they circled and looped through her body.

She started to merge back into her body but hesitated. The freedom of the data network nagged at her mind. It would be so easy to simply forget and return to that incredible place. The desire was overwhelming. After experiencing such freedom and immensity she was loathe to return to the confines of her organic mind.

Katherine looked at the data surrounding her. Accessed them and tried to see what was there. The com system was buzzing with activity.

"Their moving in on the left flank!" she heard Goody yell.

"Barnes is hit; I need help on the left... now!" Staff Sergeant Colfax said as explosions and plasma interference buzzed in the background.

Where is Shia she thought. The bright silver thread of data flickered and caught her attention. As she looked at it Shia's voice came on the com faintly.

"Goody, I can't hold them... I've ..."

Katherine watched as two bright streaks of plasma smashed into Shia.

She needs help... Katherine thought frantically.

Commander Helen Dower
Medical Bay Alpha, Deck Four
Nyx, Clare System
332.0188 FCUDT 19:47:12

"My head!" Helen suddenly croaked through a dry throat. It was throbbing and pounding intensely.

Brynn leaned over her, "Easy Helen, the pain will subside," she said placing a medical patch on Helen's forehead.

"What happened?" Helen asked quietly.

"You don't remember?" Brynn asked softly.

"I... it's all sort of a blur. I remember terrible nightmares, demons and monsters," Helen said scared.

"You took a serious dose of radiation about a month ago. We didn't know about it. It caused you to develop a rather nasty tumor in your brain. I suspect that is the source of your nightmares and likely the memory problems. Hopefully your memory will return soon," Brynn said smiling.

Helen looked confused for a second, then alarmed. "Radiation! you have to check Breaker, the pilot who brought me back from the damaged freighter. We flew right through a cloud of nuclear debris," Helen said quickly then clenched her teeth and moaned.

"Stay calm Helen, your blood pressure will cause your head to hurt worse," Brynn said cautiously, "Breaker, the pilot? I will have someone get him in for a scan, relax."

Helen closed her eyes, "How am I?" she asked.

"Doing well, we managed to shrink the tumor by ninety percent and it should be completely gone in a day. The radiation poisoning on the other hand will be trickier. Several months of treatments will keep you from having any relapse but it could be years before it's gone entirely. Being in space won't make it any easier, any more radiation and you will suffer permanent damage," Brynn said softly, "You're going to have to be careful."

"Be careful in combat... really," Helen said sadly.

"Yes, Helen. Don't be a hero. You've already proven yourself more than once," Sam said walking up.

"I'm no hero," Helen said even more despondently.

"I'm glad you're up, Xander is climbing bulkhead worrying about you," Sam said smiling.

"Xander..." Helen said fighting tears.

"Helen, he's worried sick about you. I had to order him to leave so he could get some food and rest. Otherwise he'd be sitting here in the bed next to you getting fluids for exhaustion," Sam said seriously.

Brynn put her hand on Helen's shoulder- "Get some rest, Xander will be here when you wake up," Brynn activated the med control and Helen slipped back asleep.

Brynn sighed, "She'll be fine Samantha."

"We need her back soon," Sam said concerned.

"I know but she has experienced a rather severe traumatic episode. She seems ok now but much of her actions cannot be explained by the tumor alone. Her depression and anxiety was triggered by the destruction of the engineering bay," Brynn explained, "I can't tell you if she will be capable of duty until she has recovered a bit."

Sam nodded, "Do your best Brynn."

Captain Kelli Anne Vellius
Captain's Quarters
FCS Revenge, Briton Space London System
332.0188 FCUDT 22:39:37

Kelli walked back to her cabin on *Revenge* numbly after finally finishing the last planning session in New London. She closed the hatch and stripped her formal uniform off scattering it across the deck haphazardly. She barely made it to the bed before she collapsed sobbing and curling up into a fetal position under several layers of blankets. Finally, after an hour she fell into a fitful sleep with her face in a wet pillow.

In her dreams she was chasing Josh down the passageway in her morning runs but could never catch him. Her leg jerked involuntarily in her sleep.

The com tone chirped and woke her up. She opened her eyes painfully.

"Captain, I'm sorry to bother you. Admiral Dunkirk wishes to speak to you. Captain? Captain?" her XO called from the com.

She lay there a second before responding, "I'll be out in a moment," she said to the empty room. She sat up and ran her hands through her messy half wet hair. Stepping onto the wash room the sudden light burned her eyes and she blinked at her image in the mirror. Tying her hair back she washed her face and grabbed her pressure suit.

Several minutes later she walked out onto the Bridge. She saw the crew was busy setting up the procedures for attaching to the Briton ships. Commander Tristan Reese nodded at her arrival, "Ma'am Admiral Dunkirk for you on your personal com," he said indicating at the command chair.

"Thank you Tristan," she said dully and stepped up the dais headed for her chair. Admiral Dunkirk appeared on the com- "Sorry to keep you waiting Admiral," she said trying to look presentable.

"Captain, sorry it's so late but I needed to speak to you before my command ship approached," Admiral Dunkirk said.

"Is there something wrong Admiral?" she asked concerned.

"Captain, the destroyer I have been assigned is command classified secret. It possesses technology we assume you are unaware of. We call it graviton slip stealth. I didn't want you or your crew alarmed when we approached your ship," she winked, "You have your secrets we have ours."

Kelli grimaced, "Indeed Admiral. I am so notified. Approach at your leisure," Kelli looked at Tristan, "XO Briton destroyer on approach it will be unusual. Hold all tac channels."

XO Reese nodded, "Aye Ma'am."

Suddenly directly in front of them a ship shimmered into full view. It was extraordinary. A long faceted cylinder with six thick fins that circled the main body. The fins glowed green as they floated tens of meters from the body of the ship. As they watched the fins moved sliding down the body to form two flat wings on either side of the ship.

The communications Petty Officer snapped straight, "Ma'am, com. Greetings from the HMS *Seraph*. Ready to link for docking."

The crew sat staring at the ship in amazement.

"Admiral, I'm impressed, your ship is very beautiful," Kelli said tearing her eyes off the sight.

"Thank you Captain. The slip wings can reposition for attachment to your ship. We are transmitting limited engineering data for the hardpoints."

Kelli nodded as the data flowed in, "As soon as you're

attached we can depart. I'd love to have you here on our bridge for the transit, I'm sure you will find it most enlightening."

Admiral Dunkirk tipped her head in minor disbelief, "I would be honored. I will alert you when I can board," she said grinning happily, "Until then Milady Baroness Clare." She said winking.

Tristan chuckled, "Never thought I would see the day a Briton Admiral called a Federation Officer, Baroness..."

"Stow it XO, get that ship locked on," she growled at him. She took a deep breath and sat up straight- "Alright people I want this ship locked up tight, every department owes me a green light before we leave. You have four hours," she said to the open com.

Tactical and navigation opened their consoles and began linking to the *Seraph*. Engineering was scouring the holo that showed the hardpoints for both ships. She looked at the engineers.

"Let me know when you have an ETA for the link up," she said to them.

"Aye Ma'am, preliminary look says three hours to lock them on. Displacement is less than our calculations. No problems with the pending transit," the Officer said.

"Thank you," leaning back, she closed her eyes and gritted her teeth. I will make them pay she thought. The Ottoman's will die. Her depression suddenly turned to anger and pain that boiled up inside her.

Tapping her com she connected with the master gunner.

"Yes Ma'am," he answered immediately.

"Guns, I want nuclear tipped ship killer, CT anti-matter flechette missiles and triple our inventory of nuclear and graviton mines," she said to him.

"Nuclear Ma'am? But the Morrow Accord..." he said pausing for a moment. Seeing the look in her eyes he nodded, "Yes Ma'am, right away."

The Morrow accord was an agreement on the rules of war between many nations in the spiral arm. It was so old that nations today don't even realize they abide by it. It states that the destructive power of ship carried weapons is limited to a certain level. Nuclear weapons are not enabled inside a system limit and that mines will self-destruct after a certain time frame. In effect it kept warfare humane. What Kelli just ordered violated that accord. She is going to fire nuclear missiles very close to a planet, drop non timed nuclear mines and use one of the deadliest missiles in the Federated inventory.

The Carbon Titanium Anti-Matter Flechette was designed at the closing of the Colonial war as a last resort weapon. When fired it closed on the target and burst into millions of tiny missiles. Singular these tiny missiles could do little but they were small enough to evade point defenses and slip right through shields. Once they penetrate, the tiny shards mass and impact in waves boring through the hull of the target with antimatter. Inside a ship they cause incredible devastation eating it from the inside.

Flipping the com over to the Master at Arms, he looked up as it activated, "Master Chief, I want every crewmember armed and at level two armor in four hours. We're going to war."

He nodded, "Aye Captain I have already begun issuing weapons. Level two may interfere with a few jobs..."

"Level two. Everybody. This is going to get close and personal. If someone refuses, leave them here. Four hours," she said flatly.

"Done Ma'am!" he said smartly.

XO Reese glanced at her carefully. Her face was clouded and dark as she stared back at him.

Four hours later Kelli stood in level two armor at the main airlock as it cycled and opened. Admiral Dunkirk stood tall and confident in front of two Briton legionaries in level two armor.

"Welcome aboard *Revenge* Admiral," Kelli said as she saluted smartly.

271

"Thank you Captain. The *Seraph* is tucked in and ready for transit," the Admiral replied returning her salute.

"If you'll follow me we can be underway. Your sentries can join the marines at the Bridge hatch if you like," Kelli said as they stepped away.

Admiral Dunkirk nodded at the legionaries and they followed, "I see you're ready for combat," she said indicating the crew in armor.

"Yes, I intend to prove to the Ottoman's we are not to be trifled with," she said with a predatory grimace.

Admiral Dunkirk looked at her with approval, "A stateswoman and a warrior. I knew I liked you Kelli."

They stepped onto the Bridge and the Admirals tone sounded. The crew snapped to attention.

XO Reese snapped a salute, "Admiral the Joint Federation Briton crew of *Revenge* welcomes you to the Bridge."

The Admiral returned his salute, "Thank you XO, and thank you to your excellent crew. The docking procedure was handled with precision that reflects you and your Captain. Please carry on."

Reese turned to Captain Vellius, "Captain?"

Kelli nodded, "Take us out XO."

"Aye Ma'am, twenty minutes to gravity limit," he turned to navigation, "Nav send course to the core, Tactical clear the surrounding space, Com get our departure clearance from traffic control, Engineering prepare to charge the drives," he ordered with precision.

"XO extending the joust," Engineering called out.

"Bringing up *Seraph's* bridge on port holoscreen," Com called out. To their left the Briton ships bridge appeared. Its crew looked all attentive.

"Give me an all station status check," XO Reese called out.

"Helm is green. Navigation is green. Tactical is green, course clear. Com is green, departure approved. Engineering is green, Dower coming up, stress in limits, reactors at one hundred, all ships report ready for transit," came the associated replies.

Tristan turned to Kelli, "Ma'am the ship is green, ready for transit at your command."

Kelli nodded and looked at Admiral Dunkirk, "You showed us your secret, now I am going to show you ours," Kelli watched the timer count down to the gravity limit, as it reached zero she nodded at XO Reese- "Engage transit to Clare."

"Engineering, engage the Dower Drive!" he called out.

One kilometer in front the ship an invisible field formed, fed by the emitters mounted on the bow. The aft rods vibrated as invisible energy from the center of the field expelled out behind the ship in a dizzying display of blue. As the energy readings dropped below the threshold the superconducting accelerators fired concentrated gravimetric particles from the reactors directly into the center of the void.

The gravimetric particles began to spin into a vortex faster and faster forming a torus. As the torus stabilized the third stage initiated. The CoNeE drives created a graviton spike that drove right into the center of the torus.

As the graviton spike was fired a blue circle formed expanding to two hundred meters in diameter. The huge release of energy burst from the outer edges of the circle. Super charged particles discharged perpendicular from the blue ring in a brilliant iridescent shower beginning blue and moving through the spectrum as they burned out in their second-long lifespan. As they dissipated a pencil thin blue line enclosed a fisheye lens that shined back at them.

Admiral Dunkirk's breath caught in her throat, "My lord, it's an Einstein Rosen..." she looked at Kelli in awe, "This will change everything."

Kelli grinned, "Yes it will, Admiral."

"Navigation course confirmed, gravity bubble collapsing," Engineering announced. The ship was propelled forward by the narrowing gravity well behind them. They slid past the event horizon and into another form of space.

"ETA to Clare nine hours seventeen minutes. All ships report green, no damage from transit," Engineering called out.

Admiral Dunkirk chuckled, "I always imagined wormhole travel would be instantaneous."

"Yes but unfortunately there is actual relative distance between the event horizons. Also we can only use the built up inertia from the initial gravity pulse to cross that distance. Any graviton emission could disrupt the geometry and throw us out... literally anywhere in space between entry and exit," Kelli replied.

"Delicate maneuver."

"Extremely," Kelli nodded.

Cadet Katherine Carroll
Western Barrier Mountains
Alesia, Clare System
333.0188 FCUDT 10:37:19

I'm coming Katherine thought as she plunged into her own mind. The expansive data fields receded and suddenly everything went blank. Time stopped.

Slowly Katherine became aware of cold prickling in her cheeks and lips. The words 'status check complete' floated through her mind. She felt the data connection in the quantum core open and suddenly she could see darkness. Not the darkness of her mind but actual sight. Her neuro link connected to her suit and began the power up sequences as she tried to figure out what was going on.

She tried to remember where she was and how she got here but got nothing. What's the last thing I remember before this she thought slowly.

I was injured... my spine, she thought.

Her suit connected and data streamed through her mind as the suit slowly came online. She had to check the date

274

twice to make sure it wasn't a mistake; I've been in the network seven days! She thought alarmed. Concerned she tried to move and realized she couldn't feel her body. Couldn't move her fingers or hands. Panic began to build in her mind. She couldn't feel herself breathing or her heart beating...

She forced herself to calm down. She explored the data in her quantum core. Finally, she found it. Medical data popped into her mind. Yes, she thought as she saw it. I severed my spinal cord and burst several organs. She plunged into her medical implant and checked her current status. Organ damage repaired, spine reconstructed... She tried to suppress the sudden irritation she felt over the limited power of her organic mind. Why can't I move! She thought.

Suddenly her memory flooded back in a tidal wave of emotion. She squeezed her eyes closed tightly as she painfully remembered telling Shia to leave her in that field. She was dying, she remembered. Why am I not dead? Seven days ago I should have died. She turned her attention back to her cybernetics.

Something must still be wrong, I can't move. As she sifted through the data she found a new subroutine in her suits control systems. Without a second thought she activated it.

Searing pain flashed through her body and she squeezed her eyes shut as the pain crashed into her. In seconds it subsided. Slowly she opened her eyes and looked out at the darkness again. She concentrated and tried to move her arm.

Nothing. She could feel the air currents swirl and move around her. She suddenly realized she was not alone. She could hear someone standing beside her.

"Something's happening! We must have triggered the internal power systems," a heavily accented voice said.

"Monitor it. All we need is for some self-destruct system to go off," a deeper voice said.

"No Colonel its low power, like a computer core," he said.

Katherine suddenly realized her suit was translating for her. The voices were speaking Ottoman. Impossible she thought. Was I captured? Katherine initiated a subsonic ping and mapped her immediate surrounding with sonar.

"Dear lord! The suit just fired off a sonar ping," the man said alarmed.

Katherine explored the digital map of the sonar ping. She was in some sort of vehicle. There were two people standing by her side and not much else.

An alarm gently brought her attention back to her body. The Ottoman male was attempting to pry open her chest piece. Ridiculous she thought its nanite sealed composite armor. It takes a graviton field to release the bonds. She instinctively focused on her chest piece and felt the armor respond to her mind. Odd she thought.

"Did you see that?" the man cried out.

The Colonel leaned over him, "What?"

"The armor, it rippled or something," he said pointing at it.

"Do what you were doing again, let me see," he replied.

He reached out and positioned the pry bar on her chest.

Katherine mentally recoiled against the intrusion. Suddenly her armor responded. A sharp half meter long spike grew out of her chest in the space of microseconds. It pierced the man directly through the heart and retracted back to normal. The man stumbled back against the Colonel gasping.

"What's wrong?" the Colonel demanded alarmed. "What just happened?" he asked as the man fell to his knees. Coughing up a lung full of blood he collapsed dead on the floor of the vehicle as the Colonel stood above him in shock.

Katherine was stunned. She couldn't believe what had just happened. The armor seemed to twitch and vibrate around her. Her body began to buzz and the vibrating intensified. She activated her helmet and it slid back exposing her head. She forced her eyes open and found herself staring in the dark brown eyes of an Ottoman Officer.

Those eyes instantly went wide and the Colonel lurched back against the bulkhead in total shock. "Impossible," he uttered. "The scans all confirmed death." He said to himself.

Katherine tried to move but the suit just convulsed violently. She thrashed about for a second then mentally forced herself to stop moving. The Colonel stood rooted in shock watching her struggle. She very carefully tried to isolate the movements in order to sit up. Her armor instantly complied and she found herself once again staring at the Ottoman Colonel.

He stared back at her, "You're, you're dead," he said in hollow voice.

Katherine opened her mouth but couldn't speak. She suddenly realized she wasn't breathing and panic flooded her mind again. Breathe she screamed in her head. Her body immediately took a breath. After a few breaths she began to relax. I can do this she thought. Breathe in, breathe out, she recited in her mind. She remembered the Colonel and looked at him again. He was trying to pull out his handgun.

"That won't do you any good," Katherine managed in perfect Ottoman.

The Colonel froze and slowly looked back up at her. "Dragur. God save me," he croaked in fear. He finally managed to pull out his handgun.

Before he raised his hand Katherine snapped out and grabbed his arm. Her suit convulsed again and her whole body followed her hand. She slammed into the Colonel with a violent shudder severing his arm cleanly off between the bulkhead and her suit. He stumbled back away from her as blood poured out of the wound.

Katherine slammed into the bulkhead again as her arm

swung violently in front of her. She smashed her hand down on the table and forced herself to stop moving. Activating her quantum core she scrolled through diagnostics. Something is wrong she thought frantically. Every time I move the suit goes crazy. The diagnostics returned without any errors. She tried to move her hand off the table but couldn't. Looking down at it she saw that the suit had extended several spikes into the metal of the table locking her hand to it. She stared at it in amazement. She yanked it with all her force and the suit reacted violently again. The table snapped loose from the bulkhead smashed into the ceiling still attached to her hand.

"Let go!" she shouted angrily. The spikes suddenly retracted and the table crashed to the floor. What is going on she thought standing in the wreckage of the small blood splattered room. After a few seconds she took a long breath and looked at the wounded Colonel. Ok, I can do this she thought. She carefully stepped over to the Colonel and grabbed the wall to keep the suit stable.

"Where are my Marines?" she said in Ottoman.

The Colonel stared up at her with fear- "Please," he said quietly.

"I'm not going to ask you again," she said evenly.

He winced visibly- "Outside, we have them pinned down," he nodded to a terminal on the wall, "There you can access the information. Please Dragur, don't kill me," he pleaded.

Katherine looked at the terminal and wirelessly connected with it through her cybernetics. In seconds she had all the Ottoman data. They're all ok, she thought in intense relief. She also found the Ottoman operations plan. They were set to overtake the Marines. Well let's see how they deal with this, she though as she hacked into the armored vehicle network. She triggered the automatic defense systems and reset the friend or foe identification system. The vehicle she was in suddenly identified five enemies in range. Unfortunately for the Ottoman those enemies were fellow Ottoman vehicles. Katherine grinned wolfishly as the vehicles powered up their weapons and opened fire on each other.

"Good morning Helen, you look much better," Sam said as she entered the medical bay.

"All thanks to Doc Driscoll, she'll probably start charging me if I get hurt again," Helen said darkly.

"Oh we have a bill; Captains just been paying it for you..." Sam teased her as she sat down next to Helen's bed.

"Oh Sam, I can't remember what was real and what was hallucination," Helen said seriously, "Last thing I remember as being real was Captain Stuart telling me to fix the power problem... after that it gets really strange."

Sam put her hand on Helen's arm, "Don't worry about it. Your fine now and that's all that matters," Sam grinned, "Besides you must have fixated on that order because you built some weird looking thing in the Engineering bay," she said lightheartedly.

Helen froze. She looked at Sam in disbelief.

"Oh Helen I didn't mean to..." Sam started.

"I thought that was a hallucination. What have I done?" Helen interrupted Sam.

"It's ok Helen. In your own way I think you were trying to fix our power problem," Sam said.

Helen groaned and curled up into a ball.

Sam smiled and put her hand on Helen's shoulder- "It's too bad we can't just use the higgs to jump across the system and recharge the reactors," Sam said casually.

Helen turned and looked at Sam wide eyed- "That's a good question," Helen said quietly.

Sam raised her eyebrow, "Can we?" she asked.

Helen looked at her like she was crazy, "No of course not. The curvature of space-time prevents time paradoxes like less than a light year jumps..."

Sam looked confused, "Ok, I don't know what you just said but it sounded pretty technical."

Grabbing her nearby tablet, she opened her personal files. In a few seconds Helen was absorbed in theoretical physics and seemed to forget Sam was there.

Sam sat there for a bit watching Helen to be sure she was doing ok before she left. On her way out she saw Brynn in the passageway.

"How is she?" Brynn asked Sam.

Sam looked back through the window at Helen and felt badly for her- "She is having pretty wild emotional mood swings. She got absorbed in her math so I left her alone."

Brynn nodded- "She is avoiding dealing with things. The abstract is a wonderfully easy escape for her," Brynn looked at Sam, "Give her time."

Sam frowned, "Unfortunately Doc we don't have much left."

Alarms sounded and Asteria looked up at them in the conference room, "Captain, a brigantine has slipped through the sensor net. It is enroute to the planet. Three corvettes are in pursuit."

"XO let's go," Adam said to Sam.

As she ran onto the bridge Sam looked at Simay- "Update!" she called out.

"Ma'am one Ottoman Brigantine is on full burn to the planet. There are three Clare corvettes on intercept and the planets defense platforms are spooling up," Simay reported.

"Good, has the hole in the perimeter been plugged?" she asked.

"Yes Ma'am, SDPs have been restructured, nobody else is coming through," Tactical replied.

"Corvettes entering engagement range, fighters detected! Three, no four Ottoman fighters on ballistic course for the planet. They're going to get through."

"Damn, get an alert off. We need to tell Alesia to expect company," Sam said.

"Sorry Ma'am, still no communication from the planet," Joe said from the com console.

Sam dropped into her command chair heavily- "They'll be ok..." she said to herself quietly.

Cadet Katherine Carroll
Western Barrier Mountains
Alesia, Clare System
333.0188 FCUDT 10:37:19

Antimatter warheads slammed into the Ottoman vehicle next to Katherine as she staggered away like a drunken adolescent. Her armor just wouldn't cooperate with her mind. As bright bursts of plasma flashed past she jerked and staggered around oblivious to the Ottoman Soldiers who ran past in confusion. She collapsed to the ground and in exasperation tried to crawl away. The ground seemed to move in front of her. Spatial disorientation spun her around and she gagged as her mind reeled in bewilderment.

Behind her one of the Ottoman vehicles went critical and exploded in sudden fury. She started laughing at the pure insanity of the situation. Relax she told herself as she opened her helmet and took a deep breath. Slowly she stood back up and continued on in starts and stops. Suddenly she toppled over again and thrashed about in frustration. Lying on her back she studied the data from her suit desperately looking for the fault that was causing this. I must have done something wrong with the nanites. Fear and anger spiked through her mind. Just to be sure she looked at her neural connection data and suddenly saw it. The connection speed was three hundred times normal.

That's impossible she thought.

If my connection speed is so fast I'm not going to be able to control my body with my organic brain, she reasoned. She rolled her eyes, of course, she chided herself. I'm not using my cybernetic core. I have only been activating it to run diagnostics.

I've been afraid to fully open the connection because I'm afraid I'll not be able to resist returning to the network she realized. Laying there she gritted her teeth in resignation. She would have to face it and try to remember why she was doing this. By reprogramming the nanites after getting hurt her body now required control by the quantum core in her head. It also threatened to whisk her away into oblivion.

Katherine mentally triggered the core and in a sweeping mental move she plunged into the massive flow of data. Her body jerked and shuttered. Her awareness flashed out beyond her body and into multiple wavelengths. Her physical body was barely a flicker in her awareness. Her mind shrieked at the sudden loss of her body as she was swept away in the onslaught of information. Suddenly she could see, hear, and feel everything all at once. Electromagnetic signals, data streams, cosmic radiation, pulsar bursts, and even the faint data stream from the AI data net crashed into her. If she was breathing she would have gasped.

Fighting to filter the flow of data she reached out in the hurricane looking for something to hold onto. She found Shia's signal that shined brightly in her awareness, and she latched onto it. She forced her mind to explore that signal and slowly expanded it into single pieces of data. She lost it a time or two before she finally was able to hang on to it.

Suit diagnostics, com logs, ammunition inventories, biomedical information, and Marine operation plans appeared out of the data. Katherine felt intense relief as she remained in control of both the quantum core and her organic mind. She activated the com signal and after a second the signal confirmed.

Shia, are you there, she sent via neuro com.

Katherine! Is that really you? Where are you? Shia sent back immediately.

I'm just inside of the Ottoman position. I'm having a few difficulties, Katherine sent with relief.

How is that possible? I... we... I had to leave you Katherine, I so sorry! Shia replied.

I don't know how to explain. I woke up in an Ottoman vehicle this morning. I slowed them down a little and escaped. I am having some difficulties, there's something wrong with me.

The explosions! That was you? Hold on Katherine I'm coming, Shia replied.

Commander Samantha Leeane
Bridge
Nyx, Clare System
333.0188 FCUDT 10:45:28

"Captain there is a gap in the system defense platform network. I cannot cover the entire sector any longer," Commander Asteria Hypnea reported.

"What's the status of the enemy fleet?" he said rapidly.

"They are moving to engage; they will be inside the limit in thirty minutes," Asteria reported.

"Navigation, plot an intercept. Com, alert the remaining Clare vessels," he ordered. He slapped his com, "Jacob, tell me we have enough power in the reactors. We have to move, now!"

"Sir, I can give you three hours max.... Running test sequences now. I'll let you know," Jacob replied stressed.

"Don't let me know just do it!" he said.

"Captain course in, intercept in thirty-six minutes," Lieutenant Binici called.

"Callis engage!" Adam called out.

"Aye Sir, engaging," Major Kane replied as the ship jumped into motion.

Sam jumped up and ran to the tactical holo in time to see the first ships turn towards the gap in their defenses. "Corvette inbound," she reported.

"Guns, I want a full broadside on the first ship to enter

that hole," he said to Lieutenant Commander Volkov-Delaney.

Alarm sirens sounded throughout the ship bringing them to level one alert. The automated point defenses extended and missile covers retracted.

"Ten minutes to intercept," Lieutenant Binici called out, "Sir I have additional ships entering the system..."

"What?" Adam demanded.

Captain Kelli Anne Vellius
Bridge
FCS Revenge, Interstellar Space
333.0188 FCUDT 10:50:49

Captain Kelli Vellius stood silently on the bridge waiting. She glanced over at the port holoscreen and saw Admiral Dunkirk doing the same.

Admiral Dunkirk looked up at Kelli and nodded- "Twelve minutes," she said quietly.

Kelli nodded. They had twelve minutes to detach the *Seraph*, one corvette and half the fighters, get clear and transit back out of the system. It was cutting it very close but time was essential for the plan to work. They needed to catch them by surprise.

"Event horizon in ten seconds," announced Engineering.

There was a slight shudder and the holoscreens popped to life.

"Transit complete, twelve minutes to recharge," announced Engineering, "Beginning separation."

Admiral Dunkirk smiled, "Captain, see you in twenty-four minutes."

Kelli nodded, "Good hunting *Seraph*."

The Briton destroyer slowly slid away from the *Revenge* and as it cleared the shields it suddenly vanished into stealth.

"*Seraph* away. Corvette *Titan* is away," Engineering announced, "Clear for transit in four minutes."

Kelli studied the tactical data as it came in on passive sensors. Two Frigates of battle cruiser size, five Barques of destroyer size, and ten Brigantines of corvette size. They were circling the graviton limit like sharks in bloody water. She saw the gap in the system defense grid and the vectors of the enemy altering to head for it.

"Looks like they just found a hole in the SDP grid. *Nyx* is powering up to engage. They're going to break through," XO Reese said quietly.

"Engaging Dower Drive, transit in two minutes," Engineering called out.

Kelli nodded, "Look at the data readout. They're extremely low on power. They won't survive the next engagement."

"Stars, it must be extremely uncomfortable on that ship." Reese said in awe.

"Transit!" Engineering called out, "position verified, recharge in twelve minutes."

Kelli sighed, "Ok, we're ready," she said as she walked back to her command chair. She reached down and activated the control panel. Alarms sounded across the ship. "All crew secure stations for high G combat maneuvers, repeat all crew secure for high G combat maneuvers," she announced. She turned to the bridge crew and stared hard, "Ladies and Gentleman this is what we train for, you all saw our comrades in trouble, you all saw the enemy, now they will see us. They will pay for this treachery and it is us who will exact that price. Secure all stations and go to level one alert," she sat and activated her chairs restraints.

"Ma'am, Dower online. Ready to enter system on your command," Engineering announced.

"Let's go," she said calmly.

CHAPTER NINE
Legionary

Master Chief Shia O'Connell
Western Mountains, Marine Firebase
Alesia, Clare System
333.0188 FCUDT 10:48:59

Shia jumped out of the defilade and pulled up the tactical map. Katherine's personal transponder suddenly popped to life on the map two point six kilometers away. Katherine I'm on my way, she thought. Triggering her com she spoke to Master Sergeant Goody.

"Goody, I made contact with Katherine. Her transponder just went active; I'm going to her," she said hurriedly.

"Shia that's not possible. Have you lost your mind? It has to be a trap, the Ottomans picked up her body," Goody instantly said back to her, "You need to stay in your position."

"She sent me a neuro com message, that can't be faked Goody," Shia retorted.

"That doesn't mean it isn't a trap, she must have been compromised somehow. Shia this is crazy, we saw her bio scans, and she was gone," he snapped back.

She turned and looked at his position twenty meters away- "We're pinned down! You saw the explosions and they have fallen back. This is the only chance we're going to get!" she said setting off across the northeast plains.

"Shia! Don't be stupid we don't have any intel!" he said loudly.

"No. No we don't! I am going to retrieve our commander," she said with force.

"Cole take Jimmy and go get the Master Chief! She has apparently lost her mind!" Goody said on the open channel.

"On it Master Sergeant," Cole said briskly as he jumped out of the defilade, "Jimmy, move out."

"Don't bother Cole," Shia said.

Cole trotted up to Shia and nodded, "Chief are you positive about this?" he asked her kneeling down behind cover.

"Don't even try to stop me," she said defensively.

He kneeled there looking at her, "Well let's go take a look then. Come on Jimmy," Cole said.

She looked up- "Thank you Cole."

"No problem Chief. Believe it or not I don't think we should leave her here regardless of her condition," he said seriously.

Sporadic plasma fire flashed past them as they creeped into the Ottoman line. Up ahead an armored vehicle exploded in a fury of antimatter splashing the surrounding area with shrapnel and shredding several hapless Ottoman Soldiers. Cole leaned out and shot an Ottoman rifleman as he ran for cover.

Shia sighed and looked at her tactical map to check her progress and noticed the emergency com signal flashing. Stars Goody! What now? She activated her com and Goody immediately linked with her.

"Shia! We have inbound fighters. What is your status?" he said quickly.

Shia updated her tactical map and saw the inbound vectors of several Ottoman fighters.

"Goody, we're right in front of Katherine. What's the plan?"

"We're moving to better cover. There are some rock canyons to our north west that should do the job. I encourage you to quickly do the same," he said concerned.

Shia looked at the map carefully- "Good choice, I'm going to get Katherine and I'll meet you there."

Goody paused for a second, "Fine, you better hurry," he said in resignation.

Shia was already running as she acknowledged his transmission.

Commander Samantha Leeane
Bridge
Nyx, Clare System
333.0188 FCUDT 12:40:38

"Tactical what do you have for us?" Captain Stuart demanded, "Seven minutes to intercept, weapons coming online, shields charging!" Asteria said turning to her console.

"Course is two-five-seven up sixteen, velocity at point four light," Simay called, "We're going to flash past them at seventeen thousand kilometers."

Captain Stuart nodded, "Alright let's stay in this. Flip and burn, I want to curve back in on them after we pass," he sat back down and looked at the crew.

"Sir, inbound contact! It's as showing as an Ottoman brigand with a Higgs drive. Position three-four-four down ten, just outside the limit," Asteria said looking back at the Captain.

Captain Stuart's head snapped over to Asteria, "What!"

"Sir, friend and foe identifies it as... the *Revenge!*" Simay said surprised.

Sam brought up the tactical plot and looked at it carefully, "Two minutes to contact!" she said.

"All right focus. Natalia, full broadside. I want that ship stopped. Com hail *Revenge* as soon as we pass and update their tactical data," he sat back down, "Looks like the tide is turning."

Captain Kelli Anne Vellius
Bridge
FCS Revenge, Clare System
333.0188 FCUDT 12:45:22

"Captain systems updating. *Nyx* is engaging the lead brigand at two-four-seven up seventeen. They will be out of position in four minutes. Two frigates are in position to enter the inner system," Tactical called out.

Kelli looked at the plot with venom, "Helm I want full burn straight at the lead frigate. Cross their bow at one-nine-four down two."

"Ma'am that will put us less than three hundred meters..." Helm said looking at her.

"Do it or get off my bridge!" she said glaring.

He turned and programmed the maneuver, "Aye."

Kelli activated her com, "Guns, I want every tube loaded with ship killers. We're going to drop them ballistic as we go in," she triggered the com and turned to her weapons officer, "Program the missiles to go ballistic until they independently acquire target."

"Ma'am, passing point three light. Intercept in twenty-eight minutes," Navigation announced.

"Ma'am, *Nyx* is on com," the communications Petty Officer called out.

"On screen," Kelli called out. Captain Adam Stuart and Admiral Lune appeared on her holo, "Greetings, Admiral, Captain. Can I offer assistance?" Kelli said looking at them.

"Kelli, we're quite surprised to see you. I see you're on your way in," Admiral Lune said smiling.

"Yes Ma'am, I have much to update you on," Kelli said. She nodded to the com Petty Officer and Admiral Dunkirk appeared on the com- "Admiral Lune, may I introduce Admiral Dunkirk of the Briton Royal Fleet. We are here as a joint task force to secure Clare for the Federation."

Admiral Lune raised her eyebrows in surprise- "Well, it's a pleasure Admiral."

"Likewise Admiral Lune, I've heard much about you," Admiral Dunkirk replied smiling.

Kelli nodded at them, "We have arrived with two destroyers, two corvettes, and twelve fighters. To keep things simple Admiral, I suggest we refer to you as Commander of Clare forces and us as supporting joint task force."

Admiral Lune nodded, "Yes, I agree. Continue with

your current model and we will sort this obvious change in situation when the dust settles."

Admiral Dunkirk looked at them, "Agreed, Admiral Lune my ship is in route to the planet for inner defense, due to certain sensor enhancements my velocity is limited. I can best serve here at short range. I will be in orbit in ten minutes."

Captain Stuart looked up, "Admiral we have Marines on the planet. We have not been able to contact them can you support. There are Ottoman Soldiers marching on the settlement as we speak."

She nodded, "Of course Captain. I have a squad of legionaries with air support. I will dispatch them as soon as we arrive."

"Excellent, I am sending you my command codes to authenticate," he said.

Admiral Lune looked at Kelli, "What's your move Kelli."

"I'm inbound to attack the lead frigate; they will not survive. How do you feel about a crossfire Adam?" Kelli replied coldly.

Adam looked at her a moment, "Good idea, I will alter vector and join you after you attack."

"Ma'am, approaching drop point," Kelli's XO said.

"Ladies and gentleman I have an attack to perform," Kelli said bowing sarcastically.

Admiral Dunkirk smiled, "Good hunting Kelli."

Admiral Lune and Captain Stuart noticed the familiarity but stayed silent about it. "See you on the other side Captain," Admiral Lune said, "Admiral Dunkirk, thank you for your assistance, we will join you shortly," they all nodded and the com dropped.

"Ma'am, drop in twenty seconds," her XO said.

Kelli's head snapped to the Tactical Officer- "Drop the missiles!" she ordered.

Outside the dark predatory ship ten large nuclear ship killer missiles ejected from their ports and drifted away. The ship continued to power out in front leaving them behind despite their inertial speed of point five light. They all linked together and began scanning for the frigate in front of them. With no power signatures they were impossible for the Ottoman's to see. Silent deadly killers reached out and found their target.

"Missiles away Ma'am," the Gunnery officer said quietly.

Kelli watched them for several seconds before turning to the helm- "Engines to all stop, turn the ship to heading zero-nine-one down ten degrees. Standby for full thrust," she flipped the ships com, "All stations prepare for high gravity combat maneuvers."

Her XO stepped up and leaned over, "Cap, we're extremely vulnerable. Our engines are less than two hundred meters from their guns... Are you sure about this?"

She turned and looked at him with murderous eyes, "Yes," she said emphatically.

He stepped back stood straight, "Aye Ma'am."

The crew sat in uncomfortable silence watching the Ottoman frigate quickly approach. Threat icons burst to life on the tactical holo and still Kelli sat perfectly still watching the plot. After several agonizing minutes Kelli looked up at the helm, "In ten seconds go to one hundred and twenty percent on the thrusters. Maintain course. Guns, load tubes with flechettes," she said calmly and coldly.

Alarms sounded as the automated systems alerted the engine overload- "Shut that off," the XO ordered.

Everyone buckled their harnesses and prepared. "Engines to one twenty," Helm announced. They ship began to hum and slowly built up to a heavy shuddering. Kelli felt the inertia smashing her into her chair as the graviton plates fought to counter the acceleration.

"Missiles in space, impact in twenty-seven seconds," Tactical announced.

"Guns get the point defenses out and take out those missiles," Kelli ordered.

Outside the ship the plasma from the engines spewed out in a furious rage. The *Revenge* slid sideways across space approaching the oncoming frigate with the engines pointed straight at its nose. As the ships aligned subatomic particles from the *Revenge's* engine slammed into the frigate in a massive wave. The oncoming frigate instantly lost their forward sensors and communications as they vaporized in the subatomic wrath. The forward hull was illuminated in multiple spectrums as layers of armor blasted into particles.

The oncoming ship killer missiles spotted the sudden brilliance and ignited their engines. Already at point five light they accelerated at over one hundred gravities toward their target.

The oncoming missiles from the Ottoman ship lost contact and switched to the far inferior internal sensors. They were no match for *Revenge's* point defenses.

"Ma'am, ship killers inbound at speed," Gunnery announced.

Kelli looked up, "Helm crash turn to one-eight-two!" she ordered, "Follow the curve, inbound debris field."

The ship rattled and screeched. Kelli felt her insides twist and roll as the ship suddenly turned. Behind them the ship killers screamed into the target at point seven light. No shield known to human kind could stop an object moving that fast. Nine nuclear missiles detonated in a sudden magnificent blossom of fusion. For a few seconds there were two Suns in Clare as the incredible energy flashed out into space.

"Ma'am, impact, frigate is eliminated. Incoming debris field," Tactical called out with difficulty as the acceleration crushed at them.

Radiation sensors sounded and Kelli gripped her seats armrests. Come on hold together, Kelli thought as she looked for the next target. The ship suddenly heaved as the shock wave crashed into them.

Captain Mercan stared at the tactical display as the *Distania* erupted in a massive nuclear blast. His body went cold as he realized the he had lost the initiative. The arrival of the *Revenge* with two corvettes and the loss of the frigate didn't bode well for him.

He suddenly looked around the bridge for Captain Kartal as fear crept up his spine. He lurched to his feet and looked at his executive officer- "You have the bridge; I need to take care of something," he said absently, "Continue with the primary mission."

"Yes Sir!" the sub Captain replied.

Mercan strode to his ready room and dogged the hatch. He looked around to ensure he was alone and crossed to his desk where he kept his sidearm. Taking a deep breath, he locked the charging handle back and clicked off the safety. Sitting down he gripped the weapon and waited.

I have one shot he thought. My aim must be perfect.

Just as Mercan was beginning to doubt his conclusion the hatch unlocked. He took a deep breath as adrenaline ripped through his body. Senior Captain Kartal stepped into the room and stared at Mercan impassively.

"What are you doing in here Mercan? Shouldn't you be on the bridge?" he demanded.

"I had something to attend to. We're at least thirty minutes from weapons range," Mercan said blithely, "What can I do for you Kartal," he said noticing Kartal's sidearm.

Kartal stayed near the hatch and stared at him- "What is your plan to salvage this disaster?" he asked sarcastically.

Mercan tilted his head and half smiled, "I plan on taking a Brigand and leaving this system as soon as possible," he said shrugging.

Kartal was speechless, "That's going to be difficult..." he began.

Mercan raised his weapon and shot Kartal in the throat. Kartal stared at Mercan completely shocked. He gurgled once and collapsed to the deck in a heap. Mercan had to steady himself on the desk as he stood up on wooden legs. He quickly crossed to Kartal and shot him three more times to ensure he was dead.

I have to be quick he though as he holstered his sidearm and hurried to the hatch. As he opened the hatch his executive officer jumped.

"Captain, I heard something," he said quietly.

Mercan saw him notice Kartal's body on the floor and the very slight smile twitch on his mouth. He shut the hatch and looked at his XO- "I have to attend to something," he said carefully.

"I would be honored to assist Captain," his XO replied.

Mercan stared at him and slowly nodded. Without a word to the bridge crew they stalked off the bridge leaving the remaining officers staring questioningly at each other.

"What do you think they will do?" the XO asked.

"They will do what they are trained to do Captain Kosta, keep fighting to the death," he said confidently.

Kosta nodded as they headed for the shuttle bay.

Cadet Katherine Carroll
Western Plains
Alesia, Clare System
333.0188 FCUDT 12:02:07

For the past thirty minutes Katherine had carefully focused on the data flow. She slowly sorted and compartmentalized it. She was awestruck at her ability to maintain her hold on her own mind. She kept a small piece of her awareness firmly attached to Shia's signal.

Four Ottoman fighters popped up on the network and were inbound. Lying in the grass she reached out to their data feeds and connected.

A second tactical map overlay appeared from the Ottoman fighters. She saw the two groups of ground forces moving in. One was on the verge of attacking the settlement. She explored the data searching for weaknesses for several minutes.

"Katherine, are you ok?" Shia said as she dropped next to Katherine. Cole and Jimmy took up position next to them.

Katherine's attention snapped back and she opened her eyes- "Shia, we're in trouble. The Ottoman forces are closing on us and preparing to attack the settlement," she said calmly as she retracted her helmet.

Shia's eyes went wide as she saw Katherine's face- "Katherine what happened to you... you... look different. Katherine it's all my fault I should never have left you! We were being overrun and I couldn't get to you...!"

She connected to Shia's suit and looked at herself from Shia's video feed. Her skin was porcelain white. Her red hair was still very closely shaved as it had been weeks ago. The most startling change was her neuro implant. It no longer only traced a line from her left ear to her chin. It now continued around her chin to her right ear and both eyes. Her neuro implant glowed bright crystalline blue. Delicate filigree branched off of it at her temples.

She disconnected and looked at Shia, "I'm... I reprogrammed the nanites to keep me alive," she said flatly.

Shia nodded slightly and grabbed Katherine's hand, "Katherine, I'm so sorry for leaving you..." she started.

"Shia, it's ok, I'm ok." she said looking at her.

A fighter thundered past them- "We have to go," Shia said quickly. "Goody is nearby. Can you walk? We have to find cover from those fighters"

"The fighters. Hold on, I can take care of them," Katherine said to her, "Don't leave me this time," she smiled at her.

"That's not funny," Shia said with a lump in her throat.

Katherine closed her eyes and reached out through the quantum network for the fighters again. As one passed close she managed to access its com signal. In seconds she had invaded the Ottoman ships computer. Onboard the fighter the artificial gravity suddenly deactivated and the ship went into an incredible turn. Inside the pilot's brain blood vessels burst and hemorrhaged.

Katherine triggered the fighters twenty missiles and armed them as the fighter streaked toward the Ottoman Soldiers position. She set the ships course and disconnected.

She opened her eyes and stared at Shia smiling as the fighter impacted less than a kilometer away. The ground shook as the missiles erupted in a massive explosion.

"Have I said you're amazing," Shia said to her.

"I think so," Katherine said as she mentally reconnected to her armor and that powerful electric shock tore through her body again. She reeled from the increased data flow as all the sensors suddenly went online- "Ok step back, last time I killed someone by accident," she said cautiously.

Shia stood and gave her a concerned look.

"Long story," Katherine said smirking.

She carefully rose up and staggered forward a few steps then stabilized. Taking a long breath, she relaxed and her armor remained under control. The cybernetics flowed seamlessly through her mind and into the armor.

"Ok, I'm ok. As long as my cybernetic implant is fully online I can control the armor," she said watching Shia's concerned expression.

"It's good to see you walking again Ma'am," Cole said walking up to them.

"Thank you Cole," she said nodding to him.

As the four of them rose an Ottoman close attack fighter roared in overhead and slowly settled to the ground. It lowered its loading deck and sat quietly.

Katherine strode off toward it as the others looked on wide eyed.

"Ma'am! What are you doing?" Cole asked shocked.

"Getting us a ride. Come on," she said smiling. She walked up the ramp and into the cockpit as the others ran after her. Dragging the dead pilot out of the seat she activated the ship and it lurched off the ground.

In minutes they had covered enough ground towards the other Marines that the com signal came online.

"Goody, I have Katherine we're closing on your position. The Ottoman forces behind us have been eliminated," she called to him.

"You have her? Is she..." he replied in disbelief.

"She's a little different but apparently ok," Shia responded.

"Different?" he asked.

"We'll explain later, get ready we're inbound in an Ottoman ship," Shia said, "The remaining forces are closing on the settlement. We're going to stop them."

The ground around them rose and grew rocky as they approached the entrance to a small canyon. Above them a fighter streaked by slashing the ground in a barrage of kinetic impacts. Rocks and dirt rained down around them as they pushed onward. Katherine locked onto the fighter and sent several antimatter missiles after it.

"Goody touching down get onboard quickly," Katherine called.

"Ma'am... I... we... Are you ok?" he said unsure.

Katherine smiled, "Goody I'm ok, yes. What is the status of the squad?" she asked even though she had a complete data link with every Marine and already knew.

He ran into the cabin and stared at her for a second, "Um, power levels at fifty percent, full up on kinetic rounds and explosives but plasma cannons are suffering. Two have significant armor degradation," he reported efficiently.

Kinetic rounds smashed into the mouth of the canyon again as the fighters strafed.

"Goody, fighters inbound we need to get airborne," the Lance Corporal reported.

"We're good to go," Goody reported as he continued to stare at Katherine.

She nodded and the ship jumped into the air evading the incoming fighters.

Katherine felt an odd itching sensation in the data flow. It drew her attention away for a moment. Plasma rounds flashed past the ship snapping her attention back.

"Hold on we're twenty minutes out," Katherine said as the ship rocketed off.

Incendiary explosions cracked off above them the ship buffeted violently.

Goody shook his head and ran to check on the Marines in the cargo bay.

The itching feeling returned. Suddenly it cleared and a com signaled active.

"Federated Marine Clare, this is Briton Royal Ship *Seraph*. Are you receiving?" she heard through the hiss of plasma interference.

She triggered her com and looked up at the sky, "*Seraph* this Federated Marine Commander Carroll."

"Commander Carroll I am Admiral Dunkirk, we are in orbit and ready to provide assistance. Command code alpha seven sierra stuart two," came the answer.

Katherine's quantum core automatically authenticated the codes and it flashed green- "Admiral the settlement is about to be compromised. They are about to be overrun. I'm afraid you're too late. I officially request a kinetic round on this location, stop the Ottoman Admiral," she said stoically.

Shia looked at her in shock.

Katherine pointed at the canyon walls, "Kinetic granite, it will protect us from the impact."

"Denied, Commander we are not going to lose you, the settlement, or Clare. I have a squad of Legionaries inbound to your position, they are atmospheric now. ETA four minutes via atmospheric drop," Admiral Dunkirk said sternly, "Hang in their Commander, we're coming."

Katherine breathed heavily, "Aye Admiral standing by."

"I am connecting you to the Legionary Commander. Keep your heads down Marines," Admiral Dunkirk said.

"Ma'am, say last again," Goody called out to her.

Katherine stared at the sky, "Marines, we're about to get reinforced. Prepare for a drop into a hot landing, four minutes to arrival."

Lieutenant Colonel Daniel Gerry
Drop Bay
HMS Shuttle Seraph One, Clare System
333.0188 FCUDT 13:19:24

"The situation is rapidly escalating Colonel, they don't have long. Two hundred enemy are about to overrun their position. I am leaving the final call to you. I won't order you to your death, there are options for your insertion other than dropping in on their position. We can retake the settlement after the system is secure," Admiral Dunkirk said flatly.

Colonel Gerry looked at the tactical data- "If we don't drop in with them they will die and we lose all those civilians?" he asked.

"Tactical says that is correct," the Admiral said sadly, "Their Marines, they knew this could happen. We can still accomplish the mission by dropping outside the engagement area."

"Ma'am, we're dropping in to assist them," he said confidently, "They are willing to die for this. So are we."

"Colonel..." the Admiral began.

Colonel Gerry looked at her, "We will stop the Ottoman. Legionary one out," he said and disconnected.

He activated his com, "Legionaries, our Federated allies require our assistance. We will assist. You all see the tactical data. Drop in ten seconds!"

He turned and stepped into his drop cradle. His massive combat armor was similar to the Federated commandos.

They were developed to directly confront the commandos in fact. He activated the link and his armor connected to the cradle. He was lowered into the drop port and rotated into position.

"Colonel, we're at eighteen thousand meters, ready to drop at your command," the pilot said to him.

"Thank you for the ride," he said and punched the drop sequence.

He was ejected feet first out of the bottom of the shuttle and his stomach lurched. He rotated and lay flat facing the rushing air. His speed increased as gravity pulled him down and contrails traced vortices off his fingers.

He cleared a few wispy clouds and got his first clear view of the battle. Green blue flashes of plasma popped in and out down below. He activated his com- "Federated Marine Commander Carroll, Legionary Commander Gerry inbound ten thousand meters above your position."

"Commander Gerry we're approaching the landing zone, it's hot and taking fire. Hope you have a great pilot," Katherine said.

"Copy, we're dropping in high altitude thruster insertion. No shuttles. I have your tactical data. We will be at your command in one minute ten seconds," he replied.

"HATI, copy, we will counter the mortar fire in one minute to clear the LZ," she said flatly.

Gerry watched the battle down below as the ground rushed up to meet them. He rotated into position for deceleration and bit down on the rubber mouth guard in his helmet. The automated systems alarm sounded. Thrusters ignited and he was slammed into his suit. Stars swarmed and his vision narrowed. In what seemed like an eternity he waited, then suddenly he slammed into the ground.

The Ottoman ship jerked and heaved as it took an antimatter missile strike. The controls flickered and the ship suddenly dropped.

Katherine dropped the payload of missiles as they streaked across the Ottoman ground forces. Massive explosions ripped across the unsuspecting Soldiers on the ground.

"Clare settlement this is Marine Commander Carroll we are inbound in an Ottoman ship to assist. Standby," Katherine called out to them.

Another missile struck the rear of their ship and the power flickered out.

"Everyone hold on we're going in," Shia yelled to the Marines.

The little Ottoman ship slammed into the ground eighty meters in front of the Clare settlement and careened across the dusty ground. Engines and hull plates blasted off the ship as it rolled and slid. Stopping and settling everything went silent. Katherine could hear the popping and creaking of the metal as it cooled. She looked around as her cybernetics picked up the inbound Legionaries from above.

She climbed out of the ruined cockpit and into the cargo bay. "Shia, are you ok?" she asked helping her to her feet.

"Thank the stars for combat armor," Shia replied looking at Katherine, "Are you?" she asked concerned.

"Yes, come on we don't have much time." Katherine said looking for a way out of the wreckage.

"Ma'am, over here," Goody said from up ahead.

Katherine and Shia crawled through the ruined bay to Goody who was prying open the bent cargo ramp.

"The Ottoman forces are right behind us. Legionaries are dropping in. ETA is two minutes," Katherine said as they climbed out to the ground.

"Aye, Ma'am. Marines shake it off we got company. Let's go, get to the settlement walls now!" he ordered.

Katherine turned and looked up just as the legionaries drop thrusters thundered down in front of the settlement. They smashed into the ground with a tremendous boom as dust and dirt bloomed up around them. A single legionary stepped out of the dust cloud and dropped his external cradle. "Legionaries, take positions, move!" he called out.

Seven armored Britons sprinted to the walls out of the dust and joined the commandos.

The single legionary walked up to Master Sergeant Goody and opened his helmet- "Commander, Legionary Commander Gerry at you service," he said loudly.

"Commander, welcome. I will save the nicety for later as we are about to be attacked."

Gerry looked at Goody confused, "Where is your Commander?" he asked?

"Goody, the enemy is upon us, get ready for close quarters combat," she said into her com.

Master Sergeant Goody turned and pointed out to a figure one hundred meters away. Standing in the middle of an open field facing the oncoming enemy.

"Commander, time to defeat our enemy," Katherine said to him over the com. She looked back at Shia and lifted her arm as a meter and half long scimitar blade grew out of her armor.

Above them the Briton Legionary shuttle fired a lethal blast from their plasma turrets into an Ottoman fighter. The fighter caught fire and slammed into the settlement wall above them with tremendous force. Commander Gerry dove to the ground as it flashed just meters above their heads and cart wheeled along the ground. A thundering explosion shook the walls as it burst apart behind them. Dirt, smoke, and burning debris rained down.

Katherine's helmet snapped shut and she charged into oncoming fire at the nearest enemy Soldiers. Plasma snapped and crackled in the damp smoky air all around them.

Katherine drove into the surging Ottoman troops. She cleaved four in half as she slammed into them. Triggering her plasma cannon she fired into the line of Soldiers behind them. All around her the commandos and legionaries fought back with fury at the oncoming enemy. The Ottoman Soldiers surged into the battlefield.

Commander Samantha Leeane
Bridge, Deck Five
Nyx, Clare System
333.0188 FCUDT 13:41:52

Sam watched in horror as the Ottoman frigate blossomed in nuclear destruction. Radiation alarms sounded across the ship. "Oh my stars!" Sam said quietly.

"Admiral, *Revenge* evaded the nuclear shock wave. Two destroyers are pursuing," Asteria called out.

Adam looked at Sam, "Engineering is not responding, get down there and check on them"

"Captain, we have a destroyer tracking an intercept. Currently twenty minutes out," Asteria said calmly.

Sam nodded at Adam, "On the way," she said as she hurried off the bridge. As she hurried down the decks she saw Chief Ben Zucco come out of Medical.

"XO, we got Helen back to medical," he said quickly.

"What do you mean back to medical? How did she get out of medical?" she asked confused. Sam pushed past him and entered medical expecting the worst. She saw Doctor Driscoll standing in the surgical bay.

"Brynn, what's going on?" Sam asked concerned.

Helen lay unconscious on the table beside Brynn- "It's ok, she passed out. She sneaked out while I was busy and returned to her quarters. The radiation poisoning is advanced and it will continue to attack her until I can get it under control. She needs to stay here and rest," Brynn said giving Sam a reassuring smile.

Sam frowned, "Brynn we need her help before we run out of power," Sam frowned at Helen.

Brynn frowned, "I'm sorry Sam. She isn't going to be any help for some time. Jacob brought her in, he returned to engineering."

Sam looked at Helen and nodded, "Well, we'll just have to figure this out," Sam turned and hurried off to engineering.

As Sam entered the old engineering bay she stopped cold as the hot air seemed to prickle at her face.

Jacob looked up as she approached, "XO, were trying to keep the reactors from shutting down. Unfortunately, it doesn't seem to be that easy."

"What's wrong? We're moving. Shouldn't we be getting reactor mass now?" she asked.

"No, well yes but it's not nearly enough to sustain the reactors. Plus, inside the graviton limit the density of particles is very low. Sam, we're going to shut down in less than two hours."

Sam looked around and sighed, "Well we will just have to be careful. But losing the *Nyx* is unacceptable."

"Sam... We're in trouble and there is nothing we can do about it."

Sam braced herself against the bulkhead as she returned to the bridge. The ship rattled as it took enemy fire and tried to stop the missiles with point defenses. Captain Vellius was back on the port holo screen as they joined forces with her. Kelli's left eye looked like a black marble from retinal hemorrhage. High gravity was taking its toll on her as she forced her ship beyond its tolerances. In the hour of battle Kelli had eliminated five Ottoman ships but the price was getting high for her.

"We have less than two hours. Jacob said there is nothing he can do," Sam said quietly to Captain Stuart.

Adam looked at her disappointed, "Wonderful," he

looked at the tactical plot and indicated their position. "We've been trading shots with the last frigate, Kelli is moving into position now. We have to take them out."

Kelli looked at them through the holo, "You need to leave the system," she said roughly.

"Yes, but it's doubtful we can even charge the higgs," Sam said.

"Then back off your attack run, I'll move in to cover and you can run," Kelli said.

"No, we're already committed, stick to the plan," Adam said frowning, "Natalia get ready."

The *Nyx* streaked toward its intercept with the Ottoman frigate and rolled to bear its missiles.

"Enemy missiles in space," Asteria called calmly.

"Natalia get the point defenses on those missiles and protect the port side. Let nothing through!" Adam ordered.

The missiles popped out of existence one by one but it wasn't enough. The *Nyx* shook under the impact of the anti-matter assault. Alarms sounded and hatches slammed shut to contain damaged sections. Sam saw red indicators flash across the damage control console.

"Hull damage on decks four and five, we're venting atmosphere. Sections contained but we going to have to reroute some systems," Simay called out.

Suddenly the ship lurched violently as a missile impacted the port hull above the bridge. Lieutenant Binici's console exploded as the power surged. She flew across the bridge and slammed into the bulkhead as sparks showered the small space.

"Sir, the reactors! We're getting overloads in multiple sections," Chief Zucco yelled from Engineering.

"Put that fire out," Captain Stuart said calmly, "Get us back in position. What's our status?"

"Second salvo in space, impact in twenty seconds," Asteria called out.

"Point defenses are cycling, engaging new threat," Lieutenant Volkov called out.

Sam looked at Adam worried, "We can't take another hit like that," she said.

"Captain the offensive network has crashed we're trying to reroute! We have no weapons control," Natalia called alarmed.

Sam stared at Adam in alarm.

Adam sat heavily in his chair. His com chimed and he looked down. Helen was looking back at him sadly.

"Helen? What's wrong?" he asked concerned.

"Sir, I was monitoring the feeds... Use the higgs," she said quietly.

"Helen, Jacob said we don't have the power to transit," he said annoyed.

"No but we can initiate a field... like the grasers," she replied looking at him with tired eyes.

He looked at her for a moment before he turned to Chief Warrant Kila Zucco- "Kila bring the higgs online!" he called Jacob on the com. In seconds Lieutenant Lavagnino was staring back from the holo.

"Sir," he said quickly.

"Jacob I want to use the higgs as a graser. How do I do it?" he said seriously.

"Um, Sir..." He hesitated then began typing on his console, "Sir, it will require perfect alignment on the target and millisecond timing. It will also deplete the reactors."

"But it will work?" Adam asked.

"Yes Sir," he said confidently.

"Program it, you have ten minutes," he said.

"Sir *Revenge* missed the planned course alteration, they are inbound at speed!" Asteria said suddenly, "Ten seconds to impact," Asteria called out.

Suddenly the *Revenge* streaked into the path of the oncoming Ottoman missiles. Its point defenses saturating the area. Impacts blossomed around the ship as the missiles altered their targeting. Black hull plates buckled and ripped free in the savage blasts. *Revenge* ripped past trailing debris and damage.

307

Alarms screeched again across the bridge. "Rotate sixty degrees! Bring our hull to bear!" Adam called out.

The ship shuttered violently under them as missiles slammed into the bottom of the ship.

"Multiple hull breaches! Missile bay and aft engineering have fire alarms. Sections are going into emergency shutdown and venting," Asteria called out, "We're going to lose number four CoNeE."

"Sir, in range of frigate," Natalia called out.

"Callis get us in line with them, point the nose straight at them and hold it!" Adam ordered loudly.

Sam stared hard at Adam as cold fear gripped her, "If you do this we're going to be dead in space," she said concerned, "We'll be wide open with no defense."

"If I don't that frigate will destroy us," he replied, "If we do then there's a chance we survive," he looked at Jacob on the com, "It's up to you."

"Coming online!" Jacob said.

The bridge lights flickered as the higgs powered up and began to draw energy out of the space in front of the ship.

"Captain, we're in position!" Callis called out.

"Field at maximum, CoNeE charging, standby!" Kila called.

Jacob looked up, "Firing Sir!"

The CoNeE let loose a massive graviton beam and as it intersected with the higgs field it was instantaneously accelerated to superluminal speed. As the gravitons fired the last reactor shut down. The crew of the *Nyx* didn't see the higgs field suddenly collapse due to the power loss nor did they see the superluminal graviton beam slam into the Ottoman frigate. The *Nyx* streaked helplessly toward Alesia under emergency battery power as an Ottoman destroyer turned to pursue them.

The world was erupting out of control all around him. Legionaries and Commandos snapped commands and requests on the com channel in terse precision. There was too much going on for Gerry to keep track of it. He glanced at his tactical map and a plasma bolt smashed into him knocking him to his knees.

A Commando dragged him to his feet as he ran by, "Watch your step Sir!" Master Sergeant Goody said returning fire.

He disappeared into the chaos before Gerry could respond. Gerry activated his rail cannon and kneeled behind cover. He leaned out and triggered a burst of seventy rounds into a squad of Ottoman. Waves of smoke washed across the space where they were fighting. Plasma flashed through it lighting it up in brilliant purple hues.

As the smoke lit up Gerry saw Commander Carroll standing in the middle of the firing zone. The plasma pulses lit the area up like a strobe light. He watched in awe as Commander Carroll moved in stop motion.

She spun and jumped firing her cannons in midair. Diving right she drove her scimitar through multiple Ottoman Soldiers and simultaneously fired her plasma cannon in another direction. Gerry watched riveted as she danced with deadly precision. He never thought a suit of powered armor could move like that. She flowed gracefully back and forth from engagement to engagement using multiple weapons at the same time. And she was so fast, impossibly fast.

At the same time explosions ripped at the settlement walls and Soldiers appeared and disappeared in the smoke like apparitions. Another damaged Ottoman fighter thundered into the ground showering the area with burning fuel and debris. He watched in amazement as the flames engulfed Carroll. She continued to fight in the inferno like it didn't exist...

Commander Samantha Leeane
Bridge, Deck Five
Nyx, Clare System
333.0188 FCUDT 14:21:02

Sam held on to the console in front of her tightly. Under emergency power the artificial gravity suddenly dropped to half power throwing everybody off balance. Sam fought to suppress the nausea that lurched in her stomach.

"Sir, basic course data puts us on a collision course with Alesia," Callis called out quietly, "We have emergency thruster maneuver capability, maybe thirty minutes of power in them."

"Short range com only Sir," Joe said looking back at them.

Asteria stood next to her deactivated console, "Last tactical scan before we lost power had an Ottoman brigand in pursuit. Time to range is unavailable..." she said staring at them.

Sam looked at Kila, "How long will life support hold out?" she asked concerned.

Kila looked up with a scared expression, "Not long Ma'am. We will run out of air before the temperature falls below the survivable threshold but we'll impact the planet before both. We took a lot of damage in that last attack."

Adam nodded, "All right, I want you to gather up your departments and get to the lifeboats. Prepare to evacuate the ship. We will drop the boats at the closest approach to the planet," he looked at everyone seriously, "Program the boats to head for the settlement and take as much supplies as you can fit," he sighed deeply, "May the stars protect us."

An Ottoman Soldier fell to the ground gasping as Katherine slid her blade out of his chest. Snow was falling again as the air around the battlefield cooled from the lack of plasma fire. The bodies of the fallen Soldiers began to get covered in the glistening white snow. Katherine looked out at the Marines and Legionaries as the battle slowed to a halt. She carefully walked over to the opening in the settlement wall.

"The final Ottomans have retreated to the edge of the south field. Eighteen enemies remain," Master Sergeant Goody said from his position.

Katherine looked behind her at the Marines. Commander Gerry was directing sweeps with the commandos along the walls. Shia walked up behind her.

"We held them off. Katherine, you held them off," Shia said raising her faceplate.

Katherine nodded- "So far, yes."

Shia looked at her confused. "Those eighteen cannot threaten us, they must surrender."

Katherine looked down at them, "The Ottoman do not surrender. This is not over."

"Then we should go finish them," Shia said taking a step toward them.

Katherine snapped her hand out and stopped her. "No, something is wrong," Katherine stared hard at the Ottoman position below them.

Shia looked at Katherine carefully, "What is it?"

Katherine continued to watch them not answering Shia.

"Katherine, what?" Shia asked concerned.

"Run!" Katherine said seriously.

Shia hesitated, "What?"

Katherine turned and looked at Shia with fear in her

eyes. "Nukes," she said, "The walls, run!"

As Shia took off at a sprint toward the settlements entryway alarms in the Marines and Legionaries suits began screeching.

Katherine triggered her com, "Into the settlement, the kinetic granite will protect us. Run!" she yelled at them.

Katherine headed for the entryway watching the Marines sprint in front of her. Shia and Staff Sergeant Colfax were the last to near the narrow entrance when Katherine saw a bright flash pop around her. The ground vibrated beneath her feet. Her suits sensors picked up the approaching shock wave and she realized Shia wouldn't make it in time. Without thinking Katherine ran full sprint. Time stretched out and in milliseconds she caught up to Shia. She reached out and caught her then hurled herself into the small entrance. The shock wave slammed in behind blasting debris into them at the speed of sound.

Katherine snapped awake in the dark. She dragged herself out from under the debris switching on her suits lights. Dust and dirt clouded the air and the light from her suit reflected off in a blinding glare. "Shia, where are you?" Katherine called out.

"Ma'am, we read you. Are you ok?" Goody asked.

"Is Shia with you?" Katherine asked.

"No Ma'am, sensors pick her up near your position," he replied, "The entrance collapsed between us; we're working on it. Hang in their Ma'am."

Katherine froze when she heard his reply. She stood still for a moment and activated all her abilities. Every sense in her body reached out and filled the small space. Every smell, sound, and movement crashed in on her, the movement of the dust traced chaotic patterns as it moved through the air. She concentrated and sorted the onslaught of data streaming in. Then she heard it. A heartbeat, slow and weak. She scanned the area slowly. There, she thought.

Katherine dove into the rubble and heaved a large rock

off Shia's body. She yanked her body out and lay her carefully down. "Shia, can you hear me?" Katherine asked. She connected to Shia's suit and accessed the medical systems. Shia's suit was severely damaged, errors and failures cascaded throughout. Got it, she thought. Trauma. Penetrating injury to the right thorax, right lung collapsed, multiple system failure Shia's suit reported. Katherine rolled Shia over and saw the injury. The plate that covered her right shoulder and scapula had malfunctioned many days ago. Shia had fixed it in place to maintain coverage of her armor. It must have detached during the battle and left her unprotected. There was a fist sized hole just below and right of her shoulder. Blood poured out in dark black streams. Katherine went cold inside as soon as she saw it.

"Shia no!" Katherine breathed. Katherine tried to stem the flow of blood by compressing it with her hands. She stared terrified as Shia's blood flowed through her fingers unabated. She glanced at the wound on her own arm and watched seal by itself.

Katherine triggered her commando armor and shook off her heavy glove. She held her nanite gloved hand up and closed her eyes hoping. Then she carefully reached down and laid her hand over the wound. Concentrating she willed her body to heal Shia. Please she pleaded. Please.

Katherine opened her eyes and looked down. The flow of blood slowed and stopped. She tried to remove her hand but couldn't. Slowly her hand peeled away and left a green imprint behind. It slowly absorbed into Shia's back and disappeared. Her vital signs began to stabilize and Katherine collapsed against the wall in relief.

Captain Kelli Anne Vellius
Bridge
FCS Revenge, Clare System
333.0188 FCUDT 14:45:22

The power flickered on the bridge as the ship careened

into the inner system. The bridge crew hurried to reestablish control of the ship. Kelli watched the damage control center readouts. Hull damage across the belly of the ship was extensive. Several reactors had shut down and the navigation control system was slagged. Worse was the damage to the drive core.

"Ma'am, tactical, weapons, and com are back online. Engineering is working on the drives. Medical is evacuating the wounded," her XO said from his console.

"What's the status of the enemy ships?" she asked.

"Ma'am, four brigantines remaining. Three are scattered around the inner limits and one is maneuvering against the *Nyx*." Tactical replied.

She nodded studying the holo data.

"We're on a ballistic trajectory through the inner system. We will pass the planet in thirty-seven minutes," the navigator called, "The Nav system is nonresponsive we are transferring to sub systems. In nine hours we cross the graviton limit."

"Plot a manual course to bring us to relative zero on graviton drive once we're clear," Kelli ordered.

"Ma'am, Admiral Dunkirk is on the com," the PO called.

She activated the holo, "Greetings Admiral," Kelli said.

"Captain, what's your status? That was a bad hit you took," Admiral Dunkirk said worried.

"We're working on it. Damage to the hull and engines," Kelli said sending her the data.

"You're headed in system without engines. I think you have attracted some attention," the Admiral said casually.

"We will be fine shortly. Engineering is working on the drive," Kelli replied.

"Ma'am three brigantines inbound, intercept in twenty-seven minutes," Tactical said.

Admiral Dunkirk looked back at Kelli with a raised eyebrow- "I am just off your port side Kelli. Get your ship back online we'll cover you," she said grinning.

Kelli nodded, "Thank you Ma'am."

She looked over and saw Tristan wrenching the deck plate off behind the Nav console. Joining him she kneeled down and they pried it open.

"Damn, the main input feed is fried." Tristan said reaching into the access port. "We can't switch over to the subsystems."

"Yes we can, here let me in. If the secondary is still good we can just switch the inputs." Kelli climbed into the access port and searched for the conduit leading the primary processor. "There it is." She mumbled as she yanked it out of the socket. Climbing back out she handed the disconnected conduit to Tristan.

He yanked the damaged primary out and plugged in the conduit Kelli had handed him. The console chimed and booted up.

Tristan looked at the console and smiled, "Sometimes Cap you amaze me."

"I didn't make Captain because I was dumb XO," she said getting back up.

Kelli closed her eyes and took a deep breath, "Ok I'm going to go crazy, are the engines fixed yet?" Kelli said exasperated.

Her XO looked at her smirking, "Cap it's only been ten minutes."

Kelli sighed, "Guns get ready. What's the status of the point defenses?"

"Ma'am, PDC is at forty percent," the weapons officer called.

Kelli frowned, "Ok, let's be about this. Target the inbound ships. Don't forget the *Seraph* is out there."

"The Ottoman are approaching on zero-nine-six up twenty-four degrees. Velocity is point three light," Tactical called.

"Load flechettes, prepare to fire," Kelli called out.

"Missiles in space, Cap, impact in thirty seconds," Tactical called.

"We charge into the throat of the beast," Kelli

murmured. She watched the crew move restlessly as time ticked by.

The *Revenge* glided through space and crossed the oncoming Ottoman ships. Her point defenses valiantly fought off the oncoming missiles. Just as the incoming missiles were about to impact the *Seraph* de-cloaked. Point defenses lit up the surrounding space in a massive barrage. Kelli gritted her teeth as she watched the oncoming missiles slowly winked out of existence.

"What about fire control!" Kelli yelled above the alarms.

"Still online, but we can't take any more of this," he answered.

She looked at him fiercely, "Fire!" Kelli ordered.

The last five missiles streaked past the *Seraph* and slammed into the *Revenge*. Alarms wailed throughout the ship and the power flickered.

"Cap, four impacts starboard side. Severe damage to the upper gun deck and secondary engine control. We're out for the count. We're venting plasma and atmosphere. Multiple casualties coming in..." her XO was cut off as the fifth missile slammed into them. The starboard bulkhead of the bridge crumpled and ripped away. Anti-matter snaked through the bridge as the atmosphere exploded out the side of the ship.

Kelli's suit helmet slammed shut in emergency decompression. She was crushed into the side of her chair as it tore from its mooring. She crashed into the bulkhead and her suit alarms screamed as it was tearing open. The last thing she saw as she lost consciousness was the beautiful blue planet of Alesia shimmering beneath her as she floated away from the ship.

Despite the damage, *Revenges'* flechette missiles burst out of their tubes and streaked out after the Ottoman brigantines. Just outside the Ottoman point defense range the missiles burst apart and millions of meter long spikes were released. Their simple computer brains linked creating a neural network and they spied their target ahead. At an incredible fraction of light speed, the spikes dove into the enemy ships concentrating on a single point of entry. Millions became hundreds of thousands as they dove into the ship in suicidal frenzy. Each wave dug deeper into the hulls of the hapless ships. By the time a hole large enough for the spikes to enter the ship was created there was less than two thousand left. Unfortunately for the enemy those spikes dove into the inner ships and ravaged the fragile metal of the internal structure. They never even saw the thirty missiles that *Seraph* had launched. Three Ottoman brigantines erupted in a mass of flying metal and gasses that showered the inner system in debris.

Admiral Dunkirk looked at the tactical map as *Revenge* spun out of control. "Search and rescue now!" she ordered.

Cadet Katherine Carroll
Western Mountains, Marine Firebase
Alesia, Clare System
333.0188 FCUDT 15:47:01

Katherine sat next to Shia in the snow outside the settlement entrance. Shia lay sleeping comfortably. Her vitals were strong and steady. In front of Katherine stretching for twenty kilometers the ruined hills of the prairie lay bare. What remained was burning, creating thick black smoke that filled the air in toxic ash. The ground at the point of ignition glowed from residual heat and radiation. Most of her commandos had to remain back in the settlement because of the intense radiation. Their suits no longer sealed completely. Katherine felt the radiation smashing into her. It felt like static buzzing through her. Similar to the static on the com.

Commander Gerry kneeled down next to her, "We should get her inside, radiation and all."

"She's fine don't worry," Katherine said without looking at him.

He looked at Shia then up at Katherine, "She's like you?

Enhanced?"

Katherine turned and looked at him with her blazing artificial blue eyes, "Yes but not in the same way as me."

"Are all of you...?" he asked looking into the settlement.

Katherine smiled, "No, don't worry. There are only a few of us. They were all modified out of medical necessity except for me, becoming... this... was voluntary for me."

He nodded, "Well, if it makes you feel better I'll fight by your side any day. I will never fight against you for the same reason. What I saw you do was simply incredible."

Katherine looked down at Shia, "Thank you Commander." she stood and looked to the north, "Now what?" she said absently.

Gerry turned and looked up, "What is it?"

"Inbound shuttle, I can't get a reading on it. Too much radiation interference," she said.

"More Ottomans?" Gerry suggested.

Katherine shook her head, "I don't think so. I saw their operations plan and there were no shuttles dedicated to the planet."

"You saw their..." he started disbelieving.

As the shuttle came closer Katherine got a good view of it. Her cybernetics immediately identified it- "It's a Briton combat shuttle," she said.

"How do you know that?" he asked.

Katherine raised her hand and pointed at her face- "I'm special," she said sarcastically.

The com squealed as they approached, "Clare forces, this is Briton pinnace *Sword*. Do you copy?"

She heard Gerry take a breath of relief.

"*Sword* this is Commander Carroll we copy. Transponder active," Katherine replied.

"Copy we have you, inbound for pick up. Are you in need of medical assistance?" *Sword* replied.

"We have two in need of assistance but stable, we'll be ready," Katherine said calmly.

The pinnace circled above and its thrusters roared as it

settled down toward them. A massive cloud of dust and snow enveloped the area and slowly cleared as the thrusters shut down.

"All right everybody let's go!" Master Sergeant Goody called out. The Marines and the Legionaries moved in twos covering each other and headed for the cargo ramp. Master Sergeant Goody and Legionary Warrant Officer Harmon walked up to the two officers.

"You two seem to have become friends," Gerry said to them as they strolled up.

"Marines are Marines doesn't matter what planet they were born on Sir," Harmon said, "Briton Royal Marine Legionary or Federated Colonial Marine Commando. We fight when called."

Goody slapped Harmon on the back, "Well said Harmon."

They smiled wearily and followed the rest of the battle scarred Soldiers onto the pinnace.

Katherine kneeled down next to Shia, "Shia wake up. We have to go."

Shia wearily opened her eyes looked up at Katherine and smiled wanly, "Your still here."

"Yes but now we have to go," Katherine said plainly. She nodded at the two Marines and they lifted her up on the stretcher and carried her to the pinnace.

"I can walk! You don't have to carry me," Shia protested.

Colonel Gerry nodded to Katherine, "After you Commander."

"All right! I'm Chief Petty Officer Watry, Legionnaire Armorer. Commandos the power systems have been modified to recharge your suits. Place any loose weapons in the center racks and step into the cradle. Please identify yourselves to the armor cradle and you will receive the proper signal. Lock yourself down and we will be on our way shortly," A tall man in the center said loudly.

Katherine and Gerry walked up to him. Katherine retracted her helmet and looked at him. Petty Officer Watry stared at Katherine transfixed.

"Watry, this is Commando Commander Carroll," Gerry said over the roar of the thrusters coming online.

"Um... Ma'am, it's a pleasure. Your seats... are, um, right there," he said flustered, "We're at your service."

"We need to get to the main settlement," Katherine said.

"Yes Ma'am, no problem," Watry replied.

Katherine nodded and stepped into the cradle. Static screeched and errors in her cybernetics flashed across her mind. Computer firewalls slammed down around her as the pinnace's computer shrieked. Katherine closed her eyes and reached out for the Briton ships computer. In seconds she had disabled its security and invaded the main core. She felt the presence of another mind. Somewhat simple but aware and hiding from her.

You don't need to hide I won't hurt you, She sent to it.

What are you? she received after a few milliseconds.

I'm Marine Commander Carroll.

Odd name for an AI.

I'm not an AI, I'm a human.

No human can be in here. You're lying.

I am a cybernetic enhanced human. I have a quantum core in my brain.

I don't believe you, there is no record of that being possible and you have no biological vital signs.

Maybe, but I am not lying, I could have destroyed you but I did not.

Get out of my core! You don't belong here!

Fine but if you try to firewall me again I will be back, Katherine withdrew from the mainframe and settled into her cradle. No biological vitals she thought.

Sam stood on the dark quiet bridge and stared at the limited navigation data. The Ottoman brigand was just entering engagement range.

Adam walked up to Sam and looked at her carefully- "Sam please take Admiral Lune and get to your shuttle," he said.

"Adam, we can't just leave the *Nyx*," she said.

He stared at her- "Yes you can. Do it, now," he said.

Sam stared back at him seriously, "What are you up to?"

"Don't worry about. I need you to get Coline to safety," he said quietly.

Sam nodded sadly and turned to the bridge crew- "Ok let's go! Simay you're with me. Move people!" The crew numbly locked up their consoles and hurried out. Simay stepped up to Sam and nodded. Sam turned and nodded to Adam- "Captain," she said and stepped to the hatch. She paused and looked at the bridge sadly. They hadn't been aboard long but it felt like she was leaving her childhood home.

"Are you ok Sam?" Simay asked quietly.

She looked at Simay, "Of course, let's go get the Admiral."

As they entered Admiral Lune's makeshift fleet command center they saw her standing by her chair alone.

"Ma'am, we need to go. Where is your staff?" Sam asked.

"I sent them to the shuttles," she said quietly.

Sam stood straighter, "Good, now it's your turn."

Simay looked up at her surprised by her forceful tone of voice.

Coline turned and looked at her. "I know what he's doing," she said softly.

"Then you know it's your duty to leave. You're the system Admiral and the system needs you," she said taking a step closer.

Coline looked at her impassionedly.

"Now Admiral," Sam said.

Coline nodded slightly and squared up her shoulders- "Fine," she said and followed them out of the room.

Cadet Katherine Carroll
Crew Cabin, High Orbit
Pinnace Sword, Clare System
333.0188 FCUDT 17:21:41

Katherine looked up as a com signal came in to the pinnace's array. She had been monitoring the ships sensors trying to piece together the situation in the system. It was total chaos. Multiple destroyed ships both Ottoman and Federation. There was a peculiar Briton ship running search and rescue on a strange Ottoman destroyer. She shook her head in frustration and waited for the com signal.

"Commanders we have an incoming signal for you from *Seraph*," Watry announced.

Katherine stood up and stepped next to Gerry- "Put it on screen please," he called out.

Admiral Dunkirk turned and smiled. As soon as she saw Katherine she froze- "Commanders... are you..." she took a breath and tried again, "What's your status Commanders?"

"Ma'am, we are down two Marines with minor medical. Currently recharging suits but operability is degraded by at least fifty percent for the Federals and ten percent for the Britons. Our overall status is at seventy percent with fourteen combat capable Marines," she replied flatly.

Admiral Dunkirk stared at her carefully for a moment.

"Ma'am, Commander Carroll has my complete confidence. Her performance was beyond exceptional," Commander Gerry said proudly.

"Very well, the situation up here is coming to a close.

We are currently getting the *Revenge* back into stable orbit and picking up the crew. The *Nyx* has experienced some difficulty and is not responding to hails. We are not in a position to assist before they pass the planet but are planning to intercept shortly after. I need you to secure the settlement. They are going to need you down there."

They both nodded, "Yes Ma'am."

"Good, do your best. I will be in touch as soon as I know more," Admiral Dunkirk said sighing, "Hang in there."

The pinnace glided out of the clear sky and circled the settlement.

"Clare space port this is Briton Shuttle *Sword* inbound with Federated Marine Commando support. Request permission to land," the pinnace pilot called.

"*Sword* stand by," came the terse reply.

After a few minutes the pilot called back to the Marines. "Excuse me Commander the Governor would like to speak to you," she said.

"On screen please," Katherine replied.

Grace O'Malley appeared in the screen with a fierce scowl on her face. As soon as she saw Katherine she immediately looked concerned, "Commander! What happened?" she asked quickly.

"Ma'am, we have stopped the Ottoman forces. Unfortunately, they detonated a nuclear device before we could stop them. The planet is secure at the moment," Katherine reported.

Grace stared at her, "You're in a Briton ship?"

"Ma'am, the Briton fleet and Legionaries came to our assistance, without them we would have failed. The Federal ships in system are significantly degraded. There has been a treaty issued in regards to joint defense of your system," Katherine said.

Grace's eyes narrowed, "Permission to land. Commander I want all Britons to be unarmed until I get this straight."

"Yes Governor, thank you," Katherine said seeing Gerry nod his acceptance.

"Katherine welcome to Clare, we owe you and your Marines enormously. What assistance can I have standing by for you?" she said smiling at Katherine.

"Thank you Ma'am, we have a few medical issues and some real food would be appreciated," Katherine said smiling at her.

"Of course, right away. See you soon."

Captain Adam Stuart
Bridge, Deck Five
Nyx, Clare System
333.0188 FCUDT 20:06:42

Adam sat on the dark bridge alone and listened to the shuttles and life boats depart the ship. He looked down at the simple navigation holo and saw the brigand's missiles streaking in at them. Only four he thought, I should be insulted. As he brought up the helm controls to program a trajectory that would bring the *Nyx* abruptly to the surface of the planet he heard the hatch open.

He turned and saw Callis and Asteria standing there looking at him.

"What are you doing here?" he demanded.

"Not letting you do this alone. That's what," Callis said.

Adam got up and stared at them angrily, "Get to a shuttle now!"

"No. Asteria believes we may be able to save the ship," Callis said looking at her.

"I don't care, get to a shuttle," he repeated.

A tone started chiming on the holo- "Too late," Asteria said as she hurried to the Nav console. "Callis get the thrusters online," she said quickly.

He ran to the helm controls and activated the system. "Ten seconds," he said.

"Give me a burn on axis one-six-four, three seconds... now!" she called.

The ship slowly rolled as the missiles tore past them. The ship shuttered and the three of them held on.

"What are you doing?" Adam said alarmed.

"Sir we have altered course. Inbound to the planet on a ballistic trajectory. We have twenty-nine minutes of thrust available," Asteria said turning to him.

"More than enough to set her down on the planet," Callis added.

"What... that's insane! This ship isn't rated for atmospheric flight," he said to them.

"Well then I guess I just have to crash it softly," Callis said, "That was your plan right."

Adam sat and put his head in his hands- "Fine, why not," he said in resignation.

"Excellent, twenty-eight minutes to atmosphere. Callis get ready for a de-orbital burn," Asteria said.

Cadet Katherine Carroll
Governor's Office, Clare Settlement
Alesia, Clare System
333.0188 FCUDT 21:01:31

Katherine walked into Grace O'Malley's little office in the settlements biggest building. Grace smiled and walked up to her.

"Katherine, thank you again," she said relived.

"Ma'am, it was nothing, really," Katherine said.

"From the look of you and your Marines that is not the case, but I understand," she said, "So now, what has happened to you. Your far paler and didn't have artificial blue eyes the last time I spoke to you..."

Katherine looked at her and smiled, "I died. I'm actually technically still dead I think," she said plainly, "I am being kept alive by nanites and a quantum computer that is implanted in my brain."

Grace waited for a second and seemed to be expecting Katherine to admit that she was joking. "Um, ok?" she said obviously not believing what she was hearing. "What about the Britons? Why are they here?" she asked changing the topic.

"I can't really say any more than what I already told you. I was contacted by Admiral Dunkirk and the Legionaries dropped to assist us. We would have been overrun if not for their assistance. She was assisting Captain Stuart in the systems defense."

"And how do you know she didn't lie to you?" Grace said suspicious.

"Admiral Dunkirk gave Captain Stuart's command verification code," she replied, "He submitted to my command when he arrived. They are very capable Soldiers."

"You trust him?" she asked.

"Yes Ma'am."

"Very well, he is your responsibility. They are granted access to the settlement. Don't be surprised if they aren't very popular," she said shrugging.

Her com sounded interrupting their conversation, "Governor there is a ship inbound. A big ship. I think it's... crashing." the com operator said uncomfortably.

"On the way," she said quickly.

As they entered the planetary control room Katherine stumbled. The data ripped into her from the large computers.

"Katherine! What's wrong?" Shia asked suddenly concerned.

She had forgotten her constant connection to Shia. Her mind relaxed and she focused on that connection. Slowly she regained control of herself.

"Shia, I'm fine. Thank you..." Katherine finally replied.

"For what?" she asked.

"Nothing, I'll explain later. There is a ship inbound. It's the *Nyx*."

"What! They can't enter the atmosphere." she said concerned again.

"I think they are in trouble. Get the Marines back to the pinnace we may need to go back out," Katherine said studying the data.

"On the way," she replied.

Katherine stepped up to Grace who eyed her suspiciously- "It's the *Nyx*." She said to her.

Grace frowned, "How do you know that?"

"Ma'am, transponder reads *Nyx*," the controller said looking up a from the holo data.

Katherine just stared at Grace for a moment.

"Hail them," Grace ordered.

"No response, we've been trying since we picked them up," the controller answered, "Their trajectory puts them three hundred kilometers to our north east."

Grace turned to Katherine, "Katherine, I seem to need you again."

"On the way Madam Governor," she said turning to leave.

Commander Samantha Leeane
Command Shuttle, Cockpit
Alesian Orbit, Clare System
334.0188 FCUDT 20:29:10

Sam sat silently as the *Nyx* began to trace plasma trails across the atmosphere of Alesia. May the stars protect you she thought silently.

"They'll make it," Simay said to Sam, "I'm sure they will."

Sam's heart sank, "Yea, I'm sure they will."

"Ma'am, the Ottoman brigand," the pilot said alerting her.

She studied the tactical holo, "What are they doing?"

"It looks like they are running. They are headed out at full power," he said.

Simay looked at the data, "Impossible. They don't run," she said disbelieving.

"Never the less, that is what it looks like," Sam said.

She looked at the pilot, "Regardless of what they do we need to get to the planet. Please set the course."

"Aye Ma'am. Locked in," he replied, "There is a call coming in from *Seraph*," he said as he inputted the course.

Admiral Lune stood up and leaned on Sam's chair- "Put it up," she said calmly.

Admiral Dunkirk's piercing green eyes stared back at them- "Admiral Lune I see your having difficulties. I'm sorry for being late," she said.

"It's ok Admiral, you were busy. Thank you for getting to the *Revenge*, how are they," Coline replied.

Admiral Dunkirk sighed, "Better. We managed to stabilize the *Revenge's* orbit and evacuate most of the crew. There were many casualties. Captain Vellius was gravely injured. She's in our sick bay."

Coline closed her eyes tightly- "I don't know how to thank you Admiral."

"Please you can start with calling me Tabbitha. What's your plan? Do you need my assistance?" she said seriously.

"And you can call me Coline. We're on course for the settlement. I imagine your quite full at the moment with two crews," Coline said, "Don't worry about us we'll get to the planet. I'll contact you when I reach Governor O'Malley."

Tabbitha nodded, "I'll send my shuttles as soon as the system is settled," she said.

"Thank you Tabbitha" Coline replied smiling.

Katherine stood on the shuttle pad and looked up at the sky. *Nyx* was burning an arc lighting up the sky as it streaked toward the surface.

"Oh my stars! Is that them?" Shia said in shock as she joined Katherine.

Katherine nodded slowly- "They must be severely damaged because I can't pick up their data core transmissions," she said quietly.

"We're ready to go Commander Carroll," Commander Gerry said approaching them.

Katherine nodded, "Let's go," she said as they climbed aboard the pinnace.

As the pinnace lifted off Katherine's com chimed- "Katherine, the *Nyx* has altered course they seem to have some control. Best estimates of touchdown are now a hundred kilometers to our south. They are aerobraking and coming in very fast," Grace said concerned.

"Thank you Ma'am, we have visual and are holding nearby," Katherine said staring at the *Nyx* as it thundered in towards them.

Shia connected to Katherine on her personal com- "What's up with Goody? I admit I have been touchy around him since we... left you, but he is outright avoiding me now," she said confused.

Katherine looked at him across the cargo bay, "He has said very little to me as well. I don't know. He hasn't even asked about the changes."

"Do you think the crew got off the *Nyx*?" she asked changing topics.

"I hope so..." Katherine replied.

Adam gripped the armrest tighter as the ship violently shuddered around them. He looked up as Callis was fighting to control the ship as it fell through the air towards the planet.

"Losing attitude control on the port side!" Callis yelled over the roaring of the reentry.

"Redirecting the systems to compensate," Asteria said calmly, "Fire in the starboard CoNeE nacelle. We're going to lose it."

"Just get on the ground in one piece!" Adam croaked.

"Six thousand meters to surface contact. Asteria get ready to fire the deceleration thrusters," Callis said through gritted teeth.

"Copy, we have about eighty-four seconds of thrust. That should be enough to get us on the ground," Asteria said looking up at them.

"Four thousand meters... Ready... now!" Adam called out.

The ship heaved them forward violently as the deceleration forces crashed into the ship. Adams vision narrowed to pin points as the blood rushed into his head from the force.

"Impact," Asteria called out.

The ship slammed into the soft ground and the thrusters shut off. The power suddenly went out and the bridge was eerily dark. Adam could hear the hull screaming as it crashed over rocks and soil underneath his feet. The ship continued to heave and shake as it careened forward. Suddenly the ship slammed to a stop and everything went dark as Adam lost consciousness.

"Commander location confirmed. *Nyx* is on the ground and powered down. We're inbound," the pilot said over the com.

The holo activated as they approached the *Nyx*. Incredibly the ship was mostly intact. It lay at the head of a kilometer-long trench that the ship had plowed into the surface as it bled off kinetic energy. Terrible combat damage was visible as Katherine scanned the hull. Multiple hull breaches on the topsides and the engineering deck was almost completely gone. Sudden concern for Commander Dower spiked in her mind. The plating across the starboard side was severely burned and buckled in many places.

"Oh my!" Shia gasped as the pinnace circled to port. CoNeE number three was gone.

"Look at how the strut is twisted from the base of the number two all the way to the hull! That must have been a terrible hit," Shia said quietly.

"Unbelievable..." Gerry said quietly as he watched.

As they got to within three hundred meters Katherine suddenly accessed the *Nyx's* computer. Warnings and errors cascaded through her mind as she accessed the various systems. She focused on the internal sensors. Two biological life signs appeared on the bridge as did Asteria's unique signature. The data network collapsed as the power systems overloaded and shut down.

"Commander Carroll, we have a voice only message from Admiral Lune," Gerry said to her for across the Pinnace.

Katherine looked up and nodded.

"Commanders we are on approach to the *Nyx*. What's your status?" Admiral Lune said to them over the ships com.

"Ma'am, we're in position to begin recovery. I was able to access the ships network for a moment and there are three crew aboard on the bridge. Their status is unknown. The settlement is currently not being threatened," Katherine replied.

"Excellent Commander, can you confirm there is no Ottoman presence on the planet?" the Admiral replied.

"Ma'am, there is likely small isolated pockets of Ottoman scattered throughout the area. During our various engagements we did observe some forces retreating from the area."

"Very well, since you're the only Marines on the planet I would like you to remain airborne in case we need a quick reaction force. I have dispatched several inbound shuttles for recovery of the Captain. The remaining shuttles and drop pods will rendezvous at point delta and set up a holding area," the Admiral said over the com.

Katherine looked at Gerry and nodded.

"Acknowledged Ma'am," Gerry replied nodding.

Cadet Katherine Carroll
Nyx Crash Site, Interim Camp
Alesia, Clare System
336.0188 FCUDT 14:30:01

Katherine stood in the blue green grass silently watching the crew set up temporary shelters. Over the past eighteen hours a proper camp had been established several hundred meters off to the west of the crashed ship.

"The sensors are all in place on the south side," Staff Sergeant Colfax said as his small team approached.

Katherine nodded, "Excellent Cole, good job. Go inside and stand down until third watch. Get some food and rest."

Cole grinned, "Yes Ma'am!" he looked at the other two Lance Corporals with him, "You heard the lady, move. Get up that gangway and get your armor off. I want you cleaned, fed, and into bed in one hour!" he said chasing them toward the scaffolding that led to the airlock.

"How can he be so ridiculous after so many days of this?" Shia asked watching Cole tease his Marines.

Katherine turned to see Shia walking toward her.

"Come on Katherine, Cole was the last team. Commander Gerry and his Legionaries are on station let's go get this armor off," Shia said.

Katherine activated the sensor network and scanned the area. The local area scan returned negative. She stared at the data carefully.

"Katherine, our people will be fine. You need some down time," Shia said concerned.

Katherine looked at her knowing what she was inferring. They hadn't spoken much about the changes she had experienced nor how they seemed to be able to sense each other. She could almost read Shia's mind. Not in the way two people who know each other can but literally.

"Ok," Katherine said feeling Shia relax as she nodded. They turned and walked through the bustling camp toward the *Nyx*.

Commander Samantha Leeane
Hell Hold Armory, Deck Three
Alesia, Clare System
336.0188 FCUDT 15:42:27

Sam watched in awe as Katherine and Shia stepped off the loading lift and into the armory. Katherine's armor was horrific. Deep plasma scars and gouges dotted her entire body. Her entire left side was charred and burned. Sam couldn't believe Katherine was still able to use it. Shia hadn't fared any better. An entire plate was missing on her back. All around missing plate dried flaking blood and dirt gave hint to a hideous injury that lie beneath.

"Katherine, Shia! Stars, I'm so proud of you two. You look like you've been through..." Sam said as they stepped out.

"Ma'am, it's nice to be back despite the ships location," Shia said grinning.

Sam smiled, "Yes, there is that... We have managed to get power back to this level for you so you can de-armor and get some rest. Most of your Marines have already cleared the armory and medical. You two are the last."

Katherine nodded, "Thank you Ma'am," she turned to Shia and looked at her.

Shia nodded and without a word stepped into the green graviton field. It lifted her up and with a disturbing cracking sound her armor disengaged. Shia winced in pain as the back plate popped off revealing her blood soaked pressure suit underneath.

Brynn appeared next to Sam, "Shia hold still while I run a scan. Are you in any pain?"

"Nope, it just felt like ripping a bandage off for a second. I took some shrapnel where the plate was missing. Katherine fixed it," Shia responded.

Brynn looked at Katherine, "Fixed it..." she began.

Tones began going off on the terminal. Sam looked down and her eyes went wide, "Nanite alarm?" she asked shocked.

Brynn studied the readings for a second- "Isolation now," she said to the medics standing nearby. "Shia, I have to take you to medical in isolation. The scanner says you have class three nanites in you system."

Sam noticed Shia look at Katherine alarmed. They seemed to almost have a silent conversation and then Shia visibly relaxed. The medics slid a white stretcher in and Shia slowly slid into it. It hissed closed and the telltales signaled green.

"Take her up, I'll be up in a moment as soon as we scan Katherine," Brynn said to the medics.

Sam watched as they carefully pushed the stretcher out. Katherine stepped up to the armor station and looked at Brynn, "It's my fault. I used the nanites to save her life. We were trapped in a collapsed tunnel and she was critically injured."

"It's ok Katherine. I'll get her sorted out. You did what you had too," Brynn said smiling, "Now your turn."

"Ma'am, you're going to need another isolation stretcher. I had to use the nanites on myself as well," Katherine said in resignation.

Brynn looked confused, "Katherine it's not possible to use them on yourself. There is no way to reprogram class 4 medical nanites."

Katherine looked at Brynn as she stepped into the armor station, "I found a way," she said flatly.

CHAPTER TEN
Recall

Cadet Katherine Carroll
Medical Isolation Bay, Deck Three
Nyx, Clare System
346.0188 FCUDT 06:30:00

Data streams flowed past in magnificent multihued ribbons. Odd clicks and chirps sounded from far off. Below the ribbons of data, a massive churning ocean of information boiled. Katherine merged with the local data core and listened to the thousands of data points from the around the planet. She let the data sieve through her mind and picked out the brightest most brilliant silver thread. As she merged with the data she instantly felt the soft heartbeat and breathing of Shia O'Connell. Shia shifted gently in her sleep and Katherine felt the movement from both Shia's hand and her own arm where Shia's hand lay.

Katherine had realized that whenever she began to get lost in the data it was always Shia that brought her back. She could always find her. She was a brilliant silver beacon amidst the hurricane of data.

She opened her eyes and looked at Shia as she slept next to her. She searched for Lieutenant Commander Hypnea amid the data stream.

Katherine? Asteria responded.

I have a question if you have a minute Commander?

Of course.

I don't understand my emotions, I feel unusual. I don't know what to do about... it, her...

Asteria paused, *I see. I think you need to remember that you have changed on a fundamental level. That includes how you experience emotion. Just ask yourself how you perceive this person in your mind.*

Katherine could see the brilliant silver string among all the others.

I think I understand Commander. Thank you.

337

They both withdrew from the data and Katherine looked at Shia again.

"Thank you," Katherine said quietly to Shia.

"Humph," Shia mumbled in her sleep.

Shia turned her head away and breathed deeply. Katherine noticed the pale blue glowing line behind Shia's right ear. Guilt flashed through her in a burning streak. Katherine had somehow transferred the nanites to Shia permanently. Over the course of the past week Shia had slowly transformed. They now could literally hear each other's thoughts and feel each other's emotions. The growing blue implant was the first physical indication that Shia would soon have the same physiological enhancements as Katherine. The only thing that kept Katherine from feeling massive guilt was that Shia welcomed the change. Their relationship had only gotten stronger. Shia grounded Katherine in the physical world.

"I'm also sorry," she whispered quietly.

After a moment she sat up and carefully got out of bed so she didn't disturb Shia.

Shia opened her eyes and looked at her- "You should put on your armor," she said sleepily, "You're technically naked."

Katherine looked down at herself. She did look like she was painted green.

Upon returning to the ship after their last mission the Marines had removed their armor. Before leaving the Armory they all had to pass a full biological scan that prevented them from contaminating the crew from anything they may have picked up. As Katherine and Shia passed through the scanner the unregistered nanite alarm triggered. Katherine was taken to medical and Brynn thought that removing the nanite combat suit would fix the nanite contamination. It turned out that in order for Katherine to survive the suit had incorporated into her body. The suit was now literally her skin. Nanites now performed all her bodies biological functions. She had no heart beat and no need to breathe except to speak. Federation protocol was to place them in containment isolation. Brynn was completely perplexed by Shia's contamination until Katherine told her about saving her with the nanites.

"You're right," she closed her eyes and her level two armor grew out of her suit.

"Better?" she asked quietly.

"No... I'll be up in a minute," she said smiling.

Katherine raised her eyebrow as she briefly glimpsed Shia's imagination.

"We have to be ready in an hour," Katherine said softly running her fingers across Shia's cheek.

"Umm, yea in a minute," Shia said half asleep.

Captain Kelli Anne Vellius
Medical Bay
HMS Seraph, Clare System
346.0188 FCUDT 12:41:55

Kelli felt the rise and fall of her chest as she breathed. She felt heavy and very tired. Why didn't I die? I just want to be with Josh she thought. She opened her eyes and immediately started choking on tubes in her throat.

"Just relax," a calm heavily accented voice said.

She felt the tubes being removed and she gagged and coughed. As they came clear she took a ragged breath.

"There you go. Just relax and focus on breathing," the voice said to her.

Her vision cleared and she looked at the man above her.

"Hello Milady, I am Doctor Alban. You have been injured in combat and are aboard the *Seraph*. Please don't try to move you're in a regeneration pod. You sustained serious damage due to decompression and exposure. Can you talk to me?" he said softly.

Intense sadness flooded her. Tears flowed down her cheeks- "Why?" she choked.

Doctor Albin's face softened, "It ok Milady, and you're going to be fine."

Kelli closed her eyes and cried until she finally fell asleep. All the emotional trauma of the past month crashing in on her. Losing Josh, getting her ship destroyed, and fate was cruel enough to let her live.

Commander Samantha Leeane
Executive Officers Office, Temp Shelter 32
Alesia, Clare System
346.0188 FCUDT 19:09:00

Data chips lay scattered in little piles across the desk as Sam looked for a spot to put her coffee down. She took a harried breath and set her cup down in a clear spot.

"A bit disorganized," Adam said from the door as he surveyed the tiny office.

Sam rolled her eyes at him, "So you know, this part of the job really isn't that fun."

Adam laughed, "You have a minute to talk about the crew?"

"Of course, I would offer you a seat but..." she motioned at the cluttered space.

"So how are they?" Adam asked.

Sam looked at him suspiciously- "Can you be more specific?"

"Helen, Jacob, Katherine, Shia... all of them," he said.

Sam nodded understanding, "Well Helen is shattered. She won't leave the hospital. Brynn says she is suffering from post-traumatic and the severe radiation poisoning isn't helping. She spends all her time deeply involved in theoretical physics. She barely talks to me when I go see her. Doesn't matter how I try she refuses to rejoin the engineering crew."

"Does Brynn think she'll recover?" Adam asked.

"She is unsure. Matters of the mind are difficult. Physically she is getting better and will be fine eventually.

At the moment she is unpredictable at best,"- she leaned back and sipped her coffee- "Jacob is dealing with it but the stress is building. He is one of the best engineers I've ever seen and the only one that actually understands Helen's designs. We need them to figure out how to work together."

"You're proposing we let Helen do the theories and Jacob do the work?" he asked.

"Seems like a possible dynamic," she said in resignation, "The ship is in total disarray; Jacob is somehow holding up. How long, I can't say."

"What about Katherine?" Adam asked.

Sam shook her head, "I assume you've been briefed by Brynn about her medical condition?"

"As much as I can understand. She is being kept alive by nanites that are controlled by her cybernetic core. It was a reaction by the quantum core to her biological requirement. It was the only option open to the core so it hijacked the prototype nanite suit and used it to create an external life support system." He shook his head. As soon as she came in from mission the nanite security net protocols required her to be placed in electronainte isolation."

"Well you know as much as I do. She is an amazing Marine. Totally capable and a stupendous leader... but she is also basically on life support and full of nanites. I don't have to remind you that nanites are one of the most feared technological inventions of our time for that very reason." She said frowning. "Also it appears as though Shia is changing like Katherine."

"What? How is that possible, she doesn't have a cybernetic core?" Adam said surprised.

Sam sighed, "In the closing of the fight on the planet Shia was mortally injured. Apparently Katherine directed the nanites in her body to heal Shia. She told Brynn it was out of desperation. It worked apparently but now Shia is a host to those nanites. According to Brynn, Katherine and

Shia are... linked somehow. She doesn't know what would happen if they are separated. Asteria says that they can stay linked over large distances but different systems are a stretch."

Adam ran his hand over his head, "That presents a few issues."

"Well it gets more so. They seem to be in some kind of relationship as well," Sam said smiling, "It certainly isn't the normal kind like Edward and I..." she said to his raised eyebrows, "I have kept them together because I can't get a straight answer from Brynn on what's up with them."

"That explains why I got Shia's resignation. Dumont told me she wants to be the Ranger liaison to the Commandos," Adam said frowning.

"Did you accept it?" Sam asked surprised.

"Not yet but Dumont said he would approve it from his side."

"If it matters the Marines approve of them. Goody wants to retire so you could assign her as the senior enlisted officer," Sam said shrugging.

Adam nodded, "That's a possibility," he stayed silent for a moment, "Who else?"

"We have twenty-seven crew that are classified permanent non-combat capable. Eighteen that require more than a month of rehab. Forty-nine deceased," she said sadly.

Adam leaned heavily against the bulkhead- "Well we'll just have to do our best."

Senior Captain Mercan
Alesian Settlement, South Gate
Alesia, Clare System
347.0188 FCUDT 18:27:51

The blue green grass waved in the evening wind out in front of Mercan. He watched a small group of settlers moving about their camp. Unconscientiously he ran his fingers over his sidearm. Tonight he thought.

He glanced over at Kosta and their eyes met. Kosta nodded at the unspoken message.

They had been remarkably lucky so far. It was unfortunate that the Briton corvette had forced him to abandon his plan to take a Barque but he would find a way make this right. Somehow their landing had been unnoticed as well as their approach to the settlement. Now they just needed to find a way through the gates and into the city. These unlucky people were just what they needed.

Mercan snapped his chronograph shut exactly at midnight. He drew his sidearm and thumbed the arming lever to active as he silently stepped from his hiding spot. He slowly crept up to the sleeping group and paused just long enough to ensure Kosta was in position. Nearly simultaneously they aimed their weapons and shot the four people

"Quickly Kosta, we need to get rid of them," he said quietly.

Mercan stripped the man in front of him. He had judged carefully picking the settler that most resembled himself. When he was finished he drug the body down to a hole they had dug the day before and heaved the dead man into it. Kosta followed behind doing the same. In a few short few minutes they began filling the hole that now contained four settlers.

Later that evening Mercan stared into the fire that burned their Ottoman uniforms. He looked down at a set of identifications in his hand.

"My name is Terrell McCormick," he said to Kosta, "From the freighter *Perihelion*."

"I'm Jacob Daughtery," Kosta replied in heavily accented universal.

Mercan now Terrell scowled, "Your accent is wrong. Talk as little as possible."

"Yes Sir," he replied.

Terrell nodded, "Now let's get going, and don't call me Sir."

"After you... Terrell," Kosta said with difficulty.

Commander Samantha Leeane
Executive Officers Office, Temp Shelter 32
Alesia, Clare System
346.0188 FCUDT 19:09:00

"Colonel Gerry is on the way back with three Ottoman detainees," Senior Master Chief Tameria Heirdahl said to Sam.

"I just needed a moment," Sam murmured.

"A moment? Are you ok?" Tameria asked from the door.

Sam looked up at her. "I'm fine," she said smiling at her, "You know Shia well?" Sam asked.

Tameria looked down at the floor of the tiny office- "Yes, we met many years ago and teamed up doing security on interstellar shipping freighters. We had similar experience in the Rangers."

Sam looked up at her- "Have you seen her since the ..."

"Since she came back?" Tameria finished the sentence. "Yes Ma'am."

"Is she different. I mean besides the unusual new implants."

Tameria shrugged, "A little I guess, she's actually more relaxed now that you mention it. She has always been a little angry or intense I guess. Not so much now. But other than that she's not any different. I'm not really the one to ask though, we've always been professional. Josephine has been more of a personal friend to her."

"Of course you're right Tameria. Thank you," Sam said standing and looking at her, "Please ask Lieutenant Binici to meet us at the detention center."

Sam stared out the window of the atmospheric shuttle at the wasteland created by the nuclear blast as they crossed the one hundred ten kilometers from the little camp. The scorched ground still smoked from residual fires. It was a bleak reminder of the fierce battle Katherine had somehow managed to win.

Sam felt a pang of guilt for Katherine and Shia's isolation. They didn't deserve to be locked up this way. Admiral Lune had rebuked her for opposing the order and Sam still felt burned by it. She sighed heavily and tried to focus on the task at hand.

They headed toward the shuttle pad in the center of the settlement and landed some distance from the main space port. As they walked through the settlement the people they passed avoided looking at them. They both heard the hushed whispers people said about them. After two weeks most of the settlers had accepted their presence but all of them kept their distance.

The Briton shuttle thundered in overhead and circled above- "Alesian port *Seraph* alpha requesting landing clearance," Sam heard on the local com.

"Alpha your vector is clear, permission granted to pad six," local traffic control responded.

"Commander Leeane we have three detainees. I'll bring them to interrogation," Colonel Gerry called to her.

"Excellent Colonel, we'll meet you there. Good work out there," she replied.

"Thank you, if there is anyone else, they won't last much longer without support. I think we're pretty much done out there," he said happily.

"Getting tired of sweeping up the trash Gerry?" Sam asked him laughing.

"Oh no, this is a great mission, soft beds, good views, and wonderful company," he said laughing back.

As Sam and Tameria approached the new building that housed the Joint Clare Command they saw that the Marines had already taken the detainees inside. They entered the building and took the lift to the detention level. Colonel Gerry was waiting for them as the lift doors opened.

Tameria instantly began laughing at the sight of him. He was covered in dark brown mud and had a ridicules grin on his face, "Wow, you smell," Tameria said grinning.

"Hello Commander," he said as he tried to ignore Tameria.

"Daniel," Sam replied looking at his armor.

"They were in the swamps to the southeast," he explained, "Cell six," he said stepping off to the side.

Sam looked at him suspiciously. He was being pointedly obtuse about this. She nodded and headed for the door silently.

Pausing at the door she looked inside through the one-way glass. Inside sat an Ottoman officer. He had only one arm. She looked at Gerry surprised.

"This one keeps repeating one word, Dragur," he said to her, "Do you know what that means?"

Sam looked up as Binici approached- "You're the only one that knows the answer to that."

Simay grinned, "Long story."

Sam and Tameria stepped into the cell behind Simay and looked at the Officer. They stood there for several minutes silently watching him. He stared at them with a flat expression.

"Why are you here Colonel?" Simay asked him in perfect Ottoman language.

He just sat there staring at the floor quietly.

Tameria triggered her helmet and it retracted into her suit smoothly. The Colonel looked up at the sound and froze as he suddenly recognized her dark face outlined by the glowing blue of her neuro implant. His face contorted in fear as he let out a piercing scream.

He looked at Sam and dropped to his knees, "Please don't let the Dragur kill me," he pleaded to her, "Please!"

Sam triggered her helmet and looked down at him with

the same pale skin and glowing blue eye as Tameria.

He shrieked again and flung himself into the corner. Collapsing he curled up in a fetal position whimpering- "Please god, please save me!" he cried.

"What Dragur?" Sam asked.

He stared up at her, "The one who returned from the dead, she removed my arm. She wore armor like hers," he pointed at Tameria.

"Why are you here?" Simay repeated.

He looked at her from the corner of his eyes as he trembled in the corner, "I'm being punished," he whimpered.

Sam stepped closer, "Answer and I will leave you," she said.

"I was... I was ordered to secure the planet," he said hesitantly.

"Why is the Ottoman in Clare?" Sam clarified.

He stared at her in fear, "Looking for a ship. A fast ship," he stammered, "Impossibly fast. The Emperor demanded we find it"

"You didn't come to start a war?" Simay asked in Ottoman language.

He stared at Simay as if he forgot she was there- "We left the fleet, left the war to come here. We were supposed to fight somewhere else," he said shaking, "We didn't know Dragur!"

"Know what?" Sam demanded.

He shrunk into himself as she spoke, "Didn't know God protected this planet, didn't know he would send Dragur..."

Tameria looked at Sam, "He's crazy," she said.

"Where is the rest of your fleet?" she asked him.

He looked at her with panic in his eyes- "I... I can't,"

Sam drew a long blade from the forearm of her armor and her implant flared brilliantly blue, "Where is the rest of your fleet?" she demanded.

"The Transit!" he cried, "The Perseus Transit..."

The holo recording ended with Sam and Tameria leaving the Ottoman Officer's holding cell. Simay sat in her seat silently staring at the image. Emotions surged through her after seeing the interrogation again. She wasn't upset about the treatment of the Ottoman; she was concerned for Katherine. She fidgeted in her seat uncomfortably.

Captain Stuart, Commander Leeane, and Commander Hypnos were all present. Katherine was on the com from her isolation room. She looked up at them wide eyed.

"He seems to be telling the truth," Sam said sighing.

Captain Stuart nodded, "What do you make of his statement Simay?"

She stared at Captain Stuart for a second- "He is a Ground Commander, a Colonel according to his uniform." She said getting more comfortable- "I wouldn't think he had much knowledge of fleet operations. What he said is most likely a mix direct observation and ship gossip."

"So you think he is guessing about the fleet location?" Sam asked.

Simay shook her head, "No he probably knows that information. It would be pertinent to his ground plans. The stuff he said about looking for a ship and the emperor is likely gossip. Ground troops tend to gossip a lot. Some of it is possible because he apparently was given this mission last minute. That doesn't happen often. The Ottoman rely on planning from the officials in the empire, they don't rely on Commanders in the field to improvise."

Commander Hypnea activated a holo map of the Federated Colonies. "If they are at the Transit then they are poised to attack Elysium," she said.

"They could penetrate the entire territory," Sam said.

Simay shook her head again, "No, they wouldn't attack

348

in more than one system at a time. They would depend on the transit delay to give them time to secure the system before any reinforcement arrived. Once the system is captured they would move on to the next."

"Yet they attacked here," Asteria observed.

"Something they thought was important enough to divert combat forces for..." Simay added.

"So if they planned on capturing Clare as a flanking maneuver do you think he would admit it?" Sam asked.

"No... I mean yes I believe he would have told us if he knew that to be true. No I don't think they intended a flanking maneuver. It would be unsustainable to fight on two fronts and the chance of inadvertently bringing in Briton is something they wouldn't do," Simay reasoned.

Captain Stuart rubbed his face with his hands and sighed, "So they probably came looking for us."

Asteria nodded, "And from the way the Colonel said it I assume they want the Dower drive technology."

Simay nodded, "It does give us a significant advantage, and I can't imagine they don't see that as well."

"Something important enough to divert forces," Sam quoted.

Adam looked at the holo for a second, "Why does he keep referring to 'Dragur'? What is that? He said it was protecting the planet."

Simay looked at the table embarrassed- "It's... um... he's referring to Katherine and Master Chief O'Connell," she said quietly trying to avoid looking at Katherine on the com.

"I don't understand, is that a word for Marines?" he asked.

Simay looked at Katherine painfully, "No Sir, a Dragur is... it's mythology from the old Empire. It's a story about a planet of peaceful people who revered God. They lived simply and harmed no one. One day a large army arrived and attacked them. They were driven only by blood lust. They attacked a holy monastery with seven monks in the rectory. They killed them during their prayers. In the morning they found the seven monks standing in a field blocking their way. They were raised by God in retribution to the sin and transgression of the invaders. They are immortal and imbued with the power of God because they are dead. The myth goes on to describe the total destruction of the invading army by the seven. They are called Dragur."

Adam nodded reluctantly, "There are some similarities."

They all looked at Katherine on the com, "I like it. It worked to our benefit although I don't think I have the power of God..." she said plainly.

Sam laughed, "Are you sure?"

"Ok, we need to get this data to the Fleet," Adam said dismissing everybody. Katherine disconnected as the lights brightened.

Sam looked at Adam, "Did you notice Shia?" she asked.

"Yes, I'm concerned. Have Brynn scan both of them. I want to know what's going on and if it's a problem," he said reluctantly. "We can't have the whole crew being ..."

"Dragur?" Sam said frowning.

"No... colonized by nanites," he said firmly.

Captain Kelli Anne Vellius
Medical Shelter 12
Alesia, Clare System
355.0188 FCUDT 09:01:50

Reaching out Kelli wiped her hand slowly across the condensation covered mirror of the small shower room. Water ran down the mirror in thick streaks. Her mind instantly jumped back to Amesbury. She lay on the ruined steps of the Briton mansion in searing pain. Blood pooled in front of her and ran down the steps in long crimson rivulets.

"Josh!" she screamed in pain. "Josh, help me!"

She reached out and tried to crawl to him but her hands slid through the pools of thick blood. She couldn't get a grip on the slick stone. Suddenly she was being pulled out of her ship. Deep cold space closed in around her. She flailed trying to stop but couldn't.

"Don't leave me," she cried.

She opened her eyes and found herself lying on the cold wet deck of the shower. She curled up in a ball raked with shuddering sobs as she cried. It felt like there was a deep empty pit in her chest that ached in agonizing pain.

The door to the small room slid back as the command override was triggered. Doctor Brynn Driscoll kneeled down next to her.

"Kelli what happened?" Brynn asked softly.

Kelli looked up at Brynn with a stricken face- "Please make it stop. It hurts so bad..." she pleaded, "Make me forget, please."

Brynn carefully helped Kelli up- "It's going to be ok. You're going to be ok," she reassured her. She helped Kelli back to her room and eased her into bed- "What happened just now?"

Kelli looked away in fear- "I keep; I keep seeing him die. I can't move, I can't help him. Everybody is dying. Please make it stop Doctor, please."

"Your mind needs time to process, you need time to heal. You're going to get through this," Brynn said to her in encouragement.

Kelli rolled over and curled up into a ball on the bed. Tears silently ran down her cheeks.

"I'm going to give you an anti-depressant Kelli. It will make the pain less. You have to give yourself time," Brynn said as she injected Kelli in the arm.

Kelli lay curled up staring at the wall trying with all her might not to think about the past month.

She closed her eyes and she was back in her quarters on *Revenge*. She stared into Josh's eyes painfully- "I'll be with you soon love," she whispered.

Terrell sat in a rundown café staring out a dirty glass window. He winced at the taste of the cheap bitter fluid they called coffee here.

"Nasty stuff," he spat setting it down.

Jacob smirked, "Might have to get used to it. They seem to enjoy it immensely."

He glared back at him. Jacob nodded to his right indicating something out the window, "There they are."

Terrell looked back and saw two people walking down the street.

"That's the Governor and Captain Adam Stuart. Apparently they are a couple," Jacob said quietly, "At least according to the talk on the street."

Mercan's face darkened. That's the man who destroyed me he thought. He stared out the window as the anger welled up inside of him.

Jacob reached out and stopped him from standing- "We shouldn't be rash. We need a plan. I don't think bringing attention to ourselves would be prudent," he hissed.

Terrell yanked his arm free and rose from his chair, "I'll do what I damn well please. That man ruined me," he said angrily. Jacob watched him cross the room and step out into the street.

He straightened his tattered jacket and casually crossed the street falling in behind Adam and Grace. Mentally he identified four guards in the crowd as he followed. The group paused on the corner and Terrell watched them in the reflection of a shop window. This is my chance he thought as the guard crossed the street and entered a local shop.

He continued toward them as they waited at a corner and carefully drew his sidearm. Just as he closed to an acceptable range a plasma shot flashed across the street.

The guards sprang into a defensive position around Adam and Grace looking for the attacker. Three more shots flashed into the group striking one of the guards.

Captain Adam Stuart
Alesian Settlement, City Center
Alesia, Clare System
355.0188 FCUDT 19:43:27

Adam watched as one of the guards dropped to the ground from a plasma shot to the chest. He dragged Grace down behind cover as two more plasma shots flashed passed.

"We have get to better cover!" Adam said to Grace.

Grace looked around as plasma splashed into the wall behind them. "Over there," she pointed to an alley entrance twenty meters away.

The guard nearest to them leaned over- "Go, I'll cover you as best as I can then join you," he said heavily.

"Ok, get ready," Adam said.

"Stars who is doing this?" Grace grunted as debris rained down around them.

"Has to be an Ottoman, they are the only ones who use those wretched cold plasma weapons," he said.

"How did they get into the city?" she said angry.

Adam looked out past the metal bin they were behind- "Now!" he said.

They staggered out and ran in a crouch towards the alley. Plasma crashed into the ground around them causing them to fall to the ground. Adam's side arm skittered across the ground and into the street.

"Leave it!" he said hauling Grace back up, "Move!"

As they neared the alley a shot ripped into Adam's bicep. Pain coursed through his body and he gasped. They turned the corner and collided with the far wall.

Grace grabbed him and looked into his face- "You're hit," she said trying to compress the open wound.

"It's fine, keep going," he grunted in pain.

Plasma skidded off the wall above then shattering the façade. Bits of concrete blasted into them cutting into Grace's face. Blood spouted out of several small lacerations as they rolled to the ground.

Shaking off the debris they struggled back up and staggered further down the alley. Behind them one of the guards crashed into the ground at the entrance of the alley with a plasm shot through his abdomen.

Leaning against a recycle bin Adam tried to catch his breath as the fighting behind them quieted.

"I think they got the attacker," Grace said through quick breaths.

Adam looked up and saw someone standing a few meters away. He was dressed in local fashion but there was something about him that instantly sent a cold shiver down Adam's spine. It's his eyes Adam thought. He reached for his sidearm before remembering dropping it in the street.

He watched as the man raised a nasty looking firearm and pointed at them.

"What do you want?" Adam said harshly.

The man grinned back at them, "To finish this. To be free."

Grace looked up at the sound of the man's voice, "Who are you?" she demanded.

He laughed harshly, "I am formerly the Ottoman Fleet Commander... but now. Well I'm nobody now," he spit.

"You could have just left. Why are you doing this," Adam said.

He smirked back at them, "This is me becoming a new person, my rebirth if you will."

Adam tensed his body getting ready to go after the man.

The Ottoman frowned at them and shook his head.

Adam yanked Grace to the side to push her behind cover as a bright flash of purple plasma illuminated the small alley. Adam's body instantly went numb and he lost control of his legs. He crashed into the ground in slow motion as a second flash washed over him. His head rolled to the side and he watched Grace collapse to the ground next to him. He stared into her dilated eyes as his body convulsed. Not like this, he thought, not this way. Their thick blood pooled beneath them as Adam slowly lost consciousness

Terrell/Mercan was already running toward the opposite end of the alley before Captain Adam Stuart and Governor Grace O'Malley fell to the ground.

Commander Samantha Leeane
Medical Center Alesian Settlement
Alesia, Clare System
356.0188 FCUDT 12:01:25

The glaring white room seemed too bright. The air seemed to burn her skin and she felt her heart thudding in her chest. Sam squeezed her eyes shut to close out the offending light. She could hear the chaos on the other side of the door as people demanded to know what was happening.

She looked up as the din of voices suddenly increased and saw Dr. Brynn Driscoll step through the door. Her face softened at the sight of Brynn.

"Tell me this isn't happening Brynn," Sam said quietly.

Brynn stepped over to Sam and frowned sadly- "I'm sorry Sam but it's reality."

"What were you doing Adam? Out in the open and look what happened…" Sam said under her breath, "Now what are we going to do?"

Brynn put her hand on Sam's shoulder, "We'll do what we always do and keep moving forward."

"He was more than our Captain; he was Adam Stuart. The war hero, rebel leader, and interstellar explorer. Nobody can replace him," Sam said looking up.

"Sam he is not being replaced he just moved on."

Sam sighed, "But somebody has to take his place.

Who?"

Brynn looked at Sam concerned for a moment before the back door to the little sitting room swung open.

Alesian Security Chief Calvin Flanagan, Ranger Jeffery Dumont, and Admiral Coline Lune stepped quickly inside rapidly filling the little space.

Sam stood and straightened herself, "Admiral, please tell me you know what happened," she said nodding to the others.

Admiral Lune frowned, "Sam, it's still pretty chaotic. Jeffery and Calvin have done their best," she said heavily, "How are you holding up?"

Sam looked up for a second, "I don't know, I don't think it has hit me yet. I have no idea what I'm going to tell the crew."

Admiral Lune nodded, "Calvin and Jeffery can bring us up to speed," she said motioning for them to go ahead.

Calvin nodded, "So what we know is both Captain Stuart and... Mrs. O'Malley were killed by an unidentified assailant," he said emotionally, "So were two of my best security specialists that were assigned to guard them. We managed to kill one of the assailants but we believe he was only a diversion. Medical has confirmed he was an Ottoman or at least of the same region. The weapon used to commit the act was also Ottoman in origin."

Coline squinted, "How do we know that?"

Jeffery opened his tablet, "Ma'am, the wound was identified as a cold plasma weapon. Only the Ottoman manufacture those type of weapons."

Sam nodded, "Those bright purple plasma weapons?"

"Yes, very destructive. Also causes radiation damage to the user. Federation and allies don't accept that kind of residual damage to its people. Only governments who don't care about its people use them," Dumont said distastefully.

"Anything remarkable about the individual that was killed?" Brynn asked.

Calvin shook his head, "No, nothing except he had

identification that he didn't gene match to. Stolen from somewhere but did belong to an actual person who was at some time in system."

"So what are we doing about this?" Sam asked frustrated.

Calvin activated his tablet and showed the group a map, "We have the city in lockdown all entry and exit points are being gene scanned to match identification. The local area is cordoned off so we can investigate. I have plenty of man power to do this but I lack the professional resources. I'm hoping Mr. Dumont can assist."

Dumont looked at Sam and Coline, "In the past weeks I have found a few who qualify for Ranger training but their still very new. I'm only one person I can't handle an investigation of this magnitude by myself," he looked at Sam carefully, "You have two of my very best Rangers in your crew Commander," he said that as an observation but was inferring permission to have Tameria and Shia.

Sam sighed heavily, "Tameria can be assigned to you without issue. Shia on the other hand is beyond my reach," Sam said looking at Admiral Lune carefully.

"No. I have been directly ordered by Federation Headquarters to keep her isolated," Admiral Lune said emphatically.

Sam swallowed a defiant protest. She had been vocal about her feelings concerning the isolation of Shia and Katherine. Tension washed over the small group. Jeffery and Calvin were very good friends with Shia.

"Very well, Tameria will have to do. Can I request access to Shia for consultation?" Dumont asked carefully.

Coline nodded, "Of course, as long as it doesn't violate the isolation. I'm sorry Jeffery, it's the best I can do."

"Thank you Ma'am, I understand," he said respectfully.

"That's all we can do?" Sam asked surprised, "Start an investigation."

Coline looked at Sam surprised, "We have to follow the straight and narrow here Sam. The fate of Clare is hanging by a thread. The protectorate status is tenuous at best. The loss of Captain Stuart is terrible and tragic but the loss of Governor O'Malley places Clare in a tremendous political spotlight. This has the potential to tear a rift in the political fabric of the entire arm. She was the one who sought out the status and convinced the population is was the right thing to do. The Federation placed its confidence in her leadership. The stars only know what Briton will do when we inform them. If both side pull out from the deal, all we have worked for, all our people from both sides, will have died for nothing," Coline said strongly.

Sam tensed, "Yes Ma'am," Sam had never seen Coline become so rigid even during her protest of Shia's treatment.

Coline looked at the two law enforcement heads, "Calvin, Jeffery. Please keep us informed if you will and let me know if you have any further need I can assist with. I will brief my counterpart Admiral Dunkirk. I am sure she will offer any assistance as well"- she looked back at Sam, "If you'll excuse us? Commander Leeane and I have to inform the Federation and Briton governments."

"Yes Ma'am, thank you," Calvin replied as he and Dumont moved to depart.

"Sam, we need to get back to the *Nyx*, please have the quantum communication system readied for us. I will contact Admiral Dunkirk and have her and the Briton government linked in."

"Aye Ma'am," Sam replied professionally.

Cadet Katherine Carroll
Marine Officers Quarters, Deck Three
Nyx, Clare System
356.0188 FCUDT 14:56:20

"How long do you think they will keep us locked up?" Shia said from the far side of the small sitting room.

Chief Warrant Officer Josephine Santiago looked back at her empathetically through the electromagnetic field wall.

"You're not 'locked up' Shia. It's protocol for nanite isolation. They just want to be sure your safe and…"

"Not going to start a nanite apocalypse," Shia retorted.

Josephine gave Shia a look of consternation- "Really Shia you don't have to be so trite about it."

Shia looked at Katherine.

Katherine felt Shia's embarrassment and discomfort.

"It's ok, this is my fault," Katherine said to her.

Shia shook her head, "You know that's not true. I'm upset at their reaction not your actions. I would still be upset if it was only you in here. Besides, I'd be dead otherwise," *I don't think of us as separate people any longer*, Shia thought.

Neither do I Shia, Katherine thought back to her. Katherine felt Shia relax and smiled.

"You two are bit scary. Not like nanite scary, I mean like you seem to communicate with each other on a whole different level," Josephine said smiling.

Katherine felt the data network suddenly flood with data. She explored the data and absorbed the information. She suddenly went rigid and sat up.

Shia froze and looked at Josephine as she caught bits of the information from Katherine.

"Shia! What's wrong?" Josephine asked alarmed.

"Something has happened to Captain Stuart," she snapped her mouth closed in surprise as the data passed into her mind- "He's been killed! Along with the Governor!"

"The Ottomans…" Shia said concentrating on the data. She turned and looked at Katherine seriously. Shia was stunned by the powerful emotions pouring out of Katherine.

This is my fault, Katherine thought in desperation.

No it isn't. They have us locked up, Shia reasoned with her.

It was my responsibility to secure the planet. This is my fault.

Shia frowned, *Katherine, you stopped an entire army! You did your job.*

Not well enough, Katherine's emotions spiked as she rose

and stared at Shia.

"No, we aren't allowed to leave," Shia said to her feeling her make a decision.

"You know we can find them," Katherine said to her.

Josephine stared at the silent exchange in confusion- "What's going on?" she asked.

"We're leaving," Shia said in resignation to Josephine.

"You can't, the field! I can't let you out Shia," Josephine said.

"You don't have to," Katherine said as she walked unimpeded through the electromagnetic field wall. There was a slight tingle and the nanites immediately responded protecting her.

Josephine stood in the small room with her mouth open in shock as Shia stepped through the field wall.

Katherine turned and walked out of the room toward the passageway that led to the nearest airlock outside. Shia followed right behind her. As they neared the airlock the hatch popped open and Admiral Coline Lune and Commander Samantha Leeane stepped out in front of Katherine.

"Katherine! Who let you out of isolation?" Admiral Lune said surprised.

"Ma'am, they walked right through it! The containment doesn't work," Josephine said quickly.

"Where are you two going?" Sam asked.

"Ma'am, I failed to secure the planet and Captain Stuart has been killed. I am going to complete my mission and find the remaining Ottoman before anything further occurs."

Admiral Lune stared at Katherine, "That's not your concern any longer. I understand you have the best intentions but you have been ordered to remain in isolation. We will take care of this."

"Ma'am, we are far better equipped than any others on this planet. We can find them," Shia said.

Sam looked at Coline carefully, "She has a point Ma'am."

Coline stared at them hard for a moment- "Commander Carroll you are the most capable combat commander I have ever seen but there is much more to being an Officer than destroying an enemy. Did you learn nothing in Asteria's charge? How can a General win a battle if her Junior Officers don't follow orders?"

Katherine looked at the deck embarrassed. The memory of the simulations flashed through her mind- "I'm sorry Ma'am," she said quietly.

Coline heaved a heavy sigh and looked at them- "Fine, but we're going to do this the right way. You two come with us. I can't promise anything but I will try to get you released," she pointed at them, "Unless you're telling me that your no longer Federation Officers! In that case I will have you locked up for real..."

Katherine looked at Shia for a moment and felt her pleading for her to do as they say- "Yes Ma'am, we are Federation Officers I'm afraid I lost better judgement."

Coline nodded, "This isn't over. It bothers me that you had to think about that! Now, up to bridge all of you."

Katherine followed the Admiral through the passageways up to the command deck silently. As they neared Sam placed her hand on Katherine's arm.

"It will work out Katherine, have patience," she said with encouragement.

Katherine nodded, "Thank you Ma'am."

Admiral Lune and Sam sat at the communication console as it came active.

"Ma'am, Admiral Dunkirk is online. Three minutes to Federation link," Josephine called out from the terminal.

"Tabbitha thank you for joining us," Coline said as Admiral Tabbitha Dunkirk appeared.

"Of course Coline. I so very sorry it is under these circumstances. Briton link is active in two minutes," Tabbitha said sadly.

"You read my brief? Do you have any questions before we begin?" Coline said.

"No thank you, it was very informative. I understand Gerry is assisting in the situation?" she replied.

"Yes, he is aiding the Security section chief in securing some of the more sensitive areas of the settlement," Coline said appreciatively.

Katherine watched the Officers in the dark conference room from the far wall behind a small viewport. The two of them stood outside the communication room waiting. Katherine got the distinct feeling that if either of them said or did anything rash they would be in rather hotter water. She fought to contain her fully flowing mixed emotions. Embarrassment over failing the mission and not following orders, anger towards the Ottomans, resentment towards the Admiral for holding her back, depression for dragging Shia into all this, shame for almost betraying her Marine code of Honor...

"Ma'am one minute to quantum connection," Josephine said quietly.

Suddenly Katherine felt as yet another emotion seize hold of her mind. Fear. The quantum connection would allow her access to the entire Federation network. Her fear was rooted in that deep longing to access the massive network. To get lost again and swim through the nearly infinite data. The overwhelming sense of desire caused her to flush and begin sweating.

She suddenly felt Shia grasp her hand in the dark. Realizing that Shia was feeling the same emotions as they flooded out she closed her eyes tight.

You'll be ok. I'll be here with you, Shia thought, forcing Katherine to calm a little.

Katherine concentrated on her fear, steeling her mind against the pending connection. Remembering Lieutenant Binici's words about using fear as a tool. She mentally blocked herself in and fortified her connection. Squeezing Shia's hand, she looked up ready.

Sam looked at the quantum com as the Federated Fleet Admiral Donald Birch appeared. Sitting next to him was Intelligence Chief Admiral Tabitha Matthews, and Special Operations Chief Admiral Samuel Thomas.

"Greetings Admiral Birch, we will be joined by the Briton representation in thirty seconds. I have Admiral Tabbitha Dunkirk and Commander Samantha Leeane with me," Admiral Lune said formally.

"Admiral Dunkirk, Admiral Lune," Admiral Birch said in greeting.

In moments another holo winked on and Prime Minister Bethany Scott and Admiral Sir Geoffrey Younger appeared.

"Prime Minister, Admiral Younger, we are joined by Admiral Birch and his staff as well as Admiral Lune and Commander Leeane," Admiral Dunkirk greeted them formally.

"Greetings Admirals," Bethany replied.

"I'll begin by recapping the initial brief. Both Grace O'Malley and Captain Adam Stuart passed away from injury sustained in the attack. We have continued to support the established government in securing the settlement. There have been no further aggressive acts since the initial report. Nor have we apprehended the primary attacker," Coline reported.

Admiral Birch nodded, "You can positively say the main threat to the planet is eliminated?"

Admiral Dunkirk nodded, "Yes Admiral, I am patrolling the inner and outer system with a joint crew of Briton and Federated fleet assets. We have had no contacts in the past several weeks. Our intel estimate is that only a few dozen Ottoman are still in system, all on the planet itself."

"What is the current status of the *Revenge* Admiral"

Bethany asked looking up.

"Fifty percent combat effective. It is currently being staffed as a communication and control asset in Alesian orbit. Repairs will take time due to the damage to the system infrastructure," Admiral Lune replied.

"Good, you should have Briton assets in seven weeks to help fortify the system," Bethany said looking at Admiral Birch.

"And you should have Federated assets in about that same time. We have sent a fabrication ship as well to aid in the rebuilding," Donald added.

"Prime Minister, we have already begun receiving demands from other system nations about the replacement of Governor O'Malley. This is going to be difficult," Admiral Matthews said.

"Yes we also have received similar messages," Bethany replied, "Our primary concern is that we have a leader that can handle the civilians of Clare and support the joint nature of our agreement."

"We are of the same mind Prime Minister. Unfortunately, according to Federated law there has to be an election," Admiral Matthews said, "We really don't have control over who wins."

"Can you not appoint someone interim until an election is held sometime in the future?" Admiral Younger asked.

"Yes but by law an election has to take place within one hundred eighty days of appointment," Admiral Matthews answered.

"Whoever we appoint will draw the line of allied support. I'm sure all here can come to an acceptable agreement but the other system nations are not so easily appeased," Admiral Birch said heavily.

"Admiral our knowledge of civilians within Clare is incomplete at best. It will take some time to find someone," Bethany stated.

"Does it have to be a civilian? We have full dossiers on Fleet personnel," Admiral Younger said frowning.

"I doubt that they would take to an Admiral appointee very easily. We have a good reputation for the work we have done but these are people who chose a life outside the network after all," Admiral Lune said shaking her head.

"I wasn't referring to an Admiral, what about Captain Vellius? She has the support of the Briton people and is a decorated Federated Officer," Admiral Younger replied.

Admiral birch nodded, "What do you think?" he asked looking at Coline and Tabbitha.

"On paper she is a good choice. In reality she is suffering from severe post-traumatic stress. Her actions in the battle were excellent... as well as reckless. We would need medical to approve," Coline said sadly.

Sam sat silently and watched the interplay between the two governments. Her intelligence training gave her insight to the actions of both sides. It was immediately obvious that she now sat in the middle of a very intense political situation. Coline had been right about toeing the line. Any misstep could alter the balance of power in the coming war. Nations were taking up sides in what was looking like a very serious situation. The assignation of Governor O'Malley was just the thing to tip it all off.

Finally the talks came to an end. Sam could barely stand the ache in her back from sitting in the tiny chairs. We have to replace these she thought to herself.

"Before we go Admiral Birch, I would like to say something. It is with mixed emotion I offer my condolence for the loss of Captain Adam Stuart. He is not the most popular Federated Officer in Briton. Despite that, it is a disgrace to every person in a uniform for such a legendary Naval Officer to be gunned down in a dirty alley. May he find peace among the stars," Admiral Younger said solemnly.

"Thank you Geoffrey," Admiral Birch replied.

The Briton com flashed out and they were left alone with the Federation connection.

"Now for the military side of things," Admiral Birch said

looking at them, "It is of consensus here that Commander Samantha Leeane is to be immediately promoted to the rank of Captain and placed in command of the *Nyx*. Congratulations Captain Leeane."

Sam's throat closed and her heart slammed in her chest- "Um, thank you Sir," she managed to choke out. Her head was reeling. Me! The Captain… she thought in shock.

"Further the *Nyx* is to be repaired as quickly as possible. We invested heavily in your ship and it is needed. Forward your crew assignments as soon as you can."

"Sir, I would like to request the release of Cadet Katherine Carroll and Master Chief Shia O'Connell. I believe they are uniquely suited for the apprehension of the remaining Ottoman forces," Admiral Lune asked formally.

He looked at Admiral Matthews and back to Coline.

"Denied," Admiral Matthews said flatly, "According to the reports the nanites were passed on through contact. That is unacceptable. We will not be responsible for that kind of destruction. They should be happy I haven't yet ordered them to be disposed of."

"Excuse me Admiral! Katherine Carroll has proven to be an incredible asset. She led her Marines, eight of them, to defeat an entire Army of ground forces. Her situation is the direct result of a mandate from your office to 'modify and investigate' cybernetic enhancements. We have come dangerously close to violating the human rights act!" Admiral Lune said offended.

Admiral Matthews stared at Coline, "Well according to the medical reports she is technically dead and therefore has no rights according to medical precedents. We don't even know if it is human."

"You have no right to make that determination!" Coline refuted.

"Are you challenging my authority…" Admiral Matthews began.

"Enough. Admiral Lune as the local Admiral the ultimate authority is yours. As long as you follow protocols you face no repercussions. That said, we know that nanites are on your ship and you will not be cleared into Federated space until you pass a nanite scan or have them in isolation per protocol," Admiral Birch said staring at Admiral Matthews "Now, the rest of your orders have been transmitted. Contact us if there are any updates," he looked at the other Admirals, "We have to report to the congressional board so we're letting you go. Keep up the work Coline help is on the way."

As the com flashed out Sam sat staring at Coline.

"Point of fact Sam, I happen to agree with everything you said in protest of Katherine and Shia's treatment. Unfortunately we are in the Federated Fleet and have to follow orders. Even the ones we don't agree with," Coline explained.

Sam averted her eyes, "Of course, I know that. I just feel like sometimes someone has to say it. As the XO it was supposed to be me."

Coline sighed, "Well, now as the Captain you have to find someone to remind you like you reminded me."

"I have great respect for you Admiral, there's more to you than I realized," Sam said.

Coline laughed, "There's a time to stand back and a time push forward. The hard part is knowing the difference," she said getting up, "Tell Katherine and Shia they are assigned to assist Dumont in the apprehension of the attackers."

"Yes Ma'am, thank you," Sam said formally.

An hour later Sam stood in the passageway next to the main airlock with Katherine and Shia.

"Ok, I expect perfect Military bearing, you are not mercenaries, you're Marines. Dumont is expecting you. Keep me informed of your progress and status," Sam said to them.

"Yes Ma'am," Katherine replied.

She looked at them carefully, "Please be careful. The last

time you died it caused a lot problems... Gear up and get out of here."

Shia unzipped her pressure suit and began to strip it off. Sam looked at her in question.

"Don't need it anymore," Shia said in explanation.

As she exposed her torso Sam saw Shia's skin was green and matched Katherine's, "When did this happen?" Sam asked shocked.

"A week ago I realized it was happening. I now have full nanopolymer skin like Katherine," she said.

Sam watched as Shia straightened up and suddenly level two armor literally grew out of her dark green skin, "You two are incredible. And a little bit scary. I suggest you don't do that in front of anyone else or you may find them less than acceptable."

"Yea, if I hadn't watched Katherine go through it I would be totally freaked out too," Shia said elbowing Katherine.

Katherine handed Shia a pistol and they stepped out through the airlock.

Sam watched them walk down the long scaffolding and into the small camp where the crew lived. That camp was rapidly turning into a proper town. Sam looked up and felt the hot rays of Clare shine down on her face for a moment. When she looked back down Katherine and Shia were gone.

Her com chimed, "Captain Leeane I need you in Engineering," Lieutenant Lavagnino said.

Captain she thought, how quickly we adapt.

"On the way Jacob," she said taking one last look at the camp below and stepping out of the brilliant sunlight back into the ship, her ship.

~

EPILOUGE

Captain Leeane and Lieutenant Katherine Carroll walked across the *Nyx's* shuttle bay toward the modified combat pinnace. It's dark fiber skin seemed to absorb the normally bright lights of the bay. Five disembodied wings floated several meters from the predatory body of the pinnace. The soft green glow of the graviton fields that held the wings bathed the area in an eerie light. The aft ramp hissed open as the two approached and Senior Master Chief Shia O'Connell stood inside waiting.

"Katherine please be careful," Sam said looking over Katherine.

She stood there in her non armored nanite skin. After the past year Sam had grown accustomed to seeing Katherine this way. She appeared to be nearly nude but completely green all the way up to her chin. Her short red hair stood out in stark contrast. In reality her actual skin was pure nanopolymer. Her pale face was outlined by shimmering crystalline blue bioneural implant. Sam still couldn't quite get used to the implant. All Federated citizens had one but only on the left half of their face. Katherine's traced her entire jaw and made both her eyes brilliant blue.

Katherine smiled, "Yes Ma'am," she stood there for a minute looking at the magnificent ship.

Sam's com chirped, "Approaching drop point Ma'am. Two minutes to combat translation," Warrant Officer Josephine Santiago-Kane reported.

"Thank you Joe," she activated her com calling her Executive Officer.

Instantly Commander Tristan Reese looked back at her. "Yes, Ma'am?"

"Tristan, I want us back in graviton space as soon as *Alastor* is clear. They are prepping now for drop," Sam said looking at him.

"Aye Ma'am, one-thirty to translation," he said nodding.

Sam looked up at Katherine, "Get out of here Katherine. I'll see you at the rendezvous in three months."

Katherine saluted Sam smartly then turned and walked up the ramp.

Shia smiled at Katherine as she joined her and they walked up to the pinnace's small cockpit. *Alastor is ready.*

Are you ready? Katherine thought.

As long as we're together Kat.

Katherine smiled and linked her cybernetics to the pinnace. She felt Shia do the same and they activated the ship's system. Receiving the electronic departure clearance they released the dock clamps and the thirty meter pinnace lifted off the deck.

Outside the *Nyx* flashed out of graviton space with a burst of color. The subatomic particles flashed out of existence and the ship glided out into empty interstellar space.

The pinnace *Alastor* silently glided out through the grav curtain of the shuttle bay and powered up. It slowly accelerated away from the *Nyx*.

"*Alastor* you're clear of *Nyx* local space. Your mission is go. Stars protect you," Sam said from her bridge.

"Copy *Nyx*, clear and mission is go," Katherine replied.

As the *Nyx* crew watched, *Alastor's* disembodied wings slid forward and spread out evenly. It then simply vanished.

"Stealth systems operational. Going silent, *Alastor* signing out," Shia reported over the com.

On the *Alastor* Katherine activated the engines and the pinnace streaked out invisibly toward Elysium.

Several hours later *Alastor* decelerated into the outer system of Elysium. Shia stared out the pinnace's viewport at the massive Ottoman ship of the line. They were silently gliding past only two hundred ten meters from it. She could feel the foreign Ottoman computer network as they passed through its electromagnetics.

Careful, the Ottoman AI is very dangerous, Katherine warned

Shia. Shia took a quick breath as she again felt the cold emotional memory of Katherine's last brush with an Ottoman AI. The tactical system chimed alerting them that the system had completed its passive scan.

"One hundred seventy ships of various types. Forty ships over fifty thousand metric tons," Katherine observed.

"Stars! Forty ships bigger than battlecruisers?" Shia said in disbelief, "Fleet is going to have a nasty fight on their hands."

Katherine brought up a detail scan on a single ship, "This must be the command ship. It registers as one hundred six thousand metric tons and is three hundred thirty-seven meters in length."

Shai looked at it in amazement, "I've never seen a ship that big. It's bigger than a lot of stations. I pity the crew who will have to fight that monstrosity."

Katherine nodded slowly as she programmed a safe route through the tangle of ship traffic. Finally she disconnected and stepped over to Shia.

"I think we can take a minute to ourselves..." Katherine said reaching out to Shia. She put her hands on Shia's waist carefully. As soon as they made contact their cybernetic implants linked and their minds almost completely merged. Katherine felt Shia's heart slow and time seemed to nearly stop. They stayed like that for a solid minute and in their hyperawareness it seemed like hours.

"No matter what happens Shia, you'll always be the thing that keeps me here. My silver beacon of light," Katherine said directly into Shia's mind.

Shia smiled slightly, "And after all my one hundred years of searching, I have found you and will never lose you."

They slowly separated and Shia looked down at the navigation console. A small green icon blinked as it indicated their insertion site. Outside the cockpit the planet Cronus slowly grew larger as they approached. Shia sighed loudly and nodded to Katherine.

"Cronus is no Alesia. The planet itself is as nasty as the

people who live there," Shia said frowning.

"Yes but those nasty people are Federated Colonial Citizens," Katherine pointed out.

"Fine, let's go get them ready," she said in resignation.

As they stepped into the open crew deck six Marines looked up at them. Three Federated Commandos and three Briton Legionaries. Their pale faces and bright crystalline blue eyes held steady on their Commander. Katherine felt Shia connect to their limited cybernetics and got a full system update. In front of them sat the most elite highly evolved combat Soldiers in human history. Every single one had a fully integrated nanobiological quantum core similar to Shia and Katherine's. Every Marine here volunteered for cybernetic enhancement. They were the joined. Shared thoughts and actions. They performed teamwork on a whole new level. In combat there was no commands, only shared consciousness. They were a single organic being.

"The mission parameters are on the network. There are one hundred fifty of our fellow Marines down on Cronus and they need our help. We are their only hope. Our mission is to infiltrate under complete stealth, locate the holding facility, recon and asses. In other words we will rescue them," Katherine said to the group, "During that time the Federation and Allied fleets will counter attack in the system."

Shia stepped towards them, "Gear up. We begin insertion in two hours."

The six silently rose and moved to their assigned duties for landing preparation.

Katherine watched them with efficiency and felt Shia's approval.

The early morning red light of Clare shined from behind the eastern mountains as Kelli stood on the veranda high above the city. She stared off toward the Port of Nyx. The bustling little town looked so different now that the Federated destroyer *Nyx* had left a month ago. A stab of regret flashed through her. She had retained some hope that she would return to active status and be sent back out to command a ship while the *Nyx* was still in Clare. That hope had died when she watched the massive ship lumber back up into orbit and depart the system. She had to face the reality that she was confined to system governorship for the time being. Below her the city was coming alive with traffic. People moved about their daily lives as Kelli stared wistfully up at the fading stars.

The door chimed as Assistant Governor Theobald O'Malley arrived. Kelli looked over her shoulder as he came into her office.

"Good Morning Milady," he said smiling, "You're up early, is everything ok?"

Kelli turned and walked back inside headed for the fabricator- "Morning Theo," she greeted him. "Everything's fine," she replied thinking about how she still couldn't sleep through the night. The memories of the nightmares made her shiver involuntarily. Inevitably she would wake up covered in sweat after dreaming of being blown out into deep space. It was the same dream every night. The *Revenge* being attacked by the Ottoman and her helplessness as the ship was crippled. The hole in the bridge looming in front of her as she was ripped out of her command chair.

She shook off the thought and picked up a cup of coffee. As she turned to the conference table the two system

Admirals entered her office with soft smiles on their faces.

"Good morning Milady Vellius," Briton Admiral Tabbitha Dunkirk said setting her tablet down on the table.

"And to you Tabbitha. I'm glad you could come down to join us," Kelli said giving her a hug.

Tabbitha returned her hug then held her at arms-length, "Are you ok? You look a bit distracted..." Tabbitha asked concerned.

Kelli frowned slightly, "No more than normal Tabbitha. I'll be ok." Kelli said quietly, "It's good to see you."

Federated Colonial Admiral Coline Lune stepped up next to them and smiled, "Oh, you get a hug... She never hugs me," Coline said in mock seriousness.

"We'll you just need to spend more time floating around the system," Tabbitha said teasing her.

The Admirals had split their duties with Tabbitha being the operational Admiral up in space and Coline the administration side down at the Joint Headquarters here in Bayhaven. The situation worked very well and the two were very good friends. The situation placed Kelli and Coline in frequent contact but Kelli rarely saw Tabbitha.

Kelli grinned at the twos teasing and motioned at the conference table, "Please take a seat and we can get started."

As they all sat Theo activated the holodisplay, "Admiral Lune if you would like to start," he said happily.

"Of course Theo, thank you," she said bringing up the data for her brief, "As you can see we have started construction on the Allied Military Forces training academy down on the southern ocean. The location is excellent. The mountains behind the academy will offer extremely varied terrain for training. The ocean to the south makes this the first Military training facility for both Briton and the Federation that can offer traditional planetary ocean warfare training. I expect the construction to be complete in six months and the first trainees to begin within eight."

"That's excellent news. Once we get the dry dock completed we can begin staffing our own warships," Kelli said looking at the building plans.

"Speaking of the dry dock, Hielo Corp has forwarded the contract. They agree to thirty percent Clare citizen personnel. That should bolster our economy quite well. They are planning on staffing their administration offices in the Port of Nyx with local workers. They already have one hundred and four personnel from the Federation on the way and one hundred two from Briton. That means they are hiring a minimum of sixty one from the local population. The labor and industry director believes we can support that level without difficulty," Theo added.

"When are they planning on beginning construction of the shipyard?" Tabbitha asked.

"As soon as the freighters arrive with the proprietary equipment and workers. I believe they should be here inside of three months," he said smiling.

"So we're about year out before we can have our first small tonnage ships and two out for destroyers and cruisers," Coline pointed out.

"Looks like it..." Theo began.

The building rumbled and the windows pressed in as a pressure wave crashed into them. A tremendous roar thundered outside. The group shot to their feet in shock.

Kelli rushed to the veranda and looked outside. Not two blocks away she saw an expanding cloud of smoke and flame.

Her emergency com chirped and her Senior Planetary Security Chief appeared, "Madam Governor are you ok?" he asked concerned.

"Yes Calvin, I'm with Theo and the Admirals. What just happened?" she said staring at the black smoke.

"Ma'am, it appears there has been an attack on the commerce building. Stay where you are I have a team on their way to you," he said and signed off.

Admiral Lune stood next to Kelli, "It's been six months, why would somebody attack now?" she said in shock.

"More importantly, who..." Tabbitha said concerned.

~

ABOUT THE AUTHOR
Jack Edward

Jack Edward is a former Military combat helicopter pilot recently turned freelance science fiction writer. He specializes in Military space novels and his varied experience in the Middle Eastern conflict gives his writing a flair of reality.

As an avid adventurist Jack Edward has traveled extensively gaining experience across the globe. Jack has spent his life dedicated to the service of the general public. Throughout his journeys he has been a Park Ranger, Remote Emergency Medical Technician, Search and Rescue Technician, Helicopter Pilot and Crewmen, Swiftwater and Technical rescue specialist, and instructor of several of these disciplines. No stranger to high risk activities Jack's hobbies range from white water kayaking, rock and ice climbing, triathlons, surfing, offshore sailing, big mountain snow skiing, and paragliding.

Employed as a professional mountain climber he spends his time dedicated to search and rescue. When not at high altitude Jack sails his forty-foot ketch across the pacific in search of sun and surf.